PRAISE FOR DREAM LONDON

"*Dream London* is a sweetly dark satire
shot through with Occupy-era indignation and
a bizarre dream logic in which everything makes
sense as long as you accept that nothing makes
sense. This is as strange and unclassifiable
a novel as it's possible to imagine, and a
marvellous achievement."
The Financial Times

"Tony Ballantyne's *Dream London* is one of
those unclassifiable gems that crop up from time
to time... The novel shares the surreal, absurdist
whimsy of *Alice in Wonderland* and Chesterton's
The Man Who Was Thursday."
The Guardian

"The world of altered aesthetics, reengineered
roles and unfamiliar fundamentals is so deeply
disconcerting that identifying what's wonderful
about it, and what's just window-dressing,
takes time—but once you get into the swing of
things, Ballantyne's exceptional new novel goes
from strength to strength... Smart, stylish, and
as alarming as it is indubitably alluring, *Dream
London* deftly demonstrates that the weird still
has a thing or two to prove."
Tor.com

"A real feat of the imagination, this is a
really exceptional book, unlike anything
I've ever read before."
Chris Beckett

TONY BALLANTYNE
DREAM PARIS

First published 2015 by Solaris
an imprint of Rebellion Publishing Ltd,
Riverside House, Osney Mead,
Oxford, OX2 0ES, UK

www.solarisbooks.com

ISBN: 978 1 78108 360 4

A CIP catalogue record for this book is available
from the British Library.

Designed & typeset by Rebellion Publishing

Printed in Denmark

DREAM PARIS

TONY BALLANTYNE

SOLARIS

L'homme armé

L'homme armé doibt on doubter.
On a fait partout crier
Que chacun vienne armer
D'un haubregon de fer.
L'homme armé doibt on doubter.

The armed man should be feared.
Everywhere it has been proclaimed
That each man shall arm himself
With a coat of iron mail.
The armed man should be feared.

Traditional,
15th century

SILVER

THE SOCIAL WORKER

THE SKY WAS the colour of an unpolished euphonium, tuned to a dead key.

I paused. It didn't do to let odd thoughts pass by unexamined. Dream London may have passed away months ago, I may have been living in plain old London once more, but strange thoughts still curled into the mind and tried to take root. If you wanted to stay sane, then those thoughts had to be examined, checked and classified. *A dead key*, I thought. *Exactly what colour is that?*

The colour of this January evening, when there is no life to the world. When it's cold, but not winter cold. When the air doesn't burn the cheeks or fill the lungs with icy excitement, when the streets hold a chilly dampness that can't commit itself to rain. That's the colour.

I resumed my walk home. Beneath my duffel I wore a vest, a thick shirt and jumper. Hot sweaty air puffed from the neck and cuffs as I walked, but I didn't unbutton my coat. They may have been relaying the gas pipes, but they'd yet to make it to Hayling Street and so it didn't do to waste warmth.

The workmen had dug a service trench across the entrance to my road some weeks ago and had then, typically, forgotten about it. Yellow pipes lay curled up at the bottom, wrapped around piles of gravel, half submerged in puddles of dirty water. Nothing unusual in that, the whole of London was being reconnected to the rest of the world, pipe by pipe, wire by wire. I used the narrow plank bridge to cross, jumping over the sickly puddle that covered one end, my heavy carrier bag banging my leg as I landed.

IN DREAM LONDON, one of the many thoughts that had taken root in people's minds and flourished was that females were incapable of looking after themselves. Many of the people living in Hayling Street no doubt still imagined I needed a man looking after me. I could see the curtains twitch as I made my way down the street. Funny that, all that concern about *my* moral wellbeing, whilst other neighbours were left to go hungry.

I rang Mr Hiatt's bell.

"Corned beef," I said, holding up the carrier bag as he opened the door. "I tried for some milk but there was none left."

"Maybe next time," he said, pulling out his wallet. I could hear music playing softly in the background, and I shuddered. Mr Hiatt handed across a couple of Dream London dollars, the once bright patterns faded to dull mustard.

"You're a good girl, Anna. How's your Mum and Dad?"

"Still missing."

"I heard that they found another whale skeleton under Cooper Street. That makes four."

"I heard that, too."

The sound of violins playing on the radio wove their way through the house. Violins weren't so bad, I told myself. Still, I felt myself trembling.

"I wonder what's buried beneath our houses?"

"Best not to think about it, Mr Hiatt. Look, I've got to be off."

"Thank you for the food. Goodbye, Anna."

"See you, Mr Hiatt."

He closed the door, gently. I crumpled the worthless Dream London dollars and dropped them on the pile of rubbish overflowing from the dustbin, making a mental note to take some of his waste to the communal tip down on Katherine Street.

I continued home, turning to pass beneath the dark yews guarding the garden. The house was still too tall, just like all the others in the street. Workmen had been through and erected scaffolding a few months ago, making things safe: propping up a wall here, throwing polythene sheets over the spaces where the tiles had separated on the roof there. They'd even gone to the trouble of placing braces beneath the bedrooms that had grown outwards. One of the workmen had taken a shine to me, he kept asking if I wanted to go for a coffee after I'd finished school. His gaffer had told him to leave me alone, said he wouldn't like to think of one of his daughters living by herself. He took offence when I asked him how he'd feel if it were one of his sons, and I pointed out that there were lots of people worse off than me in London. At least I had somewhere to live.

The evening shadows made my home look as if it were dying. In the middle of this scene of unchanging stillness, the sudden movement of the woman waiting by my door made me start. She was drinking tea from a plastic cup. Something about that relaxed me a little. When she saw me, she drained the cup and quickly screwed it onto the top of a thermos flask.

"Can I help you?" I asked.

"Anna Margaret Louise Sinfield?" She pushed the flask into a large bag, speaking all the time in a broad Brummie accent. "I'm Petrina. I've come to check that everything's okay."

She fumbled in her pocket and produced a laminated card bearing her name and photograph.

"Social Services," I read out loud. "I suppose I shouldn't be surprised."

Petrina was back in her bag again. That irritated me. It's not so difficult to keep things organised. Perhaps if she'd got herself a briefcase with separators instead of that impractical handknitted ethnic bag...

"Sorry to take so long, but as you can imagine we've been very busy! Oh, where is that... ah, got it! You know, I haven't had a moments rest since I was – bloody pen's leaked everywhere – seconded here last week. Ah!"

She looked up and smiled, a pad and pen in hand. "Shall we go inside?"

"I don't think that will be necessary. I'm perfectly okay, thank you. I don't need any help."

Petrina made a show of looking up at the crooked house. It was dim in the shade of the yew trees, the scaffolding further enfolding us as the January evening descended.

"I saw from that notice at the end of the road that this house isn't back on the grid yet."

"It will be in March. In the meantime there's plenty of candles at the distribution centre. And we're fortunate enough to have fireplaces and chimneys here..."

Petrina scribbled in her pad. She was going to patronise me, I just knew it.

"Anna, I don't think anyone would say that you've not been doing a fantastic job of looking after yourself. You don't need to tell me – oh, is it too much to ask for a pen that works? Ah, that's it – tell me about how brave you've been. But you're – how old, I had it written down here – sixteen, was it?"

"I'm seventeen. I'll be eighteen in two months' time."

In other words, old enough to be legally responsible for myself.

Petrina pushed her pad under her arm and fumbled some more in her bag

"Seventeen!" she mumbled, pen clasped between her teeth. "Sorry, this is bloody ridiculous! They expect us to do all this extra work without bothering to update the records..."

I tried being polite. "I can see that you're busy. Why don't you just skip me and go on to your next client? There must be far more urgent cases than mine."

It didn't work. Petrina gave me that look that some adults give when they think they're cleverer than you.

"*Everyone* is important, Anna." She turned her attention back to her bag. "Now, I've got your school records in here somewhere. According to them, your parents are missing..."

"They got sent to the workhouse on the last day of Dream London. They were marched into the parks..."

Petrina glanced up from her search.

"Marched into the parks? You're the third person today to say that. Is that some kind of euphemism? Are you saying that they're dead?"

"No. I'm saying they were marched into the parks. Didn't they brief you about how Dream London ended?"

Even if they had, it wouldn't have mattered. If you weren't here, if you didn't live through the changes, if you didn't experience how the streets moved around at night or how people's personalities were subtly altered, if you didn't see the casual cruelty, the cheapening of human life, the way that easy stereotypes took hold of people... If you weren't there, you're *never* going to understand what it was like.

Petrina adopted her experienced persona. Didn't she realise it would have had more credibility if she was dressed in a suit and not a baggy tie-dyed skirt?

"I'm from Birmingham Social Services. I was seconded here to help sort out the mess. Look, this would be a lot easier if we went inside..."

I was tired of standing in the cold, and she clearly wasn't going away. I opened my duffel coat and pulled out the heavy door key that I wore around my neck on a piece of string. Dream London had turned the door into a gothic arched portal of dark timber. There's a knack to opening the door: pull on the handle, a half twist and then push with your shoulder as you turn the key the rest of the way.

I tumbled into the hallway.

"Wait there, while I get some light."

Petrina wrote something on her pad as I felt for the box of matches on the shelf by the door. She really began to scribble as I struck the match and began to light the candles. Yellow pools of light sprang up one by one, illuminating a hallway that was slowly creaking its way back to its walnut-panelled glory.

Petrina followed me gingerly inside, careful where she trod. A line of orange Le Creuset pans marched down one side of the hall, ready to catch the drips from where the room above was separating from the rest of the house. Drips *plip plip plipped* into the pans at random, in A-flat, a quarter tone above E, a little too flat for middle C.

"It smells so damp." Petrina wrinkled her nose.

"That's because the house is leaking. It's okay in the kitchen."

I led her there. The warmth from the Rayburn smelled so good.

"I've always wanted one of those," said Petrina, crossing to take a closer look at the oven. Her face glowed orange, and I saw that she was really quite pretty when you stripped away the worry. I thought I knew her type: she'd spread her compassion wide and shallow, rather than engage on the specifics. Or maybe I was being too harsh. She was here, after all. She was trying to do the job.

"Where do you get the fuel from?" she asked.

"There's a bunch of sheds in the back garden. I've been pulling them apart."

"Why did your parents have a bunch of sheds in the back garden?"

"They didn't. The sheds turned up when Dream London was dying. You really don't understand what it was like, do you?"

Petrina didn't like that. She didn't like being told that she didn't understand. She placed her bag on the table and took a careful look around the kitchen, noting the unopened cans arranged in a line, the clean plates on the drainer by the sink, the opened cookery book on one of the counters.

"You're feeding yourself properly?"

"I get free lunch and dinner at school as part of the Emergency Support Grant. I also get a food ration twice a week from the distribution centre." I didn't mention that I shared some of it with Mr Hiatt. She was here to see me, Mr Hiatt was someone else's problem. Actually, Mr Hiatt was no one's problem. That *was* the problem.

"What about water?"

"The water still runs. The downstairs toilet is working." The upstairs toilet had been blocked with mackerel. I'd scooped out as many of them as I could and buried them in the back garden. The section of the pipe that I couldn't reach was now filled with rotting fish, but I didn't feel the need to share that information.

Petrina seemed to remember something at that point. She was back in her bag, rummaging. I can't begin to tell you how irritating that was.

"Always too many – what's that doing there – got it!"

She pulled out an orange plastic folder and began to flick through it. I read the words on the front: *London Disaster Zone Protocols, Ver 1.1*

"I'm sure I saw it in here… prostitution, dog attacks, native and non-native birds… Ah! Here it is. Water supplies… I see. Thought so. It says here that not all water supplies can be trusted. Do you know if yours has been verified?"

"I always boil the water before drinking."

"It might be better if you were to get your water from somewhere else." She paused to suck her bottom lip, to look concerned. "To be honest, Anna, I'm not that happy with you living here on your own. What if someone were to break in?"

"Did you see the door? I'm safer in here than I would be in most places in London."

"What happens if you get ill? What if you need help?"

"My boyfriend's family makes sure I'm alright. I go round there sometimes."

Petrina perked up at that. I could almost see her thoughts, her excitement at the thought of teenage sex.

"And does your boyfriend ever stay the night?"

"No, his parents won't allow it."

"But you'd like him to?" she prompted, a little too eagerly.

"What? So I can have unprotected sex in a damp house followed by the possibility of pregnancy and a delivery at what used to be Dream London Hospital? Yeah, now you mention it, that would be a far better choice than studying Physics at university. Thank you Petrina, I think I'll give him a call right now and get him round here."

Petrina smiled.

"I can see you're a sensible young woman."

"Don't patronise me."

"I'm sorry… but you say this is a damp house?"

"Of course it's damp! All the houses in London are damp. The buildings are slowly shifting back to their normal form and now nothing fits properly. This house is as dry as anywhere else."

She shook her head.

"It isn't, Anna. There are places that have been fixed up." She was looking thoughtful now. She was solving a problem. I felt my stomach tighten. "To be honest, Anna, you shouldn't be living here on your own. I think you'd be happier in a teen hostel amongst people of your own age."

"I can look after myself."

"Even so, that's what I'm going to recommend."

"Why?" I was struggling to remain calm. Start shouting and she'd mark me down as a hysterical little girl. I had to remain calm. "Why? I've managed on my own for nine months. I'll be eighteen in March; in eight months' time I'll be at university. Don't you have more deserving clients to visit?"

Petrina's mouth became a hard line. She wasn't listening. I ploughed on.

"But I suppose they don't have such nice houses. I'm sure you'd rather be sitting here in this kitchen than in one of those flats on the Broomfield estate with the druggies downstairs and two drunk parents spoiling for a fight in the room with you."

"Anna, I think…"

"You don't *want* me to be able to look after myself, Petrina. You'd rather that you could help me, because that's how you validate yourself. Well, I'll tell you when I needed help: back when Dream London ended. Tell me, where were you then? Back home in Birmingham, no doubt. You know where I was? Marching into the parks! Whilst people like you just sat at home, I was marching into the parks!"

I could see by Petrina's face that she didn't understand what I was talking about, but it didn't matter, I was angry now. Angry at Petrina, angry at all the people like her…

"You're all here now, all the people who were nowhere to be seen at the end. You weren't there when we were fighting in Snakes and Ladders Square. But you're here now, and *guess what?* You all know what to do! You're all here with your advice about how we should have done things! All the politicians, all the bankers, all the parasites. All the people who allowed Dream London to happen in the first place and then ran off to hide when it was spiralling out of control. It's always the same, isn't it?"

"Anna, I think you're getting a little emotional. I'm only here to help."

"But you don't get it, because you weren't here! And if you were, I know where you would have been. You wouldn't have been marching, you'd have been getting pissed or fucking or fighting, or writing letters to the Dream London newspapers. Well, I was out there trying to make a difference. I saw half my band killed. I walked in another world. Then I came back here only to see the same old people taking control again. It makes me sick!"

I was shouting now. I was red in the face. I couldn't help it. You hold in the anger as long as you can, and then suddenly it all comes spilling out.

"You saw people killed?" said Petrina, flicking through her folder once more. "... Trauma, trauma... here it is..."

She read the passage, nodding as she did so. "I realise it isn't nice to get so angry, Anna. I realise that later on you'll feel bad for shouting at me like that, and I want you to know that I don't blame you. No, I don't blame you. It's just a reaction to the stress that you've been under. Perfectly normal, nothing to be ashamed of. But you need help, Anna. That's why I must insist that you go to live in a hostel. Somewhere you can be looked after properly."

I folded my arms.

"No. I don't see how you can, anyway. I'm over sixteen."

"That was before the Emergency Act. Anyone under eighteen living alone is our responsibility."

"Of course they are," I scoffed. "And what happens to the properties they vacate? Who takes control of them?"

"That's nothing to do with me, Anna."

"I bet it isn't. They wouldn't let do-gooders like you know what's really going on. You'll go home thinking you've done a good job and meanwhile some shyster will have taken control of my house."

She became indignant.

"No, Anna, it's not like that..."

"Are you going to drag me away?"

"I could return here with someone to escort you..."

"I don't think that will be necessary."

We both jumped at that. Neither of us had noticed the tall, dark stranger who had slipped into the house. The stranger who now stood in the doorway to the kitchen. Not looking at us.

Petrina's eyes widened in terror as she gazed at the intruder. Petrina hadn't been in London for very long, after all. No wonder she found him so... unusual.

TWENTY-THREE

ADOLPHUS TWELVETREES

"Who are you? How did you get in here?"

"The front door was open," said the tall, dark stranger. "My chauffeur knocked, but there was no reply, so I had him bring me through here. Perhaps I should have had him announce me, but I didn't want to disturb your conversation."

He spoke with a deliciously low voice that set off a rumble somewhere in my tummy. Where Petrina gave the impression of a girl acting like a woman, he was clearly a *man*. Everything about him was perfectly groomed, from his precise haircut with the touch of grey at the temples to his manicured nails. His clothes spoke of power and money: the cut of his suit, the colour and the thickness of his shirt, the way he knotted his tie. He carried a white cane in his left hand, his silver signet ring clearly visible. He was the picture of a sophisticated gentleman, except for…

"What happened to your eyes?" asked Petrina.

His beautiful long lashes flickered a little as he half blinked. His eyelids couldn't cover those large jewelled eyes that bulged like a fly's. I'd seen people like him before, back in Dream London.

"Something I ate, I think. I'd rather hoped that they would return to normal with time, but some changes appear to be permanent. I can see shapes and nothing more. I can't read, I can't recognise faces. All I can see are blocks of light and dark. You don't mind me staying?"

The last sentence was directed at me. I did mind him staying, but I wanted to demonstrate to Petrina that I decided who was welcome in my house.

"You may stay. Would you like to sit down?"

"If you would be so good as to take my arm? As I said, I find it difficult to distinguish objects."

I led him to a seat at the breakfast counter.

"There's a stool just in front of your hand," called Petrina. I guess she'd worked with blind people in the past.

He felt its shape with one manicured hand, he used the other to find the counter surface and then he sat down. Just for a moment, those fly eyes seemed to settle on me, to look directly at me.

Petrina seemed to have regained some of her professional composure.

"This is what I mean, Anna. You have people just walking in your house. Can I ask who you are, Mister...?"

"Twelvetrees. Adolphus Twelvetrees." He produced a card from a pocket and laid it on the counter. I caught the little portcullis logo, read the words *Her Majesty's Government*. "Now, if you'll excuse me, Ms Kent, I have some business to discuss with Anna."

"I'm sorry, Mr Twelvetrees, but I can't allow that. This young woman is currently under my care."

"I'm sorry, Ms Kent, but you don't really have much of a part left to play in things."

He fumbled in his pocket and pulled out a large brass pocket watch. I noticed the bumps on the surface, watched the way Mr Twelvetrees felt the face. "Ms Kent, it is currently

4:50. I'm sorry to have to tell you this, but in thirty-five minutes' time, you'll be dead."

Something clicked inside me, and for a moment I was back in Dream London. Back in the world where such pronouncements were commonplace. Petrina seemed more irritated than upset. She'd not experienced the Dream World. Her voice was perfectly level.

"Are you threatening me, Mr Twelvetrees?"

"Merely stating a fact, Ms Kent." He reached inside his jacket pocket and pulled out a cream scroll tied with red ribbon. I gasped, despite myself.

"What?" said Petrina.

"That's a fortune scroll," I said. I felt sick inside. I didn't like what was coming.

"It's your fortune, Anna. That's why I'm here."

"I don't want to see it."

"A fortune scroll?" scoffed Petrina. "There's no such thing."

"There was in Dream London." My voice sounded flat. "But surely they don't work anymore..." I forced myself to speak firmly. "Take it away."

"That's your choice, of course."

"You mean you really believe in that thing?" asked Petrina.

"A fortune is a fortune," said Mr Twelvetrees. "Though it's true that the scroll's power is not what it was. This fortune will state where Anna will be at one particular point in time or it will describe her emotions and movement at some unspecified moment. It will never do both. Miss Kent, please note the first and fifth items on the list. You may find them distressing."

He unrolled the scroll a little.

"Or so I'm told," he said. "As I said, I can't read anything anymore."

Petrina took the scroll from Mr Twelvetrees and read out loud.

"*Anna and Mr Twelvetrees sit in the kitchen of the Poison Yews, London Temporary Zone Code B54 F11, on Thursday 11th January at 5:25pm.*"

"You shouldn't have touched it, Petrina," I said.

"Why? A stranger walks into the kitchen with a piece of paper and you just accept what he says without any... oh..."

"What's the matter?"

It took Petrina a moment to find her voice. When she did, it sounded strained.

"It says here that *Anna looks on in horror as Petrina dies.*" She ran her finger down the scroll, she licked her lips. "It doesn't say when, though."

"It won't," said Mr Twelvetrees. "The fortune gives positions or emotions. Never both at the same time."

"Then how do you know that I'll die by 5:25?"

"Because you're not present in this room at that time."

"But I might have left the room at that moment! I could have left the house!"

"What, and left Anna alone with me? Does that sound likely?"

Petrina clutched her bag close to herself.

"No! I don't know what sort of game you're playing, Mr Twelvetrees..."

"This isn't a game, Miss Kent. This is simply how it will be. Anna, I'm distressed to say, is fated to see you die. And, sadly, this will happen in the next thirty minutes or so."

It didn't sound as if he thought this was a sad thing. Something in his tone suggested that he was taking pleasure in her discomfort.

"No! I'm not having this!" Petrina rolled up the scroll, pushed it towards him. "I don't know who you are, Mr Twelvetrees, but I want you out of here. I don't want you anywhere near my client!"

"That's as may be. But I'll still be here at 5:25. You won't."

That air again. That charming bastard air. There were boys like him at school: good-looking, intelligent, arrogant. They knew what they wanted and they just took it. But with Mr Twelvetrees there was something else, too. A touch of cruelty...

"Where did this scroll come from?" I asked. "Why do you have it?"

Mr Twelvetrees's fly eyes were disconcerting. You couldn't tell which way he was looking. So what if he couldn't see; you didn't know where his attention was fixed. His reply seemed to be directed at the corner of the kitchen.

"The scroll was found in the ruins of Angel Tower. Someone noticed my name was written on it and they passed it along to me. And here I am, just as it says."

Petrina licked her lips.

"That doesn't prove anything. You read Anna's name, you turned up here."

"True, true."

"So you came here because the scroll said so?" I interrupted. "I find that hard to believe. There must be so much junk blowing around London. Lots of scrolls, lots of people's names. Why come to me?"

"Look at the scroll Anna. You'll see why I came to you."

"Leave it alone, Anna," warned Petrina. I couldn't help myself. I took it, unrolled it.

"The bottom's torn off."

"I know. That's how we found it. Don't procrastinate. What does it say?"

I took a deep breath. I looked at the scroll.

Anna and Mr Twelvetrees sit in the kitchen of the Poison Yews, London Temporary Zone Code B54 F11, on Thursday 11th January at 5:25pm.

Walking towards the ruined castle on the hill, furious at your companion

Anna moves through the crowd, terrified. What if they were to recognise her for who she was?

"Recognise me for who I am? What does that mean? When does this happen?"

"Who knows? I told you, you can know when, or what. That's the nature of this fortune. Read on."

"*He is so gorgeous! He strokes your breast as he...*"

I broke off as I realised what I was saying. I felt the blush spring to my face. Mr Twelvetrees's mouth had curled a little at the corners. He'd tricked me. The bastard had tricked me into reading it out loud.

"What does it say?" asked Petrina. Even amidst the strangeness, I could see her eyes dancing once more at the thought of teenage sex.

"I'm not saying."

He is so gorgeous! He strokes your breast as he thrusts into you. You are coming, again and again.

I had the distinct impression that Mr Twelvetrees was looking at me. He knew what was on the scroll, he knew what I was reading. He knew!

"What does it say?" asked Petrina.

"It doesn't matter. I'll go on."

Such was my distress that I read the next line before I registered the words.

"*Anna looks on in horror as Petrina dies.*"

Petrina said nothing. Mr Twelvetrees was smiling properly now. I scanned the next line before reading it aloud.

"*Nivôse 22nd. You are sitting in the* Café de la Révolution."

"Nivôse?" I said. "What's that?"

"Ah, yes," said Mr Twelvetrees. "The benefits of a private education. That comes from the French revolutionary calendar. It's the month of December or January."

"The French revolutionary calendar? Why should it give dates according to the French..."

But I'd already read the next line.

"*Anna sits down to a meal in Dream Paris.*"

Dream Paris.

It was important not to show any emotion. But I felt hollow, like if you blew across my lips I would sound a note, deep and low.

"It says here I'm in Dream Paris. I... I don't want to do that."

I was struggling to speak. Were you in Dream London? If so, you'll understand what I was feeling. How would you feel if you were told you had to return to that place?

"I'm sorry," said Mr Twelvetrees. He didn't sound sorry. "But I'm not sure that you have a choice."

"Of course she does," snapped Petrina. Good for her. "She's not going to this Dream Paris place."

But I was. I'd just read the last line.

Nivôse 23rd, Dream Paris. Anna is arguing with Margaret Sinfield.

Margaret Sinfield. That was my mother, last seen being taken off to the workhouse. I'd spent the last few months wondering if she was alive or dead. Now I knew the answer. She was alive. She was alive in Dream Paris.

Petrina and Mr Twelvetrees were arguing, their words reverberating in the hollowness inside me. I was terrified, but I knew then that I was going to Dream Paris. Of course I was. My mother was there.

TWENTY-TWO

DREAM PARIS

MR TWELVETREES FLICKED open his brass watch and felt the dial. I read the hands. It was 5:10.

"Less than fifteen minutes, Ms Kent."

I was becoming more impressed by Petrina. She was obviously frightened, but she was keeping it together. Perhaps I had been too harsh on her earlier. She may have dressed like a girl, but here, when it counted, she was acting like a professional. I sometimes think that's the difference between adults and children. Adults are better at acting.

Petrina was firm. "I don't know what sick game you're playing, Mr Twelvetrees, but I'm not leaving you alone here with Anna. The poor girl is terrified."

"She's not a girl, she's a young woman. And I'm not playing games. I'm merely showing her what's written on a piece of paper."

Nonsense! He was showing me my fortune. He'd been in Dream London. He knew what that meant. Even Petrina had some idea, now. She was licking her lips, eyes flicking this way and that, no doubt looking for the thing that was coming to kill her.

What if it were already in the house?

"Stay here," I said.

I hurried from the kitchen. The front door was closed, no doubt pulled to by Mr Twelvetrees' chauffeur. I ran upstairs and did a quick check of the rooms, looking under the beds (there were bells under them, silver bells that would tinkle if anything moved), opening cupboards (the smell of dried flowers still lingered), peered around the corners into the corridors that led nowhere (mouse traps and caltrops left scattered on the floor). Nothing. There was nothing in the house that I could see that should present any danger to Petrina.

I returned to the kitchen, the sound of a trumpet fanfare in my head.

"Run, Petrina," I said. "Get out of here."

"Not without you, Anna. I can't leave you alone here with this man!"

Of course she couldn't. She was doing her job. My admiration for her increased still further.

"Then let's go now," I said. "Both of us."

"That won't make any difference," said Mr Twelvetrees. "You'll still be back here at 5:25."

He was right, of course. I picked up the scroll again, ran my finger down the fortune.

"It doesn't mention my father. Does that mean he's dead?"

"It doesn't mean anything," said Petrina. "A stranger walks into your house and shows you a piece of paper. That doesn't mean anything, Anna."

"You don't understand, Petrina, I've seen these scrolls before. If one says my mother is in Dream Paris, then I'm going to go to Dream Paris. How could I not do so? She might be trapped there!"

"*If* it's a genuine fortune scroll. And even if your mother *is* trapped in Dream Paris, it's not your responsibility to sort out her problems."

Did she think I hadn't heard that a hundred times before? That's the worst thing about people like Petrina. They come out with the same old platitudes and they think they're saying something profound. It annoys me so much! And yet, I couldn't be too annoyed with her. If the scroll was true, Petrina had around ten minutes to live...

As if on cue, Mr Twelvetrees spoke up.

"5:15. Ten more minutes to go!"

"Stop that, Mr Twelvetrees!" snapped Petrina. "You don't frighten me with your piece of paper." Her voice suggested otherwise.

"I'm not trying to frighten you. I'm warning you. And as for what could happen to you, well, why not ask Anna?"

More cruelty. He knew how to push people's buttons. Petrina took hold of my arm.

"What could happen to me, Anna?" she pleaded.

"I don't know! Have you eaten any street food? Anything from the stalls? Some of it is left over from Dream London. People live on it for weeks, and then whatever it was in the food that was holding it to this world just slips away. The food vanishes and so do the nutrients in your body. A couple of months ago a boy in our school starved to death in front of his classmates' eyes."

Petrina kneaded the top of her bag, squeezed the knitted material between her fists. "I've only been here a week or so. I've mostly eaten in my digs."

"Do you know where the food comes from? Never mind that. There are other ways. Sometimes buildings just collapse. Whatever it was that was holding them together just vanishes. Or maybe a hole will open in the ground. That happened to a whole family. Their son was in my year. There was a crashing noise in the night and the next day the whole house had gone, vanished down a sinkhole."

Petrina looked down at the stone flagged floor.

"You think the floor will open beneath me and me alone? What if I came and sat by you?"

"You know they found metal creatures in the soil?" said Mr Twelvetrees "Like squids with spears for arms, frozen in place as they swam to the surface?"

"It's true," I said, unhappily. "They keep digging them up. A whole army of them, they were almost at the surface when Dream London ended."

Petrina was looking at the floor in horror. "Anna, whose side are you on? You must see I'm only trying to help you!"

"I know that, Petrina!" I felt close to tears. Darkness had gathered outside. This safe, ordered, quiet place that I had built was no match for the horror of the outside world. "I know that! But I'm trying to help you, too! You don't know what it's like, Petrina! You don't know what it was like back then! I don't want to go back to all of that! And yet it says that I will, right here on this piece of paper. It's not that I have a choice, it's going to happen!"

"Five minutes to go!" Mr Twelvetrees held up his watch.

"I don't care," snapped Petrina. "I'm staying. I don't care what you say, Mr Twelvetrees, this poor girl is terrified."

"And so are you," smiled Mr Twelvetrees.

"Yes, I am. But I'm not leaving."

No matter how wrong-headed she was, the woman was brave. Petrina took hold of my hand.

"Don't worry, dear. I'm staying with you." You could hear only the faintest tremor in her voice.

"Four minutes."

"You still haven't said why you're here, Mr Twelvetrees. Why bring Anna that scroll?"

"Her Majesty's Government needs people like Anna. It

wants to find out what happened in Dream London, it wants to prevent such incursions happening again."

"And what's your part in this?"

"A number of people still remain unaccounted for after the changes. It's known that most of the people who sailed down the rivers to other lands never returned when the changes came to an end. Many soldiers and spies have been sent to look for them, few have returned."

"My parents," I said. "You're looking for people like my parents."

"Precisely. See, Petrina? I'm not such a bad person. I'm here to help Anna."

"It sounds more like she's helping you."

"Where's Dream Paris?" I asked. "I've heard the news. There's been no mention of any changes happening in Paris."

"There haven't been, so far as we know," said Mr Twelvetrees. "I think Dream Paris is a different place from our Paris."

A different place.

"You think? Don't you know?"

"We know very little. You'll need to find a way back into the Dream World."

I shivered as he said the words.

"Dream Paris will be in there somewhere. We know that the Dream World has broken through to our world in the past. We suspect that Dream Paris is a remnant of a former incursion."

"So I'm to go into the Dream World and look for Dream Paris. But you don't know where it will be."

"No. If we did, we would have gone there ourselves."

Looking back, I really should have thought more about what he'd just said. But at the time I was too distracted. All I was thinking was that I was going to see my mother again.

"And then you found this fortune scroll." I looked at the paper. "I'm your route to Dream Paris."

"She's not going to Dream Paris! She's…"

Petrina paused, pressed a hand to her head.

"I don't feel so…"

"What's the matter?" I said.

"I think this is it," said Mr Twelvetrees.

Petrina was looking at her hands.

"How many fingers…?" she murmured.

"Petrina, look at me."

She wasn't listening. I was trying to see her eyes. Blue checks, square pupils… What was wrong with her?

"Everything is wHoLe. EveRyThInG iS sepArAtE…"

What was the matter with her voice? She sounded like she was being auto-tuned, her voice stepping up and down between pitches.

"EvErYtHiNg iS mOvInG aPaRt."

"What's happening, Anna?" That was Mr Twelvetrees. He sounded eager, excited.

"Her eyes! They're like little television screens. Mr Twelvetrees! What's going on? Do you know what's happening?"

"I'd step away from her if I were you, Anna."

I didn't know any better than to do so. I wasn't a sadist, I took no pleasure in the death of another human being.

"AnNa, tAkE mY hAnD! HOlD mE to tHiS wOrLd, I…"

She looked at a hand that had turned into a cluster of pink boxes and was silent. Her head was a cube sticking from her knitted jumper. She was a badly made Guy, a collection of cuboids slumping to the floor, dead.

"5:23," said Mr Twelvetrees. "What is it? What's happened?"

The sound of music filled my head, brass bands blaring. The thing that had been Petrina Kent lay on the floor. What the hell had happened to her?

"What is it?" said Mr Twelvetrees.

A soprano cornet was screaming in my head. I imagined a vault, thick walls, a heavy door, and me, inside, in the silence. It worked. It worked a little. The madness receded, the sound of it dulled by the walls.

"What can you see?" repeated Mr Twelvtrees.

"She's like a computer woman. An ultra low resolution picture of a woman."

I looked around the kitchen. My beautiful, spotlessly clean kitchen. I didn't look at the floor. I sat down on a stool next to Mr Twelvetrees. It was 5:25.

"I can't stay here," I said. "I need to go to Dream Paris to find my parents."

"The scroll only mentions your mother," Mr Twelvetrees reminded me, cruelly.

I was convinced. He was a sadist. And I was in his hands.

EAU DE NIL

THERESE DELACROIX

Mr Twelvetrees said that I wouldn't need anything, that everything would be taken care of. I wasn't having that. That's a trick that men play on women, one they instinctively seem to know. "*No need to bring anything, it will all be provided. Hey, dinner's on me! It's okay, I'll run you there. No need to bother learning how to fix it, I brought my tools…*"

They call it chivalry, they call it being a gentleman. Really, it's just a way of keeping you in their power.

I stood in the doorway, looking everywhere but at the shape on the floor. (Who would tell her family? What would happen to the body?)

"I want to fetch a few things," I said. "You wait here."

Mr Twelvetrees was gazing at nothing, fly eyes glittering like jewels in the flickering candlelight. The dull warmth of the kitchen, the smell of the Rayburn, the thick oak door that kept out the night… I didn't want to leave this place.

"Don't be too long," said Mr Twelvetrees. "We're on a tight schedule."

The salesman's trick. Make up a deadline. Still, I ran up the uneven stairs, taking care not to trip on the carpet that had buckled where the treads narrowed. The upstairs landing creaked as the house shifted, the rain pattered on the ill-fitting windows. I ran into my room and grabbed my old hiking rucksack and started throwing things into it. Underwear, clothes, penknife. My own script, the one I kept locked in a box.

My walking boots stood on my cornet case, tucked at the bottom of the wardrobe. A note sounded in my head and I remembered poor Petrina's pixellated form.

Think of the silence.

I found a pad half filled with maths notes and I tore off a few blank sheets.

Dear Ben, I wrote. I paused, pen in my mouth. What was I going to say?

My mother is alive in Dream Paris. A man called Mr Twelvetrees came to my house and told me this. He says he's going to help me find her. He gave me this card. (I placed the card at the side of the note, ready to be sealed in the envelope.) *I don't know if I can trust him, this may all be a trick, but what else can I do?*

What else could I put? I signed it *Anna.* Quickly, I scribbled out a second note to Mr Hiatt. And then a third, to Ben again. I sealed these notes in envelopes and addressed them.

I returned to the kitchen to find Mr Twelvetrees sitting where I'd left him, blank eyes turned towards a floor that danced with orange stars in the glow of the Rayburn. He looked up as I entered the room, hearing the bump as I caught my rucksack on the door frame.

"Ready? Splendid! Now, would you mind taking my arm, Anna?"

"Just a moment," I paused, thinking. "I can't just leave like this. What about Mr Hiatt? What's he going to do for food? What about Ben and his family? They'll worry if I just vanish."

"Who's Ben?"

"My boyfriend."

Perhaps that was too grand a title. To be honest, Ben was more of a convenience. A box ticked, something that prevented offers and enquiries from other men.

"... and then there's school. What about my exams?"

And that was the big thing. I had my future to think of. I needed my grades to get to university.

Mr Twelvetrees waved a hand dismissively.

"You're doing work of national importance. Trust me, all that will be taken care of." He looked in my general direction. Or was it all a lie? Could he really see me? I wasn't sure. This was where I found out. I placed the first letter to Ben in the middle of the table, in full view. Mr Twelvetrees didn't seem to notice.

"I'm sorry, Anna," he continued. "You read the fortune. You speak to your mother on Nivôse 23rd. According to our research, that's in five days time."

"And you only just came to me?"

"The scroll was only found on Monday morning. It took us a day to find out which Anna it referred to."

"It had my address on it."

"We wanted to know something about you."

Why? It's a fortune. What difference would it make? But I kept my thoughts to myself.

"I'm sorry. We can talk about such things later. Now, would you mind taking my arm?"

I did so, and I led him from the room, casting a backwards glance at the letter to Ben I'd left on the table. How long before someone saw it? Or would it just lie there, forgotten?

* * *

THERE WAS A dark car parked outside The Poison Yews; a heavy old thing, all polished chrome and shiny black paint. As we approached it, a tall young man with a broken nose got out.

"Thank you, Darren," said Mr Twelvetrees.

Darren held open a door, and the scent of the oily red leather interior wafted over us both. I felt sick: the car smelt of Dream London.

"Ladies first, Anna."

I ducked into the car through a cloud of acetone breath. As he closed the door, I noted that Darren was missing some fingers. Then he was gone, around the other side to help Mr Twelvetrees into his seat.

Mr Twelvetrees waited for the sound of the driver's door closing.

"The base, please."

"Certainly, Mr Twelvetrees."

The car pulled away gently. I noted that someone had laid down a metal sheet over the pipeline at the end of the street to allow car access. People like Mr Twelvetrees were not to be inconvenienced.

"Any news of your wife, Darren?"

"Still none since this morning, Mr Twelvetrees."

"It must be awful. I suppose the worry increases every day."

So why mention it?

"Darren put his wife up as collateral for a loan, back in Dream London," explained Mr Twelvetrees. "He was behind on the payments. They took his kidneys, too. Isn't that right, Darren?"

Darren grunted.

"He's on dialysis every night. But we look after you, don't we, Darren?"

I'd gotten into a car with a sadist. What was I doing? I reached into the pocket of my rucksack and pulled out my souvenir of the last days of Dream London.

"Can you read this, Mr Twelvetrees?"

I pushed the script into his hands.

"I can't read anything, remember," he said, feeling the edges of the sheet. "What does it say?"

"Never mind." I couldn't keep the disappointment from my voice. I'd hoped it would still work.

"Is this a truth script, by any chance? Do you think I'm lying to you, Anna? I've not said anything that wasn't on your fortune."

I reached to take back my script, and his hands tightened upon it.

"I don't think I should let you keep this."

"If you don't give it back to me, I'll get out of the car right now."

"And miss out on the chance of seeing your mother?"

"Don't treat me like a fool. If the fortune scroll is correct, I'll end up seeing her with or without your help."

Mr Twelvetrees smiled.

"Clever girl." He released his grip. I tucked the script into my coat.

We drove in silence through the broken streets of London. We passed through freshly restored areas lit up with electricity, shop windows steamy with central heating. We plunged into the gloom of less fortunate districts, where the broken shell of London was lit by nothing more than moonlight. In one such zone I saw a silver tube train, brand new and shiny, zooming on its way, full of passengers relaxing as they headed home from work. The train glided by against a backdrop of ruined Tudor houses, cracked open like eggs.

"Why me?" I whispered. The words were spoken to myself, but Mr Twelvetrees answered.

"Quite simply, because we know that you are going to find your way there. Maybe you can find your way back. If you can bring some people back with you, that would be a bonus. But just knowing a route would be a start."

"Why?"

"Because if we're going to help all the lost people, we need to know where they are. We need to know the route back home. You remember how things were in Dream London."

I certainly did. The city changed a little every night. Roads and railways had a habit of drifting off course, of connecting themselves to new destinations. Finding a path anywhere was almost impossible. There in the car I was seized with a pulse pounding fear. I felt myself getting hot, felt the sweat prickling under my clothes. I was going back to that disconnected place. I was returning to the Dream World.

After half an hour or so in the car we drove up to an endless wire fence. Lines of green lorries and Land Rovers stood behind it. Men and women in green fatigues hurried back and forth. A soldier opened a gate as he saw the black car approach.

"This is an Army barracks," I said in surprise.

"Oh, yes," said Mr Twelvetrees. "What were you expecting? You must know that Whitehall took some of the most extreme changes in Dream London. Half the buildings are uninhabitable, and we don't know if we can trust the other half. What could be listening? What's the matter?"

I was gripped with another fear, one quite different to my earlier panic. A group of men and women in bright red tunics was walking across the centre of the compound. They were carrying instruments: a bugle, two horns, a clarinet...

"I'm okay."

"No, you're not. What is it?"

"The band. They're not going to play, are they?"

"I shouldn't think so. Now, gather your things. We're in a hurry. The minister herself wants to speak to you."

The minister. I didn't register his words; I was too busy looking at the band.

EVERYTHING WAS HAPPENING in a hurry, that was obvious. I was taken to a spare meeting room, the tables down one side filled with the half-empty teacups. The flipchart at the front of the room had the letters *DP* scrawled across the top sheet. Displaced Person? Or Dream Paris? I had just begun to flick through the other sheets when the minister walked into the room. She was speaking into her phone.

"No! Cancel that meeting! I need to be in Munich tomorrow!"

She saw me and held up a hand, a brief acknowledgement.

"I'm sorry, I've got to go…" She dropped the phone in a pocket then advanced upon me, hand extended.

"Therese Delacroix, Minister with responsibility for the Dream World. Anna, I want to thank you so much for coming."

Therese Delacroix was a slight, plainly dressed woman. She gave me a firm handshake, gazing deep into my eyes as she did so. Everything about Therese suggested confidence: the minimal make up, the grey hair, the sensible shoes. This was a woman in charge, someone who did things her way. A role model to spunky, gutsy school girls everywhere. School girls like me. *See?* she was saying, *you can do it, sisters!*

I disliked her immediately.

"Anna, I'm so glad we got to meet. I'm very busy at the moment and I was afraid you'd have set off before I had a chance to thank you personally. I can't begin to tell you how impressed we all are by what you've agreed to."

"I'm not sure that I've agreed to anything. My name was on a scroll."

Therese waved a hand dismissively.

"You're going to Dream Paris. That's a brave thing to do. I'm not sure you realise how brave."

That got me.

"Really? Tell me, *Therese*, were you in Dream London?"

She didn't try to flannel me.

"No, I wasn't, Anna. My constituency is in Manchester. I was part of the Emergency Parliament located there during the Incursion."

The Incursion, I thought. *Is that what they're calling it?*

"Manchester. A lot of the ministers are still up there, aren't they?"

Therese nodded. That was when I realised that my first impressions were wrong. There was nothing plain about Therese. Her clothes, her make up, her hair. This was a woman who had spent a lot of time and money on trying to appear natural.

"Shall we sit down, Anna?"

We pulled two of the metal chairs up to face each other. The people who had been in this room before us were too important to straighten up after themselves.

"Now, Anna. As I said, we're very grateful to you for agreeing to do this for us."

"And as I said, I don't know why. It's not like I'm choosing to go."

"It's very brave of you to admit that." Therese leaned forward slightly. I'd seen this trick before. This is what some people do when they want you to think they're admitting you into their confidence. They're trying to make you feel special.

"I realise that your biggest concern is your mother, Anna, and that is right and proper. But as you're going to Dream Paris, I want to ask you to think about something else."

"Go on."

"Anna, have you ever wondered what happened when Dream London ended?"

"Wondered? I was there, Therese. I was there in the parks. I was there when they destroyed Angel Tower. When they destroyed the Contract Floor. Where were you, Therese?"

Therese smiled. Little creases failed to form at the edges of her eyes. Therese was a nipped and tucked, coloured and toned, creamed and exfoliated one-hundred-percent-natural woman.

"I like to think I did my part, too. But Anna, I want you to understand. When the freedom fighters such as yourself…"

"The freedom fighters?"

I couldn't help but laugh. Therese pretended not to notice, she carried on speaking.

"… when they broke the hold of Dream London, when they destroyed the Contract Floor, what do you think they achieved?"

"They destroyed the contracts. All that land that had been sold to the Dream World."

"That's right. The Dream World no longer owned Dream London." She sat back in her seat. "So who did?"

I opened my mouth. I closed it again. I'd never really thought about that before. "The people who used to own it?"

Therese steepled her fingertips.

"For the most part. But London is a different shape today. There is land here that didn't exist before the changes. Who owns that?"

"… the Queen?"

Therese pursed her lips and nodded.

"Actually, that's probably as good an answer as any. But even so, there are assets in this city still unaccounted for. No one owns them."

"Good! Make them common land!"

"That would be a good thing, wouldn't it? But this is the modern world, Anna. Nothing remains unclaimed for long. And that's what's happening here. The ownership of parts of this city remains unknown. We believe that some of the missing contracts may lie in Dream Paris…"

I shuddered. Dream London had started when things from the Dream World bought property in London.

"What do you know about the French Revolution, Anna?"

"That it was the start of modern Europe?"

"Good answer. But what about the Communes? The Great Fear? The Reign of Terror? Do you know about those things?"

"I've seen *Les Misérables*."

"That was much later. Anna, I won't lie to you…"

Only liars say they won't lie to you, only liars think of lying enough to mention it.

"I won't lie to you, Anna. What little we know about Dream Paris suggests that it's a dangerous place. There's no democratic government there. Rather, they have something called The Committee for Public Safety. A group of people that changes by the month, new leaders denouncing the old and putting them up for execution."

I gazed straight ahead. I'd been frightened enough at the thought of re-entering the Dream World. Now I was being told I was going to enter a revolution.

"The citizens of Dream Paris live in fear of each other. Dream Parisians live in fear of being accused as traitors by their friends and neighbours."

"I still have to go."

"You know how they show that they're suspicious of you? They hang burning fruit in the street outside your apartment."

I didn't know what to say to that.

"It will be worse for you, Anna. You'll be a foreigner. An outsider."

"I feel like an outsider here."

"You can be an outsider here and still belong. Anna, I won't lie to you, if you enter that city, you will find it very difficult to leave."

"I'm going to enter that city. It says so on my fortune. Besides, my parents are in there."

"Your mother is there," Mr Twelvetrees reminded me. He'd been sitting quietly in the corner, smiling with complacent cruelty.

"You'll need papers to get in, papers to move across the city, papers to leave. The chances are that once you're sucked into that place, you'll never get out."

"I'll see my mother."

"Do you even like your mother?" asked Mr Twelvetrees. "According to your school records you adjusted to the loss of your parents much faster than your peers."

That was a barbed but remarkably astute question. Did I like my mother? The last time I had seen her she was a lush, throwing herself at any man who came by. But Dream London had changed everyone. She never used to be like that. Once my mother had been something big in the city, she'd been a woman not unlike Therese Delacroix, back before the changes had convinced everyone that a woman's place was in the home. But none of that mattered. At the end of the day, she was my mother.

"How do you know about Dream Paris?" I asked. "If it's so difficult to get out, how do you know anything about the place?"

Therese held up a rectangular piece of paper. An old photograph, faded brown with age.

"This was found in an old book shop on Charing Cross Road. I'm sure no one thought anything of it until after the Incursion. There are lots of other sources, just like it."

I examined the image. It was a brown photograph of the Eiffel Tower. It looked as if it was under repairs, the structure wrapped in sheeting. And then I noticed the really odd thing. There was another, smaller Eiffel Tower off to the side of it. And then I spotted two more, even smaller, in front. At the bottom of the picture, written in faded black ink, I read the words *Dream Paris, 1938*.

I pulled out the truth script. It hadn't worked on Mr Twelvetrees. Maybe it would on Therese.

"Look at this, Therese..."

The script looked so much brighter here in Mundane London. The curls of colour, the fluorescent yellow, gold and scarlet seemed to light up the room. A spiral of meaning that wound out and drew your eye down to the impossible colour below. Therese was hooked.

"This is a truth script," I said. "I was given it in the parks, at the end of Dream London. Tell me, Therese, can I trust you?"

"As much as anyone else in this world."

"Hah! Am I going into danger?"

"I've already told you that you are."

I was lost. She was answering me with the truth, and saying nothing.

"Are you doing what's best by me?"

"Yes," said Therese, quite simply.

I felt quite frustrated.

"What can I do to succeed?"

Therese pulled me close.

"You've got a pretty face," she said. "Use it."

"I've got brains too," I snapped. "I don't need my looks to succeed."

Therese laughed.

"You take my advice, young lady. The odds are stacked against you in this world and any other. You take any advantage that you have and you use it."

I looked closer at Therese. She wasn't what you would call attractive, but there was something else there. Call it power, call it determination, call it sex appeal, but there was something there. Therese had *it*.

And what's more, Therese was telling the truth. She'd read the script.

"How come you know so much about Dream Paris if you've never been there?"

"You don't have to enter Dream Paris to know about the place, Anna. Its influence is spreading across the Dream World. Dream Paris is at war with everyone. If Dream London had continued to grow, they'd have been at war with us. The Dream Parisians seek to bring revolution everywhere."

"Doesn't sound a bad thing to me."

"You say that when you have a bed to sleep in every night, when you have enough food to eat, when you can walk to school and home again without fear of being denounced and sentenced to the guillotine."

I felt a flash of irritation.

"You say that you spent the *Incursion…*" – I spoke the word with heavy sarcasm – "safe in Manchester. You, who will go back to her nice safe offices whilst I set out to Dream Paris alone."

"Oh, didn't Mr Twelvetrees tell you?" Therese looked across the room. "You won't be going alone."

TWENTY-ONE

FRANCIS CUPPELLO

I'D LIKE TO say that I wasn't fooled by Francis, not for a minute. But that wouldn't be true. I was wrong about him over and over again. In a way, that's what this story is all about, I suppose. It's what every story is about, the difference between the appearance and what lies underneath.

So we'll start with the appearance. Francis looked *good*. He was almost a cliché: tall and dark, with a handsome chiselled face. Everything about him was clean and pressed and freshly shaven, that good old Army training (he told me later that the first thing the Army taught him was how to iron a shirt.) He was cocky and confident and charming and he gazed at me with the deepest brown eyes I'd ever seen and all I could think about was that fortune (*coming, again and again...*) and before I knew it I was blushing. He saw it, but he was too much of a gentleman to notice. Instead, he smiled a clear, innocent smile as he held out his hand.

I could feel Therese looking at me. She knew what I was thinking. It was only later it occurred to me that she was thinking it herself. I was inexperienced then, I still believed that others never thought about sex.

"Anna, I want you to meet Francis Cuppello. He'll be accompanying you on your journey…"

I took his hand. Francis was so big, so broad, so… pumped. I could see the way his muscles moved under his green uniform jumper. All the boys back at the sixth form seemed so skinny and insignificant in comparison.

"Pleased to meet you, Francis."

"And you too, Anna. Listen, I've got some food coming from the mess for us. I thought that you might be hungry."

He was considerate, too. The perfect gentleman.

"Oh, I am."

"There you are," said Therese. "Well, Anna, I'll leave you in Francis's capable hands. Mr Twelvetrees, shall I escort you from the room? Oh, and by the way, Anna. How long will the effect of your truth scroll last?"

"About an hour." I couldn't meet her eyes. I felt hopelessly outclassed.

"An hour. I'll delay getting back to the cabinet, then. It wouldn't do to be in this condition amongst that bunch. Best of British, Anna."

And she left, Mr Twelvetrees on her arm. They passed the food trolley as they exited.

Francis was really quite domesticated. He pushed aside the higgledy-piggledy chairs and pulled up a table from the wall, wiped it down with a cloth and then placed knives and forks and a salt cellar onto it. He set out the plates and removed the covers, then he fetched a jug of water and two glasses.

I smelled rich stew, I saw green beans, and my mouth began to water.

"Best I could do," he said.

I didn't reply. I hadn't seen such good food in months, I picked up my fork and began shovelling it down. Francis sat across the table, watching me eat.

"According to your fortune, you'll be in the *Café de la Révolution* in Dream Paris in four days time. We have to move quickly."

"You've seen my fortune?" I blushed, fork half way to my mouth. *Coming, again and again...*

"I've got a copy." Francis patted his pocket.

"Did you volunteer to escort me, or were you chosen?"

"Ordered to. I think there are other fortune scrolls. I wonder if one of them suggested I was the best person for the job?"

I noticed that he said *best person* and not *best man*. That was good.

All too quickly, I'd finished my stew. Francis pushed his plate towards me.

"Oh, no! I couldn't possibly..."

"I've already eaten. In a war, civilians never eat as well as the army."

He thought there was a war still on?

"Eat as much as you can, we're going to be busy. We need to visit the quartermaster's and then it's straight to bed."

"Bed? But it's barely eight o'clock."

"We'll be setting off first thing in the morning."

"Tomorrow? So soon?"

"Like I said, we need to move fast."

I wasn't really listening. I was too busy forking up stew.

THE QUARTERMASTER WAS a little man with a superior smile. His gaze wandered out from behind the counter and up to my chest.

"We've got these for you." He indicated a pile of clothes on the counter beside him. "We had to send out for them specially. Do you want to try them on here?"

"In your dreams."

Francis laughed, and I felt pleased at that. It was good to have a bodyguard who was on my side.

The quartermaster frowned at Francis. "They're waterproof and warm," he said, loftily. "We've got this backpack for you to put them in."

"I could be away for weeks. That won't be enough clothes."

"Don't worry, it's all been taken care of."

He opened the backpack and started to pack.

"Six pairs of knickers," he leered at me as he handled them. "Three bras, six pairs of socks, two pairs of trousers, three tee shirts, two tops, a fleece and a waterproof. Oh…"

He reached under the counter and produced something with a flourish.

"One pack of sanitary towels. You see? We think of everything."

"What else could a girl want? What about food?"

"I'll throw some Mars Bars in just in case, but like I said, we've got something better."

He produced a thick black wallet. "Will *you* sign for this?" He pushed it towards Francis.

I reached out and snatched the wallet away.

"*I'll* sign for it. Once I've checked the contents."

The wallet was divided into sections. The largest part was stuffed with currencies of all different colours and sizes. I ran a finger across them, rippling through the notes, noting the familiar British Pounds, the plastic Euros. I recognised Dream London currency, and then I was into the unknown. There were thin paper notes in lemon and white, squares of thick pink paper. There was something that seemed to be made of leather, a set of translucent notes that felt wet like onion skins, there were slivers of stone.

"We think we've covered all the major currencies," said the quartermaster.

I turned to the next section of the wallet, pulled out a silver card, the name of a well known bank printed along the top.

"Five-hundred-pound-a-day limit. You'll have to fill out an expenses form when you get back."

"What are the other cards?" I was looking at one that had a picture of a starving child on the side. It was looking up, head too big for its shrunken body. There was something written beneath it in a strange language.

"No idea," shrugged the Quartermaster. "They were brought back from the Dream World. Maybe one of them will be of some use to you."

"Thanks a bunch."

"Don't be sarcastic. Look at the last section."

He took the wallet back from me and pulled it open, showing me the last space behind the currency. A piece of parchment nestled in there.

"Dream London wasn't something new, you know."

I'd heard that. The Dream World had broken into our world many times in the past. There was just that something about our London that had enabled the Dream World to flourish in a way it had never done before.

"That parchment came from the archives. The bearer is guaranteed a good evening meal, a decent breakfast and a change of clothes. Every day."

"How does it work?"

"How should I know? Now, take care of it. That thing is very dangerous."

"Dangerous? How?"

"It would bring about the end of our society if it got into the wrong hands."

That sounded like the sort of thing my father would have said. I folded up the wallet up and put it safely in my pocket.

"Is that it?"

"Two last things."

He pulled them from behind the counter with a flourish.

"A lemon and a hipflask," I said.

"A hipflask full of whisky."

"I don't drink whisky."

"You can use it as a bribe or as antiseptic."

He seemed to be waiting for something.

"What?" I said.

"Why aren't you complaining about the lemon?"

"Because it's the most sensible thing you've included, that's why." I hoisted the pack onto my back. It weighed more than I expected, and I was glad that I wasn't going to have to carry more. A thought occurred to me.

"What about weapons? Don't I at least get a knife?"

"You get what you can handle."

And he smiled at that small victory over me. Oh, yes, that and the fact that he had got to handle my underwear.

Pervert.

"WELL DONE," SAID Francis, as he led me along a dull green corridor. "Joe's a bully. You handled him well."

I smiled despite myself.

"Thank you. Where are we going now?"

"To be issued with weapons."

I glanced at him, but he wasn't smiling.

"I was only joking about the weapons. I wouldn't know what to do with a gun."

"I doubt you'll get a gun. They'll issue you with something suitable."

"Doesn't the quartermaster give out the weapons? Obviously not. What do you call the guy who issues weapons? An armourer?"

"I usually call him Eddie."

I laughed. He was trying to keep his face straight, but I could see the smile curling at the corner of his lips.

"Eddie will want to assess you. He's a mate of mine. He's not like Joe."

We pushed our way into the armoury. It was similar to the quartermaster's stores. The same long counter, but this time there were racks of guns, rifles and knives behind it. Dark, oily metal. I suddenly felt quite worried at the thought of having to carry a weapon. Carrying a weapon meant that I might have to hurt someone. I didn't like that thought.

Eddie looked like Francis's older, only slightly less attractive brother. He didn't bother to introduce himself, he merely started asking questions straight away.

"Okay, can you speak French?"

"I got a C at GCSE."

Eddie and Francis raised their eyebrows to each other.

"Only a C," said Eddie. "I thought you were meant to be clever?"

"I'm not that good at languages. Anyway, a C isn't bad."

"I thought everyone got As for everything nowadays."

"Did you? That's interesting."

I assumed a sweet smile and left him a silence to fill. Always a good tactic.

"Okay. What other skills do you have?"

"I've got grade 8 cornet." I managed to say it without grimacing.

"Is 8 good?"

"It's the highest."

"Got any *useful* skills?"

"I'm an expert shot with a bow and arrow."

He perked up at that.

"Really?"

"Oh, yes, I used to go hunting with my father in Hyde Park when I was a kid. We were very poor, I learned how to shoot squirrels so I could put food on the table."

"I thought your father was a banker...?"

I rolled my eyes, and finally he caught on.

"Do you know any martial arts?"

"I got an orange belt in karate when I was little. Then again, everyone did. To be honest, it was more like dancing than karate."

"Do you know how to defeat someone in a fight?"

"I have the power to silence the less intelligent with withering sarcasm."

"Was that sarcasm?"

"No, of course not."

"Funny. What would you do if I challenged you to a fight?"

"I'd run away."

"That's the first sensible thing you've said since you came in here." He turned to Francis and said, "She's not getting a weapon."

"Did you seriously think she would?"

"No."

I felt quite let down.

"Couldn't I at least have a knife?"

"Do you know how to handle a knife?" asked Eddie.

"It's a knife," I said. "It cuts things."

He walked behind the counter, came back with a knife, handed it to me. I felt the weight of it in my hand. This was a real soldier's knife. It didn't have a saw edge blade or a camouflage handle or any of the other things that you saw on knives in films or in the pictures I occasionally saw the boys looking at school. This knife was nothing more than a handle and a sharp blade.

"Do you like it?" he said.

"Oh, yes."

His next movements were a blur. I felt him touch my arm, I felt myself turned around, I felt the cold point of the knife I had held in my hand now pressing against my cheek. And then he released me.

"That's why you're not getting a knife. I'm not arming your attackers."

It was a fair point.

Eddie looked at Francis.

"You picked up your equipment earlier. How's it going?"

Francis held his hands apart, palm up.

"You tell me. It seems to work okay."

They looked at each other.

"What's up?" I said.

Francis looked at his watch.

"Nothing. Look, we're all done. Really, you should go to bed, but it's a bit early. We could try for a mug of cocoa at the mess. Do you fancy it, Eddie?"

Cocoa. It was an odd thing to suggest, but maybe this was normal for the Army.

"Cocoa would be nice," I said. I guessed that as Francis and I would be spending some time together over the next few weeks, we should get to know each other. "Is it far to the mess? Only I need the toilet."

"Down the corridor, on the left," said Eddie. "We'll wait here for you."

As the door closed I heard Eddie speak.

"She'll be alright," he said. "She's got balls."

I smiled.

I FOUND THE toilet, used it, washed my hands, looked at myself in the mirror. The face that looked back wasn't the face of someone who would be heading off into another world in the morning. It wasn't the face of a heroic daughter, off to rescue her mother. All I saw was a thin, rather frightened young woman with greasy hair. I wondered if there would be a shower later on. A shower with hot water, that would be a luxury.

I picked up my backpack. It was well made, packed with clean, new clothes. Her Majesty's Government seemed to want to look after me. I thought about Francis. I was pleased that Francis would be accompanying me. Not because he was so good-looking – don't think I'm that shallow – but more because he seemed so steady, so competent. Better than that, he seemed like a good man, not like some of the pigs I'd known in the past. I remembered Captain James Wedderburn, who'd stayed at our house just before the end of Dream London. It all came back then. Captain Wedderburn, Mr Monagan the orange half man/half frog. Shaqeel, my father's gay lover… Where was my father? Why was only my mother mentioned in the fortune?

I made my way back down the corridor, placed my hand on the door, paused as I heard my name mentioned.

"… I'd fuck her…"

That was the voice of Joe, the quartermaster. I paused, waiting for Francis to defend me. But instead, Eddie spoke up.

"You're a lucky bastard, escorting that bird into France. I'd give her one, too."

"You wouldn't have to try too hard. She's gagging for it, according to her fortune scroll. And only seventeen, too. Nice tight pussy."

Joe again. I'd like to say I couldn't believe what he'd said, but that wouldn't be true. I'd heard the boys at school speaking in much the same way.

"Come on, she's young enough to be your daughter!"

"Hey, you know what they say, Eddie. If they're old enough to bleed, they're old enough to breed."

Now I couldn't believe what I'd just heard. Not the words. I'd heard stupid words like that before, stupid unthinking words spoken by stupid little boys too young to know any better. Stupid little boys trying to impress their friends. No, it's not the words that upset me, it was who had spoken them.

Francis.

Francis, who I had thought so sensible and mature. Francis, my so called bodyguard, due to accompany me to Dream Paris.

I pushed open the door, walked into the room.

Francis looked up, smooth and in control.

"Ah, here she is. Are you ready for your cocoa, Anna?"

I gazed at him.

"Actually, you were right. It is an early start tomorrow. I'd like to go to bed, please."

Did Francis and Eddie exchange glances at that? More schoolboy humour? I didn't care.

"If you like," said Francis. He led me across the camp to the barrack room where I was quartered. He chatted away, I answered his questions in sullen monosyllables. In the end he got fed up with it and we walked in silence. I gazed at his big, powerful body. Suddenly, I didn't find him attractive in the slightest.

Coming, again and again… I thought. *Not bloody likely.*

MUSHROOM

DEPARTURE

SOMEONE WAS GENTLY shaking me awake.

"Mother…" I'd been dreaming of her, remembering a time from before the changes. She'd been drinking coffee in the kitchen, getting ready to head off to work. I was telling her about my homework, she was only half-listening, most of her attention focussed on her newspaper.

"I brought you a cup of tea."

That wasn't my mother. And then I remembered. I was the sole occupant of a barrack room, somewhere in the middle of a devastated London. I was being handed a cup of tea by the revolting Francis Cuppello.

"Put it on the side."

If he heard the contempt in my voice, he didn't register it.

"There you go. I'll leave you to it, then. Take a shower, I'll meet you in the mess for breakfast. We depart at 07:45 hours."

"'kay,"

He looked at me for a moment, wondering, and then he turned and left the wonderful place they'd given me to sleep in. An empty room, metal skeletons of empty beds lined up on either side. The sound of rain on the windows.

Today was the day that I would depart for Dream Paris. I didn't want to go. Who would? If you think that you would, then you've never been in the Dream World. You've never woken each morning wondering if your personality has changed in some way, wondering how you could tell if it had. You've never seen the fear in other people's eyes as they gaze at you, weighing you up, deciding who or what you are. The Dream World is not a place where humans can live.

I was terrified. My fortune said I would meet my mother in Dream Paris. It never said anything about coming back. Back during the Incursion, as Therese Delacroix had called it, once you'd entered Dream London, you were trapped. The railway lines looped back on themselves, bringing you back to where you started. Would Dream Paris be the same?

I sipped the tea. Hot, sweet and milky. I loved this room. The bare, swept floor, the pale green walls, the metal lockers, the empty beds. It was so ordinary, so unchanging. I didn't want to leave it.

BREAKFAST WAS A dream. I can't believe I used that word; *dream* means something else nowadays. What I meant was that breakfast was wonderful. I heaped my plate with bacon, eggs, mushrooms, beans, fried bread, tomatoes, sausages. I hadn't eaten so much since, well, the night before, when I'd eaten all that stew. Francis sat opposite me, scraping the pattern off a huge bowl of porridge. I refused all attempts to start a conversation, kept things strictly business.

"So, what subjects are you studying at school, Anna?"

"How are we going to get to Dream Paris, Francis? Is it far?"

"I don't know. There's a path we have to follow."

"Where's the path?"

"Not far. A short drive." He looked unhappy. "Are you sure that you've everything you need? Wouldn't you like a couple of books to take with you? It can get boring."

"Have you seen the path before?"

And so on.

We finished our breakfast and headed back to the barracks. I sorted through my equipment for the last time, mixing things from the Army with the things I'd brought from home. I kept my own comfortable boots, but I took the Army's raincoat and over-trousers. I pulled on the dark blue oiled woollen jumper they'd provided and that was it. I took a last look around the barracks, hoisted my pack on my back and headed out into the cold drizzle.

No one paid me any attention as I walked through the busy base. Everyone was hurrying this way and that on missions of their own. We found Mr Twelvetrees waiting for us, listening to Tchaikovsky's Sixth in the back seat of his shiny black car. Darren took my pack and stored it in the boot, next to a much larger pack that I assumed belonged to Francis.

Darren turned the music right down as I climbed into the car.

"Any last questions, Anna?" asked Mr Twelvetrees.

"Why should I trust you, Mr Twelvetrees? I'm walking out on my old life on the word of a man I met barely twelve hours ago. How can I trust you?"

"You can't."

Oddly enough, that satisfied me. He wasn't promising anything.

Francis climbed in with us and we were off. The car pulled out of the barracks and we drove through a grey, drizzly London morning. A group of girls about my age walked to school: they'd shortened their uniform skirts by rolling them up at the waist, their faces were thick with orange foundation. They would go to class, chat through lessons, gossip through break, come back home and maybe get dressed up and go out for the night. Normally I would have looked at them with scorn, but today, heading off to who knew where, I felt nothing but envy.

We drove through the morning traffic until we reached a road that looked like any other. Lines of shops, pedestrian crossings, three red buses belching dark smoke. Darren brought the car to a halt. Mr Twelvetrees leaned across me and opened the door.

"And this is where we part company. Good luck, Ms Sinfield. Take care of her, Francis."

"I will, Mr Twelvetrees."

And that was it. We stepped out of the car into the misty wet day. Darren brought our packs out from the boot, nodded to us, and got back in the car. We watched as it pulled away into the traffic. I looked at Francis, dressed just the same as me. Breathable walking trousers, dark blue jumper. Both of us had on dark anoraks, unfastened despite the rain. I looked at Francis's backpack and saw that it was much larger than mine. Much, much larger. I wondered what was inside it, but didn't ask. I wasn't going to give him the satisfaction.

"Ready?" he asked.

"One moment."

The postbox was a Schindler flash of red in the grey. I dashed off down the road, posted the letters to Ben and Mr Hiatt. My only insurance.

I walked slowly back to where Francis waited and we hoisted on our backpacks – Francis with some difficulty – and we set off walking down the road. The endless drizzle formed a pattern of silver beads on my jumper. Pedestrians pushed past us, no doubt assuming from our backpacks that we were just another pair of sightseers, come to London to visit the ruins of the Dream World, come for the visceral thrill of seeing where our world had once been touched by another. I despised them, those tourists who blocked the pavements, using the heat and electricity that could have been directed to the broken parts of London whilst they searched for the vicarious thrill of the Incursion. I'd heard that some dickheads even came hoping to find a path out of our world. Which, when you thought about it, was what we were doing now.

"They shouldn't be sending you," blurted Francis. I saw by the look in his face it had been playing on his mind since he'd woken me up this morning.

"And why not? Because I'm just a girl?" I couldn't keep the contempt from my voice. I wasn't a girl. I was old enough to bleed, after all. His words. I became sarcastic. "Surely I have you to look after me? A big strong man to keep me safe? Doesn't that make things okay?"

We walked a few paces, Francis watching his feet.

"I don't doubt you can look after yourself, Anna. I don't think you should come because you have PTSD."

I don't know what I'd been expecting. An apology maybe, a blustering justification more like. Certainly not this.

"Let's be clear," I said. "You think I've got Post Traumatic Stress Disorder?"

"Yes. You marched into the parks, didn't you?"

"I did."

"That would be enough to put a strain on anyone."

So I was the problem…?

"Especially if they were just a poor weak female. Tell me, Francis, were you in Dream London?"

"At the end. I came in on the troop trains on the last day. I was there for the final push."

"So you missed it all."

"Not all of it. But I can imagine the strain you were under. I lost a friend in Afghanistan. I know what it's like. You should be seeing a doctor, you shouldn't be going back in."

I'd have laughed if it wasn't so pathetic. I overheard him being a sexist pig but *I* was the one with a problem. I felt like stopping right there in the street, dropping my backpack, jumping on a bus and heading home. And I would have done, if it wasn't for one thing.

"My mother is in Dream Paris. You understand that, don't you? Haven't you got a family?"

Francis stopped, fumbled in his pocket. Pulled out his phone. He brought up a picture of a pretty young woman holding a baby.

"That's my daughter. She's called Emily."

Okay. Score one to Francis. Even so...

"Who's the woman?" I asked.

"'Chelle. My fiancée. We were supposed to be married back in June, but then Dream London came up."

There was a note in his voice that softened me, just a little. He may have been a pig, but there was no mistaking the pride he felt in his family.

"'Chelle's very pretty." I admitted, grudgingly. "And Emily is gorgeous." She wasn't, she was a typical bald baby, but you have to say that, don't you? "How old is she?"

"Seven months." He put the phone back in his pocket.

"I know why you're going, Anna, and I don't blame you. I just don't think it's right. They shouldn't have told you about that fortune. You're not responsible for your mother."

"I'm perfectly capable of looking after myself."

He didn't reply to that. Instead he just said:

"Here we are."

We'd reached a narrow alley, squeezed between two buildings. I shivered. The alley looked like something you might have seen in Dream London: irregular brickwork; worn stone steps leading downwards; an iron post, a ring of rust around the base.

"Steps," I said, peering into the gloom. "Where do they lead to?"

"A canal."

I took a deep breath and looked around the old world, saying goodbye. The greyness, the rain, the sheer, tired, broken-down ugliness of wonderful normality.

"I'll go first," he said.

We descended the steps, my heart pounding. What would be waiting at the bottom? I imagined myself stepping into the heady, flower-scented heat of Dream London. Instead, I found myself on the towpath of a dark canal, wedged between the blank walls of two tall buildings. There was the same rain, the same greyness. Francis nudged me, pointed to the canal; the filthy, rubbish filled canal, the surface slicked with oil, the mud choked garbage soaked in moribund water. And there, amongst the garbage, a gloriously yellow orchid, a splash of sunlight in this grey day.

"That's from the Dream World," I said. "Which way do we go?"

"Downstream," said Francis. "We head for the sea, for the English Channel."

THE RAIN WAS getting heavier. I pulled up my hood as we marched on, Francis in front of me. I noted the way he walked, leaning forward to compensate for the weight of his huge backpack. What was in there?

I could still hear the traffic, echoing from the high walls that hemmed in the canal. We passed by low windows and I peered through them into modern offices lit with the glow of computer screens. There were piles of paper and ring binders, people chatting and drinking coffee. One man gazed out of a window, sandwich in hand. He saw me and winked. I scowled back.

Everywhere looked so ordinary. There were no more orchids in the canal, nothing unusual. We walked through windblown litter, we kicked coke cans, we picked our away across sections where the path had been churned to mud. We walked on one side of the canal, then crossed a little bridge and walked on the other. We passed people coming the other way, a man walking a dog, a couple arguing, an old lady...

"Did you see her?" said Francis, the excitement clear in his voice. "She had a *pigeon* on a leash! We must be getting close!"

I thought he was right. We'd walked under several tunnels already, where buildings had been built over the canal. The tunnel ahead, however, seemed different. This one seemed to emit a bluish glow.

I walked into the tunnel entrance, senses alert for any change in my surroundings. Halfway through I realised I was holding my breath. I was still holding it when we walked out into the rain on the other side of the tunnel and saw we were still in London.

"This is ridiculous," I said.

"The trail vanished when we were in there." Francis rubbed his nose. "Didn't you feel it?"

I looked around, thinking, remembering what Therese had said. They'd sold off London to the Dream World. At the end they destroyed the Contract Floor, and all those assets reverted to their original owners. But some of the assets remained unaccounted for... I looked at the canal.

"Who owns the water?"

"What?"

"The trail is in the water. Look, the flotsam is no longer there."

"We should go back to the other side of the tunnel."

Now I'd solved the problem he was quick with his suggestions. Men don't like it when you know more than they do. We turned round and retraced our steps. Now that

I was no longer holding my breath I had time to notice the source of the bluish glow. Nothing more than blue lamps, mood lighting for canals.

We emerged from the tunnel once more.

"It's here," said Francis, standing right on the edge of the footpath. I felt it, too. A muzzy, dreamy feeling, like the lift you get if you inhale from a glass of wine. Francis began, with some difficulty, to take off his backpack, the great weight defying even his build. He lurched this way and that as he slipped one arm from the loop, staggered as he brought it in front of himself then bent his knees to lay it on the ground. He unfastened a pocket at the top and pulled out a length of wire.

"What's that?" I asked.

"The path back home. They use this wire to guide missiles to their target. I've got several kilometres' worth packed in here. Hopefully we can use it to leave a trail."

Only several kilometres' worth? How far away did he think Dream Paris was?

He opened another pocket in the backpack and pulled out a tube of epoxy, then he lay on his stomach, leaned over the edge of the towpath and fixed the wire to the brickwork, just above waterline. Finally, he pulled a little box from his pocket and fixed it to the end of the wire.

He pulled on his backpack again, the wire now trailing behind him like a tail.

"Okay," he said. "Here we go."

I realised what he was going to do.

"You're going to swim up the canal?"

"Wade, I hope. I can't swim with this pack on. Besides, I'm not a good swimmer. How about you?"

I'm a superb swimmer. I'd represented my school at the backstroke, before the changes. But I didn't say that.

"I'm okay," I said.

Now he was sitting on the edge of the towpath, ready to push himself forward and to drop in the water.

"What if it's too deep?" I shouted.

Too late. Francis dropped into the canal. The water came up to his chest.

"*Fuck!*" he gasped "It's cold!"

"There's got to be an easier way…" I muttered, climbing in after him. And then I couldn't speak for the shock of the cold water. What did we expect? It was winter. For a few moments I could do nothing but gasp whilst I tried to catch my breath. I held my hands above my head, keeping them out of the icy water.

"*Fucking hell!*" shouted Francis. I'd have done the same myself if I could have caught my breath. Gasping, I began to edge forward. The canal bed was slippery beneath my feet. My foot caught a stone and I almost fell over, face first, into the filthy, freezing water.

"Be careful!" said Francis.

"*What a stupid thing to say!*" I snapped. I'd found my voice at last.

"Sorry!"

We walked forward.

"There could be rats in here. We could catch Weil's disease."

We passed beneath the entrance into the dim blue light of the tunnel, Francis slightly ahead of me again. He always had to lead the way, always watching out for the little lady.

"Do you feel that?" he said urgently.

"No, I …" And then, I did. "I can feel cobblestones beneath my feet. And I think the water is getting warmer."

Actually, there was no doubt that the water was getting warmer. The contrast to the freezing cold was as welcome as it was sudden.

"It's coming," I said. "It's coming…"

I felt sick with fear. Francis didn't know it then, Francis never knew it, but I turned around, I made to walk back down the tunnel, back home. I'd given in to my fear, but the water ran a little harder, the air filled with a spicy scent, the muzzy, dizzy feeling took hold of my body and I was walking, turning around, following Francis once more. Following him through crystal waters, following him up to the mouth of the tunnel, following him to the butterscotch glow of sunlight welcoming me back to the Dream World.

TWENTY

DESOLATION ROW

I WALKED FROM the darkness of the tunnel into the brightness of the Dream London day. Blinding loops of light rippled on the crystal waters. The Dream heat pressed against me, and I knew my clothes would be dry in an hour or so, stiff and dry and smelling of smoke and cinnamon. I was staggering, reeling, unable to deal with the sensory overload. The buildings of Dream London were welling up around me, looming out of the glare like an approaching wave...

I saw red brick terraces piled high with extra stories, brickwork bent drunkenly around skewed doorways and misshapen windows. I struggled to focus, my vision overwhelmed by the crooked chimneys teetering on the roof tops, at the grey columns of monuments rising up behind them; crammed together, each crowned with some shape: a statue, a spiked ball, a dodecahedron. And then behind *them*, coming into focus, rising up to touch the sky, I saw the skeletal remains of the great towers, their bodies burned, the vegetation that had clung to them now withered and died. The towers were dead, dark bones on the horizon.

So much visual information at once, crowding in on me. Green gaslamps and pink posters and scarlet signposts. All that colour and light was almost too much after the greyness of London. I'd grown so used to the regularity of the mundane world. Here, there wasn't a straight line to be seen, the edges of the buildings and the roads and the canal were cut out with pinking shears. I closed my eyes, I rubbed my face with the warm water of the canal.

Everything looked at once familiar and wrong: whatever power humans had held in Dream London had long been overthrown here. The towers might be dead, but the rest of Dream London was alive. The plants and flowers were running wild, they burst from the windows of the houses in riotous profusion, long green vines trailing scarlet flowers, their scent heavy on the air. The very countryside itself had encroached on the city in luxurious tongues of grass, in rounded hillocks that shouldered aside the buildings, cracking and crumbling the brickwork of the red terraces.

There was a chattering noise above me. I'd emerged into this remnant of Dream London beneath the arch of a white bridge. I waded forward a little, turned to look back at the marble spans, watched how they ran left and right into the overgrown mass of buildings that pushed amongst the green banks around us. Something was moving up there, peering out between the verdigrised models of octopuses that decorated the bridge…

"… sus fucking Chr…"

Francis waded up beside me. He seemed far more affected by the scene than I, but I suppose he'd only experienced Dream London for a short time, and that with a battle to fight. Rushing from one place to the next, watching out for enemies, he would never have had the opportunity to fully appreciate the strangeness. And now, here he stood, waist deep in water, wearing a backpack that trailed a wire back into the tunnel behind us, watching the group of blue monkeys gathered on the bank of the canal before us. They grinned and chattered and made obscene gestures. More of them looked down on us from the bridge above.

"Are they safe?" asked Francis.

I have to admit I was impressed by that. There was no false bravado with Francis: he didn't need to act hard. He *was* hard. He knew that he could stand up in a fight, he'd done it. You don't have to act when you know who you are.

"They're nasty," I murmured. "They used to torture cats."

The monkeys pointed to us with pale blue hands. They were planning something.

"Stand still," said Francis. He walked forward, wire jumping and jerking in the water behind him, scattering crystal drops. There was something odd about that wire. The monkeys on the bank observed his approach. Some of them retreated. One or two of the braver ones came forward, retreated, came forward. They were chattering and hooting. Challenging him. Still Francis walked on, coming to the edge of the canal. He looked at the crowd of monkeys, picked one of them out. Monkey and man faced-off.

"Get out of my way," growled Francis. The monkey flinched, then slowly turned around and patted away, hands and feet, as if it was bored, as if it had better things to do.

Francis began to try to climb from the canal, but the heavy pack dragged him backwards. I waded forward and helped to push him onto the sweet grass of the bank, the wire sharp on my face. I examined it for a moment: the wire looked different somehow, here in the Dream World. But I was getting wet, and so I climbed out and joined Francis at the focus of the semicircle of monkeys, lurking just out of range.

"You just have to identify the alpha male," said Francis, with some satisfaction. "Best him, and the others will retreat."

We walked forwards, and the monkeys parted to allow us to pass. Francis wore a smug expression, like I should be grateful. Like it took a man to sort out the problem. In his eyes, it took an alpha male to deal with another alpha male. Typical alpha thinking, in other words. None of them ever stop to wonder what things would be like if there were *no* alpha males.

We descended the bank onto a derelict Dream London street.

"Look," I said pointing to a line of bullet holes punctuating the brickwork of the nearest houses, the jagged teeth of shattered windows sharp in the daylight. The ground was scattered with ash and rubble.

"That's regular artillery," said Francis, thoughtfully, examining the bullet holes. I wasn't really listening, my attention had been caught by a view down the long alley between two houses. There, framed against the butterscotch sky, was something I did not expect to see in Dream London...

It looked like someone had taken the Eiffel Tower and covered it with canvas, then set fire to it. The skeleton of twisted and blackened iron girders emerged from the burned skin. The tower had died in agony, the top of it twisted around and down so that it almost touched the elongated tiled rooftops of the surrounding houses. It almost seemed to be looking at us.

"Are we in Dream Paris already?" wondered Francis.

"No, look."

I pointed to a half-burned news kiosk. The rain sodden papers and magazines that had survived were definitely written in English. *The Illustrated Dream London News*, *Arse and Titbits*, *Aardvark Fancier*.

Francis had crossed the road, the wire dancing behind him. He rubbed the ash from a street sign.

"Barking Road." He looked at me. "Which way do we go, Anna? Should we take a closer look at the burnt-out Eiffel Tower?"

I shivered at the thought.

"I don't think so. You can get lost in Dream London streets. I suppose if we follow the canal we'll be heading towards the sea…"

We walked down the road, more of the oddly changed wire trailing behind Francis. The backpack whirred with each step that he took, dispensing another length of the trail back home. I kept turning to look at the wire, observing how it ran up the green bank, seeing where it vanished over the top. How long before I returned this way, perhaps with my parents, heading for home? What was it that was so strange about the wire now? I reached out to touch it, but Francis interrupted my thoughts.

"There's been a battle fought here," he said, thoughtfully, stirring a brass rifle cartridge with his toe. It rolled across the pavement, fell clinking from the kerb. "And recently."

I looked around. "Where are the people who lived here?"

"Most of them will have fled. There will be people still hiding, though. Scavengers, snipers, people with battle shock, people who simply don't know where to go."

"Snipers?"

"They…"

He jerked to a sudden halt, staggered backwards a couple of steps, arms flung forward for balance. I turned and saw a group of monkeys holding onto the wire. They laughed as they saw us and gave the wire another yank before darting towards the closest terrace, scrambling up the vines to safety.

"How long are you going to wear that pack for?" I asked. "It seems a bit ridiculous, trailing a wire behind you."

"I have my orders," said Francis. "I'm to map out as much territory as possible."

"You're not going to map out much territory with the monkeys tugging you back."

"I can deal with the monkeys."

As he said that a plum splattered on the pavement, just by his feet. Red juice splashed outwards. Three more plums followed it, the last hitting him square on the face.

"Excellent monkey handling skills," I observed.

"Come on."

We continued down the street, the monkeys keeping pace on the rooftops, occasionally sending fruit spattering down onto the pavement near us. And then we heard the voice.

"Help me! Please, please help me!"

The sound of the monkeys stopped immediately. We stood, listening, in the afternoon stillness. The voice sounded again.

"Help me! Please, please help me!"

"She sounds terrified," said Francis.

"It sounds odd. Could it be a trap?"

"Help me! Please, please help me!"

Francis nodded. He raised a finger to his lips for silence.

We crept down the suddenly silent road. My body was still damp from the waist down with canal water, above the waist I was drenched with sweat.

"Help me! Please, please help me!"

The voice came from a dark doorway yawning in the middle of the never-ending red terrace. Francis gestured to me to help him out of the backpack.

"If this looks too dangerous, we're not going in. It's more important that I get you to Dream Paris."

"I get to Dream Paris anyway. Haven't you read my fortune?"

Francis entered the doorway. I followed him into the cracked hallway of the abandoned house. Grass grew on the carpet, vines sprouted from the ceiling, choking the light bulb. A picture of a crying girl hung on the wall.

There was a doorway at the end of the hallway. A creaking noise came from beyond.

"*Help me! Please, please –*"

Francis leaped through the door.

Almost immediately, he flung himself backward, crashing into me. Dark metal jaws snapped shut just inside the room.

"What the…" I began. It looked like the jaws of a mantrap, but much much bigger.

"Run!"

Francis pushed me onwards, the snapping noise of metal close behind. Out from the gloom into the butterscotch daylight. Out across the rubble-strewn road. There was a shriek of scraping metal. Francis and I turned to see something made from dark iron half-emerge from the doorway to the house. A brass speaker horn hanging underneath the shape whistled and then spoke once last time.

"*Please, please help me!*"

The shape withdrew back into the shadows of the house. There was a slow clicking as the trap was reset.

In the desperate silence that followed I found myself longing even for the chatter of the monkeys. Sat in that street, the endless red terrace running by us, I became aware of a tremendous emptiness. This was a dead city.

Eventually, Francis found his voice.

"What the hell was that?"

"I don't know," I said, close to tears. "They didn't have them in Dream London that I remember!"

"It looked like a crocodile!"

I don't think he was quite right. To my eyes, it looked more like a printing press.

As he spoke we heard a faint call from half way down the street.

"*Help me! Please, please help me!*"

"What? Another one?"

Francis began pulling on his backpack.

"We can't stay here," he said. "We need to get out of this part of the city."

I looked at the wire trailing behind him. It didn't look like wire anymore. What did it remind me of? Whatever it was, it made me feel uncomfortable.

"Really Francis, shouldn't we dump the backpack?"

"I have my orders," he said stubbornly.

WE WALKED ON through the city.

"The monkeys are plotting something," said Francis. "They're following us."

"How on earth do they keep picking up our trail?"

"There's no need to be sarcastic."

The canal ran alongside us, pushing through overgrown buildings of the city, occasionally shouldered aside by the hillocks that pushed their way up from the earth, lime green butterflies fluttering over their grassy surfaces. Always, the endless red terrace ran alongside us, empty windows and open doors reminding us of the people who had once lived there. Caught between the terrace and the canal, I felt like a little ball bearing in one those plastic mazes that children play with. Tilt the maze, send the ball running along, trapped in its path, all that movement to no end, lost in dull repetition.

And then we rounded another hillock and something jolted us out of our reverie.

"What the hell…"

Francis had come face to face with a life size china doll, had almost walked into its arms. He took a step back, shook his head, regained his composure.

"My fault," he apologised. "I wasn't concentrating. Not good. I'm supposed to be on guard…"

"It's this place. It gets to you."

The doll stood in the middle of the path. I stepped forward to take a closer look. It was made in the shape of a young woman, frozen in the act of walking down the street.

"It's beautiful," I said, looking at the figure's face. It was made of porcelain, delicately painted with rosebud lips, pink cheeks and blue eyes that gazed at nothing. Its clothes were made of batiste, beautifully stitched.

"Did you have these in Dream London?"

"I heard rumours of dolls like this living in Chinatown. I never went there. It was at the edge of the strangeness."

"The strangeness?" he said, deadpan.

I ignored him.

"She looks as if she was searching for something."

He opened his mouth to reply, and then we heard the voices calling.

"Mister! Mister!"

We turned around, suspecting another trap. I relaxed a little as I saw the two children approaching. A boy and a girl. I'm not good with children or their ages, but Francis later said he thought they were around ten or eleven years old. They ran towards us, following the wire. They were both filthy, dressed in ragged Dream London clothes, the girl in a torn and faded dress, the boy in grey trousers and a waistcoat. They both looked half starved and half scared to death. They were both shouting to us.

"Mister! Miss! Run! They're coming for you!"

NINETEEN

EMILY AND OLIVER

THE CHILDREN WERE called Emily and Oliver. Francis's calm manner only seemed to make them more frantic.

"Cut through the houses! The back gardens join on to the next street!"

"And take off your pack! The clowns are following the wire!"

"What clowns?" I asked.

"The clowns!" Oliver's eyes were wide with terror. "The monkeys lead them to new clients. The clowns pay the monkeys in fruit and cats."

"The monkeys torture the cats," said Emily, matter-of-factly.

"I don't know anything about clowns," I said, in answer to Francis's unasked question.

Oliver was becoming frantic. "Look, we need to move! Please!"

"I'm not taking my pack off!"

"We'll cut through the houses anyway," said Emily. "The clowns are very particular about where they walk. There are some places they don't go."

"Why not?"

"I don't know! Come on!"

The children chose a doorway and led us through the long hallway and out into the even longer garden behind it. Flowers and shrubs grew wild, narrowing the central lawn to a dark, leaf-walled passageway.

"Hurry!" called Emily.

Francis pushed his way in front of me. I didn't mind so much, imagining more printing press crocodiles waiting for us up ahead.

A woven wooden fence separated our garden from the next. Francis shoulder charged it and we found ourselves pushing through another garden and another house before emerging into another street, sandwiched between two long red rows of terraced houses. This street was quieter than the one we'd left. Something loomed over the rooftops, and I shuddered to see the burnt, twisted remains of the Eiffel Tower, now a lot closer than before. Oddly, it still seemed to be looking at me.

"Tell me about the clowns!" said Francis. "Quickly! We need to know!"

Oliver was crying. Emily took his hand.

"They turned up after all the fighting was over!" said Emily. "After Angel Tower exploded. They seemed friendly enough at first. They said they were here to help."

"Help? How?"

"They set up tables in empty buildings, laid them out with food and drink. They invited people in to eat. I remember looking in through the doorway once. There were hams, and mashed potatoes, great piles of sausages..."

"... and gravy and roast lamb, and bowls of peas with butter melting on them," said Oliver, wistfully.

"And there were drinks. The adults had beer and whisky, and there were bottles of red and yellow wine. There was lemonade and ginger beer and even Coke, like you used to get before the changes."

Ah, Coke. I remembered that. I still hadn't had it, not even in Mundane London.

"You said you only looked through the door. Didn't you eat there?"

"No," said Emily. "My mum wouldn't let me. She said she didn't trust them. She was right, too."

"They came for Mr Edwards next door," said Oliver. "Two clowns. I heard them. They said his family had eaten at their table, and now they owed the clowns a favour. They said they needed them to help in return."

"What did Mr Edwards do?"

"He said fair enough. He and his family got dressed up and off they went with the clowns. I watched Louise go off with them. I used to play with her." Oliver was shivering. "They marched them off out of the gates. I never saw them again."

"And then the word got round," said Emily. "About people not coming back. Anyone who'd eaten at the clown's table, or accepted a gift from them…"

"What sort of gift?"

"Like clothes or money, or maybe medicine or materials to mend their house. All the people who had accepted a gift were suddenly very frightened. They pretended to be out when the clowns called round. But the clowns began to knock doors down, to pull people from their houses…"

Francis was frowning. I was thinking about what Emily had said.

"Oliver, you said the clowns marched the Edwards family out of the gates. What gates?"

Oliver shuddered. "The city gates."

"I don't remember any city gates,"

"Where have you come from?" asked Emily. "You don't know about the clowns. You don't know about the city gates. You must have seen them, when you entered the city. How did you get past the city walls?"

"We didn't pass any walls. We came here from the real London. From Mundane London."

The children looked at us, open-mouthed.

"You came here from London? From before the changes?"

"From after the changes. When Angel Tower was destroyed, the old London came back. Everything went back to normal."

Oliver whimpered and took hold of Emily. He wiped the corner of his eye with a filthy hand. Emily held onto him as she replied.

"Back to normal? No! Everything got worse! There was a huge flash, and then everything jerked to the side. The colours changed. And then everything started to move even faster. The grass rolled into the city, the plants started to grow. And the clowns appeared..."

"I don't like the clowns," said Oliver.

The children were looking up and down the street. They kept glancing back through the house, back down the long hallway we'd just come down.

"Mister, we have to go!" said Oliver, urgently. "Take off your pack, or the clowns will follow the wire and catch you."

Francis became very gentle at this point. Very gentle, but very assured.

"Oliver, I can't take this pack off," he said. "But listen, there's an important reason for that. I'm here to help people. People like you."

He squatted down so that his eyes were level with Emily and Oliver.

"You know where that wire goes?" He reached back, took hold of a length of it, gave it a tug. I saw the frown that briefly flickered across his face. The wire hadn't felt right. It couldn't have done, it no longer looked like metal, more like spun cloud. Francis didn't let that bother him. "This wire is the route back home, back to the real London. If you follow that wire, it will lead you down the street and into a canal. Jump into the canal and follow the wire under a white bridge, through the tunnel. When you come out of the tunnel, you'll be back in London. Real London."

The children looked at each other, hope and fear battling it out on their faces.

"Come with us, mister. Take us home!"

"I can't. I have to look after Anna. I'm taking her to find her mother."

"I don't need looking after," I muttered.

The children didn't pay me any attention. They were completely enthralled by big, strong Francis.

"Well, at least take off that pack, mister! The clowns will follow you!"

"I need to wear the pack. If I don't, how will other people know how to find their way home?"

The children looked at each other, they looked down the length of the wire. Oliver touched it, and hope bloomed in his pale, dirty face.

"Listen," I said, "this gate out of this city. Where is it?"

"There are lots of gates. Watling Gate, Ermine Gate, Fosse Gate... I don't remember the rest."

"The Watling Gate!" I said. "That's the one we need."

Francis never questioned how I knew that. I'd guess he thought I remembered it from Dream London.

"The Watling Gate?" said Emily. "You're almost there! Follow this road, it's only five minutes' walk. But, please, take off the pack!" Emily looked terrified.

"I can't."

I wasn't going to argue with him. Nor was Emily. She folded her arms and gave us the benefit of her young wisdom.

"Then, whatever you do, don't listen to the clowns! If they speak to you, cover your ears! They're so persuasive! They'll convince you that they're doing you a favour, you'll accept what seems like a good turn and then they'll end up owning your soul."

Oliver had seen something at the edge of the street. I saw it too. Shapes, moving towards us. And now I heard the faint shriek and chatter of monkeys.

"Emily! They're coming! We have to go!"

"Follow the wire!" said Francis.

The children darted off, back into the house. I didn't watch them go, I didn't want to give away where they'd gone. I looked at Francis.

"Five minutes to the gate, they said. Can you jog with that thing on your back?"

"I'll try."

We set off down the road. The slope was to our advantage, and I followed Francis, staying to the right of the wire that played out behind him.

We hurried on down the road. The terraced houses rose higher on either side of us, eight, nine stories high now, casting a gloomy shadow over the road.

"The gate!" said Francis.

There it was. An arch of red brick at the end of the street. Beyond it I could see nothing but fields, glowing fluorescent green in contrast to the increasingly dim street.

"Come on! Last dash!"

My words were almost drowned out in a sudden cacophony of hooting and hooping. Red fruit splattered onto the road in front of us.

"Keep going," said Francis. "They're trying to slow us down."

I glanced behind and saw why. Two black and white clowns were walking down the hill behind us, following the wire. They were moving faster than we were, their odd, jerky motion carrying them along at speed.

We pushed on, the red fruit splattering over our bodies, our faces. Sticky juice ran down my face, my neck, between my breasts, soaking into my bra. Still we pushed on, the gate coming closer, a widening arch of green light. And there, standing before it, two more black and white shapes. Two more dolls.

"Keep going," said Francis. "Right through the gate."

"And then what?"

"I don't..." He was jerked backwards, landing on his backside on the cracked tarmac. Further up the road blue monkeys were turning somersaults in delight, they were cheering on their cousins as they took hold of the wire and began to slowly pull Francis back up the street.

"Dump the pack!" I shouted. Francis ignored me. He reached to one of the shoulder straps of the pack and pulled. There was a searing crackle and the monkeys shrieked and began to dance around, sucking at their hands.

"Go!" called Francis.

Too late. The two porcelain clowns had caught us up, and I recognised them for what they were. Pierrots, like in the pantomime. One of them reached out a hand to Francis.

"*Let me help you up.*" The Pierrot's face didn't move, the eyes, the lips were painted on the white china, just like the dolls from earlier. The voice echoed from somewhere inside the porcelain skull. It made me think of a jewelled insect trapped inside there, its buzzing wings amplified by the head. "*Take my hand!*"

"I'm fine," said Francis, struggling to his feet.

"*Do you know where you're going? Do you need directions?*"

Their immobile faces tilted, as if they were miming speech.

"We're fine, thank you," I said.

"*We have food, if you're hungry.*"

"*Or we can show you where there is water if you need to fill your bottles.*"

"We're okay," said Francis.

We marched onwards, heading towards the gate. The Pierrots fell into step beside us.

"*You're leaving the city? Why not rest for a while first? We can arrange transport to wherever you're going.*"

"*Or perhaps we could give you directions?*"

"We're quite okay, thank you."

We were almost at the gates. The two Pierrots who waited there stepped forwards and joined in the gentle persuasion.

"*You're leaving the city? Have you considered how dangerous it is out there? We can offer you a range of options to minimize the risk as you travel.*"

I looked out of the gate, out at the greenness beyond. I'd already had enough of the red brick of Dream London, the dust and the rubble, the chatter of the monkeys, the exotic perfume smell.

"Stand aside, please," said Francis to the Pierrot that had moved in front of him.

"*Why not just...*"

Francis didn't stop walking, he simply shouldered it aside. It fell back onto road, silk costume getting covered in street filth as it rolled, head cracking nastily on the ground. I followed Francis, under the arch and out of the gate, out into the greenness beyond.

AVOCADO

DREAM KENT

HAVE YOU EVER wondered about where cities begin?

One time I went to the States with my parents. We visited
New York for a few days before going to stay in a lovely
little town in New England, all clipped grass and white
painted houses, and all I could do is wonder how the two
places were connected. If you were to walk from that pretty
town, I wondered, where would New York start? Not in a
solid wall of skyscrapers, surely, but rather in a gradual way.
A building here, a petrol station there, a row of houses.

Not here. The red brick dust and pollen-scented sprawl of
this annex of Dream London ended in a five-storey wall of
haphazardly piled red bricks. On one side, broken buildings
wrapped in vines; on the other, emerald fields glowing in the
bright Dream sunshine, the stripes of green grass and yellow
crops, red flowers and waving rows of corn extending to
the horizon.

The country wasn't a place for clowns or monkeys. We'd
passed beyond their interest. Looking back through the gate,
I could see the street had already emptied.

"They've gone," gasped Francis. "We've left their territory."

He seemed pleased with himself; it took some time for him to register the look I was giving him.

"What's the matter?"

"Why the hell didn't you let go of your pack? We could have been killed!"

His face shifted to that quiet, emotionless expression I'd seen before.

"Why do you think I'm here, Anna?"

"To protect me."

"Yes. And that won't be done until I've returned you safely to London. How am I supposed to do that if I don't know the way back?"

"We don't need that wire to find our way back! Through the gate, across one street, follow the canal…"

"Things change in Dream London! You told me that!"

"What's the point of having a route back if we're both dead? What if someone were to cut the wire? What if someone were to just walk into it?"

"They said not to worry about that. It would be okay."

"And you didn't question them?"

"I've not spent much time in the Dream World. Things are different here."

"That pack isn't just different. It's weird."

He didn't care. He didn't want to admit he was wrong, that was the problem. He folded his arms, put on the *older experienced man talking to a silly young woman* voice.

"A soldier without a rifle is no use, Anna. I ditch this pack, and I'm no use."

"Doesn't it get a bit boring, always being right?" But then I noticed the pack, I noticed the way he was standing.

"What's the matter now?" he asked.

"How much does that weigh now?"

"I don't know. About the same…"

He got it.

"I don't understand it," I said, half to myself. Francis was flexing his knees, bobbing up and down, weighing the pack. "It looks as full as ever. Although…"

"What?"

"Things changed in Dream London. Mobile phones stopped working, electric lamps became gaslights. Something's happening to your pack, I think…"

I felt the edge of an idea. The roads moved around in Dream London. A path that was three feet long one night might be three miles long the next morning. I looked at the wire, and I imagined something, not something that unwound, but rather a lengthening path…

The wind blew, filling me with a delicious scent of freshness, of lavender and fresh baked bread. Of the salt sea and the open sky, and of everything good and natural in the world. Too good. Nothing was natural in the Dream World. Like a darling little organic café in the heart of the city, naturalness was something to be carefully cultivated.

Francis was gazing into the distance.

"How far was it from London to the channel?" he asked.

"I don't know. It used to take about an hour to drive. Sixty miles or so?"

"That's what I thought. I can see the sea."

He was right. There it was, a silver line, just tucked between the land and the sky. Why hadn't I noticed that?

"That's not four miles away," he said.

"The geography changes in the Dream World. Come on."

"Hold on! How do you know that's the right way?"

"Because, unlike most *girls*, I have excellent spatial awareness."

"Don't be sarcastic. I only asked."

"Look, over there on the hill?" You could see it, blue on the horizon, a tiny castle perched just before the sea.

"Remember what it said on the fortune? *Walking towards the ruined castle on the hill, furious at your companion?*"

"Why are you furious at me?"

"Time of the month," I snapped. I was old enough to bleed, after all. And he was foolish enough to believe me.

THE COUNTRYSIDE HAD been rucked up like a carpet. No, I've got a better analogy: it had been pulled apart, like toffee. All of the fields of that other Kent were pulled wide so that they stretched out in the middle, they became narrower and narrower, bringing the coast closer. We walked across stripes of elongated field, the hot Dream sun shimmering on bands of cabbages, rape, poppies, wheat. The narrow bands passed in orderly succession, a haze of little black flies hovering above the crops: tall tulips, yeasty smelling hops, yellow corn. There was no sound but that of our feet, of the whirring as the wire unwound from the pack that Francis adamantly refused to discard. I kept turning to look back at that wire, stretching out to be lost in the distance, reassured by the thought that back there lay the city gate, then the streets, then the canal, then the bridge, and then home.

"What's the matter, Anna?"

"Nothing."

"That's not true. Why do you keep being rude to me?"

"I'm not being rude," I said.

"If I've upset you somehow, you should tell me. It's not good to brood on things."

We walked in silence past a field of black and white roses, spider webs stretched between the blooms, the pack whirr-whirring away.

I stole a glance at Francis, plodding patiently beside me.

"Why did you become a soldier?" I asked.

"Left school at sixteen. Wanted to serve my country."

He wanted to serve his country.

"You never thought about staying on at school?"

"I don't think they'd have had me," he laughed. "I used to be in trouble all the time. Never paid attention in class. I was a fool, though, I see that now. You're doing the right thing. Studying for university. Science, too. You must be clever."

"I am," I said. I can't abide false modesty.

"Your parents must have been proud."

"Not quite."

I remembered my father. *Physics? You've got a good mathematical mind. What's wrong with finance?* He'd laugh, he'd wave his hand around our expensively decorated house. *Knowing about quarks and string theory won't earn you enough to buy all this.*

"Were your parents proud of you when you joined the Army?"

"My mum was. I don't really know my dad. He left when I was little."

"Have you ever seen him?"

"Oh, once or twice. He lives with a woman and her three kids down in Margate. She's alright."

"Okay." More silence. "Do you like the Army?"

"Love it. Taught me how to look after myself. Great mates. Great laughs. Better than being stuck working in a supermarket. And you've got to do your bit." He scratched his nose. "'Course, it's different when you've got a little one. And I've got 'Chelle to look after now."

His voice softened as he talked of his family. I remembered the picture of 'Chelle and little Emily.

"Have you ever killed anyone?" I asked.

"No."

I looked at him: he'd answered too quickly. But before I had a chance to question him further, the road bent to the left and we looked down a new stretch.

"Look!"

I saw it too. Two figures waiting, one on either side of the road. Sentinels.

"What do we do?"

"Just keep walking..."

We walked on. The sentinels were taking their duty seriously, neither moved as they watched us approach. And as we got closer, I realised why.

"More china dolls. Just like that first one, back in the city."

We stopped. The golden thread on the dolls' clothes shone in the sunlight, their golden hair shimmered in the sea breeze. Each held out a piece of paper in its right hand.

"It's a note..." I said, looking at the left hand doll. My voice almost failed me as I saw who it was addressed to. "*That's my name!*"

Can you believe me when I say that, since I had entered the Dream World, this was the most frightening thing that had happened to me? The clowns, the machine: that had been exhilarating, scary, shocking, but not terrifying, because none of that had been personal. But this, this clearly was. It took every last shred of my self-control to force me to walk up to that doll, and even then I couldn't bring myself to meet the sightless gaze of the painted blue eyes. I snatched the note from the doll's hand.

"What does it say?" asked Francis.

I read the note before me a second time, unwilling to acknowledge the words.

"It says, *Anna, don't cross the line.*"

I felt strangely light-headed. I looked at the line that had been scratched into dust of the road, running from one doll to the other.

"What's the other doll holding, Francis?"

"A letter. It's addressed to you."

The sky seemed so big and blue here, we were insignificant

figures, lost beneath it. And the world knew I was here; it had mentioned me by name. I took a deep breath and whispered, "Please open it. I don't think I can read it myself."

"It's from your mother."

I wobbled across the dusty road. Can you believe I kept to this side of the line? My mouth was so dry as I took the letter.

Anna. They showed me a piece of paper with your fortune on it. It says that you will try and find me. Don't. Turn around now and go home. You're being used. Mother.

I looked at him. I looked down at the line scratched into the dusty path.

Twenty-four hours ago I'd been heading home after a day in school. Back in London, back in the real world. In the past twenty-four hours I'd seen a woman die, I'd left my home at the word of a man with fly eyes, I'd agreed to be accompanied by the objectionable Francis to Dream Paris. All of these things I'd done at the behest of strangers. So what was I to think when I read a note written by someone I knew, someone I should have trusted?

My mother was right. Of course she was. It was obvious that I was being used. What was I doing here? Anyone with any sense would turn around and go back home right now. My own mother had told me to.

"Is it genuine?" asked Francis, sensibly. I hadn't thought of that. He held up the letter before me and I examined it. My mother had written that, I was sure. I recognised the handwriting, I recognised the tone. It was my mother's way of speaking.

"It's genuine."

"Then what are you going to do?"

I gazed at the letter. What could I do? What difference, exactly, did this letter make? I spoke slowly, marshalling my thoughts.

"I marched into the parks. I thought I might die then.

Everything since has been a bonus."

"You were being used when you marched into the parks. You're being used now."

"By who?"

"Mr Twelvetrees, the government. You're being used, Anna."

"So are you," I said. It sounded childish.

"I signed up for this. You didn't."

I looked down at the line in the earth.

"It would be nice to turn around, to go home," I said. "But then I'd never know, would I? You understand that, don't you, Francis?"

"It's got to be your decision, Anna."

I wasn't thinking of him at the time. What would Francis have wanted? To go home, of course, back to 'Chelle and Emily. He wouldn't have cared about my mother. He just wanted to do his duty, and he was conscientious enough not to try and influence me. I didn't think of that then, though. I was only thinking of myself.

"I've got to go," I said. "If I go home, I'll never know."

"If that's what you want."

I looked at him, I looked at the dolls. I closed my eyes, thinking.

I stepped across the line.

EIGHTEEN

DREAM DOVER

Dream England ended quite suddenly. The coastal wind whipped away the heat of the butterscotch sun, and we walked the shortened road with a feeling of being right on the boundaries: between earth and sky, land and sea, hot and cold, home and abroad, friendship and enmity. All too suddenly we found ourselves standing on the top of a way-too-tall white cliff, looking out at the simplest and freshest of scenes.

A horizontal stripe of dark blue flecked with white; above it, a thin, dark dividing line, and then above that a stripe of bright blue, daubed with white. The sea, the distant land, the sky.

To the side, standing on its own little island, the truncated cone of a lighthouse in alternate red and white stripes. Blue, light blue, red and white. So simple and fresh, it lifted my spirits after the fug of the Dream Country.

And then I looked closer.

I caught the flash of black and white in the water and I saw sea monsters, patterned like orcas, but much, much larger. I recognised their shapes from books. Mosasaurs – sea dinosaurs. Liopleurodons – long, crocodile-like creatures with four giant flippers. The water was so clear you could see them as they hung just below the surface – patterned bodies perfectly camouflaged in the ripples of the shifting waters – and then they would push hard with their flippers and they were gone, down into the depths after their prey.

"We have to cross that," said Francis.

"We must make it somehow. My fortune says we do."

We gazed across the water at Dream France.

"Can you see the tower?" asked Francis.

"I'd wondered if it was an illusion." The tower rose from the far shore, higher and higher into the air, blue with the distance, almost invisible against the sky.

"It's a clock tower," I said. "There's a clock on top."

"It must be miles tall," said Francis. "That can't be right."

"The towers in Dream London grew every day," I said. "They only had a year or so to grow. I wonder how long that clock has been growing?"

Francis looked at his watch.

"That clock is an hour ahead," he said. "They still keep different time, even in the Dream World."

DREAM DOVER NESTLED at the bottom of the sheer white cliffs. The ruined castle we'd seen looked down on the town from a rocky outcrop. The town was a pretty little place: buildings painted cheerful pastels, yellow-white sand, green grass lawns, red-tiled roofs. A little harbour wrapped itself around the town, though the sea-walls seemed much higher than would seem necessary. Then I remembered the black and white monsters, out to sea. Stone steps zig-zagged from the cliff-tops to the town.

Dream Dover looked trim and prosperous.

"What do they eat, though?" asked Francis. I knew what he meant. The boats in the harbour had obviously not been used in some time. They bobbed in neat rows, painted in bright colours, their decks filled with pot plants and flowers. Creepers grew from boat to boat.

"The boats aren't going anywhere," I said. "How are we supposed to get across?"

"I don't know. Look, let's find an inn. We'll need somewhere to sleep anyway. Maybe they know a way across."

We descended into the town. A girl in a petticoat stood on tiptoe to unpeg the clothes from a washing line. A basket full of hastily folded clothes sat at her feet.

"It's always the girls who do the work," I noted. I smiled at her. "Excuse me, is there an inn nearby?"

Wordlessly, the girl pointed to an alley squeezed between two houses. Another set of stone steps led downwards.

"Thank you," I said.

We found ourselves in a tiny square next to a white-painted building, its narrow windows framed by blue striped shutters. A sign painted with a picture of one of the black and white sea monsters hung over the door.

"'The Mosasaur,'" read Francis. "Shall we go in?"

"What about your pack? Are you going to leave it outside? What if someone trips on the wire in the dark? You've trailed it all the way down those steps."

"Give it a rest, Anna."

I glared at him, but he was already pushing his way inside, pack still on his back.

The bar of the Mosasaur was a nautical cliché: dark and small and filled with nets and buoys and all sorts of other fishing decorations. Three men looked up from their pints as we entered, their gazes travelling from my breasts to my face, to Francis and then back to their pints.

"Hello there, lover. What can I get you?"

The barmaid was young and buxom and clearly taken by Francis. I wondered what she imagined her chances with him would be, given that she had octopus tentacles for arms. I suppose the answer to that would depend on whether she had the same for legs. But then again, who knew? Francis was a man, and this woman had big tits and a welcoming manner. Wrap a pair of octopus legs around him and he'd probably welcome being pulled in.

"Two rooms for the night, and passage across the Channel," said Francis.

"And why's that? Why would you want to go across there?"

The words were spoken by one of the drinkers. I'm not sure which, all three of them kept their gazes firmly fixed on their pints. Francis turned to face them.

"We want to go across so we can find this young lady's mother. Do you know of someone who might have a boat?"

"You'll not find a boat that will take you across that water. Not in this port."

"I'm sorry. Would you mind looking at me when I'm speaking to you?"

I felt a little shiver at that, that edge of cold politeness in his voice. I have to hand it to Francis: he spoke the words with just the right amount of menace. I'd have quite fancied him if he wasn't such a sexist pig. One of the men looked úp. He was small and stocky, with the pale skin and smooth hands of a sailor who had not been to sea for some time.

"Try heading for Folkestone. They go hunting for mosasaur and liopleurodon in their big ships. I heard they sometimes trade with the French. Maybe one of them will take you across."

His gaze returned to his pint.

The barmaid wasn't having it. "Go to Folkestone, indeed! Why are you always so bloody awkward, Graham? There's lots of people go to France nowadays. There's no shame in it!" She winked at Francis. "Passage across the Channel can be arranged, lover. Just make sure you're in bed for eleven."

Francis grinned, and his whole manner changed. He was no longer the quiet menace, now he was the cocky wideboy, the cheeky charmer. He was hot, yes, but I find his sort of arrogance a turn off.

"My mum told me to always be in bed on time. I'm a good boy, I am." He gave a wink.

"Are you sure? My mother warned me about boys like you!"

I was fed up with this. Had he forgotten he was engaged?

"I'm hungry," I announced. "Do you serve food?"

"Certainly, *madam*," said the barmaid, suddenly all brisk efficiency. "We've got stew, eggs or pork. Oh, there might be some salmagundi."

"Two plates of stew," said Francis. "And is it okay if I leave my backpack by the door?"

It was odd, but no one seemed to have noticed the backpack until then. No-one had noticed the silver wire trailing back through the door and out into the street. Now the barmaid and the three locals were all staring at the wire, looking at where it passed through the side of the door. Now we came to look at it properly, we could all see it stretching across the room.

The barmaid shook her head. "Put your pack here by the bar, lover." She noticed me looking at her. "Are you okay?"

"Aren't you going to point out that you like a man with a big package?"

She wasn't sure what to say to that, so she settled on ignoring me. I was quite happy with that, anything to distract attention from the silken thread of the wire. Francis's face was a closed book. What was he thinking? What did he know about the pack?

The barmaid shook her head again. Finally, she seemed to snap back into herself.

"I'll get the boy to take it up to your room later. Now, do you want a drink?"

"I'd love some tea," said Francis.

"Two mugs," I said.

We sat down in a little booth, facing each other across the table. The barmaid brought two bowls of brown stew. I noticed that Francis's helping was much larger than mine. Half of his hadn't been slopped over the side, either. Still, it looked tasty. There was rich brown gravy, yellow fruit, white potatoes, chunks of meat.

"Smells good," said Francis

"Call me Lizzie, lover." The barmaid picked up Francis's napkin with one tentacle, shook it out and placed it on his lap.

I concentrated on my food.

The stew was delicious. Too delicious. There were too many flavours in there to process: the savoury of the beef, the fullness of the potatoes, the tang of whatever fruit there was in there, the richness of the gravy. It tasted so vibrant, so heady, so dangerous. There was no mistaking the fact I was back in the Dream World. Everything was so much *more* in this room; the reflections in the polished wood of the walls seemed so much deeper, the brasses glowed gold, the fishing nets were woven in strange patterns, the flames in the lamp danced to 5/4 time. Even the floorboards were over-elaborate, carved in odd patterns of fish-heads and stars. And the wire that stretched from the pack had faded into the background. I was sure that Lizzie had walked through it without noticing as she crossed and recrossed the floor...

"Here's your tea, lover!" Two mugs were plonked before us.

"Ah, the best china, I see," I said, looking at the chipped pottery.

Lizzie departed, looking hurt.

"Why are you being so rude, Anna? She seems like a good laugh."

"I'm sure she is. She seems *very* friendly."

"What's that supposed to mean? Would you prefer it if she didn't speak?"

"Perhaps."

We ate the rest of our stew in silence. I was just scraping the last of my meal from the bowl when the door to the bar opened and three women in long velvet dresses pushed their way in. I saw the purple blackness beyond them and I realised that the day had ended. Between me and my home lay miles and miles of darkness. What creatures would be coming out this Dream Night?

The three women looked around the room, deciding where to sit. One of them was looking in our direction, eyes wide with surprise.

"Francis?"

"Mandy?"

And that was it for the rest of the evening. Any chance of the return of gentleman Francis was swept away in whirl of powdered and perfumed flesh, of hugs and kisses and exclamations and coarse laughter as each of the women embraced Francis in turn. With each hug that boyish swagger grew and grew.

"Aren't you going to buy us a drink, then?" Mandy elbowed him in the ribs. "Some gentlemen you are!"

"Give us a chance, girls! Hey, Lizzie! Three rum and cokes! And I'll have a pint. Anna, what would you like?"

"I'm okay with tea, thank you."

I don't understand why people need to drink to enjoy themselves. I hoped it would be different in Dream Paris. After all, the French knew how to appreciate alcohol, they don't just use it as a means of getting pissed, like the English do.

"We've got no coke," said Lizzie. "Got home-made dandelion and burdock, better than coke!"

"Rum and dandelion and burdocks all round then," said Francis.

"We've got no rum, either. There's brandy."

"We'll have brandy and dandelion and burdocks, then."

"With an olive!" called one of the girls.

"Shove up, pet," said Mandy in a broad north-eastern accent. She pushed her way onto the bench, forcing Francis to slide up.

"Tell you what, you stay there, pet. I'll climb over you."

The other girls giggled as she wriggled her purple velvet clad backside onto his lap.

"Ooh, is that a gun in your pocket?"

"Careful! It might go off!"

Another woman pushed in on the other side of Francis. A third joined me on my side of the table, and I felt as if the booth was suddenly filled with hair, teeth and cleavage. Francis saw me glaring at him and he remembered his manners.

"Hey, Anna! I want you to meet Taylor, Cheryl and Mandy. We used to be very good friends back when I was stationed in Catterick."

I found myself on the receiving end of three appraising looks.

"And what were you doing in Catterick, Mandy?" I asked, drily.

Francis glared at me. Mandy didn't seem to notice.

"We were all part of a dance troupe. Petra's Pussycats. Did all the clubs in the area. We were doing alright until Petra started shagging our manager. The slag."

"The bitch," said Taylor.

"The cow," added Cheryl.

"So that was Petra's Pussycats down the shitter. And that was it for the money we were owed. If I ever get my hands on those double-crossing bastards…"

She paused as Lizzie arrived with the drinks. Five glasses were set out. Lizzie had brought me a brandy and dandelion and burdock too. There was a green olive floating in each, looking up with a red pimento eye.

We all took a drink. We all grimaced.

"I've tasted better piss!" said Cheryl. "It's awful!"

"Of course it's awful!" said Taylor. "It's a fucking brandy and dandelion and burdock with an olive in it. Whose stupid idea was that?"

I pushed mine away. The others drank up anyway. Mandy continued the story.

"So there we were, broke and without a manager. We were fucked, weren't we, girls?"

"Chucked," said Taylor.

"Fucked *and* chucked," said Cheryl.

"And then we heard about Dream London. It opened all sorts of opportunities…"

It took me a moment to understand what she was saying.

"You mean you went there deliberately?"

"Of course we did," said Mandy. "You've got to go where the work is, haven't you?" And she stared at me, all the girliness gone. All of a sudden, I didn't feel the Dream London sophisticate I'd thought I was. Mandy and the rest had been there too.

"You went there for work?" I stammered. "What… to dance?"

"Yes. And we had a canny good time of it until the gangs moved in. The Daddio and all the rest of them. Then Cheryl's boyfriend heard about jobs out along the river, heard you could make quite a good living doing the circuit."

"So that's we did," said Cheryl. "Caught a barge heading out through the Lowlands. That wasn't so good. Always damp, there were brown eels behind the walls, under the floors. Then we headed down through the Porcelain Cities…"

"Very pretty, but so uncomfortable. Your arse went to sleep every time you sat down," said Taylor. She slurped at her brandy, covered her mouth and burped.

"Down into Dream Orleans. We made a lot of money there…"

"But now we've had enough. We've got a bit put by. We're trying to make our way back to the Mundane World."

I was rather impressed, despite myself. These women had been out there, making it happen.

"What have you got put by?" asked Francis. "Will it have any value back in the Mundane World?"

"We've got the only thing that matters. Deeds to property, back in Mundane London."

"How did you get that?" I asked.

Mandy tapped the side of her nose.

"Ask no questions, pet."

Francis seemed delighted.

"Good for you, Mandy. I'm glad it's all worked out for you."

I sat up straighter, remembering what Mr Twelvetrees had said. All that property back in Mundane London, still unaccounted for, and here was evidence that the ownership was being traded, here in the Dream World. This world still had a toehold in ours.

THE BAR HAD slowly been filling with customers. They dressed alike in dark knitted jumpers and denim trousers and stood speaking to each other in low voices, occasionally glancing over to where we sat, eyeing up the girls in their opulent velvet dresses, the conversation becoming louder and more exuberant. Francis was a different person in their company. He was the big man, the centre of attention of those dancers, fully aware, as I'm sure were all the other men in the bar, that under those velvet clothes were lithe bodies.

Francis rubbed his hands together.

"Well, ladies. Tonight is your lucky night!"

The locals shook their heads, muttered darkly. Francis seemed oblivious.

"It just so happens that I know the way back to London. I've got it all mapped out for you, in fact. See my pack, over there by the bar?"

We looked. And Francis and I stood up.

"What's the matter?" asked Mandy.

"My pack! It's gone!"

We both saw it, laid in the middle of the room, straps splayed out around it.

"Someone must have knocked it over," said Francis, hurrying to replace it in its position by the bar. Mandy and the rest smiled as Francis returned to us. Was I the only one to notice the sullen expression on Lizzie's face?

"See the wire that comes from the back of the pack?" said Francis. There was a murmur as they all noticed the wire, as if for the first time. "Well, that wire leads all the way back to London."

The whole bar was listening now. They were looking at the pack with a thoughtful expression. Francis ploughed on, oblivious.

"Follow that wire and it will take you up the cliff face and across the grass to the fields. Go through the fields and you'll come to the edge of Dream London, then follow it through the streets. Watch out for the clowns! Keep following until you come to a canal. Jump in and follow it until you get to the tunnel under the white bridge with the octopuses on it. Go through that tunnel and you'll be back in London!"

I seemed to be the only one who noticed the silence in the bar. Mandy and the others were too taken by the thought of going home.

"We need another drink!" called Mandy, turning to the barmaid. "Have you got any Baileys? It's been that long and I'd love a glass."

"The last bottle got drunk last week. We'll have to wait for more to get across here." Lizzie suddenly smiled. It wasn't a pleasant smile. "I'll tell you what, though. Dream Breizh is back on the roads. I've got some Brittany cider back here..."

"Five glasses of cider," said Mandy. "And can we have some stew too? We'll need to keep our strength up with Francis here."

They all thought that was hilarious.

"I'll just have tea, please," I said. "I don't really drink."

"Go on, have a cider with us. We're celebrating."

"So, Anna," said Taylor, seemingly noticing me for the first time. "What are you doing here with Francis? I hope he's behaving himself!"

"I'm looking for my parents. I've been given a lead about my mother. She's lost in Dream Paris." A thought occurred to me. "Have you been there?"

Taylor shook her head.

"No way. We wouldn't go near the place. We've heard the stories..."

"What stories?" asked Francis.

"The place is like a prison. You need papers to get in, papers to move around. Papers to get out. They've got this people's committee running the place; if they take a dislike to you, they send you to the guillotine."

Cheryl interrupted.

"They're so superior! I heard that when they speak to you they always put you in your place. They have different ways of addressing you..."

"Oh, that's just *tu* and *vous*, they have that back home." I couldn't keep the edge of superiority from my voice.

"I know about that," grinned Taylor. "*Mon français n'est pas si mal que ça.*"

I felt quite chastened. Clearly Taylor wasn't as stupid as I'd assumed.

"But no, I don't just mean *tu* and *vous*. There's more to it than that. When they speak they have a way of saying just how important you are. I don't know... you'll hear it."

"So what do you do at home, Anna?" asked Cheryl. She seemed the most friendly of the three. Her accent was certainly the broadest.

"I'm studying for my A levels. I want to go to university."

"Which A levels?"

"Maths, Physics, Chemistry."

"I was no good at Maths," said Cheryl, impressed.

"I could have been," said Mandy, "but my teacher was rubbish. She couldn't keep control... I wanted to study English. I love reading."

"Really?"

"Oh, yes. I loved Thomas Hardy. He was my favourite. And poetry. RS Thomas. And Dylan Thomas..."

"I like those Andy McNab books," said Francis.

Cheryl stared at him.

"What?" he said.

Lizzie arrived, carrying a tray of tankards. She placed them on the table one by one.

"Now, this is from Dream France," warned Mandy. "Be careful..."

"I lived in Dream London," I said. "I'm used to these sorts of drinks."

I watched Francis sip cautiously at his drink. I took a deep draught, showing off.

... and suddenly I wasn't quite there in the room. I was

still sat in my chair, it was true, but now I could see myself sitting there, I could see the building we were sat in, and I could see the sea, dark and churning and flecked with black and white shapes. I could see land, and then I could feel the land, I could feel what it was like to be white dunes whipped by the wind, to be trees twisted towards the land, I could feel the pattern of roots that held onto the soil that was me, the cold of the water that soaked into me...

And then my attention was suddenly snatched back over the sea to the black and white shape cutting through the water, heading towards the town, sliding into the harbour, climbing out onto the harbourside...

I was back in the pub and everything had gone quite. Everyone was staring at the man who had burst through the doorway.

"Liopleurodon!" he shouted "Liopleurodon! In the town!"

SEVENTEEN

THE LIOPLEURODON

THE PUB EMPTIED, everyone pushing their way out into the street. I followed the crowd and bowled into Francis, who had stopped in the middle of the road, momentarily disorientated by the Dream World sky. Deep purple, rising up and up, swirls of galaxies hanging overhead. I'd forgotten how tall it was. The sky is deeper there, the stars more enfolded. You got the sense of universe after universe tucked away in the folds between the billows of the clouds, of other worlds lost amongst them, stranger than you could imagine.

And then we were swept on by the crowd rushing down the street, we found ourselves in the noise and confusion that reigned by the harbour. I saw the boats bobbing up and down on the dark waters, the plants set out on the decks glowing in the dark. I heard screams, I heard shouting (*the ropes, get the ropes!*) and then people were pushing past carrying nets. And now I could see a flash of white ahead, I could see the monstrous shape flapping its way onwards, see the great mouth wide agape, see the rows of teeth shining. I faltered, but the crowd pushed me on. Something awoke inside me and I remembered walking into the parks, back in Dream London, I remembered that calm courage that came in putting oneself to the side and surrendering to the greater good. A man was at my side. Red hair, knitted jumper, denim.

"Take this." He pushed a rope into my hands.

"What do I do?"

"We're going to try and catch it! The meat is good."

The whole town seemed awake now. I saw jaws snapping in the flicker of torches, I saw flames flickering as more hurried to join the melee, forcing the animal away from the water. I gripped the rope tighter and ran forwards.

And then the music started. The sound of trumpets and cornets. My legs gave way. I fell to the ground, hands pushed over my ears, the crowd surging over me, and I curled up against the kicking, lost in the awful, mind-turning terror. I was only half aware of someone taking hold of my shoulder, lifting me up, pushing me back through the crowd.

I WAS SAT back in the pub, back on the same bench, drinking hot sweet tea, Francis beside me.

"You okay?"

"Sorry," I muttered, hot with shame. "I lost it. You must think me a terrible coward."

"I think you're very brave. You were running towards that creature."

"I panicked."

"You have PTSD. You shouldn't be here. You should be back home receiving proper care and attention."

"My parents need me!"

"No, Anna. It doesn't work that way. Your parents look after you, not the other way around."

The door opened and a jubilant crowd pushed their way

in, Mandy, Taylor and Cheryl amongst them. They were ready to celebrate.

"They got it!" called Mandy. "Cornered it against the cliff, moved in with knives and swords and machetes and hacked it to death."

"Then they cut open its guts!" called Cheryl. "The smell! It was hanging! There was this, like, white liquid just spilling out over the ground. It made their boots steam! And then they were in there, pulling it open. One man was shouting, his hands were burning. They pulled out all this stuff. Half-digested fish. And other creatures! Like this big octopus! And other things it had eaten…"

I sat quietly in the corner, half-listening to the excited bubble of conversation. More drinks, beer and gin, they were steering clear of the cider now. The whole pub was celebrating.

"There'll be steaks tomorrow!" announced Lizzie, slamming down more glasses on the table. "Steaks for everyone! I heard that Liopleurodon was the biggest yet!"

"About time!" A big man, blood still on his cheek. Hadn't he noticed? "We've been waiting months for one of the bastards to come here!"

I looked at Francis. Didn't he think it odd? They'd waited months and one attacked the very night we arrived. Coincidence?

"What was it doing here?" I asked. Taylor misunderstood my question.

"The Dream World finds its way everywhere, Anna. It found its way into dinosaur times, and the dinosaurs carved themselves a niche in the Dream World. No one owns the water."

"You're not drinking, Anna," interrupted Mandy. She had an arm around Francis, her breasts pushing into him. She raised a glass of gin and I noticed that Francis's glass was still full. *Getting her drunk*, I thought. *Don't know why he's bothering. She's not putting up any resistance.*

"Have a drink, Anna?" called Francis.

"I think I've had enough. I think I might go to bed now."

"Good idea," said Francis. "We've got a busy day ahead." He winked at Mandy. "And Lizzie said I had to be in bed for eleven."

What had happened to all that concern of a few minutes ago? I had PTSD. I shouldn't be here.

"Well, I'm off up."

"I'll be up later," said Francis.

"Oi-oi!" called Taylor, and Cheryl laughed so much that she snorted brandy through her nose.

I rose to my feet, shaken, confused, annoyed. What about 'Chelle? Didn't Francis care about his fiancée?

"I'll see you in the morning, then," I said. "What time?"

"I'll knock you up at six."

Knock you up. Mandy and the rest thought this was hilarious.

"Goodnight, then. It was lovely to meet you all, *ladies*."

As I pushed through the merry crowd, a snatch of conversation drifted from behind.

"... *ditched little Miss Prim-and-Posh. Now we can have some fun...*"

You're welcome to it, I thought.

LIZZIE LED ME through a doorway by the bar and I stopped, wary of a trap. There was something here, concealed. Then I realised it was the wire from Francis's backpack, no doubt carried up to his room as promised. What power did that wire have that allowed it to hide itself away so, I wondered? What thread hid itself so as not to be seen?

"Ten o'clock," said Lizzie, looking at the big old clock on the wall. "Shouldn't be that much of a walk."

I followed her up a spiralling stair, wooden treads tilted at all angles, climbing flight after flight. The plaster on the walls was old and damp, there was a smell of fish and boiled mutton.

"How tall is this building?"

"Three stories," said Lizzie. "But you know how it is with stairs."

I did. I remembered my house back in Dream London. You walked up three stories to get to a first floor bedroom. Dream logic.

"And here it is," said Lizzie. The stairs arrived at a long corridor, lined with five doors painted red, green, yellow, fuchsia and aardvark. The grey thread from the backpack trailed into the yellow room. "You're in the fuchsia room," said Lizzie, opening the door. "Now, don't forget to leave by the far stairs. Try and come back the way you came and it will take all day. You'll want to check out by eleven. Is there anything else?"

I opened my mouth to reply. I was interrupted by a long moan coming from the room next door.

"Don't worry," said Lizzie. "That's just the General. She's always like that. Good night, love."

"Good night."

The door closed and I found myself in a room that was surprisingly clean and comfortable. A brass bedstead, a patchwork quilt. An oil lamp, a basin, a pitcher.

Another moan.

I opened my bag and swore. Francis had been right.

"I should have brought a book," I muttered.

It was hot. I stripped down to my underwear and got into bed.

I AWOKE TO the feel of glorious sunlight dripping down over my face. I yawned and stretched luxuriously, opened my eyes and, I'm ashamed to say, I screamed.

Two painted blue eyes gazed down at me, a porcelain face was thrust close to mine. I scrambled backwards, tangling in the bedclothes, fell backwards out of the bed. The door burst open and Francis tumbled into the room, standing over me where I lay on the floor, struggling to free myself from the sheets. Francis, stripped to the waist, shaving foam covering his face, flipping the figure back onto the bed, its golden hair flying...

"A doll!" he said. "Another doll! Where are they coming from?"

I finally got myself free of the blankets and clambered to my feet, pulling the one sheet around myself. Francis had broken off one of the doll's arms: it lay on the bed, hand turned towards me, the faint outline of fingernails.

I scratched my cheek, thinking.

"Does it have a letter?"

We went through the doll's clothes, me very aware of Francis's half-naked torso almost touching me. The doll was made of stuffed cloth, I noticed. Only its hands and face were china.

"Nothing," said Francis. I went to take a look out of the window. Gulls skipped over the harbour, skipped over the sea, just out of snapping range of the black and white Liopleurodons that jumped and played in the foaming sea of the channel. The sun was yellow and poured down like butter in this little pocket world. The sea was blue and the jumpers of the sailors were narrow stripes of blue on white. If the view was different, I was too distracted by the doll to notice.

Francis withdrew to the door. "Listen, let's get dressed and go down to breakfast."

I gazed down at the remains of the doll. A life size model of a young woman, every detail beautifully painted, from the golden strands of her hair to the cupid bow of her lips to the laces on her pretty sandals.

I looked around for the bathroom. There wasn't one. Just a pitcher and bowl and a chamber pot. Nothing there to put off a former resident of Dream London. I used the pot, covered it and pushed it under the bed. There were fresh clothes laid out, just as promised on the meal ticket in my wallet. Cotton knickers, white stockings, a grey pinafore, a straw hat. *A bed for the night, a good meal and change of clothes.* Not the sort of outfit I'd have chosen, but better than the clothes that had got soaked in the canal yesterday and had now dried to a cardboard creak.

As I finished dressing there was a knock on the door and Francis reappeared, dressed in a blue jacket covered with gold frogging. His trousers were blue with a red stripe down the side. I laughed out loud.

"I thought I looked rather dashing," said Francis with a grin. "You look very nice, I must say."

I beamed, and then I remembered Mandy last night, I imagined the lithe dancer's body wrapped around Francis.

"What time did you get to bed last night?"

"Eleven, like I was told."

Did you think of 'Chelle?

"Come on. Let's get some breakfast."

Francis's great backpack was propped outside the door, the wire trailing back down the stairs. He knelt by it and frowned.

"It's let out twenty miles of wire in the night. Those stairs have grown much taller."

We walked down the far stairs, as instructed. There weren't so many stairs going down as there had been coming up.

"It took forever for me to climb up last night," said Francis. "I almost missed the tide."

"The tide?"

"Yes. Lizzie explained it to me, you see…"

I'd figured it out for myself. Twenty miles across the English

Channel, distances changed in the Dream World. Someone had linked this floor of the guest house to the tides...

What a way to travel.

CHOCOLATE

DREAM CALAIS

WE STEPPED INTO the dining room of a little Dream French café bar.

It was obvious from the quality of the light, from the way it made the varnish of the teak-panelled walls glow, that we were in a different country. The dimensions of the room were foreign, as were the little round tables surrounded by bent wooden chairs, the blue and white enamel on the round metal ashtrays, the smell of coffee and tobacco. There was something exotic about the man who entered the room: the dark pomaded hair, the trimmed moustache, the long white apron covering his trousers. He looked like the French waiter that he was.

"*Bonjour mademoiselle, Bonjour monsieur*! *(2)Vous prenez un petit dejeuner?*"

"He's asking if we want breakfast," said Anna.

"I figured that out," said Francis, witheringly. "What's *(2) vous?*"

I didn't know. That was the first time I'd heard Dream relative pronouns; at the time I knew nothing about l'Académie Française. How can I explain the difference between *tu(2)* and *(2)vous*? The way that the intonation implies your relative status, the way that the correct pronunciation of *(2)vous* allows a French waiter to let you know that you were his superior, but only just.

Well, imagine this, you're a five-year-old child and the teacher has just walked into the classroom and caught you with your hand in her handbag. Imagine how you would feel, imagine how your guilt would come up against her authority when she asked you what *you* were doing. Well, that would be *tu(10)*. And when you spoke back to her? You would call her *(10)vous*.

The aristocracy of Dream France could invest an exact measure of authority into every conversation.

But all that's to come. The waiter had switched languages.

"Ah! English! I thought so! I saw your shoes!"

We both looked down at our feet.

"We're trying to get to Dream Paris," I said.

"The railway station is just down the road. But first, you must eat. Come! Sit down!"

Francis nodded. He must have felt as hungry as I.

We propped our backpacks against the wall and took our places at a little table.

"*Un café au lait et un croissant, s'il vous plait.*" I was showing off, putting Francis in his place after his behaviour last night.

"I'll have the same," he said.

"We have no croissants. There is coffee and *tartine*. And I will need to see your papers."

Francis and I exchanged glances.

"Papers...?" I said.

"You have no papers?" The waiter didn't seem very surprised by this. "You won't get very far..."

Francis took the hint.

"Perhaps you can help us?" he said, pulling out his wallet

and removing a couple of coloured notes. The waiter shook his head, pointed. Francis counted out more Dream Francs until the waiter suddenly beamed, closed his hand and stuffed the notes into his pocket.

"*D'accord*! And now I will fetch your breakfast!"

He bustled off, leaving us to take in our situation.

The table afforded a good view down a wide street lined with plane trees, their dappled trunks reflecting the Dream light in yellow and green and gold. There were people out there, waking up the town. People dressed a little like Francis and me in old-fashioned clothes: pinafores and uniforms and high-collared shirts. They were pulling up shutters, setting out trestle tables, hurrying to work.

"What's *tartine*?" asked Francis, unhappily.

"Bread and jam."

"I wanted eggs."

"You're getting bread and jam. It's French."

"Don't they have eggs in France, then?"

The waiter brought our breakfast. Pieces of baguette sliced lengthways, the crust golden brown, the interior soft and light and white and smelling of paradise. Two pots, one containing green jam, the other black. Two cups and a little metal coffee pot. Everything smelled so much *more*. But that was the Dream World.

I spread green jam on my bread and took a bite. A picture of an orchard filled my mind. Green leaves above green grass, people climbing ladders to pick green fruit. There were dolls in the orchard... porcelain dolls.

Francis was blinking.

"It's like that cider..." he said. "You taste where the jam comes from." He shook his head. "Was this normal? Did this happen in Dream London? The food speaks to you. You go down the wrong set of stairs and finish up in a different country?"

"The food changed you, but it never spoke to you like this. And distances... Well, they had a way of changing. Distances weren't absolute in Dream London. You could climb five stories inside a building and only be on the second floor. Francis, I saw dolls. Porcelain dolls in an orchard."

"I saw bushes, and young woman picking blackberries. No dolls."

"Dolls everywhere," I said. "Those ones in England that brought the message from my mother... Is she working for them, do you think?"

I thought about my mother, I imagined her being taken to the workhouse, stripped of her clothes, dressed as a doll, a porcelain mask pressed to her face. I shivered. It was too horrible.

The waiter reappeared.

"I'm sorry, *mademoiselle*. You appear to have dropped your papers..."

"Oh! Thank you!"

He handed across two pieces of ivory paper.

"You'd be surprised how many of our guests do that."

I took my document and examined it. My name was written there: *Anna Margaret Louise Sinfield*. I looked over at Francis's document and saw that his full name was *Francis Christopher Cuppello*.

"How did you know our names?" I asked.

"In Dream France, every object is referenced. If not then..." He open his hands. "*Poof!*"

I looked at the beautiful black handwriting, the way it covered the ivory paper. I noted that it had my name, age (17), marital status (single) and profession (*espion*).

"*Espion?*" I said. "What does that mean?"

"Spy."

"I'm not a spy!"

"Of course not!" smiled the waiter. I could have punched his smug, self-satisfied, superior Dream French face.

* * *

WE FINISHED OUR breakfast and paid the bill, the waiter helpfully showing Francis which of the notes in his wallet to use and passing him a handful of hexagonal coins as change. Then we hoisted our backpacks and stepped out into the street.

The first thing we saw was the square pillar of the clock tower, rising up from the rooftops, higher and higher into the sky.

"That's what we saw from Dream Dover," said Francis, voice low with awe. He'd never have seen something so tall before. I was from Dream London, I'd seen towers rise up way too high, but this...

"I can still see the clockface," said Francis. "It should be impossible at this angle."

"Don't look at it," I advised. "The perspectives in the Dream World can drive you mad."

"*Bonjour(4)*! *Tu(4) cherche la gare?*" The words were spoken by a man dressed in an immaculate primrose suit. Did you hear that *Bonjour(4)*? He was saying he was four social points above us. Not that I properly recognised that at the time.

"The railway station," I said. "*Oui!*"

"*Là-bas!*"

He pointed down the street, touched his hat and was on his way. He'd addressed me, not Francis, I noted. Something occurred to me.

"What does it say your job is on your papers?" I asked.

"*Garde du corps.*"

It took me a moment to work it out. "Bodyguard."

Francis shrugged.

"Fair enough."

We were in Dream Calais. It said so in golden letters over the entrance to the railway station, a building that was a joy to behold, a poem written in curved iron arches and glass, filled to overflowing with light from the Dream sun. Gentlemen in mustard and gold suits strolled through the wide entrance, escorting ladies in plum and blueberry silks. A line of statues – tall women in robes and tiaras – were arranged at the front of the station, their pedestals inscribed with the various destinations served by the station: *Dream Madrid, Dream Tallinn, Madrid, Dream Mumbai, Munich, Dream Vladivostok, Dream Oldham, Dream Manchester...*

Dream Manchester?

Dream Moscow, Dream Troy, Atlantis, Dream Atlantis...

We made our way inside and stood in the middle of the vast concourse, Francis with the long wire trailing from his backpack, running out of the station entrance and back down the street to the café and the route back to England. The hurrying French commuters stepped over the wire without seeming to notice it.

There was no clock in the station, I noticed. None was needed, not when the Dream Calais clock could be seen clearly through the glass.

Five robots stood on the concourse, looking lost. A sixth robot came hurrying up.

"Did you get the tickets?" asked one of the waiting robots.

"No. They said they'd never heard of Turing City. They kept asking if I was sure I didn't mean *Turin*."

"Come on, Francis," I said, pulling him away from the little scene. "Look! *Billets*. Tickets."

We found a little window, a woman sat behind it wearing a green and gold striped blouse.

"(2)Bonjour, mademoiselle."

"Er, *bonjour*. Er... *Je voudrais acheter deux billets à* erm... *Paris aux Reves?*"

"English?" said the woman.

"Yes," said Anna.

"Your papers, please."

Francis and I pushed our papers through the little slot in the window. The woman took her time examining them.

"I hope Claude didn't overcharge you for these," she murmured. "Two tickets to Dream Paris, you say?"

"*S'il vous plait*. Return, please."

"You are fortunate. The line to Dream Paris reconnected with this station only yesterday. There hasn't been a route to that city for weeks."

Francis opened his mouth to speak. I nudged him in the side.

"First or second class?"

"Er, first?" After all, it wasn't my money.

"That will be 300 Dream francs, or 2 louis d'ors, 500 livres or 225 euros. I hope you have enough money for your stay in Dream Paris. It costs a lot of money to bribe yourself good treatment in the Bastille."

I pushed the money across the counter and received two flowery rectangles of cardboard in return. Francis snatched them up and examined them.

"Hey! These returns are guaranteed for one day only!"

"Of course! The lines connect and disconnect. You can't expect a line to go to the same place two days in a row."

"Leave it, Francis," I said. "It doesn't matter."

"Platform *Bleu*, ten minutes," said the woman. "And you want to look after that purse. There are a lot of thieves about…"

"It's okay. I've got a bodyguard."

THERE WERE PIERROTS on Platform *Bleu*. Four of them, dressed in white silken shirts, each carrying a dark leather briefcase, looking for all the world like businessmen and -women just heading off to a meeting.

"What should we do?" asked Francis.

"Ignore them. Pretend you haven't noticed them."

We walked down the platform. They were speaking in something like German. None of them so much as glanced at us.

We found a spot to stand further down the platform, near a large family, the women and girls dressed in crinoline, the men and boys in tight serge suits. The children all held little hamster cages in their hands.

"That's their lunch!" said Francis, elbowing me in the ribs. I stared at him until he muttered a red-faced apology.

"Thank you," I said.

Our train was approaching, rounding the bend of the platform. A golden brown steam engine hissed by, sparkling with rain drops. It was a foreign-looking engine, too many domes and pieces of machinery attached to it; it sparked and flashed and reciprocated and seemed to be making way too much of the simple job of moving from A to B. The driver leaned out of the cab, his large moustache bristling, resplendent in his striped overalls, clearly proud to be driving the engine. The coaches rolled by, drab olive green with neat little windows and gingham curtains framing brass tables with lamps on them. The train bumped to a halt, and something occurred to me.

"Your pack, Francis! What are we going to do with the wire?"

He'd already thought of that. We waited for the scrum of passengers to board, each pushing the others aside with no regard for anyone else, and then Francis passed his pack through the open window of the door. He climbed on board and pulled the door closed behind us.

"What if the wire garrottes someone?" I said.

"I don't think it will. It's barely there."

"Francis, what *is* that pack? I thought you said it was just missile wire."

"That's what it was, back in London. It's changed."

"Why do you still carry it?"

"I have my orders."

He had his orders. Oddly enough, I understood. Dream London changed people, it exaggerated what was there. Francis was a man who followed orders, he carried the pack, no matter how strange that pack became. I understood Francis. And that was a worry. Because if Francis was changing, then what about me? How was the Dream World affecting me?

We walked into a carriage, the seats already filled. Whole families seemed to be travelling together, from grandparents down to little children and babies. They would take over a pair of tables across an aisle, drape them in red-and-white-checked table cloths and then load them up with loaves of bread, bottles of water and wine, earthenware bowls of salad and boiled potatoes, whole roast chickens. They filled in the gaps in between with fruit and little cakes, dishes of olives and pickles and pats of butter, platters of runny cheese and little jars of foie gras. The air in the carriage quickly filled with a delicious smell that sent my stomach rumbling. I'd only had bread and jam…

"I think first class is the next carriage," said Francis, pushing down the aisle.

I felt a lurch as the train began to move from the station: we were on the way to Dream Paris.

Francis was holding his breath, I noticed, feeling the *whizz, whizz, whizz* as the train picked up speed and the wire spooled out along its indefinite length, trailing back along the carriage and out of the open window. Slowly, he relaxed and I realised I'd been holding my breath, too.

The first class carriage was much less crowded, the seats here were much wider, two pairs on the left of the aisle, one on the right. The four Pierrots we'd seen on the platform sat around one file-strewn table. They paid us no attention.

Two old men with immaculate beards and moustaches were deep in discussion, brushed top hats sat on the seats beside them. A tall Sikh had a table to himself, where he wrote furiously on a piece of parchment. A dog sat alone at the table opposite, looking out of the window with a serious expression on its face. It was rather a handsome creature, white fur with foxy red patches. It glanced at me and I noted the wildness in its eyes.

We found seats at a table for four, opposite a woman who appeared to be travelling with her father. The pair were impeccably dressed, the old man in a dark suit and lavender shirt, his white hair and moustaches combed and waxed, the woman in a fuchsia jacket and skirt contrasting with a matched set of ivory gloves, scarf, hat and handbag. She looked me up and down in a manner that left no doubt what she thought of my appearance.

"What's your problem?" I said.

Francis placed a hand on mine and I glared at him.

"Don't touch me!"

He snatched his hand away. "Ignore her."

"Did you see the way she looked at us?"

"Seriously, Anna. We're in a strange environment. Sit back and tune in with your surroundings. Get the feel of the place."

This from a man whose backpack was unspooling some sort of Dream wire back to England.

Across the aisle, the woman said something to her father in French. He looked at me for a moment and then nodded his head gravely in reply.

"What's that?" I demanded. "What did you say?"

"Anna!" hissed Francis.

"(14)I said," said the woman, her English accent impeccable, "that there is a spy(14) sitting opposite."

Even speaking in English she managed to convey our

relative worth. *(14)I*, she'd said, putting herself 14 rungs higher than me.

"A spy? I'm not a spy."

The woman's lips creased into a superior smile.

"Young lady(14), do you honestly think you(14) are the first person that Dream London has sent this way? You're(14) going to tell (14)me that you're(14) just another young lady, looking for her(14) parents. That's right, isn't it?"

I hesitated. It was that way of speaking. *You(14)*. She was putting me in my place.

"Well... yes, but you see, I am. I've got a..."

"My father(2) and (14)I travel this line quite frequently. (14)I've lost count of the number of young men and women like you(14) that (14)I've encountered. Each of you(14) looking so earnest, so determined. Take (14)my advice, young lady(14), and turn around now. Get off at the next station and take the train back to Dream Calais and England."

I was shaken by the woman's words. Who wouldn't be? Especially when carrying papers that confirmed the accusation. Still, I rallied somehow.

"I'm sorry, *madame*. But I'm not a spy. I don't know about these other people that you've seen, but I can assure you that the only reason I'm here is to find my parents."

"Of course. And what then? Then you(14) will return home and tell the people of Dream London everything that you(14) have seen. You(14) may be an unwitting spy, but you're(14) a spy nonetheless. You(14) have the stench of it about you(14)."

And at that she sniffed the air. Her father did the same. And now other people were sniffing, too. The occupants of the carriage were all turning to look in our direction. Looking between the seat backs, kneeling on the chairs or standing up to get a better look at us. Even the dog was doing it, sniffing the air, the nostrils on its brown rubbery nose flaring as it smelled my spy-ness.

I was seized by the unfairness of it all.

"I'm not a spy! How *dare* you judge me?" Francis touched my hand again and I shook it away. Horrible creepy hand. I felt myself turning red, my voice shaking.

"All of you, judging me! This is just like Dream London, back when I was marching with the band. I saw people like you sitting around, getting drunk or stuffing their fat faces with chicken while I was marching. How dare you judge me!"

Those words struck home. The woman opposite seemed genuinely shocked. Well, good, I thought, she should be. But I'd misjudged her reaction.

"You(14) marched with a band?" she said. "Tell (14)me, what sort of band? Speak up, girl(14)!"

"A brass band."

The woman addressed the carriage in rapid French, too fast for me to follow, and immediately there was a chorus of tutting, a massed shaking of heads.

"What's the matter now?" I said. "What's the matter with brass bands?"

"The Germans have brass bands. And look what they lead to…"

You could tell by her expression that she thought me terribly naive. Silly little girl, only just old enough to bleed, no idea about the big wide world, travelling to find a mother who'd told her not to come looking for her.

"What are you talking about? What do bands lead to?"

The woman in fuchsia couldn't keep the disdain from her voice.

"Why, to war, of course!"

SIXTEEN

ERICH

THE TRAIN STOPPED at the prettiest little station I've ever seen. Yellow stone buildings, swept platforms, shiny milk churns, a little red cart stacked with suitcases. You could see a little square just behind the station, a little French town with a *boulangerie*, a *boucherie*, a *marchand de légumes*, and, best of all, a little café. Little tables spread with checked table cloths, set out in the dappled shade of the tall trees. A few customers were already seated, enjoying a glass of wine, sharing bread. It was so perfectly French, it was so delightful, it was so inviting...

"It's *so* a trap," said Francis.

"What?"

"That village, it's a trap. It's trying to lure us off the train."

"How do you know?" I said, suspiciously.

"Instinct."

The engine whistled and, as we began to move, I felt a real tug of regret to be leaving the little town behind. Like I was making a huge mistake in staying on the train. And then, just like that, the spell was broken. It was just another little town.

"You're(14) stronger than you(14) look," said the woman in fuchsia, approvingly. She reached out a hand. "(14)Mme Courbois. Please to meet you(14)."

I took her hand and wrestled with it for a moment, trying to shake it, before I realised what was expected of me. I leaned forward and kissed it. Francis did the same, only with more style. Mme Courbois nodded approvingly.

"This is (14)my father(2), M Dollé(2). You(14) will have heard of him, of course?"

"Of course," said Francis smoothly, ladies' man and born liar.

"Excellent. Now, would you(14) like to share a bottle of wine?"

Mme Courbois saw the way I was looking at Francis.

"(14)I'm not trying to poison you(14)," she said drily. "(14)I shall order a bottle of the *Belle Epoque* '89. (14)I think the perspective would do you(14) good."

The bottle was brought, brown and dusty and with a fading yellow label. Across the way the dog was served a plate of raw steak and a small bowl of pasta. It sniffed the meal carefully and then began to eat, first a mouthful of steak, and then a long strand of spaghetti.

"I didn't know dogs could suck," said Francis, watching as a long strand disappeared into its mouth.

"There's a dog who knows how to behave in polite company," observed Mme Courbois. I had the impression this was an instruction to follow suit. The waiter poured a little wine into her glass. Liquid the colour of pale straw, the scent of flowers and summer filling the cabin. She tasted it and nodded. The waiter filled our glasses.

"*Santé!*"

We chinked glasses. I noticed how Mme Courbois watched me as I sipped. The wine tasted of summer, of hot ground baking under the sun, of the heat stored up by fields of wheat, of the shade under trees...

I felt myself slipping away, slipping away like when I'd drunk the cider the night before.

"What's happening to me? What did you do?"

"(14)I've done nothing. What you(14) are experiencing is *terroir*: the combination of soil, climate and environment that gives a wine its distinctive character..."

"I feel is if I'm not properly here..."

"Drink this wine and you(14) get drunk on the spirit of the region in which it was produced. That's why everything feels so alien. You(14) don't belong here, do you(14)? You're(14) not part of the *terroir*. You're(14) not loyal to this land."

I was barely there, I was lost in a half world of sunshine, lost in the middle of the vast continent of Dream France, where the Dream sun beat down on a land that had lain there for millennia. But I was also in the train carriage and I could see the other people in the carriage smiling at me. Hard smiles, unsympathetic smiles, the smiles of those who had caught me out.

Across from me, Francis was shaking his head.

"You tricked us," he said.

"(14)I offered you(14) a little wine. It seems to (14)me that neither of you(14) can take your(14) drink."

Francis took my arm, he pulled me from my seat.

"You're(14) leaving? Don't be silly. Sit down."

"No way. Come on, Anna. Let's go."

His pack was propped up against his seat, straps hanging wide. How had it got there? I didn't know. He took hold of the pack in one hand, pushed me off down the aisle with the other.

"Everything here will try to tempt you(14)!" called Mme Courbert. "The food, the wine, even the railway stations! Everything will try and make you(14) its own, young woman(14)!"

*   *   *

FRANCIS AND I staggered down the train. I felt myself both swaying and unmoving, part travelling on the train, part the land itself. I dragged my pack along, feeling sick and disoriented, until finally Francis found us a space in third class. The people here were far more down at heel, their picnics far more organic, cold chitterlings and brawn, boiled potatoes and dishes of salt.

Francis bundled me into a seat and I sat there, looking out at the unrolling countryside. We rolled past towns of unspeakably loveliness, each one a perfect place to live.

Gradually the effect of the wine passed away.

"How long does this journey take?" I wondered.

"It depends on which line has connected," said a voice, "but I'd(5) say a good day and a half, usually."

I looked around to see who had spoken.

"Down here!"

There was a cage pushed between the backs of two seats. A fully grown man was squashed inside, his knees tucked uncomfortably up by his ears. He raised a hand in greeting.

"Er, hello…?"

The man pulled a well sharpened knife from his pocket and used it to cut a piece of sausage. He held it out to me, offering.

"No, thank you. But, a day and a half? It's not that far to Paris from Calais."

"It is at the moment. I(5) remember a time when you could walk between the two towns in an hour or so, but that was when the war with Portugal was on. (5)You'd remember that, of course?"

The last was directed at Francis.

"No. I'm sorry, I wasn't part of that war."

"Oh! (5)You surprise me(5). A soldier like (5)you. Don't deny it. (5)You *are* a soldier, aren't (5)you?"

(5)You. The man was putting Francis in charge.

"I am."

"I(5) knew it! I(5) was too, once. But what's a soldier doing accompanying a spy, that's what I(5) want to know?"

"I'm not a spy!"

"Of course (5)you're not! Are (5)you sure (5)you don't want some of this sausage? It's vegetarian, (5)you know. Very good. Made of mushrooms."

"I'm okay, thank you. Listen, can you speak without the emphasis? I find it very confusing."

"Okay," said the man, humbly. I gazed down at him, wondering if I should ask the obvious question. Francis beat me to it. He had much less tact than I.

"What are you doing in that cage?"

The man laughed, ruefully. He lifted himself a little, stretching as best as could in the confined space.

"Ah! The cage! Have you heard of Milanese Spaghetti Hounds?"

"No," I said, thoughtfully, "but I rather think I might have seen one..."

"In the dining car? Yes? That would be Uther. I bought him from a woman in Nantes. She said that Milanese Spaghetti Hounds made great pets, but that they were very strong-willed. She said I would have to be firm, that I would have to show him who was boss."

He smiled ruefully.

"I rather think that I failed in that regard."

"Oh."

"Now I(5) am (14)Uther's pet." That emphasis. He couldn't help it. "He has my house, my property and my family. He gets to eat steak and spaghetti in the restaurant car, and I'm left to travel in this cage."

"Can't you do anything about it?" asked Francis.

"Not really. It was a fair contract, I walked into it with my eyes open. Still, I can't help but wonder how many times Mme Lombard has done this. I imagine she's making quite a killing, selling Milanese Spaghetti Hounds to unsuspecting people. Let the dog take over everything and then she takes her cut. She must own a fair few properties in Dream Paris now. She wants to be careful. Own too many, and the Committee for Public Safety will start to take an interest in her..."

"So you come from Dream Paris?" said Francis.

"Oh, yes! I had a lovely flat overlooking the Seine. Just out of range of the Liopleurodons, one could sit on the balcony without risk of being snatched off for a morning snack. I used to have an important job, too, working for the *Banca di Primavera*."

He looked regretful for a moment.

"Still, look on the bright side. No more worries for me, no responsibilities. I get fed twice a day, I'm allowed plenty of exercise. There's even talk about putting me up for stud."

Francis perked up at that, funnily enough.

"How nice," I said, drily.

The man blushed, looked at Francis.

"I'm sorry, I shouldn't be speaking that way in front of your young lady."

"I'm not his young lady!"

"… what's (5)your name, anyway? My(5) name is Erich."

"Pleased to meet you(2), Erich," said Francis. He was trying. He almost got the intonation right. Almost.

THE DAY ROLLED on. Passengers got on and passengers got off, and the whizzing of the wire from Francis's backpack – now stowed in the luggage rack – counted out the miles between here and home.

The scenery slowly changed. We wound through chalk hills, cut through vineyards, followed river valleys down which great ships sailed, the decks decorated with bunting. We passed over a flat plain, running close to a wide grey city, the skies above it crowded with airships.

The train slowed to a stop at a station on the outskirts of the city, and I saw the four business Pierrots alight.

"Look," said Francis.

I saw it, over the rooftops of the surrounding city. An Eiffel Tower wrapped in olive green bandages.

Night fell and we slept fitfully, occasionally waking to find ourselves lit by the bright lights of a station, the motion of the train briefly stilled. I opened my eyes at one point to see a black train rolling by outside, keeping pace with us. Or maybe that was just a dream.

And then morning rose and we were passing through corrugated dirt fields, rolling on and on to the horizon. The passengers were getting bored now. I had a sense that the journey was drawing to an end. People always get irritable at the end. There's no point in losing your temper when there are hours to go, only when the end to the torment is in sight. I too was fed up with the shaking, the smell of stale food and sweat, of the toilets and the bundled nappies of the children.

Francis was sleeping opposite me, cuddling his backpack like a child holding onto a teddy bear. He seemed to feel my gaze; his eyes flickered open and he smiled at me.

"Wakey, wakey," I said.

He smiled at me, and then looked confused.

"Did you do this?" he said.

"Do what?"

"Put the pack in my arms."

We both stared at the pack. It suddenly seemed quite sinister, the way it nestled close to him.

"No. Why should I do that?"

He frowned, puzzled. Then he shrugged.

"I'm hungry," he said.

So was I.

"There'll be a trolley along soon," said Erich, from his cage. "Would (5)you be so good as to buy me(5) something to eat? Anything that will fit through the bars will be fine."

WE RODE ACROSS a wide plain for most of the day. I glimpsed far off towns on distant hilltops, lines of crops, neatly kept woods and forests. The sun rose up the Dream sky and slowly descended. We passed through the evening… and then, as if on signal, the passengers arose from their torpor and began to gather together their things. Blankets were rolled up, packages collected, coats were put on, papers were found and put in order.

I had a cold, hollow feeling. This was it. Soon there would be no going back. But of course, there had been no going back for some time now…

I pressed my face to the window, hoping to see Dream Paris approaching. Nothing. Nothing but darkness. And then, suddenly, an eye looking at me. A flash of white, and a splash, and I realised I was looking out over water.

"A river!" I said.

"The Seine!" said Erich. "That will be the Seine. We must be approaching the gate! Oh, I(5) wish I(5) could see!"

"The gate?"

"The gate in the wall around Dream Paris."

The Dolls' Dream London had a wall around it to, I remembered. But there was no time to think about that now, because I saw it, the long grey wall that stretched out across the plain, surrounding Dream Paris. We plunged towards it, the wall growing bigger and bigger. I thought I saw vines growing on the outside, tearing at the bricks, but then we were through the gate, travelling through darkness… Light exploded around us.

I reeled back from the window, my eyes adjusting to the sudden glare. The dark band of the river, still running alongside us, crossed by bridges, golden light reflecting in trails on the water. I saw buildings, bright lights; a searchlight, cutting across the sky. A jingle-jangle of sensation. The river turned away from us and another train curved in to take its place, pulling alongside us. Through the lighted windows I could see the passengers, men and women in brightly coloured clothes, reading little books or staring morosely into space. Dream Parisians. A golden china doll sat in a seat, staring at nothing. The other train began to pull away and I realised that we were slowing. The passengers rose and began to move towards the doors, and I realised that we couldn't stay on the train forever. This little haven of safety was now gone the way of all the others.

Francis stood up. He pulled on his backpack, the wire still unbelievably playing out behind it.

And suddenly there was daylight. No, not daylight; we were in a station! A huge station. The train stopped.

We had arrived in Dream Paris.

OLIVE

JEAN-MICHEL PONGE

WHAT WAS IT like to step into Dream Paris?

What's it like to step into any foreign city for the first time? Daunting? Exciting? Exhilarating? That sense of being out of your depth, of being in a place where everyone knows what to do and you find yourself standing hesitant at the edge, isolated, and very, very visible?

Imagine that feeling, then add the fact that you are a spy and everyone knows it (apart from you), that you're searching for your parents, one of whom has told you she doesn't want to be found, that you are in a place coveted by a powerful enemy, a place under the control of a gang of revolutionaries...

Not only that, you're in the Dream World. So, how do you think I felt? I'll tell you. I felt like crying.

But I didn't. Crying is a choice.

Let me tell you what Dream Paris looked like.

Everything had the wrong proportions. I mean everything. The longer you were there, the more you noticed it. Everything was too big or too small. Or too tall or too narrow, or too fat or too slender. Or too loud or too colourful, too plain or too restrained, too patterned or exuberant or dignified or illustrated or crenellated or striated or stellated or reticulated or arpeggiated. It was glissando when it should have been staccato, it was plain when it should have been milk.

The cups for the coffee: too small. (And the coffee too strong. I don't mean like strong like espresso is at home, I mean so strong that you could sense it before you put it in your mouth. Mere proximity was enough for you to taste it.)

The tables in the cafés: too small. Barely big enough for one person, never mind the usual four or five who tried to squeeze around at the same time.

The streets: too wide. Shop windows led onto wide pavements lined by trees followed by more pavement leading to the too-wide road, a road wider than you'd need for traffic in Britain and then you'd realise that it was only half a road because the thing you were looking at was the centre divider and on the other side was the same road only for the opposite traffic, then it was pavement-tree-pavement again.

Then there were the other streets, the ones that were way too narrow, with cars parked on either side and no space for other cars to get through which made you wonder how the original cars got there in the first place until you saw scrapes and the missing wing mirrors and you realised that they just forced their way through anyhow.

There was the way that nothing was level. Every road went up or down a slope. And they never met in a nice square. There were always at least five roads meeting, all at sharp angles to each other, and rising up or dropping down or spiralling away.

The clocks were all too big.

The lampposts were all too short.

The newspapers long and narrow, so that people sitting

reading them had to have their hands too close together, while the paper trailed between their knees to the floor.

The men's moustaches (when they wore them): too small or too big. Then there was the stubble, the brushed back greying hair, the scarves knotted carelessly around their necks.

The woman's skirts that either reached to the ground or stopped just short of the imagination.

The toilets. No two the same, in little rooms with no ventilation and dim lighting. The toilets were never white, not even avocado, but in metallic paint, mosaic or simply psycho vomit.

But all that's to come...

WE STOOD ON the platform, looking at a metal sign styled from green and yellow iron, twisted around itself like a weed.

Gare du Nord-Ouest. Paris L'Illusion

And beneath it, a temporary sign

La Révolution Reste Ouvert Pendant les Travaux

"What does that say?" asked Francis.

"I think it says the Revolution is still open during the works."

"What works?"

The arched roof of the railway station was way too high above my head, there was so much empty space up there, wasted.

"Come on," I said. "Let's get out of here."

"Where are we going?"

"I don't know. Find somewhere to stay. I'm hungry and dirty. I need a shower and a change of clothes. I hope that my meal ticket still works."

"It will work."

The crowd was thickening now, clustering at the end of the platform. A man sat at a desk there, flanked by two gendarmes. Passengers patiently formed a line, presenting their papers for inspection.

"Here we go," said Francis.

I looked at my own papers, clearly marking me as a spy. All too soon we reached the head of the queue.

"*Vos(3) papiers, s'il vous(3) plaît.*"

The man behind the desk's hair parted sharply down the centre. He examined the papers carelessly.

"*Vous(3) avez suffisamment d'argent pour votre(3) séjour?*"

"Er..."

"*La monnaie! Vous(3) avez la monnaie?*"

"He wants to know if we have enough money to support ourselves," I said.

Francis was already pulling out his wallet and showing the cash to the guard. The man nodded and picked up his stamp. He spread out my papers, ready to approve them, when...

"One moment, please."

Another man had stepped forward. This man was shorter than me, he was a little bit tubby, his chin was covered in stubble. He wore an apologetic expression as he took my papers.

"English, yes?"

"Yes..."

He examined my papers closely, nodding as he did so.

"A forgery. But a good one. And honest, too. Eh, little spy?"

"I'm not a spy!"

"But you would say that, of course. Still there are spies and spies. So, *bonsoir*! I am Citizen Jean-Michel Ponge. May I ask why you are here, Mademoiselle Sinfield?"

"To find my mother."

"Does she want you to find her?"

I thought of the message held out by the china doll standing by the road in Dream Kent.

"She's trapped here," I said carefully. "She'll want to go home."

He smiled.

"I notice that you don't answer my question. But you must understand, Mademoiselle Sinfield, that there are many people trapped here who want to go home! There are prisoners in the Bastille who would very much like to go home, but we don't allow them to! There are indentured workers who would like to go home, but until they have worked off their loans, it would not be reasonable, *hein*? Simply saying that your mother wishes to return home does not excuse you spying upon us."

"But I'm not a spy!"

"So you say! How did your mother come to be in Dream Paris?"

"I don't know! She was sold off to a workhouse in Dream London and marched into the parks. That's the last I saw of her."

"And was she legally sold to the workhouse?"

I could see where this was going.

"The law was for sale to the highest bidder in Dream London," I said, bitterly.

Jean-Michel shrugged.

"Again, I notice that you haven't answered my question. And this leads me to point out that if your mother is working in Dream Paris under a legal contract then it would be wrong of you to help her to escape from the contract, no matter how much she dislikes the conditions under which she is being held."

"The contract wasn't fair! The banks pulled in all the loans when it suited them. They left my parents destitute!"

"That's what banks do. There are banks here in Dream Paris..." Did I detect a certain bitterness in his voice? "Despite advice to the contrary, people take out loans every day here in Dream Paris. They cannot expect the Committee for Public Safety to bail them out should they be unable to pay the interest..."

"Doesn't the Committee for Public Safety care for fairness?"

Jean-Michel shrugged.

"It cares as much as it can." He rubbed the bristles on his chin. "You know, I wonder about letting you in here, Mademoiselle Sinfield, and yet I wonder if it's safe to send you away? I'd rather have my spies in Dream Paris where I can see them, rather than outside speaking to the Prussians and the Portuguese."

"I don't intend to speak to any of those."

"I'm sure. And yet if I let you in here you would go looking for your mother, and then I suspect you would do something foolish. Do you follow the law, Anna?"

"When it makes sense."

He laughed.

"And that, you see, is the problem. There are people who play by the rules. They follow the law. These people want to see others caught and punished, because if they don't then what's the point of following the law? You give away a little freedom to be protected, but what happens when people like you don't follow through on that?"

"There's no point following silly laws."

"Ah, but that's what the real criminals say. They laugh at the law, or say the rules don't apply to them. But they want *you* to follow the rules, of course. It wouldn't do for everyone to break the law."

"I don't understand the point you're making."

"People like you are a problem, Mademoiselle Sinfield. The *rebelle*. The conventionally unconventional. You're neither nothing nor something. You play into everyone's hands. You're doing it now."

"No I'm not!"

Francis and Jean-Michel exchanged a look.

"What? What does that look mean?"

"I think Mr Ponge has made a good point, Anna," said Francis. "I think that we should get our papers stamped and be on our way."

Jean-Michel smiled.

"Ah! The voice of calm maturity. Perhaps you should listen to your carer, *mademoiselle*..."

He was trying to wind me up. I saw that now. I held out my hand and spoke in my politest voice.

"Can I have my papers, please?"

"*Bien sûr*! I think that I shall allow you in, Mademoiselle Sinfield, but with certain restrictions. You are to respect the rules and the laws laid down by the Committee for Public Safety for as long as you remain here. You will report to me each day at 10am in the offices of the Committee for Public Safety in the *Grande Tour*. And you will not be permitted to leave Dream Paris without my personal approval. Is that acceptable?"

"No..."

"Yes, that's acceptable," said Francis. He leant closer to me and hissed in my ear "*It could be much worse! Stop making a fuss!*"

Jean-Michel Ponge drew out a pen and wrote something on our papers, then stamped them in red ink.

"*Voila*! I hope you find your stay in Dream Paris *très intéressant*!"

"I'm sure I will."

M Ponge raised an eyebrow.

"I know," said Francis. "She always has to have the last word."

*   *   *

WE PUSHED OUR way into the main station concourse, beneath a roof of glass. It was like a clear blanket thrown over the rose marble floor of the station, caught in the act of billowing out just before it started to fall, the glass panes glittering and flashing in diamond colours, the brilliance of the sparkles filling the station with the heady joy of the Dream World. Through the glass we could see the stars, much brighter than those of the Mundane World. But the starscape was punctuated by the regular wash of the searchlight, turning as it scanned the dark plains that surrounded the city.

"Where do we go?" asked Francis.

"There. *Sortie*: that means exit."

A young man tumbled from the crowd. He had the regulation stubble of a young Dream Parisian, the brushed-back hair, the carelessly knotted scarf. He was dressed in a blue serge jacket and trousers that looked as if they had once belonged to someone much taller and thinner, and probably of a different species.

"English, right? (1)You English, yes? (1)You new to Dream Paris? Need somewhere to sleep? Need food? I(1) have lovely room just round the corner. Only 20 Dream francs a night to (1)you, lovely lady. Double bed, just right for jiggy-jiggy."

I slapped him on the cheek.

The man looked at Francis in hurt supplication.

"Now come on," said Francis. "You deserved that." Good for him. The young man seemed amazed.

"No need to for that! I(1) did not mean to insult the lovely (1)lady! Listen, I(1) have a lovely room. *Une belle chambre*! *Tres belle*! Right above the Seine! Just out of jumping range of the Liopleurodons! Watch them feed in the morning!"

"The lady is fine," said Francis, putting his arm around me and moving me on.

"Hey! I'm quite capable of looking after myself."

"Exactly!" The words were spoken by a second tout who had seen an opening and dived in. "Listen to me, lovely lady! That man is a crook! Dream Paris is full of people like Luc, willing to take advantage of newcomers! The gendarmes, they should be keeping the station clear of such crooks, but no, they're out there making things difficult for honest men trying to earn their *pain quotidian,* rather than rounding up the worthless scroungers who prey on the innocents here."

"How much for a room?" interrupted Francis. He saw my look. "What? We need somewhere to sleep."

"Only 20 Dream francs for the night!"

"Does it have hot water?"

"All you can drink!" replied the man, despite smelling like someone who had not stood under hot water for quite some time. "But better than, it has toilets! Proper, flushing toilets! I tell you, pretty lady, nowhere else in Dream Paris will you have a more satisfying bowel movement!"

"Never mind the toilets. I want a shower and a bed."

"Of course you do. But what does one do before one takes a shower?"

He held his arms wide, waiting for my reply. He wore the expression of a man who had scored the killer point in a debate. "Well?" he prompted.

"Get undressed?" ventured Francis.

"Get undressed! Very wise! But of course, one also visits the toilet! In the *Pension du Palais*, the toilets are *magnifique*! Why, there has not been a toad climb up the toilet for at least two months!"

"Excellent," I said, by now beyond caring. "Lead the way."

"15 Dream francs," interrupted Francis.

"Ah! Monsieur! For that amount you will be lucky to find yourself a place sleeping amongst the leeches and the scum of the gutters. The Committee for Public Safety would not allow an honest landlord's children to be robbed of food. And to let a room for less than 20 Dream francs would be to rob an honest family of their croissants. But, listen, good *monsieur*, it is a good size room! Enormous! And the bed is so large…"

"I'd want two beds for twenty francs."

"I'd want two rooms," I said.

"After that doll got into your room last night, I want you where I can see you," muttered Francis.

"One room, two beds, towels so soft you can roll in them, so much hot water you could swim in it, and the most comfortable toilet in all of Dream Paris! Twenty francs."

"Fifteen." Francis folded his arms.

"I think, *monsieur*, you expect to stay at the Hotel du Palais? For fifteen francs? I think not."

"We'll take the room," I said.

Francis was glaring at me.

"What? I'm filthy, I'm exhausted and I'm hungry. I want a shower, something to eat and some sleep. If I get all that, I think I'll be much more use looking for my mother."

"Okay," said Francis to the man in the badly fitting suit. "Lead us there. But the water better be hot."

"It will be! That will be forty Dream francs, please." He held out a grubby hand.

"You said twenty!" said Francis.

"That's right. Twenty for you, twenty for her."

"Just pay the man."

Francis reluctantly took out his wallet.

"Good choice, sir! *Bon choix*! *Beau selector*!"

"You're not very good at negotiating, are you?" grumbled Francis.

"It's not my money."

"It's the principle," said Francis, but he counted out the money anyway.

* * *

WE FOLLOWED THE man out into the Dream Parisian night. Stepping from the station was like stepping into the end of a 1930s Hollywood movie. You could imagine the curtains parting, lines of women receding into the distance, each pulling back a fan, gentlemen in top hats and tails beckoning you in…

We stepped into a wide cobbled street crammed full of taxis, tall polished black boxes shaped like fat coffins standing on their ends. In place of headlights, they were equipped with what appeared to be old fashioned gramophone horns. The driver sat on a little saddle behind the horns, while the passengers climbed into the upright coffin behind. I was so lost in the spectacle I didn't notice the other odd thing.

"Look!" said Francis. "More clowns."

I saw them now. Most of the taxis were driven by black and white Pierrots. They sat upright in the saddles whilst they lined up waiting for the next customers, or they guided their little upended coffins out through the snarl of traffic. None of them paid us any attention. No one did. The square was full of people, hurrying about their business, people dressed in Dream French fashions, from the smartest velvet suits to the littlest black dresses. We saw men with their faces full of stubble, women with plucked and painted eyebrows. So many people: men in suits with no ties, shirts open at the neck, relaxed in their crumpled clothing, revelling in that touch of arrogance that allowed them to get away with not dressing properly. Francis was smiling at an attractive black woman, hair piled in curls on her head. She smiled back at him, slim and elegant. I looked away. Across the square there was a line of restaurants, tables set out on the street, waiters in long white aprons hurrying back and forth, carrying plates, cups, glasses. They collected orders, they filled glasses, they ignored the unimportant.

"Have you seen?" said Francis. It took me a while to make out the pockets of stillness. Maybe this was what Francis meant by tuning in. Take the time to absorb the scene and then they were obvious. The homeless. The men and women tucked away in the shadows, the ones who shuffled by the restaurants, hands held out for money until they were shooed away by the waiters, the little huddles of ragged people smoking by the benches along the front of the station. You could see the poverty, the hopelessness. Sitting around waiting for something to do, lined up on the benches, leaning against the wall.

"Ignore them!" said our guide. "Come on! To the hotel!"

We'd only walked a few paces when it came into view, rearing up into the deep purple Dream Paris night: the tallest Eiffel Tower of them all. Spotlights played up and down its length, picking out the blue and white harlequin pattern of its wrappings.

A beam of light speared down from the top of the tower, illuminating the square, and for a moment I felt it was looking at us, but it quickly moved on. I saw the cone of light lancing down into distant streets, flicking up to illuminate the silver shape of an enormous yellow Zeppelin hanging lazily above.

Francis was looking at all this with wide-eyed wonder. He was drinking it all in.

Me? I felt as if I'd walked into a trap.

FIFTEEN

THE PENSION AND THE CAFÉ

"Come! we are nearly at your hotel."

We'd left the bustle of the square, turning down sloping streets that drained away the busy life of the station terminus. We entered a silent street where a line of dark trees alternated with lampposts, the lamps sheltering beneath the branches and illuminating the underside of the canopy in yellow light. It looked so pretty, until you noticed the people sleeping rough beneath the trees, wrapped in blankets and cardboard. The night was hot, I could smell the familiar Dream scent of flowers and spices, but here there was a heavier musk beneath it all. The searchlight passed this way and that across the sky, occasionally highlighting the Zeppelin that turned in a slow circle high above.

"They're threatening you," said Francis. "That's a great big yellow *Fuck You* hanging in the sky."

"The Germans don't worry us," sneered the tout. "Let them send a hundred of their Zeppelins!"

Francis shook his head, ever so gently.

The tree-lined road came to an end in a five-road intersection, a stone column rising from the centre. Three scooters were parked around it, merry-go-round fashion.

"And here we are," said our guide, coming to a halt by a narrow doorway squeezed between two shops. He pushed the door open to reveal a narrow set of stairs leading upwards. I could smell garlic socks. He pointed across the five-cornered square to a dimly lit place with a sign above the door announcing it to be the *Café Lebec*. "You could do worse than to eat there."

"We could do better," I muttered.

"You could," agreed the man. "Now, go up the stairs and say that Alain sent you. Good night, *mes braves*!"

He turned and raised a hand, began to walk away, only to find that Francis had hold of his arm.

"Oh, no," he said, evenly. "You have our money, you take us up there."

"But *monsieur*! You doubt me?"

"Yes. That's why I want you to take us up."

Alain shrugged and led us up the stairs.

An old woman sat behind a desk at the top.

"Madame Calcutta, the concierge," said Alain. "*J'ai(3) deux invités ici pour (3)vous, madame.*"

"*Vingt francs,*" replied Madame Calcutta.

"*Vingt?*" I said. "That's twenty. We paid forty!" I should have kept quiet. Francis bunched his fists.

"Commission," said Alain, and at that he was gone, hurrying downstairs.

"Leave him," I said to Francis. Reluctantly, he obeyed.

Madame Calcutta was very thin. Her skin looked too big for her body. She was eating prunes from a large bowl.

"Ah! English!" she said. "I lived in England as young woman! I studied to be a doctor, but of course, such things were frowned upon back then! It was not deemed to be a suitable occupation for a young lady! Still, I dare say I knew more than most of the men. Would you like a prune?"

She held out the bowl to me.

"No, thank you."

"You speak English very well," said Francis.

"You flatter me," said Madam Calcutta. "Sadly, I have never achieved more than the most tenuous grasp on the intricacies of what remains a most perplexing language."

"Shall we go to our room?" I suggested.

Madame Calcutta led us up a narrow flight of stairs, then another, then another, each set twisting at an angle to the last. Eventually we ended up in a narrow corridor in what seemed to be the roof.

"This is the toilet for your floor." Madam Calcutta held open a door.

My heart sank. It was nothing more than a hole in the floor, two footprints set either side.

"Don't you have a sit down one?"

Madame Calcutta laughed, good naturedly. "You English and your toilets! This is far more healthy!"

"It's far more of a nuisance."

"*Non*! Squatting ensures the correct anorectal angle! One of the most import contributions to anal continence!"

"What?" said Francis.

"*C'est vrai*! Squatting reduces the pressure required for defecation! It is the approved position to ease constipation and prevent haemorrhoids!"

"Okay," said Francis.

"Indeed," continued Madam Calcutta, "in persons with anismus, the anorectal angle during attempted defecation is typically abnormal. This is due to abnormal movement of the puborectalis muscle, a hallmark of anismus. The squat toilet ensures the correct angle and thus a satisfactory bowel movement can occur."

"Well, if you say so..."

"I do say so. I had that James Joyce staying here, once. He used that very toilet! *'Madam Calcutta!'* he said to me, *'I have never been so at peace whilst at stool!'*"

"James Joyce…" I said weakly.

"Oh, yes! What a gentleman! We spent quite a delightful afternoon discussing the perfect bowel movement!"

"I'd still prefer a sit down toilet."

"You may prefer it," said Madame Calcutta, sternly, "but I warn you, young lady: the sitting position can cause the defecating human being to repeat the Valsalva manoeuvre many times and with great force, which may overload the cardiovascular system and cause defecation syncope."

"Anna, just use the bloody toilet. I want to take this pack off."

OUR ROOM WAS small, and made even smaller by the way the ceiling sloped so drastically to the floor. A tiny open window let in the sound of music playing. It sounded like accordions.

"I thought Alain said this room was massive," I complained, closing the window.

"It is," said Madame Calcutta. "Now, the shower is next to the toilet. There should be some hot water left."

I showered first and changed into fresh underwear from my backpack. The dress I'd acquired in Dream Calais was looking grubby and creased. I hoped I'd be given something new soon.

I was just drying my hair when Francis entered the room, a towel barely wrapped around his waist. His stomach was flat and ridged with muscle, his wide shoulders beaded with droplets of water. He looked good and he knew it.

"Look that way while I finish changing," I said.

"You do the same," said Francis, grinning. "I'm not having you staring at my arse while I'm getting dried."

I turned around and finished towelling myself off. A flash of blue in the corner of my eye…

"You were watching me in the mirror!"

"Sorry! You've got a lovely figure, you know."

"Really? And what would 'Chelle think about you looking at it?"

"She'd understand. It's not like I've done anything."

"You promised not to look!"

"No, I didn't. You told me to look away. That's what I did."

"A gentleman wouldn't look."

"A gentleman would have *said* he wouldn't look, but he would have done so anyway. Trust me, Anna, any man would have done the same. If he said he wouldn't, he's either gay or a liar."

"There's nothing wrong with being gay."

"I never said there was."

"I'll go and wait downstairs whilst you change."

Typical. Just when he was getting bearable, he had to go and do something obnoxious again.

"SHALL WE EAT in there, then?" asked Francis, nodding across the square to the *Café Lebec*.

I didn't like the look of the place. I didn't like the look of the unshaven men I could see through the windows, I didn't fancy drinking anything from the unlabelled black bottles I could see standing on the tiny tables. I'd much rather have headed back to the bright lights around the station.

"We could always go somewhere else if it makes you nervous…"

"The café will be fine."

Francis entered first. I sidestepped the wire and followed him in. No one seemed to notice it any more: Jean-Michel Ponge, Alain the tout, Madame Calcutta. None of them seemed to notice the grey silken thread that floated along behind us. I followed Francis inside and felt a tremendous sense of disappointment. Travelling here it had been at the back of my mind that we were heading to Dream Paris. I'd imagined grand restaurants, fabulous food paid for by Mr Twelvetrees and his wallet full of money. Here, the wooden panelling was a tired brown, the table cloths a feeble check. Two men sat at the counter drinking glasses of black wine, battered musical instrument cases at their feet. A violinist and a guitarist, I guessed. The barman looked as if he was having a competition with his bar cloth to see who could go the longest without being washed. After his gaze had travelled the length of my body, he nodded to Francis.

"*Bonsoir, (3)monsieur.*"

Francis looked at me for help. Pathetic.

"*Bonsoir,*" I said. "*Er, le menu, s'il vous plait?*"

The barman shook his head.

"*Nous ne servons plus de nourriture.*"

"What was that?" asked Francis.

"He says they're no longer serving food."

"What? But I'm starving! How about a sandwich or something?" He looked at the barman. "Sandwich? *Le* sandwich? Hamburger? *Un* pie?"

"*Un* pie?" I said, scornfully.

"Can you do any better?"

"He's not serving food. We should go somewhere else. Come on, let's go back to the station. The restaurants there looked nice."

The musicians had been exchanging looks throughout the conversation. Now the violinist, judging by the case at his feet, pointed at Francis.

"English?"

"That's right," said Francis, evenly. He recognised the threat in the man's tone.

"Your papers, please." The man held out a dirty hand and a rich scent of body odour wafted from his clothes.

"Under whose authority?" I asked, coolly.

"The authority of any citizen in Dream Paris," replied the man.

The barman said something in French, too rapid for me to follow. The violinist murmured something in reply and the barman was quiet.

"Show him your papers, Francis," I said.

Francis held the man's gaze as he took his papers from his pocket. The violinist snatched them and ran a grubby finger down them.

"These are in order. What about her?"

"She's not a *her*," said Francis. "This young woman is with me."

"A spy. Does the Committee for Public Safety know she's here?"

"I'm under the supervision of Jean-Michel Ponge."

The violinist spoke rapidly to the guitarist, who slammed his hands on the counter and swore. He seemed to collect himself and then growled a reply.

"My friend's wife's sister and her family were sold to the Germans only three weeks ago. Someone got word up to Montmartre Zeppelin Station where they'd hidden their indenture papers…"

Hidden their indenture papers? I glanced at Francis who shrugged.

"Listen," I said, "I'm sorry about that, but it was nothing to do with me! I'm not a spy! I only want to find my Mother. She was taken from Dream London…"

"Dream London?" The violinist had a dangerous edge to his voice. The guitarist spat on the ground. Even the barman was looking angry now.

"Let's just keep things calm," said Francis, easily. His hands were by his side, he wore a gentle smile. He moved so that he was between me and the other men. "We're just leaving to find some food…"

I was about to follow the wire back out of the door, but I stopped. Something had followed that wire. Something had followed us here…

Francis backed into me.

"Anna. What's the matter?"

We were trapped, caught between the customers and the figure that had just entered the café.

It was a life-sized china doll. A woman, very beautiful, with a white face and cold blue eyes painted on her face. They seemed to be looking directly at me.

OCHRE

KAOLIN

"*Merde!*"

I don't know who swore, but I heard the sound of stools scraping, of footsteps, of a door closing.

"*Bonsoir, (14)madame.*" I heard the tremble in the barman's voice.

I kept my gazed fixed on the china woman as she moved jerkily towards me. It reminded me of the precise movement of the second hand of a watch. Her blue eyes remained fixed on me, the silks and cottons of her clothes swished as she moved, their colours sparkling all the more in the dullness of the café. I smelled Eau de Toilette, and I wondered why a china doll would perfume herself. Her head twitched, moving from me to Francis.

"What's the matter?" he murmured. "Why is she looking at me like that?"

She looked from Francis to a nearby table, and I suddenly understood.

"Look at the way she's dressed. She's clearly a lady. I think she's waiting for you to offer her a seat. Like a gentleman should."

Francis pulled back a seat.

"Would you like to sit down?" he asked.

"Thank you." The doll's voice was beautiful but cold, like wind blowing across pearls in the snow. With a series of jerks, the doll moved from a standing to a sitting position that ended with her hands neatly folded on the table before her.

Francis sat down opposite her. He looked up at me, still standing.

"What?" he said. Eventually he got the hint, stood up and pulled back a seat for me.

"Thank you."

"Would you like a drink?" asked Francis.

"No, thank you," said the doll in that eerie voice. "But please, feel free to drink in front of me."

The barman was already at the table, a bottle of wine and three glasses on a tray. I got the impression that china dolls did not often visit this café. He set out the three glasses, then made to pour. The doll placed a perfect porcelain hand over the top of her glass and the barman shrugged and moved on to me. The wine was so dark as to be almost black. It looked as if he were filling my glass with oil. He moved onto Francis, and then the doll raised her empty glass.

"Your good 'ealth."

"Good health," I said.

"Cheers!" said Francis.

I took a drink of the dark wine and waited for the effects to overwhelm me. Where would I be transported to this time...

Nowhere.

I gazed at the doll. The café seemed so plain and empty in comparison. Her beautiful porcelain face, the shimmer of silver and gold, the rich redness of the painted-on lips, the depth of the blue of her eyes...

"Allow me to introduce myself. Pretty Anna, my name is Kaolin. I have come to you with a dinner invitation from the

Banca di Primavera."

"A dinner invitation? When?"

"Right now. The *Banca di Primavera* wishes to apologise for the suddenness of the invitation but unfortunately, it was let down by its staff. You will understand that in a city such as Dream Paris, things do not always function as they should."

I looked at Francis. Would he remember the children in Dream London? How their parents had sold themselves into slavery for the price of a meal? Clearly he did...

"A dinner invitation?" he said. "How much?"

"There is no cost, 'andsome Francis. You are invited as guests."

"... only I heard talk back in Dream London about people accepting favours and gifts from people like you..."

"There are no people like *me* in Dream London," said Kaolin in a voice as cold as frost. "I'm sure that you don't intend to be rude. No one could mistake me for a *Pierrot*, I'm sure..."

"Of course not," said Francis. "Pardon me, we're new here. But let's be clear. You say there is no cost?"

"You are indeed new here, 'andsome Francis, in that you ask the cost of a dinner invitation. I don't know the manners and fashions in London, but here in Dream Paris we don't invite guests to dinner and then present them with a bill."

"Hold on," I interrupted. "How do you know our names?"

"You are well known here, pretty Anna. Your fortune is the talk of Dream Paris."

You are coming, again and again. I could feel myself blushing.

"We might be able to help you find your mother."

"We?" said Francis.

"The *Banca di Primavera*. Now, the table is set, the guests are in attendance. Shall we depart?"

I looked at Francis.

"What about the wine?" he said, looking at his glass.

"Leave it for the two *monsieurs* who are standing in the broom cupboard, wishing they hadn't mistaken it for the exit."

There was an edge to Kaolin's voice, a note of amusement. Something about that convinced me. She had a sense of humour. She could be trusted.

I know. Naive.

"We should be delighted to join you," I said.

"Excellent!" Kaolin rose to her feet in another series of disconnected movements. "Then let us depart immediately!"

"Is it far?" asked Francis.

"Across the other side of the city, 'andsome Francis. The *Banca di Primavera* has leased part of the North Tower. But don't worry, pretty Anna. I have brought transport."

"Pretty?" I'd had a shower but I'd put back on the same grubby clothes I'd been wearing all day. I felt very frumpy and plain. "I don't think so, Kaolin. Not like you. You're so very pretty. So delicate."

And she was. And she knew it.

"Thank you for acknowledging it, pretty Anna. My mother was a talented craftswoman."

"You have a mother?"

I rolled my eyes to the ceiling. Francis had no tact.

"No longer. Sadly, she's now nothing but a pile of crumbling clay."

"I'm sorry to hear that."

Kaolin's painted face was immobile. I had no way of knowing Kaolin's feelings about her mother.

"This is the way of things."

"Is it? Was she badly made? Poorly fired?"

Why couldn't Francis shut up?

"We come from a river bank. A very different place to here. Much hotter, much damper. The river flows wide and slow by our bank, the okapi and tapir wander through the rainforests, the cranes wade through the river…"

"There are china people living by the river?"

"Some. But I'm talking about the beginning. Back then there was nothing but clay, clay that lay by the river bank, doing nothing. Lazy clay, without drive or entrepreneurial instinct. The sort of clay that thinks that the world owes it a living, that it can just go on being clay whilst everything around it does the hard work. Clay that was quite content to just lie there doing nothing."

"Doing nothing?" said Francis. "It was clay! What was it supposed to do?"

"Embrace the challenges presented by the modern world, of course! Join the go-ahead world of interreality commerce! Interealisation is the key to the future!"

"But it was clay! How can clay do anything?"

"By realising the opportunities offered by potential investors. The river bank was lucky enough to be visited by the *Banca di Primavera*!"

"What did the *Banca di Primavera* do?" asked Francis.

"It made us a loan of the necessary capital required in order to realise our assets."

"I don't understand. You mean it made a loan so that people could buy the mud and build factories and so on?"

"No! Much more elegant than that! It loaned the clay sufficient intelligence that it could think about ways to make a return on itself. It loaned the clay the wherewithal to animate itself!"

"You're the clay?" I said. "That's what you mean! The *Banca di Primavera* fashioned you from the clay!"

That was clearly the wrong thing to say. Kaolin flinched as if I'd slapped her. She looked down at the floor.

"I'm sure you do not mean to be so rude, pretty Anna. I'm sure that, like 'andsome Francis, you speak from ignorance, that you do not deliberately mean to hurt me."

"Oh, Kaolin! I'm sorry! I don't mean to insult you!"

"Pretty Anna, surely you have the sensibility to comprehend the world of difference between the first red worms that rolled themselves out of the clay and a young lady of refinement such as myself?"

"Of course, Kaolin. I was speaking from ignorance."

"I am not one piece of clay, slapped on the wheel and turned by the hands of some rude artisan! My body was formed of a select mix of materials including feldspar, ball clay, steatite, quartz, petuntse and alabaster! I tell you, I am not paste! There is no bone or glass in me!"

"I didn't mean to imply there was!"

"I am a young woman of refinement! I wasn't slip or shell cast. Every line on this body was shaped and reshaped by my mother's hand! I was biscuit fired in the best kiln and then removed to be painted and glazed by Sancai himself! My final firing was the subject of intense speculation! Quite a crowd gathered around the kiln door for my coming out, I can tell you that!"

"Kaolin, I've already apologised. No one could possibly mistake you for anything but the most refined of women!"

The misunderstanding had carried us from the café out into the street. Now that we were there, Kaolin forgave us.

"I understand, pretty Anna. Forgive me if I speak too much. We are all of us the way we are. Now, let us depart."

KAOLIN'S CARRIAGE SHONE light and colour onto its surroundings. A piece of blown crystal, twisted over and over, it shone from within with ruby and emerald light, sending patterns dancing over the pavement. Chameleons came skittering from every direction to bathe in the colours, sucking up the patterns to carry back to their lairs for later use.

"Look," said Francis. "China horses."

He walked to the front of the carriage and patted one of the porcelain animals, elegant in blue and white. It paid him no attention.

We climbed into the carriage and sat down on porcelain seats patterned in blue willow. The crystal walls of the carriage allowed a perfect view of our surroundings and of the purple night sky above, the yellow beam of the searchlight sweeping back and forth. The carriage began to ripple forward, and I saw the horses moving like Kaolin did, in a succession of ticks, rather than as a flowing whole.

We turned onto a wider street and then onto an even wider boulevard, and Dream Paris unfolded around us like a midnight flower opening its petals to the moon. First there was the wide space of the boulevard, filled with the mad whizzing motion of little cars the shapes of teapots and top hats, all weaving this way and that, racing recursively to fill the gap left by the previous car. There was something odd about the cars, and after staring at them for a while I realised what it was.

"Why don't they have headlights?" I asked.

"The citizens voted against them," said Kaolin, in what sounded like a sniffy voice. "They said they didn't want headlights interfering with the *Son et Lumière* that is Dream Paris. The cars use sound for navigation in the dark."

Now I understood the purpose of the gramophone horns on the front of the cars. The drivers navigated like bats. The constant sound of traffic horns resolved into something quite different.

We turned a corner and looked down the widest boulevard of all and there at the end, rising up into the night sky, the tallest of the Eiffel Towers. The master tower, standing in the middle of a vast clear space, surrounded by pools of water and fountains lit up in turquoise, more trees wrapped in silver and white lights, spotlights picking out the blue and white harlequin wrapping that swaddled the tower, and above it all, that searchlight, picking out the Zeppelins that drifted northwards to Montmartre, a white fortress on a distant hill.

"Is that where we're going?" asked Francis.

"No. That's the headquarters of the Committee for Public Safety. Our tower is not quite so tall. Follow the Zeppelin..."

She pointed upwards, just as the carriage turned a corner. Looking up we saw a Zeppelin overhead, heading the same way as us, descending, moving towards another Eiffel Tower swaddled in silver that lay directly ahead of us.

"The North Tower," said Kaolin. "We're going to Floor 105. The *Restaurant du Révolution*."

We came to a halt opposite the base of one of the vast piers of the tower. A yellow carpet led up to a pair of doors.

Francis was still straining upwards. I followed his gaze and saw the Zeppelin high above, nosing up to the docking point at the top of the tower. Ballast water fell around us as light rain.

"I think there are a lot of people expecting you," said Francis.

FOURTEEN

THE BANCA DI PRIMAVERA

WE RODE A lift to the stars, rising into a deepening purple sky. The Christmas colours of Dream Paris – the geometric lines and curves of its streets and boulevards all enclosed by the grey city wall – were a faded attraction compared to the heavens. The higher we rose, the more clearly we saw the rivers of purple and mauve and vermillion that ran through the sky. The stars that billowed like sheets lost their twinkle and assumed the shapes of spirals and spheres.

Francis was gazing out of the glass wall of the elevator, his mouth open. I realised my mouth was hanging open too.

"It's… incredible…" I said.

"Do you think so?" said Kaolin. "I don't care much for the lower reaches. It's in the 'igher 'eavens that the spectacle begins."

The lift slowed to a halt. The doors opened onto a wide room, empty of all furniture save two long wooden tables, each with two long benches on either side. There must have been nearly a hundred smartly dressed men and women, seated and waiting for their meal. As we entered the room, every man rose to his feet. The women remained seated. None of the prospective diners were so ill-mannered as to stare at us, but I saw how they watched us from the corner of their eyes as Kaolin led us to our places.

"It's like an Army mess," said Francis.

"This restaurant adheres to the principles of the revolution," said Kaolin. "We all eat together, brothers and sisters."

"That's nice," I said, looking at the pearl-embroidered dress of a woman pretending to powder her nose whilst examining me in the mirror of her compact. These people looked more like they should have been up against the wall rather than out there revolting.

Kaolin indicated three seats at the far end of the room. They were at the head of the left hand table, with excellent views from the floor to ceiling windows.

"What happened to the stars?" asked Francis.

"They're on the other side of the tower," replied Kaolin. She raised her voice. "Ladies and Gentlemen, allow me to introduce pretty Anna, the spy, and 'andsome Francis, 'er bodyguard."

The standing gentlemen and seated ladies nodded to us.

"Anna, Francis, may I introduce Monsieur André Jarre, 'ead of the Dream Parisian division of the *Banca di Primavera*."

"Delighted to meet you," said M Jarre, shaking our hands. He pulled out a seat for me and waited for me to take my place, then he did the same for Kaolin. On cue, all the gentlemen sat down.

"Welcome to the *Tour du Nord*, Anna," said M Jarre. "And to you, too, Francis. Would you like to take your backpack off?"

"I'm fine, thank you," said Francis. "I hardly notice I'm wearing it anymore."

I shot him a glance, but Francis didn't seem to notice. He turned his chair sideways and sat down.

M Jarre rubbed his hands together. "Now, shall I introduce a few of our most distinguished guests? And then we can eat."

There must have been a hundred people seated in that room, every one of which wasn't looking at us and wasn't letting us know how hungry they were.

"You've already met Kaolin, of course," said M Jarre.

Kaolin inclined her head.

"Now, going around the table we have Monsieur Duruflé, my Chief Accountant."

A well dressed gentleman with a neat grey beard, trimmed to a point, nodded at us.

"Next to him is Madame Pigalle, former courtesan."

I've never met such a thin, joyless woman as Madame Pigalle. That she was a former courtesan was not so much of a surprise as the fact she was ever a courtesan at all. She looked like a deflated set of bagpipes, and like a set of bagpipes, the thought of her being put to her intended purpose was enough to fill any rational person with a sense of horror.

"Here is Count Thomas von Breisach, attaché to the Dream Prussian Embassy. Beside him, his beautiful wife, Helène la Fée."

Thomas inclined his head, his scar covered face a marked contrast to the ethereal beauty of his wife's. Helène la Fée wore a simple white dress that draped over her superb form in a manner that indicated she wore nothing else underneath. She smiled charmingly at Francis.

"*Bonjour, monsieur!*"

"*Bonjour, madame*," replied Francis, who seemed to be picking up the language remarkably quickly all of a sudden. "You're French?"

"Parisian." She ignored me completely, I noticed. M Jarre continued his introductions.

"And this is Madame Lefevre, *le Fermier*. She represents Dream Champagne."

"*Shom-parn-ya*," corrected Madame Lefevre. She had dirty nails, a dirty dress and a dirty grin.

"*Je suis anglophone pour le bien de nos clients*," explained M Jarre. "And now the introductions are over! Let us eat!"

A number of would be diners rose to their feet at that point. They were looking towards a serving hatch at the far side of the room, looking as if they were about to slowly make their way towards it. Very, very slowly.

"Where are the waiters?" asked Francis, looking around.

"There are no waiters in Dream Paris," said M Jarre, wagging a disapproving finger.

"Really?" said Francis. "I'm sure I saw some in the restaurants opposite the station..."

Helène la Fée fixed her gaze upon him at this and gave a slow smile.

"I doubt it," said M Jarre. "There are no restaurants in Dream Paris! There is nothing more divisive than a restaurant. The idea of separating people out to eat, of saying that some food belongs to some people and not others. It's the basis of social control. That's why everyone eats together in Dream Paris. Or they should do."

Francis looked around.

"Then what's this place, if not a restaurant?"

"This is a communal dining area," said M Jarre. "We are all brothers and sisters here! We do not expect to be waited upon. We take it in turns to fetch the courses and clear the plates. So, shall I collect the first course?"

"That would be so kind," said Madame Lefevre, *le Fermier*.

M Jarre took a couple of steps across the room when a man dressed like a waiter, if such a thing were possible in a city without waiters, tapped him on the shoulder.

"*Excusez-moi, (5)monsieur. Voulez-(5)vous que je(5) (5) vous rapporte quelque nourriture?*"

"Why! How thoughtful," beamed M André, turning to explain. "This gentleman has offered to fetch the food for me! Isn't that kind?"

The helpful gentleman who wasn't a waiter looked as if he was about ninety years of age. His not-waiter's outfit looked as if it had dust on it.

"You can't expect him to get our food!" I said, rising to my feet. Instantly, every other gentleman in the room except Francis stood up. He followed suit a moment later, under the hard stare of the Count.

"Pardon me, Anna," said M Jarre. "but this gentlemen will be insulted if he feels you think him too old to perform this one little favour for us."

I looked at the old man, looked at M Jarre, and then slowly sat down, accompanied a moment later by the other gentlemen diners.

As our not-waiter went to collect our food I noticed that a number of other similarly attired gentlemen were doing the same. They all lined up by the serving hatch, and then returned to the tables with trays laden with food.

A bowl of soup was placed before me.

"Nice china," I said, fingering the gold patterned rim. "Looks expensive."

"Well," said M Duruflé, Chief Accountant, "The crockery already existed before the Revolution. Shocking though it was that the underclass were left to go hungry whilst the rich dined off such exquisite pieces, nothing would be gained by destroying it now." He raised a polished silver spoon and began to eat. The Count slurped his soup noisily. Madame Pigalle ate with a sour expression.

Kaolin had a bowl of porcelain fruit set before her.

"I do this out of politeness," she explained.

I noticed Francis eyeing the soup suspiciously.

"*Aigo Builido*," murmured Helène la Fée. "Boiled water. Eat it up, it will stiffen your resolve." I saw one gloved hand on the table. Where was the other one?

Francis sipped at the soup and nodded. The soup tasted good, much better than boiled water. There were herbs and garlic in there, and thick pieces of bread with grilled gruyere floating on the top.

A dusty arm loomed over my shoulder, yellow wine was poured into my glass. I turned to see a man even older than the not-waiter, holding a dusty bottle in his knotted, arthritic hand.

"*Merci*," I said.

"*Mon(5) plaisir, (5)mademoiselle*." I sipped the wine. It tasted deliciously of butter.

"So Anna, I believe you are looking for your mother?"

Some of the wine went down the wrong way. Francis paused, spoon half way to his mouth.

"Yes…"

M Jarre nodded.

"We may be able to help you. The *Banca di Primavera* is very interested in the human assets that have become displaced in Dream Paris. M Duruflé has made a special study of such matters."

On hearing his name, M Duruflé patted his elegantly shaped beard with a white linen napkin.

"I have indeed," he said. He placed the napkin beside his plate and leaned forward, fingers tented before him.

"Anna, I think it's becoming common knowledge around here that the Dream London venture was not at all well handled. Sudden acquisitions and speculative bubbles such as that always lead to trouble. A lot of people got their fingers burned when Dream London went – oh, what's the expression – *teets up*?"

Francis snorted.

"My accent, I think?" M Duruflé smiled. He was a bit of a silver fox, a good looking man, for a chief accountant. And he knew it, judging by that twinkle in his eye. "But yes. The result has been a complete mess. There are a lot of people from your city left here in Dream Paris, a lot of people who have been carried off to other countries against their will…"

"*Entschuldigen*!" We all turned to see the Count staring at us red-faced, spoon gripped in his hand. "I hope you're not implying something, M Duruflé? Dream Prussia employs no slave labour!"

M Duruflé gave a charming smile.

"Not at all, my dear Count. Dream Prussia is known to be a fair and honest trading partner that would never exploit the working man and woman. Dream Paris could not do business with it otherwise."

The Count nodded curtly.

"… even if it had stationed part of its Zeppelin fleet over the city in a not-so-subtle demonstration of power…"

The Count stiffened. Everyone in our little circle paused, spoons raised half way to their mouths.

"First you suggest we wish to trade with you, and then you suggest that we threaten you? You imply that we are lying in some way? Sir, do you wish to duel with me?"

Helène la Fée placed a hand on his arm and spoke to him in rapid German. The Count turned and gave a stiff bow.

"Herr Duruflé, I apologise for speaking as I did. Please excuse my hastiness."

"And I apologise for implying that Dream Prussia is threatening this city."

Everyone resumed eating their soup.

M Duruflé turned back to me and smiled.

"Where were we, Anna?"

"You said that the *Banca di Primavera* wanted to help me. I'm sorry, M Duruflé, I don't believe you. No bank ever wants to help anyone."

He permitted himself a faint smile.

"That's a little harsh, Anna. *Bancas* perform an essential service to any economy. Without loans, how would the poor ever set up in business? *Bancas* come to arrangements that benefit both parties."

"If you say so. Why do you want to help me?"

He leaned closer towards me. I could feel him turning on the charm. The smile, the body language, the lowering of the voice. Dirty old pervert.

"There are railways in London, *non*?"

"*Oui.*"

"And the houses closest to the railway stations, are they more expensive or cheaper?"

"They cost more. People can have more of a lie in before they go to work."

"*A lie in*. I've never heard that phrase. But yes, the houses closest to the railway station are usually worth more. *D'accord*! Now, suppose someone were suddenly to move the railway station to the other end of the road. What then?"

"The houses next to the station would lose their value."

"*Exactement*! And that's why the collapse of Dream London has caused so many problems. People borrowed money to buy land in Dream London. People expected to become rich. But when Dream London ended and all that land was returned to its original location people found that they weren't making the money they had expected. And now our bank is owed money from debts that can't be paid, debts that are secured on worthless land."

"You're breaking my heart. What's that got to do with me?"

"Some of the money raised went on the purchase of workers. The *Banca di Primavera* now finds itself in possession of many people from Dream London, put up as security against worthless land."

It took a moment for me to realise what he was saying.

"Is my mother one of those people?"

"She might be. We are dealing with records kept by a third party. I suspect that if we find your mother, we will find more of your countrymen."

I was beginning to understand.

"We can help them to return home. *You* can help them return home."

THIRTEEN

COUNT THOMAS VON BREISACH

WE'D FINISHED OUR soup.

"Who's going to fetch the next course?" asked M Jarre, beaming around the table. The wizened old man who had brought us our soup just happened to be passing by.

"*Permettez-moi(5)*! *Il me(5) fera plaisir!*"

"*Non, non, Gaston!*" M Jarre, head of the *Banca di Primavera*, Parisian Branch, was bubbling over with a desire to help his fellow man. "*C'est mon tour! Laissez-moi faire!*"

"*Non, (5)monsieur! J'y(5) tiens! (5)Vous avez l'air tellement à l'aise là-bas!*"

"Well, if that's what you really want." M Jarre spoke in English now, I noticed. He looked around regretfully. "I would hate for anyone to think we weren't following the precepts of the Revolution."

"Perish the thought!" said M Duruflé, cheerfully. "No one would ever accuse you of that, M Jarre!"

The old man collected the next courses from the counter and began to stagger back to our table. Francis got to his feet to help.

"Sit down," said the Count. "You'll embarrass him!"

"But he looks as if he's going to fall over!"

"It's his job!"

"Actually," said M Duruflé, smoothly, "it's not his job. Being a waiter wouldn't be very revolutionary. He just enjoys doing it."

The dishes were placed before us. Francis gazed unhappily at the contents of his bowl.

"*Tripe à la mode de Caen*," said M Jarre, noticing his expression. "Cow stomach cooked in Calvados. That's apple brandy."

Francis poked at his meal with his fork.

"It is brought fresh from Caen itself! Haven't you heard? Dream Breizh is connected to us once more! There may well be oysters later on!"

"Oysters?" said Francis, even more unhappily.

"Don't be such a *steak frites*!" I said. "That's what the French call the English, you know. They always ask for steak and chips."

"Well, I like steak and chips."

"I bet you have it cooked well done, too."

Madame Pigalle, ex-courtesan, had been watching this with a sour expression. She leaned forward and took Francis's fork.

"Here," she said, entirely failing to bubble over with sexual attraction whilst exploiting the seductive possibilities inherent in the consumption of food. "Let me help you."

She picked up a fork in one dry bony hand, speared a peace of tripe and pushed it into his mouth.

"There. *Très bon*."

"Actually, that's not bad," said Francis, chewing.

"Eat it all up. I like my men to keep their strength up."

I've never heard a line delivered in a drier, more pedestrian way.

"What, really?" said Francis, quite genuinely surprised.

"Oh yes." She looked down to his lap.

"Is that a gun in your pocket, or are you just pleased to see me?"

"It's a gun," said Francis, with great finality.

I looked back to M Duruflé, who was carefully wiping a piece of *Tripe à la mode de Caen* from his shirt.

"Careless of me!" he said. "From Jermyn Street, you know. Only the English know how to properly make a shirt."

"Never mind that. How are you going to help me find my mother?"

"Kaolin has that sorted."

Kaolin looked up from her plate of decorative food. Now she was pretending to eat a china plaice and china potatoes.

"Yes, pretty Anna. Tomorrow, after your 10am meeting with Jean-Michel Ponge, I 'ave made an appointment for you at the Public Records Office. They 'old details of all the citizens and non-citizens currently inhabiting Dream Paris. They will 'elp you locate your mother."

"See?" beamed M Jarre. "It has all been taken care of!"

I ate my tripe. It tasted good, but I was worried. I was thinking about how easy all of this was. If it was just a matter of asking at the Public Records Office, why hadn't the *Banca di Primavera* done this themselves? I looked at Francis, eating his tripe with gusto. We needed to talk, but not now.

"Not bad, this," he said, noting my gaze.

"And good for the digestion," said Madame Pigalle, in tones as sexy as a gynaecology text book. "I always ensured my clients were in the best of health. In my day, a client was sure not only of a good time, but also of a healthy, balanced and purgative diet. They were secure in the knowledge that they would return to their day with a spring in their step and a reconstituted liver."

"Good...?" said Francis.

"Oh, yes. One must keep the bowels moving. Of course, I once had a bowel movement in Orleans that... something the matter, dear?"

"No, not at all." I was gazing in horrified fascination at this clinical seduction.

"I see," said Madame Pigalle, in a voice as naughty as a labelled illustration of the female reproductive system. "All very modern to speak about sex openly, of course. One is supposed to have a relaxed attitude to certain bodily functions in London, I hear. Well, I am proud to say that here in Dream Paris we extend that attitude to *all* bodily functions."

"Were all the courtesans in Dream Paris like you?" asked Francis, genuinely interested.

"*Non*! I was the best!" And at that she popped the last piece of tripe in her mouth and chewed it slowly.

M Jarre pretended to begin to collect the plates, but again Gaston insisted that he be allowed to do it.

The next course arrived.

"Since when was lobster Thermidor the food of the revolution?" I asked.

"Well, the lobsters were dead anyway..." said M Jarre

"*Exactement*!" said Madame Lefevre. "And they practically Thermidor themselves. So what do you think of Dream Paris, Anna?"

"I don't know. I've not really seen it yet."

"Nor have I. It's rare that I get to visit. There is so much work to do, back in *Champagne*."

"So, you're a farmer," I said. "Do you employ anyone from Dream London on your farms?"

Madame Lefevre was eating with her hands. Pink lobster meat stuck to her dirty fingers. She wiped a hand across her shiny mouth.

"Ah! I can see that farms are very different where you come from, Citizen Anna."

I waited for her to continue, but she said no more on the subject.

"So, how do you know M Jarre?" I asked.

"My *terroir* is hoping to extend itself. We are discussing a loan with the *Banca di Primavera*."

"I see."

"I wonder if you do," said M Jarre, turning away from his conversation with the Count. "They do say that the *real* power around here is not located in Dream Paris but rather in the surrounding farmland. The reign of *terroir*, they call it. Would you say that was true, Madame Lefevre?"

"Of course it's true, M Jarre. Dream Paris is nothing but a system designed to produce rich manure with which to feed the crops. The plumbing of Dream Paris leads to a huge reservoir downstream, where the waste is converted to fertiliser…"

"*Bravo, madame!*" said Madame Pigalle.

"Well, I suppose that's one way of looking at it."

"Oh, no, Anna. Even in your home, the most useful crops, the tastiest vegetables, these are the ones that survive. Wheat and corn and barley conquer the world where other crops fail. Here in Dream Paris, we take this further. Taste this wine, Anna."

Madame Lefevre filled her glass with the black wine.

"A Burgundy," she said, as I took a hesitant sip. "Can you feel what it's like to wander the wooded hills?"

"I can." I thought I should be getting used to the wine's effect by now, but no, I still had to fight to keep hold of myself.

"The wine is a manifesto," said Madame Lefevre. "It's trying to turn your mind to its benefit. Remember, in Dream Paris, everything you eat and drink is a declaration of support. You drink this wine and you are pledging allegiance to Burgundy.

You take a little brandy and you are pledging allegiance to Armagnac."

She leaned in closer.

"That's why it's very important to always eat a little bit of everything. If you don't, the *terroir* will take you over and march you away. The next thing you know you will be working on a farm in the Vendée…"

Could that have happened to my mother? I wondered. I looked at Madame Lefevre's dirty hands as she tore into her lobster. *Is that what happened to Madame Lefevre? Was she press-ganged by a vegetable seller?*

Francis leaned closer and whispered in my ear.

"You lived in Dream London," he said. "Is this normal?"

"Normal? Nothing was normal there. There are similarities between here and Dream London. But there are a lot of differences, too."

"Like what?"

"I can't describe it. This place seems a lot more… ordered, I suppose. Dream London was a lot more random."

"This has all looked pretty random to me so far."

"I don't mean that. In Dream London, no one was really in charge. They thought they were, but they were just following events. Here, these people seem to be more in control…"

Around us people were politely finishing their meals, pretending they couldn't hear us. Francis scratched his nose.

"Listen, Anna. I'm not sure we can trust these people."

I felt the frustration, hot inside me. This was a man who considered steak and chips an exotic meal, a man who had to have his *Tripe à la mode de Caen* cut up by a courtesan before he'd consider eating it. He really thought *I* needed *his* advice on who to trust?

"You don't think we can trust these people," I said. "Really?"

"Yes. Just take care."

"Take care? You're the one who doesn't know how to behave in polite company."

For the first time, there was the briefest flash of anger in Francis's eyes. "Hey, I've never been to France before. I never got to go abroad when I was a kid."

"Sorry," I said, feeling embarrassed for a moment. And then I reminded myself of his words back in England. *Old enough to bleed, old enough to breed.* The man was a pig.

"Please stop whispering. It's rude." The Count's voice cut through the chatter.

"I'm sorry," I said. "All this is a little confusing for my companion. He's not used to polite company."

"No, I'm not," agreed Francis. "I'm just some stupid squaddie who doesn't know which fork to use."

"A *squaddie*?" The Count frowned.

"A soldier," I explained. The Count perked up at that.

"You are a soldier, sir! Have you seen action?"

"Yes."

"Good to meet someone who understands the meaning of service."

Was the Count going out of his way to irritate me?

"Excuse me!" I said. "Am I not here? Or do you think that women can't serve in any meaningful manner?"

"Of course," said Count von Breisach, glancing at Francis. "*Kinder, Küche, Kirche.* I could do with a little more wine right now."

Francis tried not to smile. Pig.

"Don't patronise me," I said, in my coldest tones. "I marched into the parks. I know about service."

The Count raised an eyebrow.

"You marched into the parks?" He nodded approvingly. "Well done, *Fräulein*. Well done. What were you carrying?"

"A cornet?"

"A cornet? I'm not up on British weaponry. Is that one of

the Armstrong hand pistols?"

"No, it's a musical instrument. Like a trumpet."

"I know what a cornet is. I thought I'd misheard. You mean you marched against enemy soldiers carrying a musical instrument?"

"Yes. Don't you have military bands in Dream Prussia?"

"We do, but they carry military grade instruments. What were the other members of your troop carrying?"

"Horns, baritones, euphoniums."

"But that's just a brass band. I don't understand the military advantage."

"Not all service is undertaken to gain military advantage." Have you ever had that sense of two different worlds coming together?

"And what does Dream Prussia want with Dream Paris?" asked Francis, keen to change the subject. The Count seized on the opportunity gratefully.

"Nothing more than the chance to trade," he said.

"What do you trade?" I asked.

"Machinery. A little food and drink. Ideas."

"Do you know anything about my mother?"

"*Nein*!"

He brought a hand down on a lobster claw, breaking it into fragments. He picked out bits of the flesh.

"However, Dream Prussia would like to offer to help you in your search for your mother. Should it prove successful, and even should it not, we also offer transport for you and any others you choose to accompany you back to your home."

That floored me.

"That's a very generous offer," I said, after a pause. "There must be some cost."

"No cost. Dream Prussia is always on the lookout for new trading partners. Consider this an expression of our good intentions."

He popped a piece of lobster in his mouth.

"Perhaps we should listen to him," murmured Francis. "At least he doesn't represent a bank."

"No, just a country that flies huge threatening Zeppelins over other people's cities."

"That's part of trade," said the Count. "If you want to discuss further, come to the Zeppelin station at Montmartre. Tell them you wish to speak to me."

"I'll think about it."

"Ah, Francis! I wanted to ask you something..." M Jarre turned and engaged Francis in conversation about distances: from here to Dream Calais, from London to Dream Dover. I was left with the Count. He was watching me, scarred face impassive.

"Your friend has left his lobster." he said. "He doesn't like the food?"

"My friend doesn't get out much," I said, waspishly.

"I notice that you've left half your lobster, too. Too delicate, that's your trouble. There are girls working in Parisian factories who think themselves lucky to get half a slice of black bread."

"Then they're being exploited."

"Maybe, but you're turning your nose up at perfectly good food."

"I'm not turning my nose up at it. I've just had enough for the moment."

Helène placed her hand on her husband's arm.

"Don't be rude, dear. Not everyone is as blunt as you. Anna seems like such a *refined* young lady."

I didn't need her to stick up for me. I picked up my fork and began to eat.

"I hate to see food going to waste, too. There are people back in Mundane London who would be delighted to eat this." I looked at the Count's plate. "I see you've left your parsley."

Without a word, he picked it up and ate it.

"There are places in this city, young lady," he said, "where a meal such as this would be a treat, not something to be endured."

"I eat what's put in front of me."

"Really? How about mouse pie?"

"If that's what was being served." I laughed. "When's the last time you ate mouse pie, Count? When are you ever likely to be offered it?"

He assumed a superior air.

"Young lady, right now, throughout this city, there will be families who are skinning mice, pulling flesh from the bones and dropping them in pies. Knock on the door of nearly every apartment in this city and you would see people licking mouse gravy from plates. And what's more," – he leaned forward a little – "they will be serving it tomorrow night at 7:30pm in the Old Abattoir."

Check. He spoke the words like a chess grandmaster, making a move. I couldn't back down now.

"Then why don't we go and try it? Or are you all talk?"

The Count smiled.

"I should be happy to, *Fräulein*. I like mouse pie. I doubt that I would see you there, though."

"Oh, I'll be there, *Thomas*."

I heard a groan and turned to see Francis holding his head in his hands.

"What?" I said. I suddenly realised everyone was looking at us. M Duruflé spoke up.

"Anna, are you aware that you are accepting a duel?"

"A duel? He's dared me to eat a pie!"

"You've insulted his honour, and he's insulted yours. In Dream Prussia, that's considered a challenge."

I looked at the Count's scarred face and I remembered something I'd once read, how they used to duel at university in Germany. How they'd wear padding on their bodies but no face masks, how they'd fight until one person had drawn a scar on his opponents face.

"Do you wish to back down?" asked the Count.

I would have done so, if he hadn't given the tiniest of smiles as he said it.

"Oh, no," I said. "Tomorrow at 7:30, in the Old Abattoir. Mouse pies it is."

All we were going to do was eat unpleasant food. What could possibly go wrong with that?

TWELVE

THE GRANDE TOUR

KAOLIN DROVE US away from the North Tower.

"What happened there?" asked Francis.

"Somebody has to stand up for us," I muttered.

"Stand up to who? Against what? Anna, what exactly do you think you're doing?"

"Looking for my mother."

"And starting a fight with the Germans is going to help?"

"It's not the Germans, it's the Prussians. And it's not a fight, it's a duel." And I wasn't feeling proud of myself, I knew I'd let myself down. I knew that the Dream World changed people. I'd let it get a hold on me.

"Hey," said Francis, looking out of the window. "This isn't the right direction. The big tower was over there before."

Kaolin had been listening to us argue, face as impassive as only a painted face can be. Now she raised a porcelain finger.

"The *Banca di Primavera* 'as taken the liberty of moving your things to *the 'Otel de la Révolution*. You shall stay there as our guests."

"Are you okay with that, Francis?"

"I don't see that I have any say in the matter, Anna." He folded his arms and looked out of the window. I did the same, looked at the little lights that hung from the branches of the trees that lined the road, burning brightly in the night.

"Is that burning fruit?" I said. Francis didn't answer, he was too busy sulking.

THE CARRIAGE PULLED up before our hotel. A man in a yellow-and-black-striped uniform opened the door.

"Good evening, citizens," he announced. I noticed how fine the cockade pinned to his jacket seemed to be. Red, white and blue silk, expertly stitched.

"Acting as a doorman doesn't seem very revolutionary," I said.

"Ah, but I choose to do this, *mademoiselle*. I am the equal of every man or woman who comes into this place. And if I see an aristocrat, then..."

He pulled a finger across his neck.

"Of course," I said.

We marched across the marble lobby to the front desk.

"*Chambre 113*," said Kaolin.

"*D'accord.*"

The receptionist handed across the keys with a very un-citizen like look that quite clearly distinguished between *(5) nous* and *vous(5)*.

"And now I wish you *bonne nuit*," said Kaolin. "I will return in the morning to take you for your appointment with Jean-Michel Ponge, and then on to the Public Records Office and, hopefully, your mother."

FRANCIS INSISTED THAT we both share a room. I didn't make too much of a fuss, I was worried, too. Dream London had been dangerous, but it had been my home town. I'd known people there, I'd known the rules, sort of. Here, I was a foreigner.

"They're all talking bollocks," said Francis. "Are we really supposed to believe they want to help free the British that were marched here? If they were that concerned about them, they'd never have allowed them to be bought in the first place."

"They might not have had a choice."

"Really? I thought that Committee for Public Safety ran things here. Allowing workers to be bought doesn't sound very equal."

I sat down on the edge of a seat. I felt exhausted.

"I know. I know. But they said they'd help find my mother. What other leads do we have?

"There's the fortune. Where are we up to on that?"

"I don't know. We've seen the ruined castle. We're supposed to be in the *Café de la Révolution* on Nivôse 22nd. What's today's date?"

"I don't know." He rubbed his chin. "This is the *Hotel de la Révolution*. Do you suppose the café is here?"

"I doubt it. I bet there are loads of *Cafés de la Révolution* in this city. Look, I don't like the *Banca* either, but what else am I supposed to do?"

"I know." Francis looked frustrated. "But why are they making such a fuss of us? There must be many people in this city looking for lost relatives. I can't imagine the *Banca di Primavera* rolling out the red carpet for everyone."

"But we might be the only ones who've come here from London."

"No. That woman on the train said there were others."

"Well, we might be the only ones who can find our way back."

And we both turned to look at the wire from Francis's backpack, stretched out across the floor and running out under the door.

THE NEXT MORNING dawned bright and clear, the sky a much deeper blue than normal, the sun so much brighter.

There were new clothes laid out for us. A smart yellow suit for Francis with shiny gold lapels, a white shirt and a checked red cravat that I helped him tie. There was also a brushed brown top hat and pair of white gloves. For me, an ivory silk dress with white lace at the cuffs and little blue bows down the front, a pair of black patent leather boots and a little parasol.

Francis wolf whistled when he saw me, then apologised when he caught my eye.

"We're hardly Children of the Revolution, are we?" he said.

Kaolin had changed her outfit, too. She arrived at our door just after breakfast (coffee and hot milk in silver pots, beautifully baked brioches and croissants, jam in little pots). She was wearing a yellow-and-white-striped silk dress, a white cap and white shoes.

We followed her through the lobby of the hotel and out of the entrance. There wasn't a carriage waiting for us; instead, Kaolin walked out onto the wide boulevard in front of the hotel and waited, looking at the traffic. A red Dream Parisian car trundled by, trailing blue smoke and rattling violently. Kaolin pointed to the car and it pulled to a halt. She walked jerkily to the side window and began to speak to the driver. Like all Dream Parisian vehicles, the car seemed too small and narrow. Vehicle construction in Dream Paris seemed to have evolved entirely separately from our world.

"What's she saying?" asked Francis.

"I don't know. Something about the *Banca di Primavera*. I keep hearing the word for *dress*, I think."

The man was losing the argument. He climbed out of the car looking pale, and handed the keys to Kaolin.

She turned, her white face glowing in the bright morning.

"Are you ready, pretty Anna?"

"Yes. What happened there?"

"I called in a debt," said Kaolin, quite simply.

We climbed into the car and set off, Kaolin driving.

DREAM PARIS WAS hotter than Dream London. The sky was bluer, the colours brighter, the reflections harsher. The wide squares of white gravel hurt the eyes, the flashes from the fountains and ponds imprinted lines and loops on your vision. The people of Dream Paris lived in the shade, walking in the dappled shadows of the plane trees, seated under the canopies and umbrellas of the shops and cafés. Of the homeless, there was no sign today. They must have been swept clear of the nice spaces as morning broke.

The roads widened as we headed towards the *Grande Tour*. Eventually we turned onto a wide boulevard, a line of rectangular lakes down the middle, fountains, green grass, trimmed trees. The tallest Eiffel Tower stood at the end, its covered length reflected in the waters.

"I will tell you a story about this view, Pretty Anna," said Kaolin. "No one noticed quite when the first Eiffel Tower appeared in Paris, over two hundred years ago. When first seen, it was no bigger than the tip of your little finger. When the Revolution was in full flow, a second Eiffel Tower appeared, the height of a man, just down there, where the small arch now stands. And then, at the end of the Revolution, a third grew, on the spot where the North Tower now stands. The revolutionaries tore them all down."

"Why?" asked Francis.

"The revolutionaries don't like the towers. It is a citizen's duty to report if a tower is found growing anywhere. The Committee for Public Safety will attempt to destroy it before it's rooted."

Francis still looked puzzled. He'd never lived in Dream London, of course.

"The towers grew in Dream London," I said. "They were part of the changes. It's no wonder the revolutionaries try and keep them under check."

"Okay."

"Even so," said Kaolin, "after the Revolution, it seemed a great joke for the Committee for Public Safety to build a fourth tower out of metal. I have seen the plans in the Public Records Office. It was quite a thing, a tenth of the size of the *Grande Tour* that you see there. I don't know if it would be possible to *build* such a thing..."

"Why wouldn't it be possible...?" began Francis.

"... but they certainly meant to try. They dug foundations, they poured concrete, they began to bolt together iron to make the base section, and then..."

Her voice tailed away.

"And then what?" I said.

"Some say that the world unfolded then. Just as your home recently separated into Dream London and London, Paris separated into Paris and Dream Paris. The *Grande Tour* regrew unnoticed amongst the half-completed metal construction and shouldered it aside. Perhaps, in another world, the metal copy still exists. A poor copy, nothing more than a skeleton."

"It's a universal idea," I said. "This is physics. You want to build something tall with materials of a certain strength, this is what you'd come up with. It's a mathematical form. The curve of the four pillars, the way they support each other..."

I was so busy showing off I didn't ask the important question. That was left to Francis. "Why are they all wrapped in cloth?"

"So no one can see what's underneath, of course," said Kaolin. And that was that. "I'll let you out here. They won't allow cars under the Tower."

* * *

IT WAS ANOTHER world in the vast space beneath the tower. A world that was quite definitely one of *Liberté, Égalité et Fraternité*. Every citizen there was dressed in blue or grey breeches, white shirts, blue jackets and a red Phrygian hat. If someone had wanted Francis and me to stand out amongst them, they couldn't have done a better job of choosing our clothes.

My papers were taken, inspected, re-inspected, passed on to superiors and handed back for further inspection. I was slowly ushered forward through the busy crowd to one of the pillars. At every step I was regarded suspiciously, I saw people pointing to me, I heard mutters of *Espion*. And all the time Francis – big, strong soldier Francis with his backpack trailing a wire all the way back to Blighty – was received with nothing more than a smile and courteous nod.

After what seemed like hours we made it to one of the vast pillars and were shown into a lift similar to the one we'd ridden last night at the North Tower.

"*477e étage,*" said the woman at my side. The lift operator nodded and pressed one of the hundreds of rather grubby white buttons that lined the wall. We rose into the air, surrounded by the children of the Revolution. Whereas the North Tower had been the last word in luxury, this tower was testament to the institution. As we stopped at various floors I saw corridors decorated in grey and eau-de-nil, floors laid with grey linoleum and set out with regulation furniture. The place was a hive of dynamic equilibrium as papers were moved from one place to another.

We reached the 477th floor and stepped out into yet another pale grey corridor. There was a list of names and room numbers on one wall. We found Jean-Michel Ponge's name with a little difficulty, we found room 17e with just a little more.

Jean-Michel was sat behind his desk, looking like a particularly lugubrious bloodhound, albeit one in need of a shave. There were a collection of yellow and green cubes of different sizes on his desk.

"Have you seen one of these before?"

He held up a yellow cube, the size and weight of a tennis ball.

"I've not," I said. "What is it?"

"I think it's a lemon. The green ones are limes. They were found floating down the Seine."

"Why are they that shape?"

"That is the question, *non?*"

"Who found them?" asked Francis. "I thought the river was full of dinosaurs."

Jean-Michel rose from his chair, he beckoned us to follow him to the window of his office. There was a telescope fixed there. He looked through it, adjusted it.

"Look," he invited Francis, who placed his eye to the telescope. "What do you see?"

Francis adjusted the focus.

"I see… I see men and women on the banks of the river. They're the wrong side of the guard walls. They're collecting something…"

"Mussels," said Jean-Michel.

"There's someone on guard! Something's approaching, something in the water. A mosasaur…" He swore.

"What happened?" I said.

Francis straightened up.

"There was someone on watch. They ran for the safety of the bank. The mosasaur jumped for them. It missed."

"The homeless," said Jean-Michel. "They congregate here in Dream Paris. They take any work there is, even musselling. There is little enough food in Dream Paris to feed the regular citizens." He returned to his desk. "So, how was your dinner in the North Tower?"

A point had been made.

"You knew we were there," I began.

"It was very nice, thank you," said Francis, smoothly.

Jean-Michel almost smiled at that.

"I'm sure it was. I can't remember the last time I sat down to lobster Thermidor. And I hear that the *Banca di Primavera* is to aid you in your search for your mother. Do you consider that a wise alliance?"

"It's the only help we've been offered so far," I said.

"I would have suggested the Public Records Office myself, Mademoiselle Sinfield. You know, I could instruct you not to associate with the *Banca di Primavera*, for your own good if not that of the Revolution. However, as I suspect you are already in their debt, that would be rather pointless."

"We're not in their debt," I said. "I made sure of that. The meal was free."

"A free lunch?"

"It was dinner."

"The *Banca di Primavera* is very subtle."

"Thank you for your advice. Is that why I'm here? Or can I go now?"

"You're so touchy. Why can't you allow anyone to help you?"

He looked at Francis as he said this.

"Because she's seventeen," said Francis. "And she knows fucking everything." I raised my eyebrows at the sudden passion in his voice. My reply was deliberately cool and measured.

"And because I've found that waiting for people to help you is a pointless exercise. Now, can we be about our business, M Ponge?"

Jean-Michel and Francis were looking at each other again with an expression that said, quite clearly, *women!*

Jean-Michel rose to his feet.

"No, Anna, I think not. You see, whilst you were enjoying

dinner last night, we've been finding out a little bit more about you."

"From who?" asked Francis.

"Surely that should be *from whom*?" smiled Jean-Michel. "That is the correct English, *non*?"

"Never mind that," I snapped. "Why can't I leave?"

"Because now we know the truth. Not only are you a spy, but you're the daughter of a spy. A member of the aristocracy! An enemy of the revolution!"

"No, she isn't!" said Francis. "Tell him, Anna."

He looked at me for confirmation. I said nothing. Jean-Michel was half right.

INDIGO

LA CHAMBRE DES ÉTOILES

WE FOLLOWED JEAN-MICHEL from his office down the corridor to another lift. This one was smaller, more refined. Lined with wood panelling, the buttons were polished brass. To my surprise, we were going up, not heading down to the dungeons as I'd imagined. The top button was labelled *Chambre de Projecteur*: the searchlight room. I thought about the great beam that swept the city at night, searching for non-revolutionary thoughts. Jean-Michel pressed the penultimate button: *Chambre des Étoiles*.

"You must understand, Anna," said Jean-Michel. "Revolution is the easy part: maintaining the ideal is much harder. The aristocracy constantly seek to resume power."

"Anna isn't part of the aristocracy," said Francis.

"Her father was rich. He was part of the cartel that sought to regain power in Dream London."

How did he know all this?

"He was a spy with the code name *Alphonse*."

"That meant nothing. It was just a silly game of his!"

"He was a spy. All those people who used to meet in your house, planning how they would regain power…"

I thought of Captain Wedderburn, of Mister Monagan the orange frog man, of Shaqeel, my father's supposed boyfriend. All those people who had met in our house and discussed the downfall of Dream London. Had one of them been spying for the French?

The lift doors opened and we entered the *Chambre des Étoiles*.

We were nearly at the top of the *Grande Tour*. You could *feel* the altitude. I could tell by the octagonal shape of the chamber that we were at the peak of the tower, just below the searchlight. The room was panelled in wood: dark wood decorated with golden wood, marquetry patterns forming stars on the walls and the sloping ceiling. A step led down from the wooden floor to a shallow octagonal well with a golden eight-pointed star stretched across it.

"*Formidable, non*?" said Jean-Michel. "Very few people get to see this room."

"Why?" I asked. "I thought the citizens of Dream Paris were all equal."

"We are. And this room is the opposite of equality. This is the room appropriated by the leaders who arose after the Revolution. They came here to plan for the prosperity of Dream Paris. They promised a bright new future, they promised that all men and women would remain equal."

"I've heard that before," I said. "I heard it in Dream London, I heard it in Mundane London, just before I left."

"We hear it all the time," said Jean-Michel. "They took this room as was their right, they set up their chairs and tables and their papers and they asked us to leave the room whilst they embarked on their great plans. And then…"

He walked to the edge of the room, beckoned to us to follow. We stood on the low raised step running around the perimeter of the room.

"You might want to hold on to something," said Jean-Michel. There were discreet wooden handles set into the panelling. I took hold of one just as Jean-Michel rubbed his nose and the floor gave way in two halves, hinged at the edges. I grabbed at the wall, felt a sickening sense of vertigo as I looked down and down, past the bandaged girders of the superstructure to the ground, far, far below. We were so high up I could see to the edge of the city, see the tall dark walls that surrounded it, the flat plain beyond. I felt the gust of the wind against my face.

"Close it!" I yelled. "Close it!"

"You don't like it?" said Jean-Michel, tilting that bloodhound face. "I understand. It makes you feel like stepping forward, does it not? It certainly makes me feel that way."

He rubbed his nose again, and this time I recognised it for the misdirection it was. I saw where he pressed the space on the wall that caused the floor to hinge up again.

"Cross it," said Jean-Michel. "It's perfectly safe now."

"No, thank you."

"You don't trust me?"

"Not in the slightest."

Francis laughed. There was a touch of hysteria there. Was he frightened of heights too? Then again, what sensible person wasn't?

"You get used to it," said Jean-Michel, stepping down onto the star floor. He jumped up and down a couple of times, paunch wobbling. Francis and I remained where we were. Jean-Michel ran a toe along the pattern on the floor.

"The odd thing," he continued, "the odd thing is that twenty years after we dropped the first lot down here, another group of leaders emerged. They had great plans too. They knew exactly the rules people should follow. They appropriated this room as their own, just the same as last time. To the surprise of the Committee for Public Safety, they once more set out their tables and their papers and they asked us to leave whilst they got on with their great work. And just like last time, the floor was opened and they plunged to their deaths."

"You'd think they'd have learned the lesson of history."

"You'd think so. But leaders never do, because twenty years after that, the same thing happened again. And then twenty years after that, and twenty years after that. And every twenty years ever since then."

"Oh."

Jean-Michel smiled.

"You know how long it is since we dropped the last bunch of leaders down from here, little spy?"

"I think I can guess."

"Twenty years, almost to the day." He smiled. "Come, let us descend."

WE RETURNED TO Jean-Michel's office. He took us to the window.

"A beautiful city, *non*?"

It was. I saw the river Seine running through the middle of the city, splitting in two to pass either side of the *Île de la Cité*. The river was a lightning bolt of turquoise and sky blue; even from that height I could see the ripples reflecting from the surrounding buildings, making them shimmer and ripple in harlequin patterns of turquoise and white. I saw the black and white spots of liopleurodons patrolling the river, looking for a meal of mussellers.

Francis spoke quietly.

"Why are you showing us all this, M Ponge?"

"I want you to understand. Dream London was a place of England. The people there merely accepted another set of rulers. But Dream Paris is a place of France. A place of revolution! This is the place of *Liberté, Egalité, Fraternité*."

"I just want to find my mother!"

"And this is the problem. You have a fortune scroll. You *will* find your mother. But what then? Will you simply take her home with you? What if she doesn't want to go? Have you thought of that?"

"Why wouldn't she want to go home?" But I had thought of that. She'd written me a letter telling me not to come here.

"I don't know why she wouldn't want to go. I don't know what goes on in Dream Paris."

Jean-Michel ran his hand through the bristles on his chin. He didn't look as if he had slept much last night.

"I should just send you to the Bastille right now and have done with it!"

"But you don't want to, do you, Jean-Michel?" I smiled at him, did my best to appear open and helpful. "Let me go and find my mother! That's all I want! I'll leave, straight afterwards, no matter what!"

"And what about your father?"

That brought me up short. Francis was quick to intervene.

"The scroll only mentions her mother. There's no point getting in her way. She's going to find her."

Jean-Michel nodded.

"And what then? What about the Prussians? Count Thomas von Breisach is very interested in you. Why would he wish to find your mother?"

"I don't know!"

"The Dream Prussians seek to develop the ultimate weapon. Our spies tell us of something called an Integer Bomb..."

"My mother knows nothing about weapons!"

"Perhaps not. But here in Dream Paris we are surrounded by enemies. There is the jewelled city, Dream Prague, that sends out a jewelled path to entice our citizens to itself."

"I'll watch out for the jewels..."

"Or Dream Moscow. The booms of its cranes reach out for

hundreds miles, a hook is lowered and it captures someone, maybe a child. People rush forward, they take hold of the child, they try and pull it back to safety and then suddenly they find themselves hundreds of feet in the air, too high to let go. They can do nothing but hang on as they are carried away to another city…"

"I'm sorry about that!"

"And then there are the older cities, far, far away, the land stretching as long ago as time. Dream Troy, Dream Luxor, Dream Ur…"

"That's not my problem!"

"But it's *my* problem! And then there are those within the city who seek to overthrow the established order! Every man, woman and child who is enslaved, indebted or simply homeless runs to Dream Paris, runs here, only to find that they are presented with nothing more than the opportunity to starve to death. Every army or commercial interest or bank who has been restricted in its own territory sees Dream Paris as a new market to exploit. Everyone wants to come to Dream Paris, no one wants to leave it as it is! And now you walk in here looking for your mother. An aristocrat, a spy, the daughter of a spy. Looking for a vanished woman who everyone seems to have an interest in. What am I supposed to do?"

I didn't know what to say.

He looked at Francis.

"What would you do?" he asked.

"I'd lock her up," he said. He turned to me and shrugged. "Sorry, it's true."

"And I should do that too," said Jean-Michel. "But there is the fortune. She's going to meet her mother anyway."

He sat down at his desk and shook his head. I felt my heart pounding.

"You've seen the *Chambre des Étoiles,*" he said. "You know what happens to aristocrats. To leaders. Remember this."

Was he letting me go? I felt Francis's hand on my arm, felt him pushing me from the room before he could change his mind.

"Don't push me!" I called.

"Just shut up and go," hissed Francis.

I did. He was right.

For once.

ELEVEN

THE PUBLIC RECORDS OFFICE

We walked from the shadow of the tower into the glare of the Dream Parisian morning. Looking across the wide apron, I saw that Kaolin hadn't sought the shelter of the shade like the other Dream Parisians. She stood waiting in direct sunlight. You could feel the heat radiating from her as we approached.

"And what did Jean-Michel have to say?" she asked.

That we shouldn't place ourselves in your debt, I thought.

"Just the conditions of us being here in Dream Paris," said Francis, smoothly. "Shall we go?"

Kaolin had a different car waiting for us, one more befitting her station. This one was long and black, its high blue windows revealing velvet upholstery.

We climbed in. Francis didn't even bother to remove his pack now, I noticed. He just sat sideways in the seat, the wire playing out through the closed door. Kaolin drove. Down one boulevard, past a wide set of stairs leading up to a church, children playing in the playground set off to the side. Around a corner, down a hill, swerving around a woman riding along on a bike, her child balanced in front of her, safe between her arms…

... and then we were plunged into traffic hell. Cars, lorries, bikes, scooters. The sound of horns, the wail of sonar, a maelstrom of metal, a maze of movement.

"There's our destination," said Kaolin, pointing. "The *Place de l'Étoile.*"

"Both hands on the wheel," muttered Francis.

The *Place de l'Étoile* was the focus of any number of wide boulevards: the target of most of Dream Paris, it seemed. The Public Records Office was marooned on a roundabout in the centre, the Dream Paris traffic constantly circling it like Dream piranha. Kaolin swerved and swooped through the melee, gradually getting closer and closer to the middle. She eventually pulled to a halt on a little parking bay at the edge of the roundabout. The rest of the traffic whizzed by in a hooting roar.

"I'll wait for you here," said Kaolin.

"Thank you," I said, climbing out of the car on shaky legs.

"This looks familiar," said Francis

He was right. Not the Public Records Office as such, not the overly ornate stone building, the rounded corners of its green copper roof, not the elaborately decorated portholes or the pale green louvres around the windows. Nor the glare of sunlight on the white flagstones of the paved island in which the building sat, nor the perimeter of thick lampposts topped with overlarge lanterns.

No, it was the people who swarmed around the building.

"Like ants around a heap," said Francis. The citizens who bustled in and out of the Public Records Office were dressed, men and women alike, in dark suits and white shirts, their hair greased down on their heads and parted down the centre.

We hurried through the glaring heat to the building.

"Do you get the impression Kaolin isn't welcome in the official parts of this city?" said Francis. "That's twice she's waited outside."

I followed him into the blessed coolness of the building, pausing as a woman pushed in between the two of us. She caught herself on the wire trailing from Francis's backpack, muttered something under her breath, pushed the wire up over head and continued on her way.

"And yet the cars drive through it unhindered," I said.

"I don't understand it either," said Francis.

MUCH TO MY surprise, the Public Records Office was an efficient operation. A few simple enquiries in broken French were enough to get us to the *Département des Étrangers (Britanniques)*.

A tall man waited behind a counter, oiled hair, toothbrush moustache.

"*Oui?*" he said, in a not entirely unhelpful manner.

"Do you speak English?"

"A little."

"I'd like…"

"*Nom(11)?* Name?"

"Er… Anna Margaret Louise Sinfield."

"And you, *monsieur(11)?*"

"Francis Christopher Cuppello."

The man nodded and turned to the wooden card index that filled the wall behind him, pulled open a drawer and ran a finger down the cards and selected one.

"*Bonjour, Monsieur Cuppello(11). Et maintenant, mademoiselle l'Espion(11)…*"

"I'm not a spy!"

He smiled. It wasn't an entirely unkind smile.

"*Mademoiselle Sinfield*, you are a foreigner, here to seek out information about a citizen of the republic! You are a spy!"

"I'm trying to find my mother!"

"Have you considered that perhaps she does not want to

be found? Many former citizens of Dream London are quite happy to live here in Dream Paris."

"Then what's the problem with her having a conversation with her daughter?"

"None whatsoever!"

He turned back to the card index and searched through once more.

"You have the right to examine the cards of every citizen," he said. "This is a principle of the Republic. We all watch each other. *Ah*! *D'accord*!"

He pulled some cards from the index. "We have three women with that name," he said, sliding them across the counter.

I looked at the cards. The first read *Marguerrite Sinfield*. Aged 72, born in the Manufactory District, second-generation collateral on a loan taken out by her parents to buy enough food to get through the winter. I glanced at the wooden drawers before me, briefly wondering what other stories they held.

I turned to the second card and felt my heart judder. Margaret Sinfield had died three months ago of food poisoning brought on by eating an untreated mouse pie.

"What's the matter?" asked Francis.

"It's okay!" I said, relaxing. This wasn't my mother. This Margaret Sinfield was too young, she came from Winchester, not London. She had been marched into the city just before the end of Dream London and indentured to an eel re-boner.

I turned to the third card.

"It's her, isn't it?" said Francis, hearing my gasp.

I held the card tightly, beaming as I read it.

Margaret Lauren Sinfield (née Wallace), formerly of the Poison Yews, Egg Market.

"Where is she?"

I read the card. The current address was blank.

"*Er... Excusez-moi, monsieur*," I began.

"*(11)Monsieur*!" he corrected.

"I'm sorry. It's this card. There's no current address."

The man looked at the card and turned faintly pink.

"I'm must apologise, *mademoiselle(11)*! This has never happened before. I can assure you, the Public Records Office never makes mistakes."

"Never?"

"Never!"

"There's something written on the back," said Francis.

I turned the card over. I recognised my mother's handwriting.

Anna. If you're reading this card it means that you've ignored my advice and come to Dream Paris anyway. As it will now be too late for you to escape, the only advice I can give is this: use your common sense! Regards, Mother.

WE WALKED FROM the cool efficiency of the Public Records Office, back into the glaring heat and noise of the *Place de l'Étoile*.

"'*Use your common sense,*'" said Francis. "What does she mean?"

"Just that," I snapped. It wasn't fair to be angry at Francis, I know, but I felt stupid and rejected. I was lashing out. "She was always saying things like that. 'Use your common sense. Don't be so hysterical.' She's telling me that I've been silly coming here."

"I don't think so," said Francis, slowly.

"What? You knew my mother, did you?"

"No, but I know you. You *always* use your common sense. You're Little Miss Sensible. Why would your mother need point that out to you?"

"Weren't you listening? That's what she always did to me. State the obvious."

"If you say so."

We saw Kaolin waiting for us in the little traffic bay. Our transport had changed again. Now it was a sleek silver roadster.

"Did you find your mother?" asked Kaolin.

"No." I folded my arms, defensively.

"You found something, though."

"What I don't understand," said Francis, "is why you brought us here. I can't believe that the *Banca di Primavera* hadn't checked out Margaret Sinfield's record already. It's available to everyone. That's what the man said."

I'd been so wrapped up in finding my mother, I was so disappointed at being told I wasn't wanted once more that I hadn't been thinking straight. Francis was right. He was also sharper than I'd given him credit for.

And Kaolin had given him credit for. You couldn't read a porcelain face, but Kaolin didn't seem quite so impassive as usual. There was a certain hesitation to her answer.

"It would be impolite to read another's record," she said.

"Why?" asked Francis. "They certainly didn't seem to think so in there. They almost regarded it as a citizen's duty to keep tabs on other citizens."

"What are you implying, Francis?" Kaolin's tone was as dry as crumbling clay. Francis turned to me.

"Anna, listen to me, I'm not happy with any of this. Why would the *Banca di Primavera* want to help us? When did you ever hear of a bank helping someone for no reason? And think of all those china dolls we saw on the way here..."

That was the wrong thing to say.

"What china dolls?" asked Kaolin.

Francis looked at me for support. Kaolin's hand snapped around Francis's throat, so swiftly I didn't see it move.

"Answer me," she said, in that same emotionless voice. "Describe the china dolls you saw on the way here."

"Let go of him!" Francis's face was turning red, he was gasping for breath. "I said let go of him! How can he speak when you're holding him like that?"

"You can speak for him," said Kaolin. "What china dolls? I thought you only saw Pierrots!" Her tone lowered, became drier. "Or were they like me?"

"I don't know!" I said. "They didn't move like you do. They were frozen in place. One of them was in my bedroom when I woke up in Dream Calais!"

"What did it look like?"

Francis's face was an unnatural shade of purple.

"Let go of him! You're killing him."

"What did it look like?"

"Like a china doll! I don't know!"

"What colour was its hair?"

"I can't remember. Blonde?"

Kaolin let go of him and became perfectly composed again. A pretty china doll, with blue eyes and painted smile. Cold, beautiful. Composed.

"Thank you, pretty Anna. And now I must now report back to the *Banca*."

She climbed into the little silver car.

"I will return to pick you up. In the meantime, do not mention anything we have discussed. Do you understand this?"

"Why not?" I said.

"Do not attempt to leave the island. This is for your own safety, you won't make it through the traffic. Pretty Anna, do you understand this?"

"No, I don't. Why should I remain here? You're not in charge of me."

On the ground, Francis was rubbing his throat, gasping for air.

"You will wait here, pretty Anna. Do you understand?"

The air of menace in her voice was unmistakable.

"I understand," I said. I didn't say I was going to follow her instructions...

"Good."

She clashed the gears and the roadster darted into a gap in the traffic, leaving us both marooned.

I bent down to help Francis.

"What happened there?" he gasped.

TEN

THE ROUNDABOUT

THE MIDDAY SUN beat down on the roundabout. The heat was almost unbearable.

"There'll be a way off," said Francis. "Someone will give us a lift."

I was only half paying attention. I was thinking about my mother's message, about Kaolin, about Jean-Michel Ponge…

"This place isn't like Dream London," I said. "In Dream London everything was shifting and growing. There, it was like the city was moulding people and places into what it wanted to be. Here, it's like the people are stronger. They fought back against the changes, they moulded things to suit themselves."

"You mean the Revolution won?"

"I don't think so. The people at the restaurant last night certainly didn't seem like revolutionaries. They were just playing a game. I think the Revolution is ongoing. Everyone speaks in its name, but they all have their own agenda. I can't believe that the *Banca di Primavera* wants to give power to the people."

"No." Francis rubbed his throat. "Why do you suppose the *Banca di Primavera* is so interested in your mother?"

"Why is everyone so interested in her?"

We resumed pacing around the roundabout. There were other people doing the same; visitors to the Public Records Office, no doubt. Two children ran by holding *pains au chocolat* in both hands. They climbed onto a pair of benches with difficulty, and then sat eating, legs swinging.

"Why would the *Banca* be so interested in her?" wondered Francis. "What did your mother do?"

"In Dream London? She was a housewife. That's all Dream London allowed her to be."

"But before Dream London. What was she then?"

"A banker. A very successful one, too. Before Dream London, she was doing far better than my father. She earned far more than he did. She used to point that out to him all the time."

"And now she is somewhere in Dream Paris, and the *Banca di Primavera* is looking for her. The *Banca* is looking for a banker..."

"And she doesn't want to be found..."

"Now you're using your common sense."

The traffic noise seemed to be getting worse, the heat was almost unbearable. I was thirsty, I was uncomfortable. I didn't want to be here. I looked at Francis's backpack and the route back home.

"Have you noticed how insubstantial your backpack has become? No one even notices it anymore, and yet still the line trails out behind you..."

I gazed at Francis and something shifted inside me. Maybe it was the bright sunlight, but he looked different. More like the handsome, decent man I'd first seen. The man who had followed me, uncomplaining, all the way to Dream Paris. The man who was doing his best to help me. At that moment, I felt a little guilty at my treatment of him.

"How did you get chosen to accompany me?" I asked.

"I don't know. They just told me."

"You've got a partner and a child."

"I know that. But I signed up to serve my country. I want to make them proud."

"You want to serve your country?"

The words sounded odd, old-fashioned. It wasn't the sort of thing that people said any more. It was the sort of thing that my father would have sneered at. And my mother. The woman Francis had come here to help save. What had my mother said about people like him, people serving their country?

They're suckers, Anna. That's the sort of thing you feed people to make them easier to manipulate. You don't hear anyone in my bank talking about serving the country. We serve the shareholders, wherever they come from. We serve profit. At the end of the day, we serve ourselves. That's all there is to it. Anyone who says otherwise is a fool.

I'd joined a band and marched into a park along with a bunch of other kids. What would my mother think of that? I knew the answer. She'd think I was a fool.

"You think there's something wrong with that, Anna?"

His words surprised me. There was a glint in his eye. He didn't often challenge me, he left me to do my own thing. Obviously I'd touched on something important to him.

"I don't think there's anything wrong with that. I marched with the band, remember?"

"Yes, you fought for your country."

"Not for my country, no. I fought because it was right. And I'm not a soldier. I don't know if I could kill someone…"

"What if someone were to attack you in the street?"

"I'd run away."

"What if you had to kill one person to save five people?"

"I'd kill them. That's nothing to do with patriotism. That's just logic."

223

"What if you saw Adolf Hitler raping your grandmother?"

I began to giggle. Partly hysteria at my situation, partly because of the question.

"What's so funny?"

"They say that, don't they? I never thought about it before. What sort of bizarre train of circumstances could possibly have led to Adolf Hitler invading England, ignoring all the women available in London and making a beeline for Worcester and my grandmother?"

He laughed. There, marooned on a roundabout in the middle of Dream Paris, we both laughed together. We laughed so much we had tears in our eyes.

"I suppose it does seem a little unlikely," he agreed.

And there, for the first time since that night I'd overheard him discussing me with his friends back in Mundane London, I really warmed to him. I saw the human side to him. Maybe he wasn't so bad after all, part of me admitted.

SOMEONE WAS CALLING to us. A young man and woman, hurrying up behind us.

"Excuse me!"

"Yes?"

The young couple ran up. They were dressed in the blue serge trousers and jackets of the Dream Parisian workers.

"You're English, right? We heard you talking."

"Yes," I said. "We're English."

The man squeezed his partner's hand.

"You're newly arrived here, aren't you? You've come from London. Real London!"

"That's right."

They looked at each other.

"Then it's true! You've brought the road back home with you!"

I turned and looked at the wire stretching out behind

Francis. It wrapped its way around the Public Records Office building, tracing our wanderings.

"Well, yes. I suppose we have. But I warn you, it's a long way..."

"It doesn't matter!" said the woman. "It's a path. We were lost. We didn't know which way to go!"

"Who are you?"

"Oh, I'm sorry. It's been so long."

She stretched out a hand.

"Jane Hardman. I used to live in Barking. I was a teacher, that was before..." Her voice trailed off.

"Steve Orlowski," said the man. "From Putney."

He used his left hand to shake mine, his right remained in his pocket.

"Were you a teacher too?" I asked.

"Me? Oh, no. I owned a restaurant. Jane and I didn't know each other back in... we met here..."

"In Dream Paris?"

"Dream Paris?" said Jane, looking up. "No! Not Dream Paris! We ran to Dream Paris from the manufactories!"

The manufactories. I'd heard that term back in Dream London. Another name for the workhouse.

Jane shuddered, spoke in a low voice. "You don't know what it's like. Sleep in a single-sex dormitory, too tired to speak. Bussed from Clichy to work all day on the machines, surrounded by people but lonely. Oh, so lonely! Excuse me..." She pressed a hand to her mouth. Steve gripped her other hand, he made no other move to comfort her. He was shaking too, I noticed.

"You escaped from the manufactories and you chose to come to Dream Paris?" Francis couldn't keep the surprise from his voice. "Why? This place is a prison. It's run by revolutionaries."

"You're a soldier," said Jane, eyes narrowing suspiciously.

"How can you tell?"

"You stand up for the establishment."

"Why do you say that?"

"You don't like revolutionaries."

"Only the bad ones."

"How do you know which ones are the bad ones?"

"They're the ones who don't believe in freedom."

"The people here fought for freedom. Just like the French did in our world."

"We didn't have a revolution in England." Francis seemed to think he'd scored a point.

"Perhaps we should have done," answered Jane.

"The people of England didn't want revolution," said Francis. "They fought against it. What about Waterloo?" He smiled, obviously thinking he'd won. Jane shook her head.

"Don't let anyone ever tell you that the common people of England fought against Napoleon. They *wanted* him to invade, he was the one they hoped would free them from their servitude."

"Were you a history teacher, by any chance?" I asked. It didn't matter. Jane was warming to her theme.

"All the way across Europe, the downtrodden welcomed Napoleon. But the rulers turned the working classes on themselves as they always do. They sent in the soldiers."

"She worked in the East End," said Steve, apologetically. "All the teachers there are lefties."

"All soldiers support the established order," said Jane.

"And those who don't are labelled as spies," I said.

"What's up with your hand?" asked Francis. He was obviously irritated with being labelled a tool of the establishment, so he was changing the subject. Steve seemed pleased to go along with him.

"This? It's what you get working in the manufactories."

Steve held up a hand that looked as if it had been dipped in granulated sugar.

"We made car parts. You've got to be very precise with the measurements, and that's the problem…"

"I don't get it."

"What's five divided by two?" asked Steve

"It's two and a ha – Two and…" Francis frowned. "It's blue."

I could see the confusion on his face. Dream Maths gives you vertigo, the first time you run up against it. It doesn't get much better afterwards, to be honest.

"The Dream World doesn't allow fractions," I explained.

"But that's ridiculous!"

"Don't think about it. Trust me, I've been doing my best not to do that since I first came here. Your mind fills up with colours and other concepts. You start to think in different ways."

"It can send you mad," said Jane.

"The mathematicians back in Dream London committed suicide," I said.

"But what happened to your hand?" asked Francis.

"I don't know," said Steve. "You try to measure parts in millimetres, but sometimes you need to think smaller than that and, I don't know… This world doesn't like it."

I looked at the hand, wondering.

"Blue," said Francis. He was frowning, trying to understand.

I was thinking about Petrina, falling dead in my kitchen, thinking about her pixellated eyes. Perhaps she had looked at something too small. Something that didn't want to be a fraction.

Francis shook his head, clearing it.

"This is a distraction," he said. "Listen. Why did you come looking for us? How did you know about us, anyway?"

Jane laughed.

"Know about you, when you're dragging that line behind you? Half the city must know about you by now. If the rest doesn't know by nightfall, I'd be surprised. Anyone wanting to find you just has to walk the streets until they find the wire. It's almost like you want to advertise yourself."

"Or someone wants us advertised," I murmured.

"We first got wind of you in the *Café de la Chausette*. Someone came in rushing in, shaking fit to burst. It took two glasses of pastis before he was calm enough to talk about it. He said there was a line leading out of the city and across the countryside, a line that leads to another world. He said there was a man and a young woman walking through the city, bringing the line to the people. There was an argument. Some say it's the road to freedom. Others say that we have freedom here, that good citizens should not be leaving Dream Paris and embracing the enemy. They say it's a citizen's duty to remain here and fight for the Revolution!"

"You've no idea the trouble your presence is causing," said Steve.

I looked around. Were there people watching us from the sea of traffic that surrounded the island? People watching to see what we would do next?

"What are you going to do now?" I asked.

"Place one hand on the wire and follow it back to England," said Jane.

"Good luck," said Francis. He looked out at the road. "You'll have to make it across there first."

"We'll hitch a lift. Pick it up at the other side."

Hitch a lift. Why hadn't we thought of that?

"Do you want to come with us?" asked Jane.

"You know a way off this place?" said Francis. "Sure."

"I don't think we'll need it," I said, looking at the vehicle that had pulled up nearby. Someone had got out and was walking towards us. "I think our lift has arrived."

PURPLE

THE ABATTOIR

THE MAN WALKING towards us was clearly German. You could tell by the moustache, the pointed helmet, the military stride. Stereotypes were deeply entrenched in the Dream World.

He came to a halt in front of us both and ripped off such a smart salute that I saw Francis half raise his own hand in response.

"Fräulein Anna Sinfield!" he barked. "Count von Breisach sends his compliments. It is his pleasure to offer you the use of his carriage in order to transport you to tonight's duel."

Francis shook his head in despair.

"Duel?" I said. "I thought we were having dinner."

The man clapped his hand across his head. "Ach! How stupid of me! You will be having dinner! Please forgive my momentary lapse of memory! I am, of course, fully aware that duelling is forbidden in Dream Paris."

"But we're not duelling!"

"Exactly! We are guests in this city! It would not do to offend our hosts by going against their perfectly reasonable laws!"

I noticed the faint scar on the man's cheek.

Francis spoke up. "We already have other plans for dinner."

The young man's eyes widened.

"Forgo dinner? But that would be the act of a coward! Who could hold their head up in any society if they were to back down from a du... a dinner invitation?"

The afternoon shadows were lengthening, the glare of the sun was fading and a sluggish heat was settling in. Evening was approaching. What else was I to do? Besides, this was a way off the roundabout...

"Oh, leave it, Francis. It's only a meal. Besides, I'm not letting that arrogant bastard think he's got the better of me. I'm willing to eat a few mouse pies in order to spite him."

THE CARRIAGE TOOK us through successively narrower streets into the poorer quarters of Paris. The buildings lining the streets were cracked and grey, covered in posters advertising concerts: *Le Jazz*, *Chopin*, *Eroica*. The homeless slept in the gaps between the tightly parked cars, they sat on sheets of cardboard, heads in their hands. The cafés and *tabacs* here were smaller and darker, the customers that sat outside dressed in blue and grey, red Phrygian caps on their heads. I saw them mutter and point. Once there was a sharp rap on the carriage, as if someone had thrown a stone at us. Eiffel Towers wrapped in rough grey bandage grew here and there from the wrecks of buildings.

"What's up?" I asked Francis. He was gazing out of the window, frowning.

"That funny little green van back there. I think it might be following us."

I looked at the wire whizzing from his backpack.

"I don't think anyone would have to work too hard at that."

We were heading towards the river, down into a region of warehouses and cranes. Turquoise ripples of light banded the buildings, reflections from the water. We passed the long body of a mosasaur, skeleton half exposed from the black and white body. A group of women, their skirts tied up above their knees, flensed it with axes and long knives. The carriage pulled up outside a huge wooden shed in a lot full of rubble. Francis read out loud the word written on the side

"Abattoir..."

We followed our German escort towards the building. There was a rank smell of old blood and flesh that made me want to vomit. Never mind actually eating mousemeat, the thought of eating *anything* here was enough to make me sick. The chatter of voices got louder as we entered the shed. A large crowd had gathered inside.

"What are they doing here?" asked Francis.

"They've come to spectate the du... the dinner!"

There was a roped-off path through the centre of the crowd. I walked down it to polite applause, heading for the table set out in the middle of the wide floor. The table was covered in a cloth decorated with green fig leaves and red berries and set with a mismatched dinner service, all good quality but no two items the same. A velvet rope had been strung at some distance around the table, keeping back the assembled crowd: mainly men in black tie, but with a large minority of women, all dressed for the occasion. More people sat on wooden bleachers set out around the walls.

"Are you really going through with this?" said Francis.

I didn't think I was. Something about the look of the crowd, the way they looked at me, as if I was a commodity, almost as if I was something to eat.

"I..." I was ready to back out. I would have done too, honestly I would have, if Count von Breisach hadn't appeared, immaculate in his military uniform.

"Ah! Fräulein Sinfield! Not about to leave, I hope?"

"Why should I do that?" Why are there some people from whom a simple 'excuse me' can be taken as a challenge? Something in the Count's duelling nature meshed exactly with mine.

"I hope you don't mind if we play out our little disagreement as part of a wider competition? I've reserved us two seats together, near this end of the table." He spoke as if he had invited me out for dinner and the theatre.

The maître d'hôtel appeared, equally immaculate in his black and white outfit. He clapped his hands once for attention.

"*Mesdames et messieurs, veuillez s'il (1)vous plaît prendre (1)vos places, le dîner est sur le point d'être servi!*"

The Count led me to the table. Francis made to follow, but a dinner jacketed waiter blocked his path.

"*S'il (1)vous plaît veuillez attendre ici, monsieur, avec les autres spectateurs.*"

I looked on helplessly as Francis was escorted to a row of purple velvet seats set out for the friends of the diners. He took his place next to a gentleman in a lavender suit. The man seemed to take an instant shine to Francis, pulling out a brown paper bag and offering him a piece of deep-fried octopus, which Francis queasily refused.

The Count led me to a seat with a good view of Francis and his new friend. There he pulled back my rather moth-eaten *Louis Quinze* chair, then took his place next to me on a wobbly pine fiddleback seat. I looked around the other diners. A pretty young woman in a yellow-and-silver-striped dress, a man with a pointed beard and a rakishly tilted bowler hat. Next to him, a man wearing a red toupee and then, towering above the diners, something that looked like a cross between a human and black bird. An elegant lady of mature years sat next to him, her hair pinned up in an elaborate chignon.

"I must admit, I am surprised that you turned up tonight," said the Count, shaking out his napkin. "Perhaps you will prove to be a worthy adversary…"

"Do you go out on many dates?" I said, lightly. Inside I felt sick. Sick at the smell, sick with worry about what was to be served… If I had any sense I would have got up and walked out there and then. But too late, the waiters were approaching the table, seven of them, carrying platters covered in silver dishes

The maître d'hôtel introduced the course.

"*Et pour commencer, la nourriture des pauvres de Paris!*"

Francis was waving, trying to catch my attention. He held up two hands; he didn't understand, he wanted me to translate.

"Poor people's food!" I called. "No problem."

A plate was set before each of us diners. On a signal, the cover was removed. We looked at the food with stoic indifference. Stale bread, a thin gruel.

"The wine of course, is excellent," said the Count, swirling his glass. "A '43 Trainee Sheep, I believe."

"'Trainee Sheep'?" I said. "Is that the correct translation?"

"*Naturlich*! I speak eleven languages."

I didn't particularly like wine, but I took a drink anyway. It helped to soften the bread.

Across the way, the lavender man placed a hand on Francis's knee. Francis visibly stiffened, one fist half-clenched. I couldn't help but smile at the sight of Francis pushing the hand away.

"Why are you so angry, Anna?"

"Me? I'm not angry." I couldn't keep the surprise from my voice. "Why do you say that? I was just smiling."

I examined the Count's face carefully, searching for signs of strategy. Was he trying to put me off the meal? But no, he just seemed puzzled.

"Even when you smile you are so very angry, and I don't know why. You can't admit the good in anyone without first enumerating their bad points. No one is perfect, Anna."

"I never said they were."

"Not out loud, perhaps."

Lost for something to say, I spooned up a mouthful of gruel and almost gagged. Not quite. I washed it down with the Trainee Sheep. I coughed.

"No. That doesn't excuse people's behaviour, *Thomas*. People are in the habit of doing awful things and then excusing it by the fact that *'no one is perfect.'*"

The Count nodded thoughtfully, spooning up gruel and swallowing stoically.

"True, Anna, but it's not always the case. Look at how you treat your companion..."

Francis and his friend were apologising to each other, shaking hands, laughing. The lavender man had signalled to a waiter and the pair of them were handed a glass of champagne. Now that I came to look, I noticed that all of the spectators were enjoying food and drink of a much higher quality than we were.

"A perfectly pleasant young man, but you treat him with contempt."

"No, I don't. And he has his faults, too, you know..."

"See what I mean? You don't accept imperfection."

"That's not true!"

"It was not such an insult. We are both that same, Anna, you and I."

I gulped down my last spoonful of gruel.

"I don't think so."

"Ah, the young never like to think they resemble the old."

"I don't threaten other countries."

"Nor do I."

"So why are your airships hovering over this city"

"Two hundred years ago, Anna, the armies of Dream Paris marched to the very walls of Dream Friedrichshafen."

"So? Just because they did something wrong doesn't mean that you have to do the same."

"Ah, Anna! You are so delightfully naive!"

"And you're a patronising creep."

He laughed out loud. It was all just another duel to him, I realised, this one of wits. *One up to me*, I thought.

One by one the diners finished the first course. I noticed the young man in a red toupee gulping down wine to hide the taste. My stomach was churning a little, but I ignored it. This was poor people's food. I'd had worse in the aftermath of Dream London.

The plates were quickly cleared and the next course arrived. It smelled rather appetising, warm pastry, something meaty with a delicious savoury bass line.

"Mmm…" said the elegant old lady with the chignon. "*Tarte à la Souris.*"

Mouse pie.

"That smells rather good," I said, an enormous sense of relief flooding through me.

"It does, doesn't it?" agreed the Count.

The spectators applauded politely as the pies were placed on the table, one pie for two diners. I wondered who'd get the spare portion.

The Count and I watched as an immaculate waiter sliced into ours. Brown gravy spilled out. I almost retched at the sight of the little mouse bodies packed inside. They had been skinned and gutted, but that was it.

"There is a problem, Anna?" said the Count, smiling. "There are many people in the manufactories that ring Dream Paris who would be grateful for a meal such as this tonight."

Was there a problem? The pie smelled good, after all. It's not like they would serve us anything poisonous…

"No problem," I said. "It smells delicious."

A waiter heaped pie crust, gravy and mouse bodies onto my plate. He did the same for the Count. The waiters all finished serving at the same time, bowed, and withdrew. We picked up our forks.

The big black bird man ate first. It didn't seem to bother him. The woman in the silver striped dress was tucking in with gusto. I began to eat. It wasn't that bad, apart from the bones. I copied the Count and piled them up on the corner of my plate.

"Of course, Anna," he said, "if the people of Dream Paris were to allow us to take over the running of their city, there would be no hunger. German efficiency would ensure all were fed properly."

"Are you saying there's something wrong with this food?"

"No, merely its distribution." Make that one-all.

The second course was soon finished and the maître d'hôtel reappeared.

"*Et maintenant, mesdames et messieurs, une pause courte avant l'événement principal.*"

"A short break before the main event," translated the Count.

"I understood that!"

The diners rose to their feet, drifted towards the velvet ropes and their friends and supporters. I returned to Francis, tummy gurgling.

"Well done," he said. "You've proved your point. Are you ready to go now?"

"I think so." I was watching them clear the table. The cutlery, the crockery, glasses, even the table cloth had been removed. Two women with wooden buckets appeared and were scrubbing the surfaces of the tabletop with stiff brushes. For some reason, I was more aware than ever of the hooks hanging from the roof, the hooks that would once have carried the animal carcasses.

"Why should we go now?" I wondered. "After all, the meal has only just begun."

"Don't be silly, Anna. The next rounds are dangerous. Albert was telling me all about it!" He pronounced the name

Al-burr. The man in the lavender suit who had taken such a shine to Francis appeared at our side. He had such beautiful, lustrous eyes.

"Ah, Anna! Eet ees true, what 'e says! You must not eat anymore! It is *dangereux*!"

I looked from Francis to Albert and raised my eyebrows.

"Oh, I know he's gay," said Francis. "It doesn't bother me. We had shirtlifters in the Army. Fine once you get to know them."

"I don't like that term, shirtlifters."

"Oh, give it a rest, Anna."

The Count marched up, glass of schnapps in hand.

"She did very well, didn't she?"

"Very well," agreed Francis.

"*Très bon*!" agreed Albert.

The Count clicked his heels together and gave a little bow.

"Anna, I concede. You have won the duel!"

I tried not to smile.

"You're very gracious, Count."

"As a token of my esteem, I would invite you to join me in Montmartre tomorrow. Perhaps we could board my airship and talk more about Dream Prussia and Dream Paris. I find your views most entertaining, Anna."

"Entertaining?"

"Oh, yes."

Somewhere a bell was rung. I saw the other diners return to the table. The big bird man was the first to resume his seat.

"Are you being intentionally rude?" I said.

"Not at all!" The Count smiled, that scar on his cheek glowing in the dim light. "And now, if you'll excuse me, I must return to the table. Our duel is over, but the contest goes on..."

He bowed and turned to walk away. I noticed the old lady with the elegant chignon staring at me.

"What?" I said.

She turned away without a word. I felt my cheeks grow hot.

"Hold on! Count von Breisach! I said wait!"

"Yes?" He turned around slowly, an amused smile playing across his lips.

"You're carrying on?" I asked.

"Of course. But do not think that you must do the same. You've already proven yourself, young lady."

The maître d'hôtel clapped his hands.

"The meal will recommence in one minute. Please take your seat at the table if you wish to continue!"

It didn't register with me until later that that the maître d'hôtel had spoken in English. He was playing with me. Everyone in Dream Paris was playing with me. If only I'd realised that at the time…

"If you're going on, so am I!"

"Anna! Don't be silly! It's dangerous!" Francis put his hand on my arm. I stared at it until he removed it.

"Thank you, Francis."

"Anna. Do not do zees!" Albert's big eyes were pleading.

"You should listen to your friends," said the Count. "This is no place for a young woman such as yourself."

"She's not much older than I am!" I said, pointing to the young woman in the silver striped dress.

"Ah! But she has experience of the world!"

"And I don't?"

"Thirty seconds," said the maître d'hôtel.

"Anna, don't be silly. Come on. Let's get out of here."

"Yes. Do as your friend says," said the Count, and he resumed his seat.

"Come on, Anna."

"Be quiet, Francis. I'm not a kid!"

I took my place by the Count just as the second bell sounded.

I immediately wished I hadn't.

The maître d'hôtel stepped forward and waited for the spectators to be silent.

"*Mesdames et messieurs!*"

He paused for effect.

"*Le premier cours du dîner de la mort!*"

The Dinner of Death.

The crowd applauded. Across from me, I saw Francis and Albert cover their eyes.

NINE

ENTRÉES

I STOOD UP.

"What's the matter?" asked the Count.

"This is stupid. I'm not risking my life for this."

"Why not?" asked the young man with the pointed beard. That rakishly tilted hat irritated me now, he seemed just too self-satisfied: the way he'd spent the first course in conversation with the young woman in the striped silver dress, as if the rest of us were beneath his notice.

"Risk your life to impress this crowd?" I said.

The young woman spoke up. "And what would you risk your life for?"

"My family. My friends."

"Your country?" she laughed.

"Certainly not."

"How about your honour?" said the young man. "Stay with us and prove yourself a true gourmand."

Everyone was staring. The ranked rows of silent spectators, the other diners, even the serving staff had paused, silver dishes in their hands.

The maître d'hôtel stepped forwards and spoke to the audience.

"*Il semble que notre petit espion ait eu des regrets.*"

"What's that?" I said. "What did he say about the little spy? What did he say about me?"

"He insulted you," said the Count. "Will you let that pass by?"

"Why not? He's a waiter in an abattoir. Why should I care for his opinion?"

"Spoken like a true aristocrat," declared the young man. "Not a popular point of view in this city of Revolution."

That gave me pause.

"I'm sorry, I didn't mean to belittle anyone. But why should I remain here?"

All the diners at the table spoke the answer at the same time.

"Respect."

I looked around at the faces of the other diners, and suddenly I recognised something there. Something familiar, something that we all shared. That sense of raging against the emptiness inside, that feeling of the meaningless of it all, that terror of the emptiness that we all knew lay beyond the edge of things. That futility which we did our best to hide from our vision, that we blocked with work and activity and duty, anything to forget that it was there.

And that's how I found myself sitting back down at the table, the spectators applauding. One by one the diners nodded to me and I knew I'd been accepted. At that time it was the most important thing in the Dream World to me.

The waiters approached once more. I could smell the next course even before the platters were uncovered. Rotten meat. The stench after the silver covers were whisked away was appalling.

No one could criticise the presentation though. Two cubes of greenish grey meat lay on a swirl of yellow sauce, a little cold bean salad piled on the side. All of the food was fresh but the meat.

"Not fair, I think," said the Count. "Carrionman will have no problem eating this."

"It's the salad I'll have trouble with," said the big feathery bird man, a single piece of lettuce speared on his fork.

"Allow me," said the Count, taking the lettuce and eating it.

The crowd applauded politely as the young woman deftly speared the two cubes of meat with her fork, popped them in her mouth and swallowed. She immediately turned and vomited into the bucket held up beside her by a waiter. A second waiter handed her a napkin and she dabbed her mouth clean.

"That's the way to do it," said the Count, spearing a piece of meat.

I looked at the meat before me. The situation was ridiculous. And yet, they were such two small pieces of meat. And I knew I was going to survive to meet my mother... It was in my fortune. But what if I were to meet her with a belly split open by food poisoning?

"All you have to do is swallow it," said the Count. He chewed, swallowed, and vomited.

Everyone was waiting for me. Everyone had eaten those cubes and vomited, they were all now rinsing the taste from their mouths with Geordie Pope wine whilst waiting for me to do the same.

I looked at the meat, patterned in an oily rainbow of green. Mix it in the sauce and the salad. Gulp it down. I was doing it before I had time to think of it. Chewing, gagging, swallowing. It was still in my mouth. The taste! I was going to throw up. No, not yet! I swallowed, felt the meat slipping down, felt the rising wave of vomit, managed to turn and throw up into the waiting bucket. The Count was there, helping me back to my seat, handing me the glass of wine.

I swilled it around my mouth. It tasted good! It actually tasted good! Someone had actually managed to select a wine that complimented the taste of vomit! What sort of sick place was this?

The crowd applauded.

"Well done," said the Count. "I knew you could do it."

"I'm not doing it again," I said. "This is ridiculous. I'm going."

I made to get up and a china hand placed itself over mine.

"Don't go yet, Anna. Surely you can stay a little longer?"

I turned and gazed into the painted blue eyes of Kaolin.

THE WAITERS AND the maître d'hôtel moved us all around the table just enough to set a place for Kaolin right next me. She took her seat; at her side, a glass painted as if filled with wine. The Count gazed at her with a look of utter hatred, his scar throbbing as if he might challenge her to a duel at any moment. Kaolin kept her pretty face fixed on me.

"I think you know more than you pretend, little spy," she said.

"I know a lot of things," I said. "But I never pretend to know less than I do. I'm not ashamed to be clever."

"Nor am I. I don't believe you'll gain as much advantage from this meal as you might 'ope, pretty Anna. Not enough to influence events."

I had no idea what she was talking about. I wasn't going to let her know that.

"All I want to do is find my mother."

"So you keep saying. And clever of you to be so direct about it. You 'ad us fooled, pretty Anna. Even so, that doesn't mean we can't still work together."

"I thought we already were working together!"

"And so we are. 'Owever, the information that your friend

revealed this afternoon – the fact that your mother is already in contact with you – that alters things."

My mother was already in contact with me? I suppose she was, after a fashion. But I wondered if Kaolin suspected there was more to it than a few notes. What was her interest? I resolved to say nothing and to listen.

"Pretty Anna, I want you to tell your mother that the *Banca di Primavera* is still interested in supporting 'er. We may yet come to a mutually beneficial arrangement. Ah! And now the next course arrives!"

And sure enough, two waiters were approaching carrying a large dish between them. The crowd went silent. Ominously so.

"What's the matter?" I asked, peering at the dish as it was laid on the table. I saw a large blue fish patterned with turquoise patches resting on the plate, yellow eyes staring out with a faintly surprised expression.

"Dream Fugu," said the Count. "Parts of this fish are poisonous."

Was that silver sheen to the flesh evidence of poison? I found I'd covered my mouth with my hand.

"We'll avoid those parts."

"You don't understand, Fräulein Sinfield. The fish must be eaten. All of it." He gazed at me. "Perhaps you now wish to leave the table?"

"Do you?"

"Certainly not." He smiled, enigmatically. Like I was missing the point. Like this wasn't as dangerous as it appeared. As if there were a way. Somebody hissed my name.

"*Anna!*"

Francis had left his seat and had come to stand behind me, just beyond the red rope.

"What's the matter?"

"Albert says the fish is poisonous."

"Only parts of it!"

"Do you know which parts?"

"No."

"Then why are you still sitting there? You can leave at any time!"

I knew that. I also knew that I was going to live through this meal. I was going to see my mother. I wasn't as frightened as I might be.

I was still frightened. My hand was over my mouth again.

I looked around the table. Everyone was watching me, waiting to see if I would leave.

"I'm not scared," I lied.

"No, you're bloody stupid," snapped Francis.

I turned my back on him. The blue fish was in front of me, its body tall and narrow, one yellow eye looking directly at me.

"Serve the fish!" I said.

"*Et bon*!" said the maître d'hôtel. "All of the fish must be consumed. I will be on 'and to ensure that everyone takes an equal portion. And so, let the meal begin."

At that point my courage almost failed me. The enormity of what I was doing came crashing down upon me. I was risking me life over nothing.

"Well," said Kaolin, "If you must continue, than I shall wish you good luck."

"Thank you," I said, without thinking.

The Count handed me a knife and fork.

"Ladies first," he said.

I glared at him, but he leaned in closer and spoke in reasonable tones.

"Anna, I'm trying to help you."

"Why?"

"This contest is a test of courage, not a fight to the death."

I looked at the scars on his face. What he said made sense.

"The dangerous portions are in the liver and ovaries," he

said. "The skin and flesh are perfectly safe. The outer part of the fish is delicious."

I'd known it. I'd known there was a trick to this. Stick to the safe parts. I smiled.

"You are too kind, Count. But I must insist. You go first…"

THE FISH DIDN'T taste that bad. Actually, I suspect it would have tasted excellent, if I hadn't been so scared. We ate our way through the fins and the skin. Once that had gone, a white suited chef stepped forwards and expertly filleted the fish, peeling the sharp skeleton from the flesh and laying it to one side.

"Do we have to eat the bones?" I asked.

"In an omelette. I will fry the bones soft."

The flesh was orangey pink and tasted a little like trout. Now the crowd were clapping and stamping and calling out advice on which parts to eat and which to avoid.

"Ignore them," said the Count, greasy flecks of fish around his mouth. "The flesh is safe."

To one side, a waiter marked percentages consumed on a blackboard, and no one proceeded to the next portion until the percentages were level. I chewed away, washing down each mouthful with a rather excellent white wine. At one point I felt my tongue going numb, I felt the sweat pricking at my forehead, but the feeling quickly passed. I wondered if it was nerves, or a mild case of poisoning.

The amount of fish was diminishing. Now the flesh had almost gone and all that remained on the plate was the internal organs, the intestines, the eyes. The noise of the crowd slowly faded until we were sitting in silence, waiting for the young woman in yellow and silver to finish a last mouthful of fish, to dab her mouth. And then she was still, her eyes gazing at nothing… the crowd caught its breath. Could this be it?

The first fatality?

But no. She drank some wine, raised her glass in triumphant acknowledgement of the huge cheer.

The maître d'hôtel stepped forward, and the crowd was immediately silent. This was it. I could see the fear, the uncertainty in everyone's face. I saw the glassy look in the Count's eyes. He felt it too. The fear.

The maître d'hôtel spoke.

"And now for the offal…"

I eyed the remaining organs along with the rest of the diners. Liver green and placenta blue. What were we waiting for? All the other diners were looking at the big bird man. Carrionman reached out with a fork.

"The liver," he said, spearing a wobbly green shape. "Poisonous to you, but it won't harm me. The remainder will be okay."

The diners relaxed, and now I understood. Now I got it. The Count saw that I understood.

"It's all about establishing trust, Fräulein Sinfield. At this moment, who else can you trust in all of Dream Paris but your fellow diners?"

We could only get through this together.

"Why do you want me to trust you?"

"Why do I want to trust *you*, Anna?"

"Why indeed, Count?" said Kaolin.

The Count turned towards the china doll.

"Somebody stole the designs for our Integer Bomb, Kaolin."

"So the Prussians 'ave said on more than one occasion, Count. The theft 'as nothing to do with the *Banca di Primavera*."

"Take an eye," said the Count to me. "They're unpleasant, but not poisonous."

I ate an eye without hesitation. Salty jelly in my throat. The waiter scribbled on the chalk board, he raised a finger.

"*Encore, mademoiselle.* One eye is not enough!"

But one egg is, I thought.

Around the table, the rest of the diners selected their portion and ate. They looked at each other as they did so, that sense of camaraderie. The fish course was almost at an end, we began to smile... The crowd began to applaud, louder and louder.

The maître d'hôtel raised his hands.

"*I think, messieurs-dames, I think that Carrionman 'as saved the table...*"

There was a roar of applause for Carrionman, who raised a glass in modest acknowledgement. The Count stood up and raised his glass to the big bird man. And now the rest of the table were doing the same. I pushed my way to my feet, a feeling of relief washing over me. I'd done it! I was still here! We were all here!

The feeling of elation died away with the applause of the crowd. Because it was becoming apparent that something was wrong. The young woman in the beautiful yellow and silver striped dress paused half out of her seat, her glass held up in her hand. The young man with the pointed beard turned to her, made to ask her what was wrong. She hadn't moved. She still didn't move, her face frozen half way to fear.

"Arlette!" he called. "Arlette! *Non!*"

"Paralysis," whispered the Count as two of the waiters hurried forward and took her by the arms. "Death by paralysis. The offal cannot have been divided properly."

"Just bad luck," said Kaolin.

"*Arlette!*" The young man had pushed the waiters away. He was shaking the young woman's elbow frantically. Her whole body rocked with the movement.

"That's it," I said. "I'm out."

I could see Francis moving towards me, pushing his way through the red rope barriers, Albert following him. And then he saw the ripple of movement and, like the rest of the crowd, he turned and looked down the aisle of the abattoir, down towards the great doors at the end that had now slid open. Something was approaching. The waiters were hurrying away in the opposite direction, hurrying to get away from them.

The maître d'hôtel spoke in hushed terms.

"*Mesdames et messieurs, le plat principal est arrivé!*"

And, having announced the course, he turned and left at a dead run, quickly gaining on the retreating waiters. The diners erupted in a roar of French. The Count was shouting in German. He saw me looking at him and he took the time to translate.

"This is not right! We did not agree to this!"

"To what?" I said. A cold china hand pulled me back down into my seat.

"You can't leave now," murmured Kaolin. "Now we can see what you're *really* made of."

All the diners were sitting down now. We couldn't help ourselves. Our gazes were drawn to the approaching meal. Six animals, the size of large dogs, trotting towards us with eager looks on their faces.

Something clattered on the table, thrown from the crowd. Six clatters. The Count took something, pushed it in my hand. We six remaining diners were now holding knives, long, thin, wickedly sharp knives that glowed in the blue light. I looked at my knife, felt the weight of it, the balance, the warmth of the bone handle. Were we really expected to use these knives on those amiably shambling animals? What were they anyway?

Calves. Little calves with woolly heads, hurrying eagerly towards us. One of them was looking at me with big black eyes. It almost looked as if it were smiling.

Fear rang through my body like a trumpet blast.

GREEN

LE PLAT PRINCIPAL

EACH OF THE calves had chosen a diner. Mine nuzzled gently at my knees, pushing me backwards, away from the table. It had such beautiful long eyelashes…

"Hello," I said. I was holding the knife behind my back, out of its sight. I didn't want it know that I was meant to kill it.

"*Hello*," said the calf, its voice speaking in my head. "*How are (3)you, Anna?*"

"I'm okay," I lied, "And how are you?"

"*Oh, I'm(3) fine. But what about (3)you, Anna? I don't think (3)you're fine. I(2) don't think (2)you're fine at all.*"

I heard the subtle shift in the way the calf addressed me. I looked around at the other diners for guidance. What were they doing? The man with the beard had pushed his seat back from the table, he was leaning forward so that his head was almost on a level with his calf.

"Oh, I'm fine," I said. "Better than fine." I thought for a moment and repeated myself, struggling to get the emphasis just right, putting myself in the superior position. "(3)I'm perfectly okay."

The calf looked up at me, amused.

"*Well, if (2)you say so, Anna.*"

"*(3)I do say so!*"

"*Indeed (2)you do. Tell me, Anna, are (2)you hungry?*"

I gazed at the calf. It looked so pretty, with its curly woollen coat and its delicate eyelashes. And yet its unctuous manner unnerved me. Looking across the sawdust covered floor, I noted how the elegant old lady stood imperiously over her calf, leaving no doubt who was boss. She wasn't hiding her knife, either, she was holding it between the calf's eyes. I felt sick at the thought that I should be doing the same. How could I kill this innocent little baby creature?

"I've had a fair bit to eat already," I said.

"*So I've(2) heard. They tell me (2)you performed admirably in the fish course.*"

I looked miserably towards the spectators. Francis was mouthing advice to me. Kaolin remained seated at the table, a china calf at her side.

"*Are (2)you a vegetarian?*" The veal calf seemed to be taunting me. "*I(1) am. Funny that, isn't it? I'm(1) a vegetarian and (1)you're a carnivore and so therefore my(1) wants automatically become inferior to (1)yours. Why is that, I(1) wonder?*"

"(1)I don't know," I muttered.

"*What's the matter? Why do (1)you look so hesitant? (1)You wouldn't have been so slow to eat me(1) if I'd(1) turned up on the plate, already dead. Is it because you're(1) a vegetarian?*"

"I'm(1) not a vegetarian."

Why was it so difficult to admit that?

"*Then you're(1) a coward,*" said the calf, scornfully. "*You're(1) someone who ignores reality. Too squeamish to wield the knife.*"

"No I'm(1) not! I'm(1) not squeamish! I(1) know where my meals come from!"

"You think you could you(1) kill your dinner? (1)I doubt it."

I'd always thought that I could. I'd heard the argument before and, yes, I could hunt for my dinner, and, yes, I could pull the lever in the slaughterhouse. Or so I'd always said...

"No! There's a difference here! There's a difference between killing a dumb animal and killing something you can have a conversation with!"

"Not from where (2)I'm standing." Across the table, the man with the pointed beard leant forward as his calf opened its mouth to reveal its teeth. Long, sharp teeth. Not the teeth of a herbivore, but long canine incisors, made for ripping flash. The calf bit into the man's neck. A flash of red. The crowd gasped. There was a half cheer, half groan. The man slumped in his seat and his calf moved in, biting, tearing apart his clothes. That bowler hat that he had worn at such a jaunty angle rolled across the floor.

"I thought (2)you said you were vegetarian!" I was indignant, I was in command once more. The calf smiled at me, baring its teeth, baring those long, sharp incisors that were just made for ripping flesh. And I realised what I'd just said. *(2)You*, not *you(2)*. I'd put the calf in charge. No.

"(2)I mean, I thought you(2) said you were a vegetarian!"

The calf licked its lips, and now its teeth were flat again. Sweet little calfy teeth.

"Oh I(1) am. I(1) am now. But what about (1)you, Anna? What are you(1)? Are you(1) the predator or the prey?"

I didn't know any more. I heard another cheer and I looked up to see that the old lady had plunged her knife into her calf's head, right between the eyes. The calf was convulsing, its legs were kicking, but still the old lady pushed the knife in deeper and deeper. The crowd rose to its feet, applauding loudly, and a cook moved forward, pushing a trolley. There was a little flame on the trolley, a selection of shiny copper pans. Oils and fresh herbs. The cook bowed to the old lady, and then he began to point out various parts of the animal.

"She's selecting cuts," I said, half to myself.

"*It's the civilised way to eat,*" said my calf. "*Perhaps that's what gives the old lady dominance. For her eating isn't just about consumption. It's about the right cut of meat, the correct oils and herbs, it's about the right sized portion, cooked to perfection. Not like us(1) calves. We've(1) got no culture. Look at (1)my colleague over there, head pushed deep into that man's stomach. Where's the grace in that?*"

I didn't want to look, but I couldn't help myself. The veal calf in question was tearing at the body, its fur matted with blood.

"*And now, Anna. What are we going to do? We can't stand here all day, just looking at each other.*"

As the calf spoke, the crowd cheered again. The Count had elegantly dispatched his calf with a flick of his knife.

"Tartare!" he loudly proclaimed to his cook.

"I(2) don't want anything to do with this," I said.

"*Few people do,*" said the calf. "*Come on Anna, (3)I can tell your(3) heart isn't in this. Why don't you(4) just put down the knife. We can talk about this.*"

"Why should I(2)? I(2) didn't ask to be involved in this."

"*You've(3) been involved in this since the day you(3) were born. Everything you have ever consumed has been a statement that your(3) body is of more importance than the food you ate. Every piece of meat, every piece of fruit. Every vegetable.*"

"We all have to eat."

"*Everything you(4) own. Those clothes you(4) wear are a statement that they are better on you(4) than as the wool on the back of an animal.*"

I sat down. I was only dimly aware now of the roar of the crowd. Somewhere I could hear Francis shouting. Ahead of me I could see the Count, arms folded as he gazed at me appraisingly, his cook busily mincing veal at his side. The Count saw he had my attention; he raised his knife and waved it slowly through the air.

"I(3) don't want to kill (3)you." I could hear how weak my words were. This was the thing about Dream Paris. French here had evolved far *be*yond *tu* and *vous*. Here, all the shades of relative importance were reflected in the vocabulary. You could measure the success of the Revolution, of *Egalité*, by listening to what people were saying.

"Listen to (5)me, Anna. You(5) know the world is not fair. Look at the Count. He knows that Dream Prussia must become strong or it will be overrun by Dream Paris, and so he has become what he has become. But that's not you(6), is it Anna? You(6) marched with the bands. You(7) believe in equality."

"I(4) believe in equality."

"But here, in the dining room, where it really matters, there is no equality. Here, there is only the consumer, and the consumed. Which are you(8), Anna?"

The calf looked at me with its big black eyes. I saw those long black eyelashes, the woolly tufts on its head. This was only a child. How could I kill it?

"You(9) were willing to sacrifice yourself(9) in the parks to save the children, weren't you(9) Anna?"

I was. The Count wouldn't have done that. The Count commanded armies. He sent other people to their deaths. And as for the old lady, what did she do? I was barely aware of my hand relaxing, of the bone handled knife slipping to the floor.

"Lean forward, Anna. Let (10)me kiss you. That way, (10) I get to go back home. (10)I will see (10)my mother again."

See its mother again. That poor little calf wanted to see its mother again. I shook my head. Mother. What was it about mothers?

"I(3) have a mother, too," I said slowly. I shook my head again, bent down. Picked up the knife. Just holding it was enough to reinstate some of my sense of my own importance

"I(1) have a mother. And what about all the lost people?"

"*What lost people?*"

"The people brought here to Dream Paris? The ones who are waiting for (2)me to show them the way home? What about them?"

The knife felt good in my hand. The knife was power. The knife was the difference between the hunter and the hunted. Tears welled in the calf's eyes.

"*Don't kill me(3), Anna. Please don't kill me(4).*"

"(5)I don't want to do any of this. But it's like you(7) said, it's consume or be consumed. And (9)I'm not squeamish."

I placed the blade between the calf's eyes and pushed it forward. I felt the crunch of bone, the surprisingly pink welling of blood. The knife began to twitch in my hand as the calf convulsed. I gripped the handle with both hands and pushed deeper.

My cook approached, wheeling his trolley.

"*Quelle cuisson?*" he asked.

"*Saignant.*" Hell, I was hungry. Ravenously, bloodily hungry. My stomach was a hollow, aching space. I needed meat.

The Count was at my side.

"Well done. I thought you had it in you."

"So did I," I said. "But it's nice to have it confirmed."

"You see?" said the Count. "You belong here."

I looked around. The old woman joined us, her right arm covered in blood. She held it out, I took it and shook it.

"*C'est un plaisir de vous rencontrer*, Anna," she said. "*Bienvenue à la Révolution!*"

EIGHT

BONE

I LEFT THE meal as a hero. Men and woman patted my back as I walked by, they shouted out good wishes and congratulations in hearty French and occasional broken English. A hero? People want heroes, they will make people into heroes despite the evidence of their lives. I would be a hero by the end of this story.

Ah, but whose hero?

There were no lights in the rubble-filled ground around the abattoir; we walked beneath a night sky filled with spiralling galaxies. The city was a distant band of light.

"Would you like a ride in my carriage?" asked the Count.

"I will take them back to their hotel," said Kaolin.

"What about Albert?" asked Francis. "We were going for a drink together."

"Albert 'as other things to attend to," said Kaolin.

"Does the *Banca di Primavera* have control over everyone?" I asked.

"The *Banca di Primavera* controls no one. We exist merely to 'elp people realise their ambitions. We cannot be 'eld responsible, 'owever, when people make bad choices."

That's the point at which Albert seemed to remember the bad choices he had made. He raised a hand in goodbye and left.

Kaolin had requisitioned a smart black fiacre to take us back to the hotel. Francis gazed out of the window, arms folded. The searchlight on the great tower picked its way across the city. It shone on a man in dirty biker leathers, sleeping on a saddle bag, two salad cartons and a half piece of bread in a pile next to him. He opened his eyes at the glare, waved a hand at the searchlight, telling it to move on.

KAOLIN DROPPED US off before the brightly lit lobby of the *Hôtel de la Révolution.*

"I'll meet you tomorrow morning at 9am. We shall discuss your next move then."

The fiacre drove off before we could reply.

The doorman held open the door, and I made to enter, but Francis pulled me back.

"*Un moment.*" Where had he picked that up from? Albert?

"What?"

"Why are we going in there? Kaolin will have us exactly where she wants us."

In the hotel we could see Dream Parisians chattering together. The women wore long silk dresses, the men colourful suits. They were chattering, laughing, drinking champagne. Could they be spies? I lowered my voice.

"But where else do we go?"

"Wherever we like. We've got the money, we've got our meal tickets."

I looked at the hotel. It looked so tempting, so comfortable. I'd rather sleep there than somewhere like the pension we'd visited when we first arrived in Dream Paris. And, correct anorectal angle or not, they had proper toilets here.

"What would we gain by running away? The *Banca* is helping us."

"They're helping us to help themselves. The *Banca di Primavera*, the Prussians, Jean-Marc Ponge and the Committee for Public Safety. They're all using you."

Francis turned and took hold of the wire that trailed from his pack. He tugged it a couple of times.

"Even the British," he said. "What could your mother have done?"

"I told you, I don't know! She was a banker. I suppose the *Banca di Primavera* could be interested in her because of that."

"Maybe she knew something about the money in Dream London."

"I doubt it. She lost her job right at the start of the changes. I told you, they didn't like women working in Dream London."

A man left the hotel, his beard shaved almost to the jawline, rising at the chin to meet the lips. He nodded to us.

"*Bonne nuit,*" said Francis.

"Albert taught me some French," he explained, seeing my raised eyebrows. "He was very interested in you, you know. He says that there have been stories of spies around here for months. He'd heard of Dream London. Everyone in Dream Paris has, he said."

"The Count said someone had stolen the Dream Prussian's Integer Bomb. He seemed quite upset about it."

I turned to face him.

"You're a soldier. Have you heard of an Integer Bomb?"

"No. Never. Would your mother have stolen a bomb?"

"Why should she do that? She was a banker, not a spy."

We stood in silence for a moment, thinking.

"I think we should go in," I said, eventually. "At least if we stick close to Kaolin we know what she's up to. And that way, she's helping us, even if it is for her own reasons."

"That makes a kind of sense, I suppose."

We entered the hotel and climbed up the stairs to our suite. Just as we approached the doors, Francis pushed me gently to one side.

"Let me check."

He opened the door to the room and looked inside.

"Run!"

A broken figure emerged from the doorway, arms reaching out beseechingly. Its head was like a broken eggshell, the space where the face should be smashed away with a spoon. There was nothing inside the head but emptiness...

Francis was pushing me, protecting me, entangling me in the wire. We staggered down the corridor, tripped, rolled on the floor. I saw the broken figure holding its hands wide. Somehow, it spoke.

"*Please! I'm here to help.*"

"Stand still," commanded Francis. "Don't come any closer!"

Immediately, the figure stopped moving

"It's a doll," I said. "A china doll. Like Kaolin!"

"*No! Not like Kaolin!*"

The broken figure was quite agitated. "*Not like Kaolin at all! I've remained true! I'm clay through and through!*"

The figure wrung its china hands together, and I saw how the porcelain was cracked and dirty. Where Kaolin was perfect in every way, from the fine stitching on her clothes to the delicate paint of her face, this figure was an essay in neglect. Its clothes were ragged, the silk of its shirt grimed with dirt, its pantaloons rent with slits. And as for its china face...

"What's your name?" I asked.

"*My name is Bone! Anna, I'm here to warn you! The* Banca di Primavera *is looking to invest in you! Don't let it do so!*"

"Thank you, Bone," said Francis. "We're not allowing it to!"

"*Come inside the suite! I can't be seen talking to you.*"

Francis looked at me.

"I go in first."

I nodded. Francis and the creature disappeared around the gold leaf door of the suite. After a moment, Francis appeared and waved me in.

Bone stood in the middle of the vast floor, wringing her cracked hands together.

"*Who is paying for this suite?*" she asked.

"The *Banca di Primavara*," said Francis. "Don't worry, we've not signed anything…"

"*You don't need to have signed anything! You'll be paying for this suite, you just don't know it yet! What else has the* Banca *given you?*"

"Nothing!" I said. "Well, they've provided us with transport around the city, but I checked, it was a gift. Kaolin said so."

"*No! This is terrible! The* Banca di Primavera *make no gifts! We must leave, right now!*"

"No," said Francis. "We're not going anywhere yet. Not until we know something about you. Why are you here?"

"*Anna's mother sent me.*"

Somehow I'd guessed that. Broken as she was, she bore a resemblance to the dolls I'd seen in Dream London, the two dolls outside Dream Dover, the one that I'd woken up to see in Dream Calais.

"How is my mother?" I said. "Where is she? Take me to her, now!"

Bone shook her broken head.

"*No, Anna! I can't! Anna, understand this, she's safe and happy as long as she remains hidden.*"

"But why? What's she done? Why is everyone looking for her?"

"*Anna, she can't say. Anna, please, just go home, now. It would be better for everyone if you were to do just that.*"

"But what about my fortune? It says I'm going to meet her!"

"*It says you will argue with her. What if you were to do that via letter? Via a go-between? You don't have to meet her in person, do you?*"

"I…"

Francis was moving his lips, figuring it out. Our eyes met. Was Bone right?

"*You never had to meet her,*" said Bone. "*You're being played with, Anna.*"

She was right.

"Anyway," I said. "I'm not sure we can go back. I don't have the papers to leave the city. The Committee for Public Safety think I'm a spy."

"*You are a spy, Anna. You're spying on your mother.*"

I crossed my arms, wrapped them around my waist.

"What are we going to do?" asked Francis.

"I don't know! I don't know! This could be a trick, too. What if my mother is really in trouble?"

"*She isn't, Anna! She is perfectly safe!*"

"Prove it! Tell me about her! What was she like when you last saw her?"

"*I've never seen her! You don't understand, Anna! They told me nothing so I could give nothing away under torture. And I didn't! They broke my face, they broke my beautiful face, and still I said nothing. They hosed my beautiful clothes in slurry, they broke my hands and stuck them back together with glue and still I kept my silence, for I had nothing to say.*"

"Who tortured you?"

"*The Banca di Primavera.*"

"But why?"

"*Do you know the history of the china people?*"

"Kaolin told us," I said. "There was a bank of mud by the river. The *Banca di Primavera* loaned it intelligence so that it *could become.*"

"*That's right. The* Banca di Primavera *loaned intelligence to a bank of mud. The mud learned how to form bodies such as mine.*" Bone paused. "*Such as mine used to be.*"

"Go on, Bone," said Francis, gently.

"*The mud learned how to use those bodies to make other china artefacts. Cups and crockery, vases and all manner of ceramics. The* Banca di Primavera *took a percentage of the profit of the sales of those artefacts as payment for the loan of intelligence. There were only four bodies back then, and they would have quickly repaid the loan, but the Banca wanted to make more money. 'Listen,' it said. 'At the moment you are making money from making cups and crockery. Are you happy with this?'*

"*'We are!' said the four bodies.*

"*'Surely this is just a lack of ambition on your part! You make some money, it's true, but over in Dream Delft they have constructed a whole village made of china. Imagine that! Houses and inns and shops and cafés all built of china! They have people travelling from all over the Dream World to visit them and to buy their produce.'*

"*'But there are only four of us! How could only four of us hope to construct and run an entire village?'*

"*'Perhaps four of you couldn't manage it, but what about sixteen of you? There is another mud bank further down the river. What if I loaned you the intelligence to craft bodies made of mud from that river bank?'*

"*'But we are happy as we are!'*

"*'But with more money, you could be even happier!'*

"*And so the four bodies took another loan from the bank and with sixteen bodies they built a village. And when that loan was almost repaid the* Banca di Primavera *talked them into taking another loan, and another, moving down the river, borrowing more intelligence to exploit more of the land. And all was well whilst there was still mud on the river, but eventually there came the time when there was no mud left. So much intelligence to pay interest on, and no more resources for expansion. And that of course, is what the* Banca di Primavera *wanted. The china people could not pay back the bank, so it took back its collateral. Now it owns all the river, and all the bodies, all the china."*

It was Francis who asked the pertinent question, but I never really thought about it until later. Much, much later.

"Where did the intelligence come from?"

I wish I'd listened, I wished I'd pressed Bone for an answer. But I didn't, I was too busy making a point.

"But surely the bank doesn't own you," I said.

Bone had no face, but I could tell by her movements that she was distressed.

"Oh, but it does! It owns me body and soul! If it discovers I have spoken to you, it will repossess me!"

"Just like the other dolls we saw..." I said, thinking aloud. "What's the matter, Francis?"

I'd seen him like this before, the way his expression changed, the way he stopped being a boy-man and turned into something else. A soldier. His face became hard, his body poised. He was looking at the door to the room, checking out the exits.

"Anna, this is a trap."

Bone became even more agitated.

"No! Not a trap! I'm here to warn you!"

Francis crossed the room, stood at the side of the window, peeked out.

"They've used you, Bone," he said. "Why torture you then let you go? They followed you. Maybe you'd have led them back to Anna's mother!"

"No! I *would never have done that! I couldn't! I don't know where she is!*"

Francis was a professional. I'm sure that, from the street, no one would be able to see him looking out of the window. But he could see what was going on out there.

"There are too many taxis out there, Anna. All driven by Pierrots."

"What should we do?" I was totally in Francis's hands, now. He was the soldier, the expert.

"We've got to go to ground. The *Banca di Primavera* will know we're on to it now."

"Where do we go?"

"Down! We go up and we're trapped. Listen, this is what we're going to do. I'm going to find a cane, you're going to put on a stole and take my arm and we're going walk out the front door, just like we're heading out for an evening stroll. We're going to brazen it out."

"What about Bone?"

"We leave her."

"No!".

"We have to, Anna. We take her with us, we'll be more obvious."

"*He's right,*" said Bone. "*Go, Anna. Go now!*"

"I want to get changed!"

I was still wearing the white dress with the blue bows down the front. A beautiful thing for a young lady out on the streets of Dream Paris. Not something suitable for a young woman making her escape into the night.

"No," said Francis. "What you're wearing is perfect!"

It was okay for him, in his suit. Women were always handicapped by their clothing...

"Goodbye, Bone."

"*Good luck, Anna!*"

We left the room, made our way down the carpeted corridor

to the wide stairs that led to the lobby.

"Too late!" hissed Francis. I saw why. Down there, down in the wide lobby of the hotel I saw Kaolin speaking to four Pierrots.

SEVEN

THE COFFEE SELLER

W E HURRIED BACK down the corridor, now very conscious of the whizz-whizzing sound as the wire unreeled.

"Your backpack!" I said. "You're still wearing your bloody backpack!"

"I can't help it," he said miserably. "They gave me my orders. Besides, I don't think I can take it off any more."

"Don't be silly! Of course you can!"

"No! I don't seem to know how."

"What does that mean?"

But I knew what he meant, sort of. The Dream World had a way of getting into your head.

"This way," he said, pushing open a plain door that was almost lost in the swirling colours of the wallpaper. "Service door!"

"They'll just follow the wire!"

"We'll just have to try and go faster than they can."

We'd have to. Still, who was I to talk about strange behaviour? We were running away from a set of china dolls that my mother seemed to be helping to liberate from slavery and my stomach was lurching and popping with the contents of an eating competition. Who was I to complain about the fact that my companion was trailing a wire behind him?

We descended a steep stone staircase, the sound of our footsteps echoing from the bare walls. Round and down, down and round, running past hallways lined with linen baskets and bottles.

"No! This is the ground floor!"

Francis took my arm and stopped me from descending into the cellar. From down there I could hear the clatter of pans, the hiss of steam. A rich smell of stew came drifting up the stairs. After my earlier meal, the thought of eating anything made me feel queasy.

"This way!"

There was a metal door to my right. I pushed it and we tumbled out into the spicy night. We found ourselves in a long alley, by the overflowing bins. Two dogs shared a plate of spaghetti nearby, clearly out on a date together.

Francis held a finger to his mouth, he pointed down the alley to where two Pierrots were standing with their backs to us. I nodded in acknowledgement and we walked the other way, wire trailing along behind us.

"*There they go!*"

The voice sounded like sugar cubes plinking into an empty china cup. I heard the odd stop motion tap-tap of porcelain feet hurrying after us, overlaid by the slap of our own feet.

"Faster," said Francis.

"I can't! This dress!"

I pulled up the skirt to free my legs and we ran, trailing our route behind us, out of the far end of the alley and into a brightly lit street. A line of plane trees ran down one side, their branches hung with apples and oranges carved with lit faces like halloween pumpkins. The shop windows opposite the trees illuminated the scene, four Pierrots just happened to be driving by in their taxis. They all just happened to see us, they all just happened to turn in our direction at the same time.

We ran. There was a roar of engines and a taxi bounced onto the pavement before us and pulled to a halt.

A pair of Pierrots got out. Another taxi pulled up beside us.

"More behind us!" said Francis. "We're surrounded!"

"*Quoi?*" A woman, sleeping unnoticed on the pavement looked up at the disturbance. She saw the Pierrots and recoiled in horror. "*Non! Non!*"

"What do we do?" I asked.

"We're outnumbered," said Francis. "We surrender. Go with them. Look for an opportunity to escape."

One of the Pierrots reached forward, something dangling from its hands.

"Are those handcuffs?" I said. They were Dream handcuffs if so; the links of chain seemed to spell out words in the air, a binding contract.

"Anna, I'll try and hold them off. I want you to run."

Francis pushed his way forward, ready to fight.

And then... And then...

I saw a flicker of movement, I heard the screech of car tyres followed by the call of a friendly voice. One that I'd heard in the past; one I never expected to hear again.

"Miss Anna! At last! I've followed that wire through the city all day!"

I looked with increasing disbelief at our rescuer. Perhaps someday it will become something of a cliché to have the characters in a story rescued by an orange frog man in a beret and striped sweater driving a three-wheel coffee truck. Well, this cliché started here. Never have I been so glad to see a coffee salesman.

"Mr Monagan! What on earth...?"

"Miss Anna, get in!"

Mr Monagan had pulled his tiny coffee truck right alongside us. I clambered inside the cabin and pressed up close against Mr Monagan's hot body. I could smell coffee, but only just.

"I can't fit in with this pack on!" shouted Francis.

"Then hang on as tight as you can!"

There are more controls in a Dream Paris vehicle than you get in our world. I counted five pedals, two things that looked like handbrakes and at least ten control stalks bristling from the steering oval. As I watched Mr Monagan pulled two levers, rotated a wheel, pushed a button and then stamped down with both feet... and we were away.

Down the wide streets of downtown Dream Paris, Francis hanging both out of the cabin and on for dear life.

"Slow down! Mr Monagan, slow down! Francis will lose his grip!"

"I can't, Miss Anna! We have to lose our pursuers!"

I looked in one of the many mirrors that festooned the cabin. The vehicle was equipped not only with rear view mirrors, but side view mirrors, forward view mirrors, under floor mirrors, slow glass mirrors that showed the view from two weeks ago and four vanity mirrors for applying lipstick and checking the back of your head. I had multiple views of the coffin shaped taxi cabs that followed us, that zoomed up and down from side-streets, that were coming head-on towards us.

"We can't lose all those cabs!" I said. "Even if we did, we're trailing a wire behind us that they can easily follow!"

"That won't matter!" called Mr Monagan, wrenching on the wheel and sending us spinning around the corner on two wheels.

"I'll try and get to the *Champs-Élysées*, we should really be able to pick up some speed there!"

"What about Francis?"

He wasn't listening.

We raced through the Dream Paris streets, swerving to the left, diving down roads to the right, roaring beneath the legs of a small Eiffel Tower lit up in bone-white and marrow-pink. I could hear the whizz of the wire, I caught the occasional glimpse of the chasing cabs. We spun around the tiniest little roundabout, nothing more than a circle of stones around a plane tree. People sat in dapples of moonlight around the perimeter, burning oranges with pumpkin smiles on their tables. I grabbed hold of Francis's jacket as he was flung outwards.

"Mr Monagan! You're going too fast!"

"I'm sorry, Miss Anna! I need to get ahead of..."

We shot past the front of a black cab that had appeared from a side street, missing its nose by inches.

"... that cab!"

I looked at Mr Monagan, at the sure way with which he handled the controls. Everything in the cab was clean and well cared for; the leather of the olive green seats looked as if it was well oiled, the dials on the dashboard were carefully polished. Mr Monagan's arms and feet were in constant motion, pressing pedals, releasing levers, tapping buttons, turning handles. We zig-zagged around another couple of corners, just ahead of the ever-present black cabs that tried to cut us off, and then we were out onto a wide boulevard, heading towards an emerald-wrapped Eiffel Tower bathed in the Dream moonlight, and Mr Monagan floored it. Francis leaned forward as far as he could into the cab, his knuckles white on the doorframe.

"How do you know this... person?" he asked.

"Mr Monagan came to my house, back when Dream London was at its height. He helped out the Cartel."

"The Cartel? Was that an organisation of orange frogs?"

"Man! Mr Monagan is a man!" He liked to be called that, I remembered. "No, the Cartel was a group of sad old men who were trying to cling onto some of their former power. My father was one of them."

"Okay."

"What *are* you doing here, Mr Monagan?" I asked.

Mr Monagan seemed quite relaxed as he drove, weaving in and out of the Dream Paris traffic that careered down the wide boulevard. A recursive weave. A taxi pulled out in front of us, and Mr Monagan sent the truck into a long three-hundred-and-sixty-degree skid, neatly turning us around the nose of it.

"Ah, Miss Anna!" said Mr Monagan, as relaxed as if he were sitting at home in an armchair, despite the busy movement of hands and feet. "Given the choice, I would have remained in Dream London, but when the end of that city came about I realised I had to move elsewhere. I was sitting in a café near Belltower End when I had my idea... Excuse me..." – he sent us on a long drift around a corner and then floored it once more – "I'd enjoyed a drink called 'coffee' in Dream London. Have you heard of the drink?"

"We served it when you came to our house."

"Oh, yes! I remember, so you did! Delicious, I thought. Very strong, as I remember, Miss Anna! Very strong indeed! Perhaps, and I don't wish you to think that I'm being rude, perhaps a little too strong?"

"Everyone has their own tastes, Mr Monagan."

He clashed the gears, sent us skidding around a Morris column advertising *Le Jazz Hot*. I reached out and took hold of Francis's jumper.

"Thank you!"

"Indeed they do, Anna. Well, it occurred to me that perhaps other people might enjoy drinking coffee. People in other cities. And so the idea grew and grew within me. And then one day I saw this truck, and I knew what I must do! I bought this coffee truck and a supply of coffee, and I took the road from Dream London, following my dream!"

"That's good to hear, Mr Monagan!"

"Thank you! And as I travelled, I perfected my recipe. I believe that my brew is unique. A very subtle blend of flavours."

He kissed his fingers, the truck veering to the left as he did so.

"And so I came here to Dream Paris! I have been selling coffee to the Dream Parisians these past few months!"

I remembered Mr Monagan from his brief stay in our house. He had thought that a plain omelette was a little too spicy; he coughed and spluttered when drinking a glass of flat soda water. And this was a man who believed that his coffee was a subtle blend of favours? I didn't want to pry, I knew I shouldn't ask…

But I couldn't help myself.

"… so, what do the Parisians think of your coffee, Mr Monagan?"

I wished I hadn't asked. He looked like was going to cry.

"… I think that they're slowly coming round to it, Miss Anna."

I didn't say anything. I didn't want to distract him from driving.

"After all, the last woman who drank it didn't spit it out directly. She merely shivered. She even pretended to swallow it."

"That's good, is it?"

"I saw her spit it out into her handkerchief."

"And that's an improvement on normal behaviour?"

"Well, at least she didn't swear at me. Or try to punch me. Or force me to drink the coffee myself."

"Well, it's a step in the right direction."

"Nor did she try and let all the coffee out of my machines, or try to drive my truck into the Seine. She didn't gain three thousand, six hundred and twenty-two signatures on a petition demanding I be kicked out of Dream Paris. So, yes, I think I'm beginning to make progress…"

Francis, who had been following this with a confused expression, pointed to a mirror.

"The Pierrots are still there."

"And there are more of them ahead of us, Mr Francis," observed Mr Monagan. I, too, had seen the wall of taxis heading towards us. "But they are too late. Perhaps, Miss Anna, you would hold on to Mr Francis…"

And his hands and feet became another blur of motion as he sent the coffee van into a long, long skid. Dream Paris slid past in a riot of lights and fruit faces and then we lurched forward, swallowed up by a great arch that spanned the road.

"Is that the *Arc de Triomphe*?" I said.

"The *Arc de Complicité*. Now, I must warn you, Miss Anna, you may find this unnerving…"

'Unnerving' was an understatement. We were looking out into infinity.

"*What… ?*" I gasped.

"The *Champs-Élysées*," said Mr Monagan.

"Whuh…"

It was like the world ran out, like the road ran from the edge of the Earth and out into space. Before us, everything was light and blackness. There was no substance. The sides of the road seemed to enclose nothingness, converging on a point somewhere beyond infinity.

"What are we driving on?" I asked.

"Oh, the road is still there," said Mr Monagan. "It's just that here, if they can't sell it, they don't bother to display it."

"Turn around! It's making me feel ill!"

'Ill' wasn't the right word. Something about the view ahead disagreed with me on a fundamental level. Things simply weren't right here…

"We won't be on this for long. The Pierrots will slow down. They don't like this end of the street. The *Banca di Primavera* has very little purchase here."

"Why not?"

"Because the Revolution owns this end…"

He pressed down a pedal and the coffee van leapt forwards. As we drove, details seemed to fill in around us, like the slow fade up of scenery at the beginning of a movie. To the sides I made out shop windows filled with regulation clothing, *boulangeries* selling regulation bread, bookshops selling regulation books, all of them closed for the night.

"How long is this street, Mr Monagan?"

"No one knows, Miss Anna. The shops become more expensive the further you travel down it. How high can prices go?"

As we travelled down the street the shop fronts began to change. The windows became wider, the produce they displayed more colourful. Again I found my eye being drawn to the point of infinity were the two sides of the street converged. I forced myself to look to the side.

"This is starting to look quite expensive," I said.

"Oh yes. We're already at 55% cocoa solids," said Mr Monagan, seriously. "We'll want to get off this road before it hits 95%."

"What are you talking about?"

"In Dream Paris the level of cocoa solids in chocolate is an indicator of the declining influence of the Revolution. It's a measure of the disposable wealth of the area. People will refuse to eat chocolate with an insufficient level of cocoa commensurate with their social standing."

"It's a bit like that in London, to be honest," I said.

The road grew wider. Now the shopfronts were brightly lit, white light spilling into the dark night. Shop assistants stood by increasingly sparse displays. Hundreds of empty square feet, and in the middle of it all, a single suit hung on a dummy, or a single bag, or a single piece of chocolate.

"That said 91% cocoa," said Francis.

"Good. The turning won't be long..."

"That shop sells nothing but combs," said Francis.

"Oh, that's nothing," said Mr Monagan. "There's a place further down the road that has nothing in it but a single grain of rice. The shop floor is almost a mile wide."

"They're taking the piss," said Francis.

"Oh, no, Mr Francis!" Mr Monagan seemed truly shocked. "Not down here! They would never *take* anything. The whole point about coming here is to pay through the nose in order to amplify class differences. You clearly know nothing about high-end shopping. Now, here we go..." He pulled the wheel to the left and sent us spinning down a side alley. The contrast between the bright light of the street and the sudden darkness left me blinking, great wobbly ghosts of shapes filling my vision.

"Can you see, Mr Monagan?"

"No. Please be quiet, Anna. There are no lights here and I'm navigating by echo."

"He's what?" said Francis.

"He's using the horns on the front of the car," I said. "It might help if you just shut your eyes." I glanced to the side. "Mr Monagan certainly seems to think so."

CYAN

THE CHILDREN OF THE RÉVOLUTION

"We've lost them," said Mr Monagan.

We were driving down a dimly-lit back street. The swaddled pillar of yet another Eiffel Tower sloped up at 45 degrees ahead of us, an angled bridge hanging in the air between the walls of two buildings. We passed slowly beneath it.

"For the moment, at least," I murmured. I looked at Francis. He wasn't complaining, but I could tell that he was having trouble hanging on. Ghostly wire still played out behind him and it seemed for a moment as if his life was ebbing with it.

"Is it much further?" he said. "I'm sorry, but I'm going to need a rest."

"Not much further," said Mr Monagan. "We're heading for the *Quartier Latin*. The Pierrots can't go there."

"Why not?" asked Francis.

"Because the *Banca di Primavera* has no assets there. Right from the beginning, the *Révolution* has refused to deal with the any of the *Bancas*."

Mr Monagan drove his little coffee van through increasingly narrow streets made narrower still by the cars crammed at the edges of the pavements. The streets were dark and olive; the walls, however, were alive with colour: graffiti and advertising posters filled the available space. The tall, narrow trees were hung with glowing fruit.

"Why the burning fruit?" asked Francis.

"A reminder, Mr Francis." He turned a corner. "Here we are. The Latin Quarter. There used to be a big school here. They burned it down."

"A big school?" I said. "You mean the Sorbonne?"

"I think that was the name."

"Who burned it down?"

"The Committee for Public Safety. The students and teachers manned the barricades to defend it, but to no effect. They were all killed, as has happened so many times before in Paris."

"But why did they destroy a school?"

"Because education is a dangerous thing," said Mr Monagan. "Especially in a place like Dream Paris. The mathematicians would not stop investigating. They threatened to tear the world apart!"

"But it was a school!"

"I know. One of the priorities of the revolutionaries is education. They will rebuild the schools and the university."

"I thought you said the revolutionaries burned it down?"

"No, the Committee for Public Safety burned it down. The Committee for Public Safety aren't revolutionaries any longer. They've been in power too long, they've become what they fought against! The true revolutionaries are fighting for freedom."

And for education, I thought. I liked the sound of them already.

The narrow street opened up into a large and handsomely proportioned square. Save for the road we'd driven down, there were no other exits.

"Should be a great place to defend," I said.

"Or to be trapped in," said Francis.

There was a railed garden at the centre of the square, a little children's playground at one corner. Plane trees grew from round beds just outside the garden, their trunks barely seen through the scooters jammed around them. Shadows filled the narrow doorways, the windows of the buildings were shuttered for the night.

There was a florist, a *boulangerie*… and on the corner of the square, a wonderfully French garage. One of those little garages they manage to squeeze into the smallest spaces, just room to park a car inside diagonally. Through the glass doors I could see a little yellow Lemoen, bonnet and boot touching the walls. There was a bookshop. Over the door were painted the words: *Au Charlotte: Meilleur Librairie*.

"Look," said Francis, pointing. I'd already seen it: a little café, painted in blue. The street lights picked up its name, lettered in gold.

Café de la Révolution.

I shivered as I heard music playing inside, the golden thread of a trumpet solo, winding through the night, the silver sheets of chords pumped out by an accordion. We passed a man pissing against a wall, yellow steam rising into the night.

"What's the date today?" I asked.

"Nivôse 21st," said Mr Monagan. "Hold on. It's after midnight…"

I knew it. Like it said on the fortune.

Nivôse 22nd. You are sitting in the Café de la Révolution.

Mr Monagan spotted a gap in the crowd of parked cars and he steered the coffee van into it, gave the steering wheel an affectionate rub as he cut the engine.

Francis climbed down from the van with some difficulty. He couldn't move his hands properly.

"You okay?" I asked.

"I'll be fine."

"Here we are! My flat is above Mme Joubert's shop!" Mr Monagan sounded so proud.

He turned a key in the lock of an anonymous grey door to one side of a bow window, through which rows of striped lollipops and bonbons seemed to glow with their own internal light. The colours of the sweets lit up the shop's interior with slowly moving fluorescent stripes like a tigers' disco. Mr Monagan ushered us through the door and up the narrow stairs beyond.

"Are you sure the Pierrots can't follow us here?" I said to Mr Monagan.

"Positive. They cannot pass the *Rue des Moulins*. Now here we are!" You could hear the pride in his voice. "Welcome to my flat!"

"It's very nice," said Francis.

"Very nice," I agreed.

The flat was tiny. A miniscule kitchen/lounge with two doors leading from it. A little sink, a hotplate, shelves filled with packets of coffee, a counter laid out with neat lines of glasses filled with pale brown liquid. There were pictures of Dream London on the walls, there were little tourist ornaments of Tower Bridge and Big Ben.

"Would you like some coffee?"

"Sleep," said Francis. "We need sleep."

"Oh, Mr Francis! I'm sorry! I wasn't thinking! Of course! You must sleep!"

He hurried over to a little chest, brought out blankets, laid them on the floor.

"We can talk in the morning."

I wasn't listening.

Today was Nivôse 22nd. I was going to a meeting in the *Café de la Révolution*. And tomorrow, I was going to meet my mother.

*   *   *

I AWOKE TO the smell of coffee, but only just.

Mr Monagan was kneeling before me, a little white cup and saucer in his hand.

"Here you are, Miss Anna!"

I sat up, took the coffee, sipped it. He smiled hopefully.

"Very… subtle."

He beamed with delight.

"It is, isn't it? Thank you! I knew you would appreciate what I was trying to do, Miss Anna! And what do you think, Mr Francis?"

"Delicious, Mr Monagan."

Francis was already up. He'd changed his trousers but not his jacket. I realised why.

"You slept in your backpack."

"I don't seem to be able to take it off."

We looked at each other, not knowing what to say.

He was standing by the window. I joined him and looked out into the morning.

"What can you see?" I asked.

"Nothing," he said. "Just an alley and the building opposite."

"Is that good?"

"I don't know. They know where *we* are. I'd be happier if I knew where *they* were."

"Madame Joubert should be here shortly," said Mr Monagan.

"Madame Joubert?"

"The leader of the *Résistance*."

"Resistance to what?" muttered Francis. "Tell me, Mister Monagan, how did you find us again?"

"I told you, I followed the wire."

"But how did you know about us?"

"Everyone knows about you, Mister Francis. Everyone knows you are here to help Miss Anna find her mother."

MR MONAGAN HAD clothes for us to change into. Of course he did. The meal ticket was still working. A plain grey dress for me, Francis had already pulled on the trousers provided. I changed with difficulty in the tiny bathroom, and returned to the main room just as someone knocked on the door.

"Madame Joubert!" declared Mr Monagan.

"*Bonjour*, Anna. *Bonjour*, Francis."

Madame Joubert was a woman completely in control, a woman of iron self-discipline. Her long grey hair was pinned up in an elaborate chignon, her slim figure suggested so many meals half-eaten, so many courses where she had taken one mouthful and pushed away her plate. This was a woman with an air of command, a woman with no doubts, a woman who I'd seen last night push a knife into the forehead of a veal calf without any qualms. I turned to Mr Monagan.

"What's going on?" I demanded.

"We had to see if you were serious," said Madame Joubert. "We had to see if you were one of us. Now, shall we have breakfast?

OUTSIDE, THE PLACE *de la Révolution* had woken up and was ready for business. A market had set up in the centre of the square: stalls selling trousers just like the ones Francis wore, fruit and vegetables, baby clothes, shoes and cheap jewellery. There were flowers set out in pots on the floor, flowers in bunches on tables, flowers in big vases. There were chickens – raw and stationary, cooked and rotating – and big pans of potatoes frying. People milled around selecting bunches of green and yellow beans; workers' clothes, party clothes, refugee clothes and kids' clothes; cheeses whole, sliced and inflated; *pains speciaux* and *normales*; eggs; insects live, stunned and pre-cooked; knives, forks, spoons and crustacean dissectors; pork and mosasaur charcuterie; bolts (of cloth, of lightning, and just plain nuts and bolts); white stacks of brains arranged in order of size from ant through cauliflower up to elephant; fresh fish, pickled fish, dried fish, herbed fish and inside-out fish; yellow, white, brown, spotted and floating mushrooms and soap.

Around the edge of the square the shops had come to life. The florist had opened wide the wooden doors at the front of her shop and was arranging a display of flowers in jars. A woman I could only suppose, given the sign above her shop, was Charlotte was setting out books on a table. The garage was open, and a man in blue overalls was climbing beneath the little yellow car inside. The shutters of the *Café de la Révolution* had been thrown open. Blue tables had been set up outside, a few of them occupied by men in blue and grey clothes, drinking their *petit noirs* and smoking.

There was a subtle change in the atmosphere as we entered. The customers looked up at Madame Joubert, one or two of them inclining their heads in acknowledgement. A fat little barrel of a man hurried out from behind the baskets of *croissants* and *pains set out on the counter.*

"*Bonjour, Madame Joubert. Si vous souhaitez entrer dans la sale. Suivez-moi, s'il vous plaît.*"

"*Merci, André.*"

André led us to a neat little back room, decorated with painted flowers. There were two people seated there already. One of them looked as if he'd been sleeping in the gutters. I recognised the other straight away. So did Francis.

"What are you doing here?"

M Alain Duruflé remained perfectly composed. He steepled his fingers beneath his neat little grey beard and looked up at us.

"Why should I not be here?" he asked. "I am a member of the *Révolution*!"

"You're the Chief Accountant for the *Banca di Primavera*!" I said.

"A man can have two roles," said Mme Joubert. "M Duruflé maintains a Chinese Wall within himself to ensure that there is no conflict of interest."

"What?" said Francis. "That's bollocks."

"It's a banking term," I said. "My father used to talk about it. It's how you keep the investment section from speaking to other parts of the bank who could use the information."

"That sounds like even more bollocks."

"My father said that, too."

"That may be true in your world," said M Duruflé. "Here there is no problem. Today I work for the *Révolution*."

"What's going on here?" I asked. "You, Mme Joubert, Mr Monagan. Is there anyone else going to turn up that I know?"

"I don't know," said M Duruflé. "Perhaps we can find out. May I introduce Paul?"

Paul looked as if he slept in the gutter. He scratched himself and muttered something we didn't catch.

"Where's Luc?" asked Mme Joubert.

"*Je suis désolé, j'étais occupé.*"

I turned and saw a man who, while I'd never met him before, I'd known about even before I set off on this journey. He was the man implied by my fortune. I'd never seen a man look so at ease with world. He walked with gentle swaying rhythm, wearing the gentle smile of a man who was pleased just to be out in the city, seeing the sights, maybe to drink a little coffee, have a little conversation. In a city that had raised 'looking smartly dishevelled' to an art form, I had just met the undisputed master.

Long black woollen coat just thrown on, black trousers, polished black boots. His white shirt was undone at the neck and I caught a glimpse of the coffee-coloured skin of his chest. Curly hair down to his shoulders and face full of stubble. He was the most relaxed, the most beautiful, the most *sexy* man I have ever seen. Even Francis felt it. He looked from Luc to me and you could see the realisation dawn in his eyes, and I blushed because it was so obvious. It seemed to me that the entire world could see it. Everyone must know what I was thinking.

And yet Luc took it all in his stride. He came up to the table and gave such a wonderful smile.

"*Hé, c'est quoi le problème?*"

"*Pas de problème*," I said, defensively.

He pulled out a seat for me, waited for me to sit and then slid into the chair opposite.

"English? Yes?"

"Yes."

He smiled again. Such a lazy smile, his beautiful eyes half-covered by the lids.

"There is a *problème*. You're so…" He struggled for the word. "*Bouchon*. Everything is… trapped inside. You need to…"

He opened his mouth, he mimed singing. "You need to play. To release. You are musical?"

"I…"

He shook his head.

"You are musical. I can tell. But all the music is trapped within you. Not good. You need to…"

He pretended to sing once more. I found myself looking at those big coffee-coloured hands. So smooth and beautiful. Musician's hands. And then I realised that I was lost in a little bubble, and that there were people outside looking at me. Francis, M Duruflé, Mme Joubert and Paul.

"Er… sorry," I said.

André coughed politely. I was relieved: it broke the tension.

"*Oui?*" said Mme Joubert.

"*Est-ce que ce sera tout, madame?*"

"*Je pense que oui. Dominique peut nous servir.*"

He bowed and left the room. Dominique entered the room like a ray of sunshine, a golden beauty of a young woman. Bright blonde hair pinned up, dress stretched over her curves. Francis spotted her straight away. Of course he did. She was old enough to breed. No, that wasn't fair. I had no reason to feel bitter. Not with Luc sitting over there, smiling that lazy half-smile at me.

Francis leaped to his feet.

"Would you like a hand with that tray?"

"My *daughter* is perfectly fine," said Mme Joubert.

Dominique blushed. Luc just smiled.

And just then, I saw what was going on.

We were being played with.

We had been played with since we entered Dream Paris. I'd been played with since Mr Twelvetrees entered my kitchen.

I felt so stupid. I should have known from the start. My mother had told me about this trick.

"*Let the other person realise that they know less than you do. Make them realise just how out of their depth they are. Do everything you can to intimidate them. Use your accent, your clothes, your position.*"

I was a foreigner, I didn't speak the language. I didn't know anyone here, and they all knew each other. Since I'd arrived, everyone in Dream Paris had been playing that trick on me. Making me think I was in control, whilst all the time they were putting me in my place, keeping me off balance, calling me *tu(14)* and treating me like a veal calf.

And I'd finally realised it.

I looked at Luc, looked deep into his amber eyes. Was he in on this, or was he just another unwitting dupe, brought along to secure my cooperation? Just like blushing Dominique, glancing at Francis from the corner of her eyes.

"Now," said Mme Joubert. "Shall we begin?"

"No," I said. "No, we won't."

Cold fury was rising in me, stronger than the embarrassment at my naivety.

Mme Joubert raised an eyebrow.

"Young lady, you're our guest. I don't think you are in a position to dictate what happens in this meeting."

"Actually, I rather think I am."

Was Francis surprised at my tone? No. He was impressed. He nodded in support. I continued, gaining in confidence all the time.

"I'm the person everyone in this city is interested in. It's just taken me some time to realise it. What I want to know is, who are *you*, Mme Joubert?"

Mr Monagan was turning a deeper shade of orange.

"Miss Anna, Mme Joubert is the leader of the *Révolution*! You can't speak to her like that!"

"Why not? Anyway, I thought that the Committee for Public Safety ran the *Révolution*. That's what Jean-Michel Ponge told me."

"Hah! Jean-Michel Ponge and the rest are so concerned with *Égalité* they are ignoring the very people who could make this city great again! The Committee of Public Safety has allowed the *Banca di Primavera* to buy up whole tranches of the city with impunity! They have allowed the *terroir* to claim people for its own! I tell you, when we regain control there will be no people sleeping in the streets! There'll be no Dream Prussians controlling our skies!"

"That's nothing to do with me. I just want to find my mother and go home!"

"That's all you want? Do you really expect us to believe you're that naive?"

She turned to Francis. He didn't look well, sitting there with that big, heavy pack stuck to his back.

"And you, why are you here?"

"To protect Anna."

"He thinks he's telling the truth," said M Duruflé. "They wouldn't have told him the full story. They'd be afraid of someone using the truth script on him."

"What are you talking about?"

"You're being used, Anna! You've opened up a path between Dream Paris and London!"

Of course, we had. Francis had trailed a wire all the way back home.

"So what if I have?" I blustered. "It's not just my mother trapped in this city! There are hundreds, thousands of other people, trying to find their way home!"

"And what might come the other way, little spy?"

"Well…"

I faltered. The other way. I hadn't thought of that.

"What do you want with me?" I asked, much subdued.

M Duruflé leaned forward.

"We want to help you find your mother, and then we want you to go home. No offence, Anna, but Dream Paris would be better off without the pair of you."

"Is that you saying that, or the *Banca di Primavera*?"

"I'm speaking for the *Révolution* at the moment. The *Banca di Primavera* holds no territory here."

Paul, the dirty tramp of a man who sat at the end of the table, perked up at that.

"The *Bancas* have no toehold here! Nor will they ever! Not while the *Révolution* is strong! Not whilst the people work to denounce those who would sell us out!"

He smashed his fist on the table.

"There was a *patissier* on the *Rue de Cygne*, he was ready to sell his business to the *Banca*. He would have taken the money and moved to the *Rue de la Petites Hotels*, left us here with the leg of a *tour* in the middle of the *Quartier*

Latin! The traitor boasted of the money he would make over wine and cards. And then…"

He drew a finger across his throat.

"A leg of a *tour*?" asked Francis.

"An Eiffel Tower," I explained.

"That's how the *Banca di Primavera* acquires land," explained M Duruflé. "Four plots, and then they start to build upwards and along. Before you know it you have a tower growing above you."

"Why are they all wrapped in cloth?" I asked.

"How else would you build a *tour*?"

"In the Paris that I know there's only one *tour*, and it's nothing but a skeleton. Only iron beams."

M Duruflé looked up at that.

"You've been to *Paris Ancien*?"

"Never mind that," said Francis. "You said you would help get us home. How?"

"Mr Monagan here will help you. Mr Monagan is a resourceful man."

"So we just need to find Anna's mother. But why should we trust you? *Everyone* wants to find her."

"We don't," said M Duruflé. "Margaret Sinfield has no part in this city. There is no record of her. There is no record of her ever having been here."

"Of course there isn't," I said. "So isn't it obvious where she is?"

At that, they all gazed at me open mouthed at that, and I *just* resisted the temptation to smile. Now who was the one in the know?

SIX

LA PLACE DE LA RÉVOLUTION

FRANCIS WAS GLARING at me. No surprise there. Men hate it when you're cleverer than they are.

"What's the matter, Francis?"

He opened his eyes fractionally wider, shook his head just a little.

"I think," said M Duruflé, "your friend is telling you to be quiet. He's wondering if you can trust us."

"I don't know if we can trust *anyone*, M Duruflé," I said, smiling.

Mr Monagan's bottom lip quivered.

I turned to Francis. "But we're going to need help. And at least these people want to build schools. That's got to be a good thing, hasn't it?"

Francis held out his hands, palms up. He shook his head. "Whatever. It's going to have to be your call, Anna."

He looked grey, a sheen of sweat on his forehead.

"So," said Mme Joubert. "Your mother. Where is she?"

I looked at her, I looked at Francis. He shrugged. Should I have said? I don't know. I was tired. And today was *Nivôse*

22nd. Tomorrow I would be arguing with my mother. I was due to meet her any time now. What was the point in remaining quiet?

"My mother is in the Public Records Office." I couldn't help sounding smug.

Everyone sat up a little straighter at that.

"How do you know that, Miss Anna?" asked Mr Monagan, genuinely impressed,

I grinned. I couldn't help it, I was little Miss Know-it-all. For the first time since Mr Twelvetrees had arrived at my house, I was ahead of the game.

"Think about it. If you didn't want to be found, where else would you go? The very place where you could alter the records. She would have access to her record card, she could remove the address herself. And then she wrote that message..."

"Of course," said Francis. "*Use your common sense.*"

"Yes. And I did."

Mme Joubert and the others were speaking to each other in rapid French. Most of their comments seemed to be directed at Paul: filthy, stinking Paul. He looked at me.

"You'll have problems getting into the Public Records Office."

"We went there yesterday, no trouble."

"You didn't have the *Banca di Primavera* looking for you yesterday," said M Duruflé. "They're very... tenacious when trying to recover a debt."

"The Germans will be following her too," said Paul.

"The Germans aren't following me."

"Not on the ground, no. They can track everything from their Zeppelins. They'll have seen your every move since you came to this city."

I looked at Francis, who nodded.

"Why? Why would they be interested in me?" My brief flush of triumph at knowing my mother's location had quickly passed.

"They're not interested in *you*, Miss Anna," said Mr Monagan, gently. "They're interested in what you represent. Dream Paris and Dream Prussia have been at war with each other for hundreds of years. And with Dream London, too, for that matter."

"No! Dream London only appeared last year!"

"Your London touched the Dream World last year." said M Duruflé. "It has touched many times in the past..."

Francis spoke up.

"They all speak English here, Anna. Think about it."

I hadn't spotted that. And I should have. The Dream World had been around for a lot longer than I'd suspected. No, that wasn't true. I'd known that the Dream World had touched ours many times in the past. I'd known that back in Dream London. I'd known about the strange cities lost in the Indian rainforest...

And I remembered Mr Twelvetrees and Therese Delacroix and I realised that their interest in Dream Paris ran far deeper than simply rescuing a few hostages.

What was I doing?

"If you're going back to the Public Records Office, you'll have to wear a disguise," said Paul.

"What about Francis?" asked M Duruflé.

We looked at Francis, wire trailing behind him.

"Is there no way you can take off that backpack?" I said.

He gave a tired smile. He looked so grey.

"Do you think I'd be wearing it if I could?"

I looked at M Duruflé "Can't you help?"

"Me?" he said, in some surprise. "Fight a Dream Spider? I'm a logician, an accountant, *Une Immortel de l'Académie Française*. I'm not a fool."

But I was, because I'd never suspected for an instant. But now that M Durufle had said the words it was obvious. Just for a moment, I saw a black creature on Francis's back, eight pink eyes looking at me, four pairs of legs wrapped around his shoulders and waist.

And then the moment had gone, and I was looking at a backpack again. Black webbing, black stitching, zips and pockets. That wire...

"Why can't I see it all of the time?" I said, slowly.

"The fly never sees the spider, nor the web," said M Duruflé.

"What's a Dream Spider?" asked Francis, his voice flat and expressionless.

"They stretch the fabric of the Dream World to make their webs. They can make a ten-centimetre strand of silk span an entire country. They can swallow armies whole, and then they can make you forget they were ever there."

"Who can make you forget they were ever there?" I asked.

"What are you talking about?" said M Duruflé

"We were talking about how we were going to disguise Francis," I said. "He can't remove his backpack."

"In that case, perhaps you should go on your own?" suggested Paul.

"Oh, no," said Francis. "I stay with Anna. I have to protect her."

"I don't need protecting."

No one spoke.

"So," said Mme Joubert, eventually. "A disguise for both Anna and Francis. I'm sure you will think of something, Paul."

"I have an idea," he said, and he rose and left the room.

Dominique re-entered the room with a fresh tray. Pretty little Dominique, there to bring more coffee when called. More coffee and bread and anything else that the men desired.

M Duruflé drank a little coffee, patted his neat moustache with a napkin.

"So, Paul will find a way to take you to the Public Records Office. And once you have met your mother, Anna. What then?"

"Like I said, I'll return home. With or without her."

"And what about us? Do you think all will be as it was before? The pathway between the worlds will be open. Neither London nor Dream Paris can ignore that. Nor Dream Friedrichshafen, nor Dream Troy, nor Dream Moscow."

"I didn't ask for this to happen! I've done my bit already! I marched into the parks! I am not responsible for everyone!"

"She's right," said Francis. "What's the problem, M Duruflé? What do you expect her to do?"

"I expect her to think. She's allowing things to happen to her, rather than controlling events."

"Why should you care?"

"I don't. But you should. She's not helping you."

"She doesn't like me."

I was shocked to hear Francis say that. I mean, it was sort of true, but to just come out and say it.

"I don't..." I began.

"Anna, it doesn't matter. I'm here to protect you. You don't have to like me."

"Even so," continued M Duruflé. "She's not helping you. She allowed you to become trapped by that backpack."

"That's not fair! I didn't know it would do that!"

"That's because you're not thinking. You were in Dream London. Now you're here. You say that you study physics, you say you're logical."

"I am!"

"Really? Haven't you taken the time to think about the logic behind this world?"

"What? And go mad?"

"Only if you allow yourself to. Start thinking. How big is pi?"

I knew pi to twenty places.

"Three point one four one five nine two seven…"

"But there are no decimals in Dream Paris. There are only whole numbers. So how big is pi?"

There are only whole numbers. I knew that from Dream London. All the numbers were wrong in the Dream World. I knew that. But I didn't want to think about it. No one wanted to think about it.

"Come on, Anna. What's pi?"

"I don't know."

"Yes you do. Pi is (a feeling of fulfilment). It's an emotion."

I didn't want to remember this! There were no fractions in the Dream World, all the numbers got squashed in your brain into too small a space and the fractions popped out as something else. They became colours, or emotions, or… *no!*

"Numbers are emotions in the Dream World, Anna. You must remember that from Dream London. Can't you count?"

I counted in my head, all the extra numbers that filled this world: one, red, two, blue, (a feeling of setting out on a journey), three, (a feeling of fulfilment)…

M Duruflé was speaking. I had to focus on what he was saying, I was lost in the numbers…

"Here there are whole numbers. Nothing but whole numbers. Do you know that the circumference of a circle is equal to (a feeling of fulfilment) times the diameter."

"How many is that?"

"You know how many, and it's a whole number. The circumference of a circle is always a whole number. So is the area. Don't you see that that changes the shape of things? Circles are always a little bigger, or a little smaller than in your world. Geometry is always different here. *Always* different. *Nothing* here is the same as your world."

I was reeling. I was trying not to think about the numbers, I was trying not think of the way that Francis's pack seemed to be looking at me. I forced myself to speak.

"Does this place seem normal to you, M Duruflé?"

He beamed at my question.

"When you allow yourself to think, you really are a clever young lady, aren't you?"

"I'm clever, full stop," I snapped.

"I apologise for my figure of speech. But you've seized the essentials of the matter. I grew up here. Surely this place seems normal to me? After all, you live in a world where you expect time to remain a constant. So shouldn't I think it normal that all circles have a whole number area?"

He rubbed his elegant grey beard.

"And this, of course, is the problem. This is why I became a logician. Because this world does not make sense! It's internally inconsistent. This is why when, as a child, I heard of the existence of worlds such as your own, I could only deduce that they were the reality, and this world the illusion. Because, as a logician, an internally consistent world makes more sense than one which is not."

"You deduced this from pure logic?"

"There are no fractions here, no decimals. No transcendental numbers. It's funny, isn't it? I can understand the concept even though they don't exist in this world. That's what makes me think that your world is real. But I try not to think too hard on this matter. One can get lost in the numbers."

"Back in Dream London, the mathematicians committed suicide."

"They will have become lost in infinity. There are no irrational numbers in this world. Everything is countable, and a mind can get lost on the path to infinity. Better to jump from a building than to follow that path…"

I looked closer at him, but I said nothing for the moment. M Duruflé wasn't telling the full story. M Duruflé worked for the *Révolution*, he worked for the *Banca*. Could he work for other people as well? And then I had it. All this talk of logical deduction was *another* misdirection. M Duruflé's shirts came from Jermyn Street. He'd told me as much. He'd been to our world. How else could he know about numbers that didn't exist in the Dream World?

And something else occurred to me.

Someone had stolen an Integer Bomb from the Germans. I didn't know what an Integer Bomb was, but I now had an idea how it worked. And so did M Duruflé.

I knew that he knew. And he knew that I knew he knew.

WE FINISHED BREAKFAST. Francis watched Dominique as she cleared the table, and Mme Joubert suggested we take a little fresh air while Paul worked out our route to the Public Records Office and my mother.

Francis followed me outside to the *Place de la Révolution*. The busy market was thronged with would-be revolutionaries doing their shopping. These were the people who would have been students and intellectuals, had the Sorbonne not been burned down. They wore revolutionary dress that contrived to be more authentic than mere denim trousers, jackets and hats. They held revolutionary conversations in front of the revolutionary bookshop, and I was struck with their sense that this was how a revolution should be run, free of the demands and petty concerns of the ordinary people.

I watched as a young woman proffered money to a man wearing a stack of straw bonnets on his head. The man took one off the top and handed it across with a smile.

I walked to a stall selling cheese and examined the orange and yellow wheels. Francis was there beside me, wire stretched out behind him.

"Why are you here?" I said. "Don't you want some time to yourself? We've been constantly together these past few days."

I felt on edge. He'd guessed that I didn't like him. Okay, maybe that wasn't as true as it had been, but I felt embarrassed by the fact that he knew it. He was going to talk about it, I didn't want to do that.

"Anna, about that meeting."

"Never mind."

"It's important. Why did you tell them where your mother was?"

"They're going to help me find her."

"*Everyone* wants to help you find her! I don't know what your mother has done, but she's obviously important, and now you've gone and told the revolutionaries where she is."

"Well, aren't the revolutionaries the good guys?"

"Not always."

"Thus speaks the soldier."

For a moment he looked so angry I thought he was going to hit me. Something about his expression made me want to push him further, to really annoy him. But the moment passed. He shook his head.

"What was M Duruflé talking about? All the numbers. Did you understand that?"

"Yes."

We continued around the square, looking at the different stalls. We came across Mr Monagan polishing the chrome of his coffee truck. When he saw us, he threw down his yellow cloth and eagerly invited us to try samples of his coffee blends

"This one is especially strong, Miss Anna! Be so careful drinking it!"

They were all insipid. How he was making a living in Dream Paris, I had no idea. I tossed them back, thanked him and moved on. I found myself outside the book shop

Charlotte: Meilleur Librairie. There was something unusual about the books on display…

"English, yes? I have some books in English inside."

I guessed this was the eponymous Charlotte.

"Thank you. If you don't mind, these books all look so… different." I ran my finger down an ivory spine.

Charlotte smiled.

"They're all covered in human skin."

I snatched my finger away.

"Why?"

"Because there are people who like to cover books in human skin, and there are people who like to buy them, and I found a way to make money by bringing the two together."

"Okay. But what's revolutionary about that?"

"Nothing. But where you find revolutions you will find opportunities to make money. In any revolution there are always far more business people than revolutionaries."

She must have sensed my disappointment, she softened a little.

"Well, it might not be true at the start, but it certainly is at the end. Take a look around inside."

And so I did. I walked around the dim shelves, and saw books covered in the skins of hanged men, a book about virginity covered in a young girl's skin, books about slavery covered in a patchwork of skins sampled from the workhouse. I saw books about animals covered in the skin of the man who had hunted them, a book of songs covered in the skin of the singer.

And I felt nothing. All those dead people, nothing but containers for paper.

Francis took the book I was holding from my hands.

"Tattoo art," he read, looking at the tattooed skin of the binding. "I knew this guy. That was Dale Jackson. He fought in Dream London with me. He was listed missing in action."

"Looks like he found his way to Dream Paris."

"Looks like a lot of people did," said Francis.

BACK OUT IN the square I paused for a moment to take in the scene before me. This was how I had hoped Dream Paris would be. Pleasant markets, sun-dappled squares. Intellectuals, trying to make a better city for everyone to live in.

But even here, at the edge of the market, I saw the forgotten people; the homeless, the dispossessed. They were always there, at the edges of the scenes, almost forgotten. I watched a mother hunting through the discarded stalks at the edge of a vegetable stand. I saw the grim desperation on her gaunt face as she seized a few bruised cabbage leaves, waved them to her two daughters, scavenging nearby.

"This city could be so beautiful," I said.

"I know," agreed Francis. "If only they could do something about the scroungers."

"Scroungers?" I was incensed. "Since when was picking food from the floor to feed your starving children *scrounging*?"

"Well, what are you going to do about it?" he muttered.

I knew what I was going to do. I marched across the square to the mother.

"*Bonjour!*" I said.

She looked at me, terrified, her golden irises slit like a cat's. She pushed the cabbage leaves into my hand, saying something in a strange, purring language.

"No. Don't be frightened." I pulled out my wallet. "Here," I said, pushing a piece of parchment into her hands.

Francis was there, fussing.

"Anna! What will you do for food?"

"I've got plenty of money," I said. "And I'll be going home soon!"

"You can't give her that!"

"Why not?"

The cat woman looked at the piece of parchment promising her a meal and change of clothes for the rest of her life. She must have understood what it was. She bowed down, once, twice, dropped to her knees and kissed my feet.

"It's okay, honestly."

She tilted back her head, yowled, and suddenly there were other people around me, all bowing, all creeping forward to kiss me.

"No! Please! It's nothing! I've still got plenty of money."

I felt so embarrassed, I was really quite relieved when Paul arrived to tell us we were ready to go.

ORANGE

THE STREETS OF DREAM PARIS

PAUL'S PLAN WAS simple and elegant.

"We make use of Francis's pack," he said. "We make use of the wire."

We'd returned to the back room of the *Café de la Révolution*. Paul had brought in two bundles of clothing. A shapeless grey dress for me, similar to, but not as nice as, the one I was currently wearing. This new dress was the sort of thing that a good citizen might wear. For Francis, he'd bought a pair of blue serge pants and a scarf to tie around his neck. No change of jacket for smelly Francis, not with the pack on his back. The stench of body odour hung around him, but that wasn't the worst part. Truth be told, I was getting worried about Francis. He was turning greyer by the hour. He was too much of a man to admit to being ill, though.

"How do we use my pack?" he asked.

"How many people do you think are following your wire back to London, Francis?" asked Paul.

"I don't know. I've seen four."

"I estimate there are currently about two hundred."

That gave us pause.

"All through Dream Paris the word is spreading. People who have escaped from the manufactories are coming to Dream Paris, searching for the wire. People who have been stuck here all these years. So many people walking its length, trying to get to back London."

"What are the Committee for Public Safety doing about them?" I asked.

"Watching them. If their papers are in order, there is no problem. Otherwise…" He shrugged, palms upwards.

Paul explained his plan, and I saw how clever it was. We were dressed appropriately, we would pretend to be just another pair of displaced persons heading home. The wire naturally led to the place we wanted to go, the Public Records Office. We knew that: we'd been there.

"But what about my pack?" asked Francis.

"We'll disguise it with this," said Paul, holding up a shapeless burlap sack. "People will think that you're carrying your possessions in it. People won't notice the fact there are two wires. The way you've criss-crossed the streets, things are getting pretty tangled already."

"Excellent," I said. "But what if the Pierrots recognise us?"

"I'll sort that out," said Paul. "Interference is my speciality."

BY THE TIME Paul had finished with Francis I didn't recognise him. He'd lost his good looks. Something about the bad haircut, the badly shaved stubble… Paul had worked on me, too.

"You look like my friend's ugly sister," laughed Francis.

"I'm sure she's a lovely girl."

"The *Révolution* knows how to forge papers!" said Paul, handing them across. "You are now Gill Marcello and Keith

Littleworth. You were brought here from Loughton and put to work in a shoe manufactory. You managed to escape three days ago and are now heading home."

I took my papers and noted that I was now twenty-one years old.

"We'll head up to the top floor and cut through the attics," said Paul. "Drop down in a house at the other side of the block. The Pierrots are watching the exits to the *Place de le Révolution*. We'll get you to the wire the back way."

He led us up a set of stairs, past rooms filled with flowers, bottles of wine, stacks of bistro chairs. Higher and higher until we came to a small room with a ladder leading up to the ceiling. Mme Joubert was waiting for us.

"*Bonne chance*," she said.

"*Merci*."

"You are a very stubborn young lady."

"You make it sound like a fault."

"It was a compliment." Mme Joubert gave a slow smile. "I brought you a sweet."

I took it and beamed. "A loveheart. I haven't had one of these since I was a little girl."

The sweet was pale pink and in the shape of a valentine's heart. There was a message written in white letters.

"*Cross the line*," I murmured. "What does that mean?" I knew the answer already, I was blushing.

"It means you are about to lose your virginity," said Mme Joubert.

Francis had the grace not to hear what she said. No he didn't. He was smirking. So much for me feeling sorry for him. For all he could be sensible sometimes, he was still a sexist pig at heart.

"I have a loveheart for you, too," announced Mme Joubert, handing Francis a pale blue sweet. I was delighted to see his horrified expression.

"What does yours say?" I asked.

"It says, it says…" he coloured slightly. "It says, *Have a wank.*"

"*Exactement,*" said Mme Joubert. "If you make it back here, stay away from Dominique." She swept from the room.

"She's got you sussed," I laughed.

WE CLIMBED THROUGH the attics, a succession of dusty rooms filled with the detritus of the years, lit by the dusty portholes set in the sloping roofs.

We passed a stuffed mosasaur, a faded heap of origami cranes folded from coloured paper, a collection of amber glasses: the usual Dream World oddments.

Eventually we reached another trap door and descended through the building, finally emerging in a hairdresser's on the ground floor.

The hairdresser sat in her hairdressing chair, eating an almond croissant. She looked so stylish and pretty with her very short hair, sharp cheek bones and earrings like large gold coins.

"*Bonjour, madame,*" said Paul as we entered the room. "*Un moment, s'il vous plaît…*"

He looked through the window to the street beyond. It was a typical scene: the building opposite covered in cartoon posters and graffiti, cars and scooters crammed into every available space. It was funny to think we'd driven down there last night, but drive down it we had. I knew it, you could see the ghostly shape of the wire trailing across the ground. Few of the pedestrians seemed to notice it enough to step over it as they crossed the road. Most simply walked straight through it.

"Stay here," said Paul.

He opened the door, slipped out into the street. We watched as he slowly lit a cigarette, took the time to piss against the wall, dropped his cigarette to the ground and ground it underfoot before coming back inside. The pretty hairdresser finished her croissant and licked her fingers, completely unfazed by our presence.

"Come on," said Paul. "The Pierrots have moved on for the moment."

We hurried out of the door, past the river of steaming piss that dripped into the gutter.

"*Doucement*! Act naturally."

We both bent and took hold of the wire. It felt warm and silken. Francis walked in the lead grasping the old trail, me just behind him, holding the new one, holding it close to the first in an attempt to hide it.

"There we are," said Paul. "And now I will withdraw. Keep walking in that direction. I'll be watching you…"

And he was gone.

We began to walk. It was funny to think that this was, in fact, the way home. Somewhere up ahead was a white marble bridge, and beneath it a tunnel, and at the other end of the tunnel a dirty little canal. How I wished I was already there!

"Just think," said Francis. "We could be going home. This could be the first few steps."

But we weren't. We were coming back here, the fortune said so. I was coming back to meet Luc, to *cross the line*, to *come, again and again*.

How do you think I felt about that? It never seemed less likely. I would have confidently said that was one prediction that wasn't coming true.

Funny little Dream French cars were running up and down the street. Sometimes the people inside banged against the windows, as if they were trapped. Stolen away by bad machines, press-ganged into life in a manufactory, perhaps? We pulled the wire to the side of the road so we could walk in the shade, out of the glare of the Dream Paris sunlight.

"Keep your head down," hissed Francis.

I saw it too. There were Pierrots up ahead. We kept on walking, pretending not to pay them any attention. One black and white china face swung in our direction. I held my breath, but the china doll moved on. We carried on around the corner and off down the street.

"How long do we have to walk?" asked Francis. "We must have driven miles when we escaped from the hotel. All the way up the *Champs-Élysées*. And then there was the trip to the abattoir…"

There were more Pierrots ahead. They seemed to have filled all the streets around the *Place de la Révolution*. We kept on walking.

"This might just work," I said. "Clever Paul."

"I don't know," said Francis. "Up ahead."

There were two women following the wire in the opposite direction, on a collision course with us. Both wore red Phrygian hats with cockades pinned to them.

"Committee for Public Safety. They'll inspect our papers. They'll see we're fake!"

"Maybe not. Just play it cool."

The women had seen us. They fixed us with a stern, officious gaze. All too soon we met.

"*Papiers, s'il vous plaît.*"

As we fumbled for our papers, there was a huge crash down the road. Suddenly there were cats running everywhere.

"*Merde!*" shouted the women, running towards the commotion.

A car had collided with a cat transporter. Orange and brown and gold shapes eeled from the wreckage, a flowing fur carpet that filled the streets. No one was watching us now.

"Keep on walking," said Francis. "Well done, Paul."

* * *

WE MUST HAVE walked two or three miles before we were clear of the Pierrots, trailing down one road after another, keeping to the shade of the trees hung with burning fruit, passing by Morris columns covered in political cartoons, pushing by newspaper stands that opened up like clams. We passed a mother watching her son playing with a ball on the pavement. He looked so sweet, trying to bounce the ball and catch it. Francis was so intent on the child that he missed what was up ahead.

"Look!"

We were approaching an intersection of roads, a five-pointed star. Ghostly wire trailed across the middle of the intersection. Three young people, a tall man and two women, not much older than me, stood there, deep in conversation. I felt a pang of homesickness at the sound of the English accents. Homesickness? I'd only been gone four days.

"So, I think you'll find it's that way," said the young man. He towered over his companions, his arms and legs way too long for his regulation serge jacket and trousers.

"I'm sure we walked down there earlier," said the shorter of the women. "What do you think, Val?"

"I'm sorry," interrupted the young man, "I thought I was the navigator. Er, excuse me? Can I help you?"

He'd noticed Francis and me listening in to the conversation. He noticed something else, too…

"You're English, aren't you?"

"Yes," said Francis. "How can you tell?"

"Dave knows everything," said the woman who wasn't Val.

The man seemed to notice me for the first time, and suddenly his manner changed.

"Don't be so rude, Sue." He smoothed his hair and smiled at me. "So, we're following this wire back to London. Do you know about the wire?"

"No," said Francis "We were just wondering what it was. Can you tell us about it?"

Dave looked from Francis to me. I could tell what he was thinking. So could Sue and Val.

"So, I think you'll find that it's the route back home. Follow it and we can walk out of the West Gate of Dream Paris."

"Where did it come from?" I asked, innocently.

"So, the British government have sent a team of people here to rescue us."

"The three of you?" said Francis, all innocence.

"No," he said, patiently. "All the people brought here from Dream London. The rescue team are unrolling a wire as they come, marking the way back."

"A wire?" I said. "That seems a little unlikely, doesn't it?"

"So, it's all to do with the way that the Dream World operates. Distance means something different here. If you'd been in Dream London, you'd have understood that."

"I was in Dream London."

Val and Sue grinned. Dave pretended not to notice.

"Well, there you are. It's all to do with the numbers here. Have you tried counting? Actually, maybe it's better if you don't. I'm a programmer. Think too hard about numbers in this world and it can send you mad."

"A programmer?" said Francis. "They have programmers here?"

"After a fashion," said Val, speaking up for the first time. "They've had us working on something more like mechanical adding machines."

"They were more complicated than that," said Dave. He flushed with prided. "We were sent to work for the *Laboratoires Garnier*."

"What's that?" asked Francis.

"Only the top scientific research institute in the Dream World."

"That's what they said, anyway," said Val, clearly unimpressed by all this. "All we ever seemed to do was reverse engineer machinery they'd got from Dream Prussia."

"It was a little more complicated than that," said Dave, haughtily.

"I don't think so," said Val. "They got us to examine this super weapon they'd managed to steal. It was nothing more than a very accurate measuring device."

"That doesn't sound very dangerous," said Francis.

"Oh, it was," said Val. "Lethal, if you understood the way the Dream World works."

"There were a lot of programmers working for *Laboratoires Garnier*," said Sue. "The Dream World likes the way we think."

"You were all programmers?"

"Val and Dave used to work for me back in London."

Dave didn't like that.

"So, we're heading to the West Gate. Do you want to come with us?"

"We're looking for the Public Records Office."

"It's down there," said Val. "Only about fifteen minutes walk. We passed it earlier."

"Twice," said Sue.

"Anyone can make a mistake," said Dave, sulkily.

WE WISHED THE three of them luck as they headed to England, and made our way up to the roundabout on which the Public Records Office sat.

"How do we get across?" I wondered.

"Let's just walk," said Francis. "I can't see there being a problem. I think everyone wants us to get to your mother."

He was right. We strolled over the wide space, cars and scooters swerving and honking around us, missing by centimetres. It was scary, but we got across and made our way inside the building.

A woman was waiting for us.

"Anna Sinfield?" she said.

I looked at Francis.

"No, I'm Gill Marcello."

"Of course you are. Your mother said you would be coming. Follow me."

FIVE

MARGARET SINFIELD

MY MOTHER HAD a well-appointed office near the top of the building. She sat behind an elegant wooden desk, equally elegant in an ivory blouse and pearls. She didn't seem too surprised to see us. She didn't seem too happy, either,

"Well?" I said. "Aren't you going to say something?"

She rose from her seat and crossed the room and gave me a sudden, fierce hug.

"Don't think that I'm not pleased to see you, darling," she whispered. "Don't think I'm not proud of you."

I burst into tears. Don't ask me where it came from. I thought I didn't care that much for my mother. I'd almost convinced myself of the fact. Something deeper inside me knew better.

We hung on to each other, I don't know for how long. The smell of her skin, the feel of her arms around me... I couldn't stop crying, floods of tears, soaking her blouse. Me and my mummy, stood in an office in a grandiose building that stood on a roundabout in the middle of a strange city, connected to our home by a long, long wire.

It seemed like forever before we broke apart. She touched the corners of her eyes with her little fingers. I was a mess, a snotty, slobbering mess. Francis handed me something. A handkerchief.

"You must be Francis."

"Hello, Mrs Sinfield."

"Call me Margaret."

She touched her hair, smoothed down her jacket and skirt, smartened herself up. My mother always liked looking good. Our moment was over, she was retreating back into her glamorous shell. She sat back down behind her desk.

"I knew you'd find me."

"I got your message on the data cards. *Use your common sense.*"

She shook her head.

"No! Couldn't you see I was telling you not to find me?"

I felt something sink inside me. I'd thought that the card was a clue to her location: my reward, that last piece of help after overcoming all the obstacles. It wasn't, it was her last warning not to look for her. She'd provided all the personal information about me to prove the card's provenance, and then the final warning. And I'd thought myself so clever...

"What about the dolls? Did none of them get through to warn you?"

I thought about the dolls frozen in place on the path from Dream London, of the doll that had almost woken me in Dream Calais before its intelligence was repossessed. I thought of poor old Bone...

"Well, yes..."

"So they made it! Why didn't you listen to them?"

"How did I know whether to trust them?"

She folded her hands together and looked up, her emotion pushed to one side. "The *Banca di Primavera* will have tracked you all the way here. You realise you've given away my location, don't you?"

"I know! I'm sorry! But what was I supposed to have done? Leave you trapped and alone in Dream Paris? Besides, they brought me a fortune scroll back in London. It said that we were going to meet."

She looked directly into my eyes.

"Who brought you the scroll?"

"A man named Adolphus Twelvetrees."

She held my gaze for a moment longer. Was there the faintest edge of a frown there? Was I being paranoid, or was she really disappointed with me?

Then she smiled.

"Would you like something to drink? I feel as if I need some coffee. Although I would much prefer a proper cup of tea."

"Me too," said Francis, with feeling.

She looked at him, eyes twinkling. She pressed a button.

"*Pourriez-vous apporter un peu de café, Claudette?*"

"*D'accord!*"

Silence descended. It filled the large room, a room where it seemed the decorations and furniture weren't quite big enough to fill it. The gold-patterned wallpaper was separated by stripes of wood, the carpet didn't meet the walls, the desk seemed too small for the little rectangle of carpet on which it sat.

"Are you okay, darling? Have you somewhere to stay?"

"I'm perfectly fine, mother. We're staying with the Revolution."

"The Revolution? I suppose they're fighting for the good of the people of Dream Paris?"

"And what's wrong with that? I once heard, Mother, that if the cause is the right one, people will rally behind the banner."

"As you get older, Anna, you'll find that people just rally behind any banner, irrespective of the cause. Especially pretty banners. Most of the time they don't even bother to read what's on it."

"I'm not going to argue with you. We've just linked up with them. They helped me to find you."

"Anna, you're very naive. *Everyone* has been helping you find me."

I knew that. I still felt foolish. I stumbled on.

"And you'll never guess who's helping them out…"

"Don't tell me. Mr Monagan?"

That floored me.

"But… well yes! But… how did you know?"

"Oh, come on, Anna. Haven't you figured out that Mr Monagan is a spy? He always turns up at the right place and time. Innocent, wide-eyed Mr Monagan. He just happened to bump into Captain Wedderburn. He just happened to turn up at our house. I bet he was there just at the right time at the end of Dream London, too. Pity I wasn't around to see it. Come on, Anna! You should knqw better!" She turned to Francis and something in her whole demeanour changed. Her smile widened, she adopted a different posture.

"What do you think, Francis? Is Mr Monagan a spy?"

"Maybe," admitted Francis.

"Definitely." My mother turned back to me. "Anna, you really don't want to know what's going on here! You're my daughter, trust me! You've found me. We'll have a cup of coffee and a chat, and then I want you to turn round and head straight back to London. There should be quite a crowd of people doing the same right now, following that line of Francis's. Lose yourself among them. The sooner you're back in London, the happier I'll be."

"And you're not coming with me?"

"No. I'm staying here."

I'd suspected it all along, of course. I'd known it deep inside. But even so it cut deep to hear it.

"Oh. Okay."

"Anna! Don't look at me like that! Think about it. Why should I go back to London? What is there waiting there for me now?"

"There's me."

"Really? For how long? You'll be heading off to university this year, won't you?"

I didn't answer.

"There. And I wouldn't want to keep you from that. And what else is there for me in London? No job, no friends. They all let me be marched off to the workhouse. No one stood up for me then. Do you think that I want to see any of them again?"

And then it hit me. You might wonder why I hadn't thought of it sooner, but you must understand that I was confused, I was reeling.But it took that long for me to ask the question.

"And Dad. Where's Dad?"

She looked down at the desk once more.

"I don't know."

"Is he dead?"

"I don't know! Do you know what it was like, being taken away to the workhouse?"

"No, I don't. I was dealing with one or two problems of my own at the time."

We'd only been together for a few minutes and already I was being sarcastic. Soon we'd be arguing. She wasn't listening. Margaret Sinfield was always primarily concerned about herself.

"They separated the sexes. Your father and I were marched off in different directions. I never saw him again."

"You make it sound like he's dead," said Francis. I raised a hand to silence him.

"So how did you end up here? This seems a step up from the workhouse."

She smiled at that.

"The good thing about Dream Paris is that there is no sexism here, no racism or old boys' network. Here they recognise talent."

"Come on, Mother. You need to add more than that."

"The books in the workhouse were a mess. I was an accountant, remember? I sorted out the finances, put that place on a better footing. Got myself transferred into Dream Paris itself. Ended up working for the *Banca di Primavera*."

That made sense. My mother could always spot an opportunity.

"So what went wrong?"

"Nothing. I was working with the dolls. I saw how unfair the deal the *Banca* had negotiated with them was. I helped them out."

"How?"

"Cooked the books. Moved the numbers around so that some of the dolls had a little more intelligence, a little more freedom. By then the Committee for Public Safety found out about me. They wanted me on their side, they arranged for me to escape. I ended up here."

It rang hollow. My mother helping out other people. Really?

"That's a pretty impressive few months' work."

"It is, isn't it?"

She smiled, disingenuously.

The coffee arrived. A *Louis Quinze* porcelain coffee pot, little cups, a plate of petit fours.

"I see the Committee for Public Safety doesn't stint itself within its own offices," I observed. "I thought everyone was equal in Dream Paris."

"Please don't tell me this surprises you, Anna. Please don't tell me you're really that naive."

Francis poured the coffee. It smelt strong. It smelt good.

We sipped our coffee and I felt so flat. All this way for a cup of coffee. Was that to be it?

No. Francis was acting oddly, looking at me, looking at Margaret. There was clearly something on his mind.

"What's the matter, Francis?" I asked.

"This," he said. He felt in his pocket and pulled out an envelope.

"They told me to keep this a secret from you. I was to give this to your mother when we found her."

It was a long, white envelope, sealed. On the front was written, in large black letters, *FAO Mrs Margaret Sinfield*.

"I'm sorry, Anna."

He couldn't meet my eyes. My mother took the envelope and held it in both hands.

"Mother?" She didn't reply. She was looking at Francis, who was looking at the floor, a red flush rising from his neck.

"Why didn't you tell me?" I said. I couldn't keep the hurt from my voice. But that wasn't the worst thing. The worst thing was the gradually dawning realisation that I wasn't as clever as I thought I was. No. That wasn't the worst thing. The worst thing was that yet again I'd started to trust Francis, to regard him as a decent guy, and yet again he'd betrayed that trust.

"Well? Aren't you going to open the letter, Mother? Don't you want to know what's in it?"

She smiled at me kindly. Patronisingly.

"I don't need to open it, dear. I know what it will be. It will be a letter asking me to help out British interests."

"How do you know that?"

"Because that's what I'd do. I'm their woman inside Dream Paris. They'll want me to help them."

"To do what?"

"Oh, Anna! There's a revolution here. There's been a revolution about to take place for two hundred years. You know what it means when there's a revolution?"

"It means that people have had enough. They're fighting for their freedom."

I felt foolish as soon as I said the words.

"Don't talk such nonsense. Revolution means that power is up for grabs. It means that the rulers have lost their grip and that everyone with an interest in power is moving in to take it."

"No, it means that the people have risen…"

"Anna! All that happens in a revolution is what happens in any battle: the common people are sent in to fight and be killed whilst the rulers watch from the sidelines."

"No! People fight because they believe what they're fighting for is right!"

"*Fools* fight."

I could see the look on Francis's face. He was one of the fools. That's what she was saying.

"The wise stand at the back and send the foolish in to fight for them. You see the same thing played out in the abattoir once a week. A group of people standing around shouting 'mine!' And now the British Government has a found a path into the Dream World they want to shout 'mine!' loud enough to drown out the sound of the Dream World shouting 'mine!' back at them."

"No! How do you know that?"

"Francis has a line all the way from London to Dream Paris. There'll be British soldiers marching down that line even now, coming here to stake Britain's claim."

"But what's that got to do with you?"

"That's what the letter will explain. I have power here, I work with the free china dolls. I have the pension funds of people back home. I've got the contracts of some of the workers back in the manufactories…"

"Open the letter."

"I will, Anna. When you're gone."

"Now!"

"I told you not to come here. I knew that you'd react like this. And I didn't want people knowing where I was. The

Banca di Primavera wants the things I took from it when I broke free of its control. They're looking to call in their debts."

I had a sudden image of my mother frozen in place, eyes gazing at nothing, the breeze stirring her hair, just like the china dolls I'd seen on my way here. I might have whimpered. I don't know. Francis took my hand. I shook it free. I didn't want the sympathy of the man who'd twice betrayed me.

"How did the government know you'd be able to help?" I asked. "What if you'd been trapped in some workhouse somewhere?"

"Our sort of people never end up trapped in workhouses, Anna. You, me, Madame Joubert, Monsieur Duruflé. We always rise to the top. How many times have I told you that?"

I didn't know what to say.

"Come on, Anna. Don't look like that."

"Like what? What am I supposed to do now?"

"Give me a hug, let me tell you that I love you, and then turn around and go home. There's a war coming here, and everyone knows it. Get out while you can."

"How can I get out of here? Everyone is looking for me."

"They won't be any more, Anna. Now they've found me, you've served your purpose. Go home. I've arranged for a taxi to take you back to the *Place de la Révolution*. Spend the night there. I'll have Mr Monagan take you to the railway station in the morning; there's a train that will take you directly to Dream Calais. And then you can head back to London."

"This all seems very organised."

"Of course it is! Oh, Anna, I still love you. I want to look after you! I'm trying to do what's best. I've had people looking out for you. I knew you were coming."

They all did. They'd all seen me coming. Every last one of them.

FOUR

THE WOMEN IN FRANCIS'S LIFE

I FELT LIKE a child. Like I'd been wandering round in the adult world, wearing my mother's shoes and clothes, pretending to be a grown up whilst everyone smiled and nodded and said what a big girl I was. And all the time everyone had been laughing at me.

"I'm sorry," said Francis. "If there's anything I can do..."

"I don't want anything from you!"

Everyone in the corridor turned and stared at us. Identical clerks with identical suits and identically parted hair, all gazing with eyes opened wide in astonishment at my outburst. I didn't care.

"How do you get out of this place, anyway?" I snapped. "Why can't they put up signs?"

"There's a *Sortie* sign there," said Francis.

"I wasn't speaking to you!"

"Sorry."

"I can't believe you didn't tell me about the envelope!"

"I was ordered not to!"

"And you always do what you're told!"

"I follow orders."

"I order you to be quiet!"

He did as he was told. I blanked him out. Tears of anger and humiliation blurred my vision as I pushed my way through the corridors, pushed my way past all of the ordered revolutionaries pushing paper for the good of their fellow men, out of the doors, out into the bright sunlight. Wire had settled in a spider web across the wide pavement. There were people dotted around it in clusters, following it back home. My mother was right. People needed lines to follow, people needed direction. People rarely thought for themselves. Who did think for themselves? Our sort of people. No. That wasn't true.

Mr Monagan was waiting by his coffee truck. He waved to us frantically.

"Miss Anna! Mr Francis! Hurry! Into the truck! I'll get you back to safety!"

"Will you? Will you really, Mr Monagan?" I gazed at him, at his open, honest face. Was he too good to be true? "Tell, me, are you a spy, Mr Monagan?"

"Me? A spy?" His lower lip wobbled. "Why would you say that, Miss Anna? All I want to do is help."

"That's very good of you, Mr Monagan. Help who?"

"You, Miss Anna!"

"Why? Why would you want to help me? What are you doing here, Mr Monagan?"

"I've come to collect you."

"My mother said she'd arranged a taxi."

"I was worried about you! I was here, waiting for you!"

That innocent face! Could it possibly be an act?

"Come on, Miss Anna! We need to get off now! The Pierrots will be looking for us!"

I glared at him, trying to make up my mind about him, the sun burning on my head, the people milling around the square. Francis spoke up

"Anna, do you want my opinion?"

"No, not really."

That didn't stop him giving it.

"You saw her, Anna. Your mother wasn't asking for help. There was nothing about her that seemed unhappy with her situation. The only thing that she wanted was for you not to be here."

"Thanks! So you're saying my mother doesn't want me?"

"I wasn't saying that! I was saying that her biggest worry was the fact that you *were* here. Listen, Anna, we've done what we came to do. We've found your mother. We've done what your fortune said. Now it's time to go home."

"What about my father?"

"What about him? Anna, your mother said it: he's gone. He could be anywhere in the Dream World. We don't even know where to start looking. Come on, let's get in the van."

"Stop telling me what to do!"

"I'm not telling you. I'm giving you advice."

"Yeah! You've done your job, you've delivered your envelope. That's what you were really here for, wasn't it?"

"No! The envelope was secondary to the main objective. Protecting you."

"Really? Is that right?"

"Yes! Anna, I know that you're upset, but you don't have to accuse me of lying, too."

I was fed up. Angry, in fact. Everyone knew what was best for me. Everyone had an opinion. Even the bodyguard.

"Why should I believe you?"

"Because it's true," he said. "What are you going to do, Anna? Get me to read your truth script? Tell you what, go on, do it. I'll read it and you can ask me. I've got nothing to hide."

I was already fumbling for my wallet.

"But I'll tell you this…" His gaze travelled to Mr Monagan, then back to me. "You're never going to have real friends if you have to resort to that. You'll never live an adult life while you hope for magic to solve your problems. Magic is for kids who don't want to face up to the hard parts of growing up."

I was already unrolling the script.

"Give me that!" He read it, the light playing on his face. I felt my stomach sinking. I'd made a mistake, and I knew it. I'd held the moral high ground right up until this point. And now, by resorting to this scroll, I'd lost it. But now I'd started I was on stuck on this road...

"Go on then, ask me a question!"

"Whose side are you on, Francis?"

"Yours."

"What did you know about the contents of the envelope?"

"Nothing."

My heart sank.

"Happy now, Anna? Now will you listen to my advice? We should leave now. I really don't think it's wise to stand out here for long. Let's get in Mr Monagan's van and get back to safety."

I felt like a silly little girl, well out of her depth.

"Do you know what, Francis? I'm really not that interested in your advice at the moment."

I shouldn't have been surprised at the anger in his face. I'd called him a liar, I'd forced him to read the truth script. But I should have realised that I wasn't the only one who felt hurt, who wanted to hurt others.

"Look," he said, in his oh-so-reasonable voice. "We're all tired. We've all had some excitement today. This isn't the time."

We're all tired. I hated that. I hated the way he was trying to depersonalise everything. Him, acting so mature, so fucking *adult*, like only he knew how to behave. Him, the sexist pig, the man who didn't have the guts to stand up to his friends. So I did the worst possible thing. I made it personal.

"Listen, Francis, I've just been told by my mother to go away. You'll excuse me if I feel just a little bit pissed off. So I'd really appreciate it if you could do one little thing for me? Could you do that? Yes? Keep your fucking opinions on how to behave to yourself."

"You're shouting," said Mr Monagan, urgently. "People are looking at you."

I ignored him. I was almost oblivious to the crowd of people gathering around us, watching.

"Look at the way you were staring at Dominique this morning! Look at the way you behave around women. And you're a father!"

"What's that supposed to mean?"

"Always looking, flirting, judging. Treating women like objects!"

"No, I don't..."

"Don't pretend you're any different to any other man, Francis. I heard you back at the barracks, that first night I met you. You said that you'd give me one. What was the phrase you used? *Old enough to bleed, old enough to breed*?"

That got him. He blushed. He actually blushed.

"You don't deny it, then?"

He waved his hands, he stammered. Totally out of his depth, unsure what to say.

"Listen... Anna. Look, I'm sorry. I didn't mean for you to... that wasn't for you to hear."

"Obviously."

"I mean, that was just men talking..."

"Oh, yeah. Man talk."

"No. I don't mean that. Well, I mean. Look, I didn't mean it. I was just joining in. You weren't supposed to hear that. I just meant you were an attractive young woman. And you are."

I was icy.

"I'm not defined by my looks. What you said was rude and demeaning and reduced me to nothing more than a sex object."

"I know that. I said I was sorry. And I've never been rude to you, have I?"

"Oh, not to my face! But I wonder about the things you say when you think I'm not listening."

Mr Monagan was looking more and more uncomfortable at this exchange.

"Oh, Miss Anna! I've never heard Mr Francis be anything other than a perfect gentleman!"

"Really? I wonder what Michelle would think if she knew how you'd been behaving?"

That got to him.

"Michelle? What do you mean?" He actually looked worried. Good.

"How do you think she'd feel if she knew about those women on your way here?"

"What are you talking about, Anna?"

That floored me. He'd read the truth script. Wasn't it working?

"Those prostitutes in Dover," I said. I could feel my ground shifting.

"What prostitutes? You mean Mandy and the others?" He laughed. "They were dancers! Why would you think they were prostitutes?"

"You said they were working girls!"

"Yes! They're hard-working girls! They get out and earn, they go where the work is."

"But... you can't blame me for thinking..." The tables were turning. No! I was the one who had been hard done by. "Even so, you were way too familiar with Mandy."

"Too familiar? I'm friendly with everyone. That doesn't mean that I'm unfaithful to 'Chelle. My family means everything to me."

I felt more foolish than ever. I should have left it there, but I was desperate to salvage some pride at his expense.

"So, what do you think of me, Francis?"

"You're very clever, a lot smarter than me. But you're still young. Everything is very black and white…"

"Do you fancy me?"

Why was I doing this? Because I was hurt, and I wanted to hurt everyone else.

"Well. You're an attractive young woman. You've got a great figure…"

"Would you like to sleep with me?"

"Yes."

"Pig!" I was back in control again. I might be immature, but he was a sexist pig.

"Francis," said Mr Monagan, gently. "Do you intend to try?"

"Of course not. Just because I find her attractive doesn't mean I'm going to do anything about it. I love 'Chelle."

"How many women have you slept with?"

"Does it matter? Too many. That was all before 'Chelle."

"You've been faithful to her?"

"Yes"

"Why?"

"I love her."

My face was on fire.

"Stop!" cried Mr Monagan. "Don't say anything more!"

I wished I'd never handed him the script. I wished I'd kept my temper. All I was doing was proving what everyone around me seemed to know. I was still just a naive little kid.

"You didn't want me to come, here did you? Because I was just a girl. You're sexist." I was grasping at straws. It sounded hollow even to me.

"I didn't want you to come because it was clear to me that you were being used. Anna, you're suffering from PTSD, you should be at home being treated."

I shook my head. I didn't want to hear this. I really didn't want to hear any of this. Something dripped onto my front. I touched my face. It was wet. I was crying, and I hadn't even known it.

"Anna," he said, gently. "Can we stop this? It's not doing you any good."

I shook my head. I didn't want to finish like this, looking weak. I scrabbled for something to ask.

"You have lied to me. Tell me now, have you ever killed anyone?"

"Four people."

"Why did you lie about it?"

"No one likes to admit to that."

"But you're a soldier. You were just doing your job."

"That doesn't mean I take pleasure in it. Anna, can we stop this?"

I'd been rejected by my mother, I'd just humiliated myself.

What made it worse was the way they were all so nice about it. They gently led me into the truck and drove me home. I kept my face down, I felt the tears dripping into my hands.

YELLOW

THE MEN IN MY LIFE

LET ME EXPLAIN.

I hadn't really thought about sex. Okay, that's not right. I'd thought about sex, I'd imagined my first time, imagined how it would be. I'd thought about it a lot. The man, the seduction, the place, the time, how everything would just be *right*. But back in Dream London everything was *wrong*. You spent your time wondering if your thoughts were your own, your body sent on flights of lust by the smell of flowers. There was that spicy musk to the air, that aching in the night, that sense of constantly reining yourself in, of not allowing yourself to falter…

And then, back in Mundane London, it was the complete opposite. There, it was an effort just to keep yourself going. The daily grind through the chill damp, trying to stay warm, always feeling hungry. The sense of isolation. That emptiness, that desire to desire.

Again, I was feeling completely alone. My mother didn't want me, Francis had betrayed me. I wanted to be wanted. I wanted someone. Anyone.

And yes, I got carried away. In my mind, I thought I'd go so far, appreciating the attention, and then I'd stop. But I was inexperienced. I didn't know what it would be like. I didn't realise that sweeping wave of excitement would be stronger than my intellect. I thought that I was the master of my body… I suppose it's true, I'm too clinical, I spend too much time living in my head. You do that, you forget that you have a body and your brain rides it. Sometimes, the body just takes over…

OH YES. AND isn't there something special about your first time being somewhere exotic? Out on an adventure, out in the most romantic city in the world. There with a *really* handsome man who knows what he was doing. Do you blame me? More to the point, would have you done otherwise? If you think so, you're either wrong, or a coward.

But this was *my* first time. It's part of the story. It happened like this.

MR MONAGAN PULLED up in the *Place de le Révolution* and turned off the motor. The coffee van shuddered to silence. I stumbled out, into a night filled with billowing stars that rose up and up forever into a deep purple sky, and the silvery sound of a trumpet floated by. I froze, terrified.

"Anna!" said Francis.

"Leave me alone."

I breathed in. I had to face this.

"Anna! You're already upset!"

"Leave her, Mr Francis. She'll be okay here in the square."

"But…"

I pushed their voices from my head. I was fed up with dancing to other people's tunes. The music terrified me. I wasn't going to let it do that anymore. I was going to face up to it.

I pushed my way into the café, into dimness lit only by candles on the tables. The music was coming from the corner. Three figures: a snare and brushes, a double bass and there in front – knees bent, curled around a trumpet – was Luc. Luc, the man from the café that morning. Beautiful, sexy Luc, blowing his soul through the instrument.

He was good. He was very good. Tone, technique, articulation, musicality. All the things that make a great player. The music he was blowing was different. Dream Paris Jazz is different, there is so little American influence. This music had evolved in a different way, only a few melodies had slipped in from our grey world. I listened, half-fascinated, half-terrified. The piece ended and there was a little applause. He noticed me, and that lazy smile was turned in my direction.

"Anna."

"I didn't know it was you. I heard the music from outside. I..."

I was babbling. His amber eyes danced in the candlelight.

"*Un moment.*" He turned to the band, said something in French. They laid down their instruments, picked up their drinks. It was break time.

Luc placed his trumpet carefully in its case and then he was at my side, amber eyes burning.

"Here. We sit down."

He took my arm, led me to a little table.

"Wine?"

I nodded.

He proffered a pack of cigarettes. I shook my head. He shrugged and placed the packet on the table. Someone had brought over a bottle of wine and two glasses. No one had ordered it. I guess it just seemed the obvious thing to do.

"*Où est Francis? Et Mr Monagan?*"

"I don't know. Back at Mr Monagan's flat, I guess."

"And you came here alone?" He nodded, approvingly.

"No! I didn't, I... I heard the music and..."

I was hot all over, sweating. My tongue felt thick, suddenly I couldn't think of anything to say. I was both embarrassed and annoyed with myself. This wasn't me! I didn't act this way!

"Well, you're here. That's good. And how did today go? Did you see your mother?"

"I don't want to talk about it."

He nodded. "I understand."

He poured the wine, picked up his glass and held it up. It glowed ruby red – ripe with the fecundity of the land where the grapes had ripened.

"*Santé*!"

"Cheers!"

We drank. This time the pictures in my mind were not so strong. This time I felt a warmth, deep inside me.

"You look so lost."

"Not lost. I'm fed up with being told where to go."

He understood.

"We all have to go our own way, Anna."

"I know that."

He shrugged and poured a little more wine in my glass.

"Why did you shrug?" I wasn't so annoyed. I thought the shrug charming, so very French. He shrugged again.

"No reason. Why do you think you have to sort things out, Anna? Why do you think you are responsible for everyone?"

I opened my mouth to reply, to say that wasn't true, but I faltered.

"Because..."

He drank a little wine, waved his free hand in an expansive gesture.

"Let it go. Anna! Let it go! Do what makes you feel good. Look at me, I just follow the music. I'm happy."

He pulled a cigarette from the pack, lit it on the candle flame. He exhaled, smoke drifting sensuously from his lips. Oh, I know that's not a good thing, I know that cigarettes are unhealthy, I knew that he was harming my health just smoking near me, but, hell, he looked so *fucking sexy*. The way he narrowed his eyes, that scent on his breath. *Hell, he looked good!*

He sucked again, and his eyes narrowed.

"And what about you, Anna? Do you play?"

"I used to."

"What did you play?"

"The cornet."

"Why did you stop? Were you no good?"

Even lost in that moment, I couldn't stand the thought of being second best.

"I was excellent."

"Then it is a crime that you stop! Here…"

He rose from his seat, went to the stage and fetched his instrument.

"No, I'd really rather…"

"Take it!" He pushed it into my hands. It felt warm and heavy, heavier than I was expecting. The trumpet was old and scratched, but it felt loved.

"What do you think of her?"

"It feels like a really nice instrument."

"Then play her."

"It's not quite the same as a cornet. The mouthpiece…"

"*Bof*! Play!"

I detected the glint of eyes in the darkness. The other customers in the café were looking at us. Looking at me.

I raised the instrument to my lips. I hadn't played for months, not since… well, you know. My embouchure had gone. I blew, and the note that emerged was breathy. I licked my lips, licked the mouthpiece, tasted him. I concentrated, blew again. That was better. Straight down the middle. I played a scale, frowned.

"Good," he said. "You can play a bit."

"I can play better than that," I snapped. The other people in the café were still watching, speaking behind their hands, smiling. They didn't think much of me. And yet I was better than that. I stood up, I was remembering how it was done. And there it was… deep breath, instrument to lips…

I began playing. *Don't know why, there's no sun up in the sky…* Verse. My lips were too tired, I was splitting the high notes. I didn't care. This was better. This was where I was supposed to be… in the moment. Not thinking of the next chord, not reading notes, just playing music. I'd forgotten how it felt to be so free, to just let yourself go and play music, because when I was playing music that's what I was doing. I was playing music…

… and I gradually realised that I'd finished, that everyone in the café was staring at me. Staring at me and applauding.

"*Très, très bon*! You can play!"

"That wasn't just me," I said, looking around. I felt dizzy, half removed from the room. "That was this place. That was Dream Paris. It was playing me…"

"*Non*! It was the other way around! You were playing Dream Paris! You allowed the Dream World into you, you allowed it to go through you, but *you* sent it where *you* wanted it. You sent it through the music. You have the power, Anna. What's more, you have the *balls* to do it!"

"I didn't! I was just feeling the music."

"Feeling the music? You were in touch with the world! No wonder the wine affects you so much. You have the courage to just let go…"

And he leant forward and kissed me. I'd never been kissed like that before. Never like that. He kissed my lips gently, and then I felt one hand touch my hair and he was kissing me more firmly, and I could taste the tobacco, I could taste the wine and I could taste *him* so close to me, the heat of him, the musk of him and it was so wild and reckless that that was the moment I thought, *Well, why not?*

The rest of the café seemed to drift away. I drank wine, I laughed, I looked into those eyes, and I allowed myself to be seduced. I wanted desperately to be seduced. Anything to help me forget this grey confusion, this feeling of rejection. We finished the wine and he led me outside. We kissed in the square, both his hands cupping my face. We kissed outside a doorway and then his hand clasped mine as he led me up a set of stairs and into a little room.

We sat down on the edge of his bed and he began to rub the back of my neck.

"Why are you still so tense?" he asked.

"I didn't think I was."

"Perhaps we should say goodnight?"

"I don't want to do that…"

He was teasing. I laughed, uncertainly.

Fully clothed, we tumbled back onto the bed. We lay on our sides, facing each other. He smiled at me.

"You're very pretty."

I smiled. I felt pretty.

"… but somewhere inside you, you're still all locked up."

"I've had to be."

"You need to trust someone."

"Why? They'll only let me down in the end. Everyone does."

"*Oui*, this is true. But it doesn't matter. The time before that happens is when life is wonderful. This is one of those times."

He placed a hand on my stomach. He bent one strong finger, dragged it over the rough grey material of the dress, dragged it down the side of the abdominal muscle. He ran the finger back upwards, I shivered as he touched the bare skin below my chin.

"Everyone dies in the end," he said. "But that doesn't mean that we give up before we start. It's the same with trust."

Now he ran that finger down me again. I could see the little puckers that his nipples made in the tight material of his shirt. I reached out and touched one, made him gasp. The heat of his body felt so good.

"See?" He said. "There are moments in life that are what life should be. When everyone behaves as humans are meant to be, and nothing else can intrude."

He waved his hand around the faded shabbiness of the room, with its faded wallpaper and trailing fern fronds.

"Now, I want you(2) to take off my trousers…"

The sudden shift in tone, that sudden command, the arrogance!

"Don't speak to (1)me like that," I said, putting all the authority I could into the words.

"Why, Anna? Sometimes you(2) must allow yourself to be led."

"(1)I… I(1)…"

"Shhh, Anna. Let (3)me show you how it's done…"

AND I LAY in the night, relaxed and contented for the first time in months, breathing the strong musky scent of the man who lay beside me.

I didn't know it then, but somewhere in the night the Dream Prussians had begun bombing…

(A FEELING OF FULFILMENT)

THE MORNING AFTER

WE WERE WOKEN by the sound of banging on the door. I heard Francis's voice, raised over a babble of French and English.

Luc rolled from the bed, slowly pulled on his trousers. He was so sanguine that for a moment I thought he might pause to light a cigarette. Me, I was busy trying to keep the sheet modestly around me as I attempted to pull on my dress.

Luc sauntered across the room and opened the door.

"*Quel est le problème?*"

Francis pushed his way in, wire spooling out behind him. "Anna!" he called. "It's your mother! She's been arrested!"

"What? Why?"

Francis didn't answer, he turned around blocking the doorway against the others waiting outside. "Get back! Let her get dressed!"

I was pulling on my dress under the sheet whilst discreetly trying to kick the used condom lying by the bed out of sight.

"Francis, what's going?"

"I don't know. It's like the revolution started for real in the night. There are people out in the streets... Another fleet of Zeppelins arrived in the night, they're dropping bombs..."

"*Silence!*"

Overweight and unshaven and looking as if he'd not slept all night, Jean-Michel Ponge pushed his way into the room.

"Miss Sinfield, I have a warrant for your arrest!"

"What! Why?" I had no time to ask for more details, others were crowding into the room now. Paul was there, speaking to Luc. I caught the word "*Révolution*" mentioned more than once. They were all shouting at each other in French. Everyone seemed to want to claim me, everyone was pointing at me, shouting. Everyone, that is, but Luc, who was pulling on his shirt, slipping on his shoes. Francis was squaring off to Jean-Michel. The scene was descending into a free-for-all. I took a deep breath.

"*Silence!*" I called, with all the authority I could muster. Given that I was semi-naked in a man's bed, I didn't do badly.

Everyone was looking at me.

"Why am I being arrested?" I asked.

"Conspiracy against the State."

"I only came here to find my mother!"

"She too has been arrested for conspiring against the State!"

I looked at Luc for support. Luc, the revolutionary. Luc, who only last night was telling me to express myself, to do my own thing. Luc who had agreed that everyone lets you down eventually. I'd expected him to last longer than a few hours before doing so.

"Sorry, Anna, You cannot fight the *flics*."

"Yes, you can," I said. He said nothing, merely shrugged and went to join Mme Joubert, waiting by the door.

"You're pathetic," I said.

"We will fight when the time is right," he said.

"People are rising in the streets, the Prussians are bombing, and this is not the time to fight?" said Francis, scornfully.

"*Allons*," said Jean-Michel. "We need to leave."

"Can I get dressed first?"

"*D'accord.*"

"It would help if you all left the room."

They slowly withdrew. Francis was the last. He nodded to me before he went.

Five minutes later Francis, Jean-Michel and I were all in a large black car, speeding through the streets of Dream Paris.

OH, AND DID you notice who was missing from the previous little scene?

THE GENTEEL BUSYNESS of the Dream Paris streets had been replaced by something quicker, something tauter, something much more on edge.

There was an atmosphere of a city holding its breath, waiting for the next move. We drove through a square filled with grey- and blue-clad workers – all turning their heads to follow our progress – then out onto a wide boulevard, the shops lining the road empty of customers, abandoned tables and chairs standing outside the cafés.

We drove past a group of people crowding around the black-and-white shapes of three Pierrots. Someone was waving a stick.

Zeppelins thrummed overhead, so low we could see their big yellow bellies almost scraping the rooftops. The people in the upper stories of the buildings looked out of the windows in awe. We hurriedly reversed from a little square where Pierrots lined up in ranks in the middle.

"When did this begin?" I asked Francis, sitting sideways on the seat beside me.

"I don't know. The first I knew anything was wrong was when I felt the ground shaking from the bombs."

"Where were you?"

"Outside your room." He spoke the words matter-of-factly.

"Were you listening?" I felt myself turning crimson, half with embarrassment, half with anger.

"Of course not. But I'm supposed to be guarding you."

There was no judgement in his gaze. I realised that any judgement about last night would come from me, anything I saw in his reaction would just be a reflection of my own feelings. And I didn't feel bad. Quite the opposite.

Jean-Michel was shouting at the driver in French. A wave of people suddenly engulfed the car, running with the flow of traffic. They blocked the light, they rocked the car. I felt my insides shrink: you could hear the anger in their voices. Gradually I realised the anger wasn't directed at us, but rather at something up ahead.

I could smell smoke. The crowd briefly parted and I saw fire up ahead, fire rising up into the sky. A ladder of fire reaching up into the heavens.

"What is it?" I wondered.

"It's a tower," said Francis. "They're burning an Eiffel Tower."

"But why?"

"*Faites demi-tour!*" called Jean-Michel.

The driver was trying to turn the car around. The anger of the crowd had ignited, it burnt so much brighter than before. I turned and twisted in my seat to see what had upset them. They were pointing to the Eiffel Tower. The canvas wrapping that had covered the main structure was burning away and the interior, hidden for all this time, was slowly revealed. And as it was revealed, so the roar of the crowd increased.

"Oh," said Francis. "Look at that. They've been lied to."

"I think we've all been lied to," I said.

A piece of wrapping caught fire, broke free of the tower and rose burning up into the air.

"That *is* what I think it is, isn't it?" said Francis.

"I think so," I replied.

I looked harder. Beneath the wrapper there was nothing more than the skeletal structure of an Eiffel Tower, just like we have back in Mundane Paris. There may have been ants in that tower, I don't know. That wasn't what was agitating the crowd.

What was whipping them into the fury was the colour scheme of the tower itself. Because as the wrapping burned and peeled away and more blue paint was revealed, as more red paint edged in white appeared, it became more and more obvious just who the tower belonged to.

"That's a Union Jack," I said.

"There's more to this than just your mother," said Francis.

I didn't answer. He was clearly right. Over on the horizon I saw another fire flickering around another tower.

THE WEATHER HAD changed. We arrived at the *Grande Tour under grey skies.* Its canvas wrappings snapped and fluttered in the wind. I'd never seen weather like this in a year of living in Dream London. Even the elements seemed to be conspiring in the change.

The *Place du Grande Tour* was empty at the moment. The rebellion was still spreading, I guessed. The final march on the centre of power was still to come.

We got out of the car and hurried across the flags, Jean-Michel at my side, calling out to the scared looking lift attendant.

"*Ouvrez les portes*! *Laissez-nous passer*!"

The wind battered us as the doors closed and we began to rise.

"What have I done wrong?" I asked Jean-Michel, miserably.

The lift doors opened and we hurried down a corridor. I recognised it, I'd been here before. I knew where we were going and I felt my stomach tighten in fear. I knew what lay in wait for us ahead.

We were entering the Star Chamber. I was terrified. *Keep to the walls!*

Jean-Michel was preparing for the big drop. He'd summoned the leaders here. All of them. Mme Joubert and M Duruflé stood by the man who'd been missing from all the events so far: Mr Monagan, the spy. No surprises there. And standing next Mr Monagan I saw Kaolin, beautiful as ever in a yellow-striped gown. And next to her...

"You!" I shouted. "You lying bastard! What are you doing here?"

"Anna!" said Mr Twelvetrees, fly eyes glinting in the light. "Is that you I can hear?"

THREE

OLD FRIENDS

THERE ARE PEOPLE who know how to pull the threads that make other people twitch at their bidding. Francis would like to have thought he was one of them, but he wasn't. He thought he was one of those big extrovert jolly-boy sort of men and he probably was, but that's not enough. You need something extra. I've seen it in men and women. My mother had it, so did Therese Delacroix. There's a type of person who just wants to control. The cream, or the scum is probably a better word, of the rugby-playing, bow-tie-and-dinner-jacket-wearing breed. The perfectly coiffed, power-dining, charity-organising type. The sporty over-achievers with voices that everyone can hear that push themselves to the front of the queue and take control, who want to be in charge for being in charge's sake, never mind if they know what they're talking about. They look down on competence and understanding, thinking it's not as important as networking and bullshitting. Mr Twelvetrees was one such man. I used to look down on people for not standing up to them. I don't anymore. When it came down to it, Mr Twelvetrees was just as adept at controlling me as anyone else.

"It's me you can hear, Mr Twelvetrees. What are you doing here?"

"You've changed," he said. He sniffed the air.

I felt myself blush. Was it that obvious? Then I remembered. He was a sadist.

"Oh, no, Mr Twelvetrees. You know the fortune, You're just making a blind reading, like a psychic. I want to know. What are you doing here?"

"I've come to help. I'm here to demand the freedom of every British citizen held here in Dream Paris."

He declaimed the words loudly, playing to the gallery. Jean-Michel Ponge shook his head, bulldog jowls wobbling slowly.

"I've told you many times, Mr Twelvetrees," he said, "Dream Paris is not holding British citizens against their will."

"Then what about my mother?" I asked.

"Your mother has been arrested for spying."

"She wasn't spying," said Mr Twelvetrees. "Her Majesty's Government has no spies in Dream Paris."

"Margaret Sinfield's citizenship is 'eld by the *Banca di Primavera*," interrupted Kaolin, staking her claim.

"This revolution has nothing to do with me and my mother!" I shouted. "Why don't you just release us both and let us go home? I promise you, I've had enough of Dream Paris."

Mme Joubert interrupted, speaking in rapid French. An argument quickly arose in the room. I noted how Mr Twelvetrees joined in in fluent French.

Jean-Michel Ponge paid close attention, but all the time he was keeping to the edge of the Star Chamber, standing on the raised lip that ran around the outside. I did the same. I was pleased to note the Francis had the sense to join me.

"What's going on?" he asked.

"I don't know. I can hear the words *armée* and *soldat*. I don't think Mr Twelvetrees came alone."

"I certainly didn't, Anna," said Mr Twelvetrees, switching back to English. "There is a relief force waiting just outside the gates of Dream Paris."

"A relief force?" scoffed Jean-Michel. "An army!"

"There are thousands of people who were marched here in captivity from Dream London," said Mr Twelvetrees to Jean-Michel. "You're surely not suggesting that Her Majesty's Government ignore their plight?"

And yet Her Majesty's Government allowed its own people to live in poverty, it allowed them to be imprisoned unfairly all over the world. Her Majesty's Government would stand back and allow the most monstrous injustices to be perpetuated both at home and abroad.

Silly, naive little me. A seventeen-year-old cynic who thought she was wise to the ways of the world, finding out the bitter truth: that teenage cynicism was nowhere near as cynical as the real world.

Her Majesty's Government only took an interest when it was to its own benefit. All governments were the same, and here they all were, moving in on Dream Paris, a city ripe with rebellion and ready for the taking.

"It's not just opportunism, Anna," said Mr Twelvetrees, reading my thoughts. "It's us or them. The Dream World almost took London. Perhaps it will next time. We need to fight back."

Why did we always have to fight? I never had a chance to ask. The argument in French had been continuing. I heard my name shouted out and I looked to see Mme Joubert and Jean-Michel, staring at me with contempt.

"Don't speak about her like that," said Mr Twelvetrees. "She came to rescue her mother, but she did so much more. She helped establish the path between the two cities!"

"That was never my intention!"

He waved a hand.

"Don't be so modest. You're a hero, Anna. You'll probably get a medal for this."

"I didn't know!" I said, seeing the angry gazes of Mme Joubert and the rest.

Mr Twelvetrees just smiled, that smug, complacent smile. They must have been searching through the old documents of London for months, searching for anything useful. No wonder they'd moved so fast when they found my fortune. They knew this was their chance to lay down a path here. I looked at Francis.

"I didn't know, Anna. Honestly, I didn't."

I believed him. He wasn't bright enough to think of this. He was just a grunt, a squaddie. A follower. We were all followers, all of us just pawns to be used by the leaders who arose every twenty years, ready to fuck up the world once more to suit themselves. Why had we been brought here? I knew why the others were here: Jean-Michel was looking at the crowd before him with utter contempt. His hand was close to the switch...

"What about you, Mr Monagan?" I said. "What do you think of all this?"

He looked at me with big innocent eyes.

"I don't know, Miss Anna! I don't know what to make of this!"

"Really? Tell me, whose side are you on, Mr Monagan?"

"Yours, Miss Anna."

Mme Joubert shot him an angry look.

"I thought you were part of the Revolution?" I said.

"All I want is for people to be free to follow their dream, Miss Anna."

"So you'll help me?"

"Yes."

"*I'm* here to help you, Anna," said Mr Twelvetrees. "I've come to take you home, you and all the other British Citizens."

"What about my mother?" I looked at Kaolin.

"Your mother is the property of the *Banca di Primavera*," she said, coolly.

"I'm sure we can come to some arrangement," said Mr Twelvetrees, smoothly. "The British Government and the *Banca di Primavera* are hoping to continue a mutually beneficial relationship." He looked at Kaolin as he spoke.

"What relationship?"

"Property acquisition," said Kaolin. "The British Government 'as been buying land in Dream Paris through us."

I thought of the tower painted in the colours of the Union Jack and I felt sick inside. Sick at how I had been used, sick at the sheer cynicism of what was going on here. Sick at the thought of what Mr Twelvetrees and the rest were to unleash upon London. I looked at Jean-Michel Ponge.

"Pull the lever," I said.

"It will do no good," said Mme Joubert. "Citizen Ponge, I relieve you of your duty. The Revolution is taking control."

Jean-Michel pulled the lever. Nothing happened. He pulled it again. And again.

"Stop that, M Ponge. The *Grande Tour* is now the property of the *Banca di Primavera*," said Kaolin.

"Since when?"

"Since last night, when the latest Revolution began."

Jean-Michel held his hands wide in despair.

"What are the people rebelling against? Themselves? They already own the city!"

"Not so much as they once did. They have been selling it to us."

We hadn't been paying too much attention to the city itself. Seen from this height, the scene was almost peaceful. Almost. You could see more and more wrappings burning on the towers, their true colours shining through. And it wasn't just the Union Jack painted on the towers. Flags of the Dream Nations were sprouting throughout the city.

Kaolin spoke. "The Committee for Public Safety may stand for *Liberté, Egalité* and *Fraternité*, but as you can see, the people prefer to take the opportunities offered by the free market."

Jean-Michel surveyed the scene impassively.

Mr Twelvetrees was getting restless.

"And now, Anna, I think it's time to move. The people of Dream Paris have spoken. They are to be aided in their quest for a new way of life by Her Majesty's Government and the *Banca di Primavera*. Mme Joubert, I think that you should take over here. Perhaps you can arrange for Jean-Michel Ponge to be reassigned to other duties?"

Mme Joubert nodded in acknowledgement.

"Anna," continued Mr Twelvetrees, "why not accept a lift to the Bastille? I intend to begin negotiations for the release of your mother."

I looked at him, fly eyes glowing, and I felt a shiver of revulsion. I didn't care that he was offering to help me, I wanted nothing to do with him. I looked across the room.

"Mr Monagan?"

"Yes, Miss Anna?"

"You promised to help me."

"Whatever I can do, Miss Anna."

"Will you stop Mr Twelvetrees from following us when we leave here?"

"Of course."

Francis had been following the conversation with an increasingly unhappy expression. He perked up at that.

"Are we going now, Anna?"

"We are."

"Now hold on, Anna," began Mr Twelvetrees. Mr Monagan stepped forward and took hold of his arm, orange froggy fingers sinking into the fine weave of his jacket.

"Take your hand off me, you filthy frog! How dare you touch me?"

"I'm sorry, sir! Miss Anna requested that I hold you."

"I thought you couldn't see," said Francis.

"I can't." Mr Twelvetrees frowned. "Why do you think otherwise?"

"How did you know Mr Monagan was a frog?"

"I'm not a frog!"

"I didn't know he was a frog!"

Ah! It was casual racism. There you go.

"Mr Twelvetrees, I'm leaving here. I'm playing no further part in your games."

Mr Twelvetrees pulled out his big silver watch and felt the face.

"You're free to do what you wish, Anna. *Everyone* is. This city is no longer ruled by the Committee for Public Safety. But you should trust me. Who else can have your mother freed…?"

He heard it first. Maybe his hearing was more sensitive than ours, given his blindness, but now we heard it too. The faint whistling, followed by the *crump, crump, crump* of yet more bombs falling.

"They're getting closer," said Francis.

We rushed to the windows to look out over the city, and I felt my heart judder at the suddenness of the sight, the imminence of the Zeppelin that hung just before the window, almost as if it were looking at us.

"Where did it come from?"

"What are they bombing?"

Down below, the river had burst its banks. I saw the black and white shapes of mosasaurs being swept through the streets.

"Biological warfare," said Jean-Michel Ponge, unable to keep the satisfaction from his voice. "The Prussians are attacking your men, Mr Twelvetrees."

(A FEELING OF SETTING OUT ON A JOURNEY)

THE BASTILLE

I WAS THERE at the end of Dream London. I was there at the end of Dream Paris.

If you were to ask me what both events had in common, I'd say it was this: no one really knew what was going on.

I'm sure that it's always been like that. I knew they say that history is written by the victors, but I think there's so much more to it than that. The whole idea that *anyone* really plans the eventual outcomes, or that events can be reduced to a story, is an illusion people give themselves. You could see it in the face of Mr Twelvetrees, that brief flicker of betrayal; you could see it in Mme Joubert's haughty disdain. You could see it in the world-weariness of Jean-Michel Ponge. All three had sought to control events. All three had been betrayed.

Only Kaolin's china face remained impassive, as it must.

The shuddering of the bombs grew louder.

"I can't see," said Mr Twelvetrees. "Tell me, why are they attacking?"

"Isn't it obvious? The Prussians don't want the British taking Dream Paris," said Kaolin.

"And what about you?" asked Francis.

"The *Banca di Primavera* treats all its clients impartially."

"Miss Anna? Mr Francis? May I suggest we leave the tower? We may be a target."

"Where shall we go?"

The situation was changing by the moment, there were no friends or enemies here, I realised. Only opportunities. I looked at Mr Twelvetrees.

"You said you could have my mother released."

"I can."

"If you're lying to me... "

If he was lying I'd what? I don't know.

"I'm not lying."

I looked at Francis.

"Let's go to the Bastille."

WE SQUEEZED INTO the lift. Me, Francis, Mr Monagan, Kaolin, Mr Twelvetrees, Mme Joubert, Jean-Michel Ponge. The sudden appearance of the Zeppelin had changed the group dynamic. No one knew who was in charge any more.

"We can take my carriage," said Kaolin.

There it was, waiting in the unnatural calm outside the pylons of the *Grande Tour*.

"It's a prison van," said Francis.

It looked like a castle on wheels, from the crenellations around the top to the thick portcullis of the radiator grille. The words *Banca di Primavera* and *Bastille* were painted in big gold letters on the side. The rear door had been lowered on chains like a drawbridge.

"Were you expecting trouble today?" I asked Kaolin.

We took our places on the velvet chairs, and we were off. Mr Monagan pressed his face to the little grille at the back, looking out.

"What can you see?" asked Jean-Michel.

"Nothing. The streets are empty."

We swayed back and forth with the movement of the carriage.

"You don't see very happy, Anna."

Mr Twelvetrees sat back in his seat, perfectly at ease. If he was still upset at the actions of the Dream Prussians, he was concealing it.

"You used me," I said. "You all used me."

"You're getting what you want. Your mother freed and both of you returned home to London. Play this right, Anna, and you'll be very well rewarded. You're an intelligent young woman, you've been to Dream Paris. Her Majesty's Government could make use of you."

"What? So I could be like you?"

He smiled. So did Mme Joubert.

"What's so funny?"

"You're already like me, Anna. Like it or not, we're both the same. We have different brains, you know, the people like us who take charge. They've done studies on monkeys. Monkeys at the top of the hierarchy have more developed regions in certain parts of their brains. I don't know if we're born this way, or if the brain grows according to experience, but people like us are made to lead."

I looked at Francis, mute in the corner of the carriage. Francis wasn't a leader. Francis waited to follow.

"I'm nothing like you, Mr Twelvetrees," I said.

"Oh, don't be like that, Anna. You're a survivor, just like me." He pointed to his eyes. "Do you know why I look like this?"

"Something you ate?"

"No. I was caught in the web of a Dream Spider, back in Dream London. Do you know about them?"

Francis was looking at me. I knew what he was thinking. He'd remembered, just as I had.

"We have a spider here with us," I said. "One of them is riding Francis."

"You spotted that? I thought you would. The Dream Spiders spin their webs throughout the Dream World. People don't see the webs – I suppose a fly never sees a spider's web."

That made sense.

"The Dream Webs are clever. Most things pass straight through them, the spiders sieve their prey from the world. A Dream Spider must have thought I was prey, it caught me."

"That was unlucky," I said. I didn't mean it.

"It wasn't. It was my fault. I was allowing myself to be prey. I allowed myself to become the fly. Look at me!"

"I am looking. How did you escape?"

"I remembered who I was. I stopped acting like prey. I took charge. I took a knife and I cut the webs and I cut myself free. Sadly, it was too late to save my eyes."

"Good for you."

"Yes, good for me. Later I thought on how I could put that Dream Spider to use. A line that stretches on forever, one that only becomes tangible to those who wish to return home…"

"I don't see how that makes me like you."

"We're both survivors. We're both clever."

And he was clever, thinking of using a spider like that, using it to lay down a path here.

Francis spoke up.

"The spider is feeding on me, isn't it?"

"Yes," said Mr Twelvetrees.

I shuddered.

"You bastard."

"Francis is a soldier. He knew when he agreed to accompany you here he was carrying untested equipment. He knew there was a risk."

"You bastard."

He smiled. He was a sadist. He was enjoying this.

"Why are you so upset, Anna?"

Kaolin's voice sounded like someone tapping a cup with a teaspoon. Sharp and impersonal.

"Why am I upset, Kaolin? Do you think it right, what's happened to Francis?"

"These are the terms Francis agreed to when 'e signed up for the job. Were you lied to, Francis?"

"No…"

"But…" I began. Kaolin spoke over me.

"When people regret the choices they make, they often blame those who offered the choice."

"*Exactement*!" said Mme Joubert.

"I know that contracts often favour one side unduly. My mother didn't choose to go to the workhouse."

Kaolin tilted her head, just a little.

"You think your mother is the innocent party here? You know whose name is on the contract she signed with us?"

"No. Whose?"

Kaolin didn't answer.

Mme Joubert said something in French.

"What's that?" asked Francis.

Jean-Michel rubbed his stubbly chin, he looked up with those hangdog eyes.

"She said that Mr Twelvetrees is right. The aristocracy is born to lead."

I couldn't believe what I'd heard.

"How can she say that! She's a revolutionary!"

"But of course! She seeks to overthrow the people's republic and restore the aristocracy. Her great grandmother held the title of Comtesse de Ségur."

"As do I!" she declared haughtily.

Mr Monagan spoke up excitedly.

"We're here," he said.

THE DRAWBRIDGE DESCENDED. A welcoming committee of porcelain-faced dolls were lined up on either side of the road.

"Welcome to the Bastille," said Kaolin.

I walked out into the shade of high walls. We were in a wide, deep courtyard, flagged in yellow stone. Narrow windows looked down at us from all sides.

"How did the *Banca di Primavera* come to own this place?" I asked.

"We don't own it. We run it," said Kaolin.

"They let a bank run a prison?"

"Who better than a *Banca* to manage debts, and what is a prison but a place where people repay their debt to society?"

Two Pierrots appeared. They locked handcuffs around Jean-Michel's wrists.

"Where are you taking him?"

"To the holding cells."

"What's he done?"

"That's to be determined. At the moment, the Committee for Public Safety do not run the city. The *Révolution* currently holds command. This may be subject to change. Mme Joubert, I think you may wish to discuss matters?"

"*D'accord*!" She nodded to me. "*A bientôt, Anna.*"

And at that she followed Jean-Michel and the Pierrots off through an archway.

"Wondering if you made the right choice in helping the Revolution, Anna?" asked Mr Twelvetrees.

I was, but I wasn't going to admit that to him. We made our way through a smaller gate into a wider courtyard beyond. Again, barred windows looked down from the high walls on every side.

"The rehabilitation area occupies most of the interior," said Kaolin. "Our offices are located in the outside walls for the most part. Our clients prefer natural sunlight."

"I'm sure the prisoners would, too."

"The prisoners are entitled to put the cost of better living quarters on their debt," said Kaolin. "The *Banca di Primavera* is not immoral."

No, I thought, you're amoral. That can be a whole lot worse.

Two prisoners walked towards us wearing neat silk clothes trimmed in yellow and white checks. Prisoners, I guessed. But clearly prisoners paying a little extra for comfort. Their uniforms were edged with lace, their hair extravagantly trimmed and coiffed. They smelt of lavender.

"*Bonjour, (2)Madame Kaolin*," said one, but his full attention was on me. He was turning up his charm, turning the full force of his personality in my direction. "*Et bonjour, mademoiselle(5)!*"

"Leave it, you nonce," said Francis.

"You're(5) English?" said the man. "I didn't realise the young ladies(5) of England were so pretty!"

And the spell broke. I hadn't matched wits with a talking veal cow to have someone like this call me a young lady(5).

"(6)We're not only pretty, but very smart, too. What are you(6) in for? Statutory rape?"

He smiled at that.

"Ah! Such fire! Would that (5)I had met you(5) eight years ago! (5)I could have taught you(5) to be a French Lady. The price you(5) could have commanded!"

"What *are* they in for?" I asked Kaolin.

"Careful, Anna," said Mr Twelvetrees. "The *Banca* will give you anything you desire, but it will charge you."

"I don't intend to charge Anna, Mr Twelvetrees," said Kaolin. "Our best customers are entitled to rewards for banking with us. M Duchamps took out a loan on the charm and accoutrements needed to build up his business. 'e proved very successful in recruiting young women and girls to his cause. Alas, 'e did not prove so successful at accountancy."

"Figures bore me," said M Duchamps. "Who would spend their time looking at books when he could be living? Don't you think, young lady, that the biggest sin is to have regrets?"

"What?" I said "Bigger than acting as a pimp for paedophiles?"

He gave a rueful smile.

"You make it sound like a bad thing."

I'd seen Francis do this before, explode from calm affability into vicious, concentrated action. The punch landed hard in the man's stomach: a glorious blow, every ounce of his weight behind it. A textbook example of how to inflict maximum pain. It was followed by two good kicks to the side. Normally I'm against violence, but I thought Francis had judged this one about right.

"That's enough," said Kaolin. "M Duchamp is guaranteed a certain amount of protection when in here."

M Duchamp was heaving up thin gruel on the pavement.

We stepped over him and walked on across the courtyard. A metallic creaking sounded from a doorway to our right.

"That doesn't sound healthy," said Francis.

"That's where the bad machines are punished," said Kaolin.

"Bad machines? How can a machine be bad?"

"A machine can be bad on a regular basis, without rest. Some are built that way. Some choose to be bad."

Kaolin made no further comment.

There was a guillotine erected at the centre of the square, sunlight flashing from the edge of the blade.

"A guillotine? How do you make a profit from someone when they are dead?"

"The bodies are worth something. Plus, the Committee for Public Safety pay us thirty-five Dream francs for each execution."

We walked through a door, the shade beyond a welcome relief. I blinked at the coloured lights before my eyes, trying to focus on where I was stepping. Kaolin led us down a set of stairs.

"You're holding my mother in the dungeon?"

Mr Twelvetrees laughed.

"You should be proud of her, Anna. Your mother has proven herself to be a very difficult woman to hold onto."

We went deeper and deeper underground. As Mr Twelvetrees explained, the dungeon wasn't a cruel place. The *Banca di Primavera* didn't have that much interest in its capital. Instead, the dungeon was a place of ordered efficiency, its inmates offered the exact amount of light or space or food or water allowed by the terms of their imprisonment.

Finally we came to the cell that held my mother.

"Open the door," said Mr Twelvetrees.

"No," said Kaolin. "If you wish to be assured that all is in order you may examine the debt through the window. When you are satisfied, we can discuss terms."

"I think Anna should have the honour," smarmed Mr Twelvetrees.

I looked through the hatch and saw my mother sitting up on a bed, reading a book.

"Mother!" I called.

Kaolin slid the hatch shut.

"Communication is extra."

"Is everything in order?" asked Mr Twelvetrees.

"She's fine," I snapped.

"Then I think we can discuss terms."

"Very well."

It was impossible for Kaolin to smile. Even so, there was something smug about her posture. "What are you offering?"

Mr Twelvetrees had an answer ready.

"Selected property in Dream London."

"Dream London is mostly gone. We would wish for property in London itself."

"That could be arranged."

"No!" I couldn't believe what I was hearing. "You can't be serious! You can't be thinking about letting them back in again! Remember what happened last time?"

Mr Twelvetrees raised a hand. *Calm down, dear!*

"Anna, this is perfectly normal business practice. We shall be seeking to establish premises in Dream Paris, too."

"I'm sure that's what they said last time! Mr Twelvetrees, you can't be serious! You can't let the Dream World in again! It will take over."

"Last time we were caught off-guard. This time the incursion will be controlled. Besides, we need to do this. How else will we get our people back home?"

"No! This isn't right!"

"You'd sacrifice your mother for the sake of your principles? I'm only trying to secure her release."

"No you're not! You're just looking for an advantage! You don't care about my mother, *or* the people trapped in Dream Paris. This is all just an excuse to exercise power. Jean-Michel was right! Anyone who shows the slightest inclination to be a leader should be taken to the Star Chamber and left to fall to their deaths."

He smiled again, maddeningly, infuriatingly.

"I imagine that's quite a novel thought when you're

seventeen. Open the door, Kaolin. Let her out. I'm sure that Margaret should be involved in these negotiations."

Kaolin opened the door. My mother was waiting, dressed in a dark business suit, looking as if she'd just arrived for a day's work at the office, not as if she'd spent the night in prison.

"Anna," she said, nodding to me. "Now, Kaolin, Mr Twelvetrees. Shall we begin negotiations? We have a city to save, and time is of the essence."

"You're going to help them?" I said. Francis put a hand on my arm. The person who turned to me wasn't my mother. It was Margaret Sinfield, hard-headed business woman, who spoke to me now.

"Anna, how many times have I told you? This is where I want to be."

"But –"

"Mr Monagan, Francis. Would you be so good as to escort my daughter safely back to England?"

Mr Monagan took my other arm. He and Francis gently escorted me up the stairs, back to the daylight, back to a city that was shaken by bombs, filled with British troops, a city that was rocked back and forth by rebellion.

I didn't care anymore. I'd had enough. I wanted to go home.

BLUE

THE HANGING

"Where are we going?" asked Francis.

"I told you. We're going home."

"I know, but how do you suggest we get there? The city is at war."

As he spoke, a dark shadow cut across the courtyard. We looked up to see the yellow shape of a Zeppelin diving towards some not-too-distant target.

"I know a way, Miss Anna!"

Of course Mr Monagan knew a way.

"There is a café at the north side of the *Place de la Bastille*. I'll meet you there with my coffee truck."

"And then?"

"We'll head for the West Gate…"

He turned and ran, through a gate in the opposite wall of the courtyard, almost knocking over a prisoner coming the other way.

"But he's a spy," reminded Francis.

"I know. But so far he's the only person who's not suggested anything I actually disagree with."

We marched through the centre courtyard to the Bastille's wide gate. A small door was set in it, guarded by two Pierrots.

"Let us through," I demanded.

They looked at each other.

"*It's not safe out there.*"

"We choose to take the risk. Let us pass."

They opened the door, and we stepped into a world of smoke and screams, of the clash of metal and the shudder of bombs.

Despite my fear, I did what Francis had told me to do: I took the time to tune in, to seek my bearings.

The Bastille sat at the focus of a star of wide boulevards, the surrounding buildings set well back as if they had recoiled from the prison in horror. The perimeter of the space was crowded with people, the citizens and refugees of Dream Paris, pressing into the cheap cafés and market stalls that surrounded the *Place de la Bastille*. They were angry, shouting insults at each other. A handful of blue caped *flics* ran for their lives, their colleagues left curled up on the ground, protecting their heads from the feet of the revolutionaries surrounding them. No one was interested in the Bastille. Yet. That was probably just as well. So far, we remained unnoticed.

"Which way?" asked Francis.

"That way's north," I said, pointing. "At least, I think it is. We'll head for the café. Hopefully, Mr Monagan will be there."

"Anna, I'm still trailing a wire behind me."

"It barely shows now, Francis. Besides, there's so much wire around now, and people are so distracted…"

There was a high-pitched shriek and a whoosh.

"Missile!" shouted Francis, throwing himself on me, pushing me to the ground.

I heard the roar of engines. The Zeppelin, water spilling from its sides onto the yellow cobbles, yawed wildly as it tried to gain height.

"It's trying to get away."

A rose bloomed on the side of the Zeppelin, and I had the sense of movement... A blast of heat washed across us, drying my eyes. I pulled Francis to his feet and we began to run, feet hard against the cobbles, ankles twisting. The great shape of the Zeppelin was falling, burning, flame running across the yellow skin, a growing shadow on the ground beneath it. On and on we ran, plunging into the mass of people, reaching the edge of the *Place*, turning down one of the wide boulevards, Francis pulling me to the walls, pulling me sideways down an alley, out of the path of any explosion and then at last we stopped, leaning against a wall, gasping for breath.

"Missile," panted Francis. "That was a missile. Army. British Army."

"This isn't a rescue! It's an invasion!"

"Anna, we could make contact with the British troops. I could get new orders."

I didn't like that idea.

"Is that what you want to do?"

"My first orders are to protect you."

I knew that too. I was using Francis, dragging him with me away from his fellow soldiers. Probably putting him in more danger. And yet, what the Army was doing was wrong. Wasn't it? I wasn't sure any more. I'd abandoned my mother, turned down safe passage home. Now I was wandering through a city under attack, all because of my principles. I didn't even know what my principles were any more...

"Francis, I don't know what to do."

I was crying. There, in the middle of the chaos, in the middle of the noise, the washes of heat, the droning and the whistling, Francis held out his arms. I stepped into them and he hugged me.

"There's nothing wrong with that, Anna," he said. "Everyone feels like that sometimes."

"Not me," I said. "Not me."

"Why not you?"

"I played the trumpet. I cured myself."

"I think you're confusing Dream Paris with Fairy Land. Anna, you're one of the bravest, most competent people I've ever met. But that doesn't mean you're never going to need help."

I couldn't answer that.

"Come on," he said, gently. "We need to move. We need to keep to the edge of the trouble. That way people are less likely to notice us."

"But where are we going?"

Francis thought.

"Downhill. That will take us to the river. We can follow it downstream to the gate."

WE MADE OUR way through the city, always heading downwards. Down alleys, the walls pasted with peeling cartoon posters, running with crowds along wide boulevards, plunging down side streets to get away from the barricades set up by the *flics*, creeping through tall arches decorated with graffiti. Always keeping our heads down, trying our best not to be noticed.

It couldn't last. We were rushing down a long cobbled road, heading for a tiny five-road intersection, when we were spotted. A big man with a blue chin had been walking beside us for some time. He kept examining me, kept looking at Francis, looking behind us, looking at the wire. I pretended to ignore him. Down the hill we marched, heading for the intersection, heading for the point where we could choose a different road and part company.

Too late.

The man spoke in French, too rapid for me to follow. I

ignored him, marched on. He repeated himself. The intersection was getting closer. If we just kept walking... but no. The man spoke again. He reached out, took hold of me.

"Let go of her!" called Francis, pulling me away. That was it. Everyone was looking in our direction now. Francis took my hand, began to pull us along, but the word was spreading through the crowd, a gradual crescendo of chatter. And then they moved in and pulled us apart, they pulled my arms up behind my back.

"*Anglaise*!"

"*Espion*!"

"Anna!"

A man staggered backwards and I saw Francis, his fists raised. He punched a woman, hard, the full weight of his body behind the blow. His elbow snapped back into a stomach, he stamped down on an instep. He was serious, he was deadly. This was Francis the fighter. But another woman flung an arm around his throat, pulled him backwards, someone kicked him hard in the balls and then he was lost in the melee.

More hands grabbed hold of me, my arms, my legs. Someone groped at my breasts, another hand grabbed at my backside. I was pulled this way and that, shouting on every side.

"Francis!" I called. "Francis!"

I could hear nothing but French, I could feel hands pulling me in every direction. My dress ripped, my right arm was wrenched in the socket and for one icy moment I thought they were going to try to tear me apart. And then a consensus seemed to develop, all at once, and suddenly the crowd opened up ahead of me and I was being dragged into the gap, dragged down the street, trying to keep my feet, slipping, grazing a knee, being pulled back up, a stabbing pain in my right shoulder.

Onwards, pulled through an endless sea of bodies. I thought I felt rain, until I realised they were spitting on me, calling out names. Flames burst in the sky; I didn't care, I was too busy trying to keep my feet. The level of noise rose, the shouting, the screaming, the boos, the catcalls. Someone was beating a drum, and somewhere ahead I heard a sudden cheer and a burst of applause. The rattle of the snare, a continuous military tattoo. The feel of the ground beneath my feet changed and I realised I was being dragged over grass, pulled along a strip of grass between trees. There was something hanging from the trees, and I cried out in terror. My captors laughed at my reaction; one of them reached out and groped me once more.

"*Eh, espion?*"

They turned me so I could get a better view of the bodies hanging from the trees. Men, women and children, bodies still swinging, still being spat at and pelted by stones.

"I'm not a spy!" I screamed. "I'm on your side! I want to help!"

They laughed, they jeered, they pulled me onwards, heading towards the sound of drums, the crowd parting to let us through… And I saw our destination and I almost lost it completely.

I was being pulled to a group of prisoners, surrounded by guards with guns. Men, women and children, looking around wide-eyed with terror. A revolutionary wearing a grubby blue scarf pointed to a woman with red hair. She shook her head, tried to back away, but the man in the scarf grabbed her and pulled her from the group.

The hangman was waiting for her, stripped to the waist and wearing a leather hood, his pasty skin glossy with sweat. The hangman asked a question, the woman's reply was lost in the jeers of the crowd. I watched as they tied one end of a rope around the struggling woman's neck, the other end was thrown over a branch of a tree.

"Please! I'm not a spy! I just want to go home."

She was English. Half-starved, no doubt marched from the workhouse to Dream Paris. About to be hanged because people like Mr Twelvetrees had decided that Britain's interests would be best served by forging closer alliances with this city. The hangman turned to the crowd, held a hand to his ear. They cheered louder. The drums suddenly stopped, and the big man pulled on the rope, hand over hand, hauling the woman into the air. The sun dappled the space below the leaves, it dappled the woman as she kicked and choked. They tied the other end of the rope around the trunk and then immediately forgot about her. They left her to die unnoticed whilst they chose their next victim. My guards shouted, they pointed to me and I was dragged forward...

And then there was a disturbance in the crowd. Francis! He'd broken free! He was a soldier, he knew how to fight. When I saw the flash of orange at his side the relief was so great I almost laughed. Mr Monagan! He was there too! Mr Monagan, who always turned up when he was needed. He was holding a large gun with a flared barrel and I watched as he took aim and fired. The rope holding up the red haired woman snapped, and she fell to the ground.

"Miss Anna! I'm coming!"

"Mr Monagan! Mr Monagan!" I was crying, tears of joy.

And then someone swung a stick at the back of his orange head and knocked him to the ground.

"No!"

The crowd fell on Mr Monagan, they kicked and punched him, they tied his hands and feet and dragged him to the leather-hooded hangman. Another length of rope was brought forward and somehow tied around his neck.

"No!" I shouted. "*No!*"

Mr Monagan had not stopped speaking during all of this time, his voice drowned out by the crowd. I could imagine his calm, reasonable tones, I imagined him explaining that this wasn't helping anyone, I imagined him asking to be released so he could go back and sell his insipid coffee. Whatever it was he was saying, it wasn't working. It took two men to pull him up into the air, but they managed. Mr Monagan kicked and kicked, and the crowd loved it.

And then it was my turn. They seized my hands, they pulled them up behind my back and tied them so tightly I felt the blood swelling at the wrists.

The hangman leaned forwards. I saw brown eyes behind the leather hood. I smelled his sour breath as he rasped:

"Any last words, *espion*?"

"I'm not a spy! Ask Jean-Michel Ponge! Ask Mme Joubert! I was trying to help!"

He laughed and then I felt the rope being pushed over my head, I felt the knot next to my ear, the scratchy feel of the coconut hair. I felt it pulling, stretching my neck...

"*Arrêtez!*"

Someone was shouting stop! I was on tip toes, the rope pulling me up...

"*Arrêtez!*"

There it was again! Why wasn't anyone listening? I was pulled into the air and I couldn't breathe. My feet were kicking of their own accord, I was spinning back and forth, I saw jeering faces, dapples of sunlight spinning this way and that. I heard gunfire, I saw the crowd surging...

I tumbled to the ground, fell on my side, the rope still too tight. I couldn't breathe. The jeering crowd was scattering, running from the men and women with dark faces, thin faces, dirty faces that were coming through the trees in good order. An army, carrying rifles. But which army? Whose side were they on?

I didn't care. Someone cut the rope from around my neck, freed my hands. I saw them cutting down poor Mr

Monagan's body.

A hand gently took mine and I jumped.

"Anna! It's okay."

The hand tightened around mine. It was Francis, his voice hoarse.

"Oh, Francis!"

"I know."

He hugged me. I hugged him.

TWO

THE NORTH TOWER

SEEN FROM THE altitude of the Ballroom Suite of the North Tower, Dream Paris seemed like the perfect city. The carefully planned boulevards, the way the sun reflected from the golden domes, the green copper of the roofs, the turquoise blue of the Seine…

Down on the streets, of course, it was a different story. The Army of the Dispossessed had taken control. For the moment, at least. They ensured that the food that was suddenly rolling into the city was shared out equally; they were rehousing those made homeless by the fighting, those who had lost their homes when the Zeppelins had crashed to the ground. And they were finding homes for those who previously had none.

They patrolled the streets, herding the mosasaurs back to the river and sealing the breaches in the walls. They disarmed the few soldiers of Mr Twelvetrees' army who were still hiding in the city and sent them on their way.

And for those people who wanted to return home, for those who wanted to return to places like London, the Army of the Dispossessed fed and clothed them, they showed them the wire, they gave them advice on following it back.

Of Mr Twelvetrees, there was no sign.

Nor of Mr Monagan. One moment his body had been lying in the park, the next it was gone.

"I wonder how long he could hold his breath?" Francis had said.

"Long enough," I said. *I hope*, I thought.

Francis was sat on a stool in the corner of the room, bent over against the weight of his backpack. He was in pain, I could tell. Count von Breisach had promised to fly us as close as he could to home the next morning.

"Perhaps, once you're back in the Mundane World, you'll be able to take the pack off."

"I hope so," said Francis, with feeling. "So, how does it feel to be the hero of Dream Paris?"

"Don't say that, Francis. It's not true."

"Jean-Michel Ponge thinks it is. You fed the homeless. You raised the Army of the Dispossessed."

"No I didn't. I gave my meal ticket to a hungry family."

And that was it, I was being written into the story. First I was to be the hero of the British for laying down the path here from Dream London. Then I was to be the hero of the Revolution for finding my mother. Now I was the Anna, who had raised an army with a few fish and a couple of loaves of bread. People were saying that I'd been in league with the *terroir* all along. When I'd given my meal ticket to the woman in the market, I'd provided a way for the farmland that surrounded Dream Paris to take control of the city.

None of it was true. None of it was planned. It just turned out that way and it was convenient for all that I be labelled a hero.

I watched Francis, chatting to a glamorous woman who simply oozed Dream Parisienne style. Her long dark hair was tied up in a chignon, her dark green silk dress followed the elegant curves of her body. Francis would always chat up women, but he didn't mean anything by it. I could appreciate that now.

Jean-Michel came up to me, as lugubrious as ever. He'd shaved, though his chin was already blue with stubble. His shirt looked a little better pressed than usual.

"Anna! You can't stand by the window all day. Come and meet my wife!"

"Your wife?" I couldn't keep the surprise from my voice. I'd never thought of Jean-Michel doing anything but his job, but now he was leading me, to my great surprise, to the elegant lady that Francis was chatting to.

"Anna, I'd like you to meet my wife, Isabelle."

She was taller than Jean-Michel, and I noted the way she looked down at her tubby little blue-chinned husband with an amused smile.

"Isabelle, meet Anna, the spy."

I shivered. "Don't say that. Not after what happened. I was never a spy!"

Jean-Michel shrugged. I had been a spy, we both knew it, albeit an unwitting one.

Isabelle took my arm. "Don't listen to him. He can never leave his work at the office."

It took me a moment to register her accent.

"You're English," I said.

"That's right. From Leeds."

"What are you doing here?"

"I used to work for the *Banca di Primavera*. I met Jean-Michel when I was transferred to the Dream Parisian branch."

I looked at Jean-Michel in amazement. Jean-Michel was short and stocky with a bulbous nose and drooping, sad eyes. He wasn't exactly ugly, but this beautiful woman was clearly way out of his league.

"He makes me laugh," said Isabelle, guessing my thoughts.
"Jean-Michel?"

She gave that amused smile again.

"Come over here, and meet some of the other expats. We're all married to Dream Parisians. We have nothing else in common but that, but it's enough."

She took me to a little group of people, all holding drinks and chatting. Count von Breisach was there.

"Anna!" he said. "I was just telling the group about you. How you saved Dream Paris."

"Please don't say that. I don't want the credit – or the blame – for what happened here."

"People want a hero."

"Not me. If the Army of the Dispossessed had arrived two minutes later, I'd be dead and this conversation would not be taking place."

"You're too modest," said an oriental woman holding a glass of champagne. "The Count was telling us how brave you were at the Dinner. How you ate all manner of things simply to infiltrate Madame Joubert's revolution."

"I didn't! I didn't know what I was doing!"

"Of course you didn't!" said the Count, and then he gave a broad wink for all to see.

"Clever of you to hook up with the Germans," said another man. "How did you know they were arming the homeless?"

I hadn't. I hadn't known anything about the plots and counter-plots that were taking place in this city. I doubted I yet knew about most of them. The only thing I could understand was that the surrounding cities wanted to maintain the status quo. They didn't want Dream Paris falling into the hands of the British, or anyone else.

"I lost half my fleet to the British," said the Count, ruefully. "I've never seen anything like those rockets they carried.

We're trying to develop them ourselves now, of course."

I smiled, I tried to appear relaxed, but all I could think of was *what have I done?* I'd come to rescue my mother, in the end I'd just helped to prolong a battle that had been fought for centuries. For millennia. Funny that, I'd marched for what was right in Dream London and I'd been forgotten. Here, I'd been nothing but an unwitting pawn and I was treated like a hero.

I heard a voice at my shoulder.

"Excuse me. May I borrow Anna from you?"

I turned and saw M Duruflé, beautifully dressed in dove grey, his beard neatly trimmed to a point.

"Hello, Alain," I said. "And in what capacity are you appearing here today?"

"*Logicien et Immortel de l'Académie Française,*" he said, beaming.

"I've heard you mention that before. What is that?"

"The charge of the *Immortels* is to work with all the care and all possible diligence to make the French Language pure, eloquent and able to treat the arts and sciences."

"Ah."

"I see that you aren't too impressed. Perhaps you don't understand. It is the Academy that developed the Dream relative pronouns, the *(5)*vous and *tu(3)* forms. You took part in the *Grand Dîner*. You defeated a Veal. You should by now realise that power lies in being able to say *mine*. Claiming something for yourself, saying that your needs are greater than others."

"Maybe here in the Dream World!"

"And in your own world. I believe in your land you're told that you're subjects of the monarch?"

"That's just convention!"

"Really? Perhaps you could learn something from the mosasaurs. They say *(17)mine*. That's all they do. All they are. They've survived 65 million years by never doubting for a moment that the world is theirs."

I gazed at him.

"But all this talk is making me thirsty. More wine? Or perhaps a little champagne? Or maybe some cheese. I see all the *terroirs* are making themselves known today."

I saw what he meant. A circular ring of tables was set out at the centre of the room, laden with cheese and meats, vegetables, shellfish, pies and pastries, sweets and souffles, wine and spirits and all of the produce of France, a pleasant reminder of one of the new powers at large in the city.

"I'm okay," I said. I'd eaten a little bread and cheese, just for hunger's sake. I wasn't ready to turn my body into a battleground just yet. Besides, there was something I needed to know.

"And what about the Revolution? Are you no longer a member of the Mme Joubert's plot to overthrow the Committee for Public Safety?"

"Oh, I am still a member."

I paused, weighing up my words.

"And Luc...?"

"He is there, too. In prison, I mean. You are welcome to visit him."

I wasn't sure if I would. I changed the subject. "What about you? Why aren't you in prison?"

"I will return to the Bastille this evening and be imprisoned. I take my various roles very seriously."

"You're imprisoned part time?"

"Oh, yes. Besides, whilst in the Bastille I will do some of my work for the *Banca di Primavera*."

"You still work for them too?"

"*D'accord*! In fact, I'm about to perform a little errand on their behalf."

"And what's that?"

He spotted a china doll across the room and waved to her.

"Excuse me," he said. "I hope we get a chance to chat later."

I didn't have time to be upset at the snub. I'd just seen the person I wanted most to speak to. She was there across the room wearing a satin blue jacket and skirt, sipping at glass of sparkling water. I hurried over to meet her.

"Mother!" I said.

RED

MOTHER

WE DIDN'T HUG, simply nodded at each other.

"What are you doing here?" I said. "I thought the *Banca di Primavera* wanted to punish you for running away. I thought they'd have you locked up in the Bastille."

"Oh, Anna! Why would the *Banca* lock up one of its best assets?"

Yet again I was left feeling naive. I had the impression that my abiding memory of Dream Paris wasn't going to be fear or discomfort, but rather embarrassment. I was wrong, though. Very wrong. I would spend a long time wishing the worst thing that could have happened here was my being humiliated.

"I'm beginning to understand something about Dream Paris," I said. "It's not a question of right or wrong, it's just about being on the winning side."

"Oh, Anna, that's true of everywhere. Now, I rather fancy some of that salmon mousse…"

I didn't. Nothing was naturally that shade of pink. Also, the fresh octopus on the adjoining dish had been helping itself to the mousse when it thought no one was looking. I took another piece of bread whilst my mother heaped up a plate of seafood.

"You're not coming home, then?" I said.

My mother smiled in acknowledgement to a woman across the room. I got the distinct impression that our conversation was just one of a number of meetings she hoped to fit in that day.

"We already discussed this, Anna. Besides, things are even more exciting now the Army of the Dispossessed is on the scene. There are a whole new set of opportunities opening up before us."

"The Army of the Dispossessed. You're going to help exploit the homeless now?"

Why wasn't I surprised?

"Oh, no, Anna. You're too harsh. The *Banca di Primavera* is going to help them. The homeless are a new business opportunity to be embraced. Clever of the *terroir* to make use of them."

"But now the *Banca* intends to do the same."

"Of course. The homeless realised their power, right at the end. They had nothing to lose, and that's why they were so powerful. We won't make that mistake again. We'll make sure they have something to lose in the future."

"I'd like to think I'm no longer surprised by your cynicism…"

"I'd like to think you shared it."

I couldn't win an argument with her.

"They're calling me a hero, Mother. I don't deserve it."

"I know. But who cares?"

"I gave my meal ticket to a hungry mother. Who wouldn't do the same?"

"Me."

"Please come home with me."

Something flickered across her face. She felt something. She wasn't completely cold. She touched my hand.

"Anna, there's nothing for me back in London. Here, I've got a chance to pursue my career properly. Besides, I've met someone…"

She looked across the room. I followed her gaze.

"No!" I said. "But he's so… so…"

She laughed.

"You're going to say 'so logical'. You think he's too clinical, perhaps?" She laughed. "One night of passion with a young stud and you think you know it all."

I blushed.

"But, Anna, my dear, you must learn to keep your eyes open. M Duruflé is very discreet, he would never boast."

"Boast about what?"

"Alain likes to think he's the premier lover of Paris. There are many woman in this city who would testify to his prowess. Why shouldn't I have my chance to see if they are right?"

"Mother! I don't want to hear this!"

"He's well-mannered, assured, intellectual. He knows how to behave in company, he will pay for your meal, never be lost for conversation, and then in the bedroom, my dear, he will make your eyes roll so far back in your head…"

"Mother! I've heard enough!"

She laughed at that.

"Stop it!"

"Aren't I allowed to enjoy myself?"

"No! Not after what you did to my father!"

That shut her up.

"Ah! So you know."

I hadn't known. Not for certain. But now, seeing her reaction I did. I knew. And she knew I knew.

"Kaolin hinted as much, back in the *Grande Tour*. You

sold him out, didn't you? You sold him out to the *Banca di Primavera*."

All around us, people spoke a little louder. They turned their backs a little towards us. They filled their plates and ate and looked out of the windows and ignored our little scene.

My mother wore an odd expression. There was a little fear there, a little embarrassment, a little defiance. And yes, a little respect.

"So you figured that out. I knew you were clever. That's what I was afraid of, I suppose. But yes, I sold him out. What else was I supposed to do? It was him or me."

"But he was your husband! My father!"

"Oh, come on, Anna, you saw the state he was in at the end of Dream London. Barely capable of looking after himself. If I'd left him to sort things out, we'd all still be stuck in the workhouse. At least this way I'm free, you've got the potential to go home, and your father, well, he's where he'd always have been."

"You took a loan from the *Banca di Primavera*, didn't you? That's how you got free from the workhouse! You took out a loan and used my father, your husband, as security!"

"Not entirely. He took on most of the debt, but I took some too."

"You betrayed him!"

"I know, but you have to understand how it happened. The *Banca di Primavera* offered us a loan to buy our debts from the workhouse. Your father and I talked about it, we knew the dangers of indebting ourselves to a *Banca*, but life in the workhouse was so bad…"

She shuddered.

"I dealt with the paperwork, and that's when I spotted the opportunity. Remember what it was like back in Dream London? Women there were nothing but chattels. Men held all the titles and deeds. It was your father's name on the paperwork, and when I saw that I thought, well... why not? What difference would it make if I signed myself away too? At least if I were free, I might be able to change things. I might be in a position to help your father, later on..."

Put like that, it all sounded so reasonable. Would I have done the same in her position? But...

"No! If that's the case, where is he? Why haven't you found him?"

"I told you, I don't know where he is. Shortly after I was freed, he was transferred from the workhouse. He could be anywhere in the Dream World by now. Don't think I haven't looked for him."

I believed her. I'm sure she had looked for him, in her efficient, businesslike way. I'm sure she'd written it into her schedule, assigned a portion of her valuable time to the task of tracking down a potentially valuable asset. I'm sure that the search was ongoing and subject to review.

We looked at each other. Our meeting was approaching its end. Across the room, Francis was chatting to Mme Ponge, nearly invisible wire trailing across the floor. Jean-Michel was looking down from the wide windows, no doubt discussing the future of Dream Paris with the ragged gentleman who stood beside him.

"What about Mr Twelvetrees?" I said, suddenly. "What was your relationship with him?"

"You've got it the wrong way round. Mr Twelvetrees wanted to establish a relationship with me. He came looking for me, following the trail your friend laid out behind him."

"What did he really want?"

"You know what he wanted! Do you remember how the world reacted to Dream London?"

I did. The world had been terrified. Terrified at being swallowed up by the Dream World. So terrified they'd tried dropping nuclear bombs upon us. Tried unsuccessfully. The bombs turned to flowers as they fell.

"They were afraid..." I said.

"Of course they were afraid! But not just afraid. They were excited, too, weren't they?"

Excited about the opportunities presented by the Dream World.

"And then you come walking in here with your little friend, dragging a great big *This Way!* sign behind you. And you didn't expect to be followed? Anna, just how stupid were you?"

She was right, of course. She'd tried to stop me, tried to make me turn back. I guess she was innocent of this one.

"I wonder what happened to him?" I said. "To Mr Twelvetrees."

"I don't know. I suspect he's back in London by now, planning his next move."

I knew she was right. She saw the disappointment in my face.

"Really, Anna, what did you expect?"

"I know."

We stood in silence for a while. This was it. We were going to say goodbye. Should we shake hands? Should we hug? I gazed at her, looked at the woman I would soon be leaving. Would I ever see her again? I wanted to drink her in as she was. So confident, so self-contained, so sure of herself. Convinced she was right about everything. How do people get to be like that? It was a mystery to me.

"Good luck with your studies," she said. "I know you'll do well at university. I hope you won't be too disappointed afterwards."

"Disappointed with what?"

"The world. The way things are. It will suck you in, too, you know."

"Not me. I'm going to make a difference."

"Really? You want to make a difference, become a teacher. Or become a nurse, or a mother, even."

"I might do that eventually. After I've done my bit."

"See? Everyone *says* they want to make the world a better place, but they don't want to do what will really make a difference. There's no glory in it. The only difference between us, Anna, is that I learned that *before* I was your age."

I couldn't think what to say. Anything I said would just start the argument again.

She held out her hand.

"Goodbye, Anna. Take care on the journey home."

I took her hand and shook it. I was saying goodbye to my mother by shaking hands.

"I'll be okay. Count von Breisach is flying us home. Part of the way, anyway."

"Good. I'll feel happier if I know you're safely away from here."

"Why's that?"

"This won't be the end. It never is."

And it wasn't.

ONE

THE REAL CHILDREN OF THE REVOLUTION

NOTHING WORKS PROPERLY with Dream Numbers
There are no fractions, no irrational numbers, no transcendental numbers. What does that mean? It means that pi there is different from our world; it means that all the circles in the Dream World are deformed, which means that space curves differently. I don't know whether it's the numbers that deform space, or the space that deforms the numbers, but if you try and do maths in the Dream World, things go weird. Well, weirder than normal. The Dream Prussians tried doing maths with mechanical computers and they changed the world. Imagine what they could have done with a computer from our world, one calculating at 2.22 teraflops. You can't imagine it?
Read on.

JEAN-MICHEL HIMSELF ACCOMPANIED us to Montmartre the next morning.
"No offence," he said, "but I want to make sure that you leave Dream Paris."

"None taken," I said. "I just want to get home."

Francis didn't say anything. His face was pale, his forehead sheened in sweat. He wouldn't admit it, but it was obvious that he was in tremendous pain. We couldn't reach home soon enough for him. Driving through Dream Paris, we seemed to encounter the ghostly grey wire on most of the streets. I hadn't realised that we'd travelled so widely.

We drove uphill for most of the journey, passing through little squares where people piled pumpkins in the corners; they cut the carved fruit down from trees. We zig-zagged up narrow alleys where people worked to scrape and peel posters from the walls. The revolution had passed again. All hoped it would be a while before it returned.

Up above us we could see the yellow cigar of a Zeppelin, newly arrived that morning. That was our ship home, I told myself.

The car swerved often, avoiding the children playing in the streets. There seemed to be more than ever this morning. I suppose their parents had sent them all out to play in the sunshine, now that the city was safe once more.

Eventually we found ourselves at the base of Montmartre, a wide square set before a steep hill. A little funfair sat in the corner, a colourful carousel chugging round and round to the sound of a steam organ. Children in neat little suits and pretty dresses were going up and down on the horses. Life was returning to normal.

"Can we take the funicular?" asked Francis, looking at the steep steps to the white-domed Zeppelin station at the top of the hill.

"Of course we can," I said. And that's when it really struck home to me just how badly the backpack was affecting him. I began to wonder if he would make it home.

We waited at the little platform at the bottom of the green hill, looking back over Dream Paris, stretched out below us in the morning sun. The painted Eiffel Towers dotted the landscape. Who owned them now, I wondered? I suppose my mother would be looking into that.

"It looks so different from here," I said. "The river, the roads, even the wall. This could be such a lovely place if only people ran it properly."

You could say that of everywhere, of course. But this morning there was something especially beautiful about Dream Paris. The sky was a little bluer, a little less, well, *extreme* than was normal for the Dream World. The sun was bright but not unbearable. The sound of the children playing was delightful. I was almost sorry to be going.

"What's that?" asked Francis. Something in his tone made me uneasy. I turned my gaze to where he was pointing. A silver speck was moving in the depths of the Dream sky.

"Is that an aeroplane?"

Francis pulled his binoculars from his backpack with some difficulty. Behind him, the children were using the wire as a skipping rope. He didn't notice, he was too busy gazing upwards.

"That's a C-130," he said. "Royal Air Force markings. How did they get that here?"

"Your backpack," I said. "Everyone is following your backpack."

The plane looked so otherworldly, drawing a line across the blue sky. So peaceful and serene, so utterly removed from the noise and heat and smell of the little French fair.

"Anna," said Francis, very slowly. "Get the children inside."

I didn't ask why. I felt it too, that deep-down sense of wrongness. I turned, spread my hands wide.

"Inside!" I called. What was the French for inside? "*Dans la maison*! *Allez*! *A tout vitesse*!"

My voice was drowned out by the music of the carousel. Not that it made much difference. The children had seen the plane themselves, they were stopping in their play, turning to face the sky, turning to watch the little silver bird. I suppose they'd never seen anything like it before.

"It's lowering the rear ramp," said Francis. "Oh, shit. They're going to drop something."

Twin brothers stood in front of me; I guessed they were about six years old. Each held an overlarge lollipop in one hand.

"*Allez!*" I said. I spread my arms wide, began to push them towards the little café at the edge of the fair. The boys shouted at me as they dodged away from my grasp. The whole playground was still, now, the faces of the children craning upwards. Even the children on the carousel turned to follow something in the sky – something falling, falling, falling...

"*Regardez! Il y a quelque chose qui tombe du ciel!*"

"Cover your eyes," commanded Francis, turning, bending. Too late for me. Something was unfolding like a paper star beneath the silver plane. Like a Chinese lantern. Like a sheet of creamy card that had been folded in half and folded in half again, and again, over and over, and was now unfolding in the heavens. It was full of holes, a Sierpinski gasket, it was...

I can't describe what it looked like. It pulled open the world and folded it into a new shape.

Francis took hold of me, pulled me to the ground. I heard the noise of the carousel, the excited chatter of the children...

The voices changed. How can I describe it? They became robotic, they became less discreet, more discrete. The back of my head and my hands stung with astringent itching. I heard a noise like water freezing, heard the creaking crackle of it, and then a sigh, and then everything stopped.

ZERO

TICK

Tick.

Tick.

Tick.

Tick.
A moment.

A moment.

Stretch and break.
Stretch and break.
Stretch and ...
I tried to raise my head, to get a better look. I couldn't move. My eyes remained closed.
"Stay DOWN, StAy KeEp yOuR head cOverrEeEeD..."

What was wrong with Francis's voice? It sounded like he was speaking through a vocoder. I couldn't open my mouth. Couldn't speak.

Then someone began to moan. Another moan, and then the eerie sound of machines crying. My eyes clicked open, one, two. I ratcheted my head upwards, *click, click, click*. Francis was looking at me.

"WhAt?" I said. "WhAt'S tHe MaTtEr?"

I licked my lips, tongue sliding out and back, out and back like a metronome.

"Is ThAt My VoIcE? Me SpEaKinG..."

I looked at the back of my hands. They were dusty, like they were covered in caster sugar. The sleeves of my jacket seemed to have melted, to have become like snake skin. I was looking at my hands, turning them back and forth, feeling the roughness on the back of the hands.

All around me the robots were crying. Not robots, children.

"WhAt WaS tHaT tHiNg? WhAt DiD tHaT pLaNe dRoP?"

Shapes were falling around us. Small black cubes, black and orange cubes, clusters of cubes, melted together like boiled sweets left in the sun.

I jerked my way to my feet. Something grabbed hold of me and I looked down into two sightless blue cubes.

"*MeS yEuX! MeS yEuX!*"

A child. What had happened to their eyes?

Francis stumbled into me. He had a tail, an icicle of different-sized cubes. He was struggling with his backpack, picking at the straps with fingers like threaded strings of cubed cheese.

"HeLp Me!"

I staggered in front of him, twitching and jerking, fumbled at the straps with sugared hands. I yanked at the straps, loosened them bit by bit. Francis was jerking like a robot, trying to separate himself from the pack, banging at it with his elbows, trying to shift it. I felt my way around behind him, nearly tripping on a child that was using my legs to support itself as it tried to pull itself to its feet

"SoRrY! *DéSolÉ!*"

Francis. Francis was. The wire that had followed us all the way from London had transmitted the full force of the bomb right into the pack, blowing it apart. It looked like a frozen explosion of building blocks.

"FrAnCiS, YoUr FrOnT…"

We both looked at his chest, at the irregular pattern beneath the blue striped shirt he wore. I fumbled at the buttons with fingers that didn't seem to work properly. Feeling came in irregular bursts. The shirt opened and I saw his chest. It looked as if it were made of pink Lego.

I placed my hand on it.

"I caN't FeEl YoUr HeArTbEaT," I said. And then I did. One pulse. A door clicking shut.

I ran a staccato finger across his chest.

"AnNa…"

"YeS."

"AnNa, tElL 'cHeLLE…"

"YeS…?"

And he died. I watched the light go out from his eyes, and his body knelt down in stop-frame motion. One, two, three.

"FrAnCiS!" I called. I took hold of one hand, I hugged his blocky form. "FrAnCiS!"

It was too late. Poor Francis. Poor Michelle. Poor Emily, another little girl who would grow up without her Daddy. Cube tears fell on him. I was crying.

Slowly, the background noises filtered through my anguish. Children crying, adults shouting. Everything heard through static. And then I felt the heat and the flame, I heard the explosion. I flung myself across Francis, eyes closed. Was this it? I wondered. Noise and heat. I was burning up.

But no. The heat passed and I looked up to see that my Zeppelin had turned to blocks and had fallen to earth. My lift home had crashed, destroyed by this strange explosion. This bomb.

"WhO did thIs, FranCis?" I asked. I'd forgotten he was dead. Just for one brief moment. "Who dId thiS?"

But deep in my gut I knew the answer.

That was an Integer Bomb. Who had stolen the plans for an Integer Bomb? I knew now.

But I didn't have time to think about that. The children needed help. The two brothers, the ones I'd tried to push to safety, were staring at their hands, eyes wide, too terrified to speak. Their hands were cubes. Nothing more than cubes.

"I DoN't KnOw wHaT tO dO!" I said. "I DoN't KnOw wHaT tO dO!"

There were children everywhere. Children crying, silent children whose faces had turned to cubes, children who sat gazing at nothing, children who screamed and screamed.

I moved through them, touching them with hands that felt in pulses, trying to comfort, not really knowing what to do, listening to the irregular bursts of tone that filled the air. What was that noise?

And I realised. The carousel. The music from the carousel. Smoothed out, reduced to whole numbers by the Integer Bomb. There were no half-tones anymore.

And then I saw the most horrible thing of my life. The thing that haunts my dreams every night. The thing that I will never forget.

The carousel was still spinning, rotating in jerks, rotating as if it were powered by square wheels. I was looking at the lucky children at the moment. The ones who had been sheltered from the blast. The ones whose hands and feet were covered in caster sugar, whose eyes had filmed over. But the carousel jerked on and I saw the others. Those caught directly by the effect.

That's when I was sick. Red cubes, hurled onto the pavement.

I FOUND OUT later that the bomb had been aimed at the *Ile de la Cité*. The bomb aimer had been told to look out for the little island in the middle of the Seine, he'd used it as a target as he'd lain on his stomach in the belly of the craft.

When I pulled myself together a little I could see the randomness of it all, the blocky head of a tree that had caught the blast and had shielded a child, the satin blue cuboids in sunlight where her sister had stood.

It was worse in the centre of the city.

The *Grande Tour* was no longer a tower, it was simply a rectangular cuboid. Three cubes sat at its base. The middle of the city was a collection of building blocks. Down there, people died in agony, died of suffocation as their blood pumped in blocks, died in agony as nerves fired incorrectly, died in nightmares as their neurons pulsed in fixed charges.

The Bastille was cubes. Madame Joubert, M Duruflé. Luc...

I walked downhill, heading towards the centre of the chaos, past a wall that had cast a shadow against the destruction. The half of the street closest to the wall remained normal, shiny cars crowded together, sunlight glinting off chrome. Past a line drawn halfway across the road, the street erupted in rising waves of grey sugar cubes.

A woman sat on a seat by a little table in a café, looking down at the place where her legs became part of the ground. She looked at me, looked back at her feet, picked up a glass of wine and drank from it.

I passed two children fused together, quite dead.

I...

I don't know how many people died that day, but Dream

Paris wasn't the first city to be bombed in the Dream World, and it won't be the last.

All that horror, I don't want to talk about it anymore.

No, I want to say one more thing. Dream Paris had been a living city. Some of the people still lived, but the city died that day. Something may have arisen afterwards, but it wasn't the same place.

No. I want to say one final thing.

Have you seen a sound wave? The shape, the humps that give it its character. What do you get when you sample a wave, take out the curves, push it into blocks? You get something that's got a noise but no character, just noise with no soul.

You get a dead note.

Dream Paris sat under a sky the colour of an unpolished euphonium, tuned to a dead note.

EPILOGUE

SIX MONTHS LATER

SHE KNEW THAT I was there, she was just pretending not to have noticed me. Well, I'd waited this long, I could wait a little longer. I watched as she finished reading the last piece of paper, as she picked up a silver pen and signed off with a flourish. She leaned back in her chair and took off her glasses, stretched and yawned, finished for the evening. She folded her glasses into their case and then sat up straight.

"Well, Anna. Don't you have something to say?"

I moved from the shadowy corner in which I'd been standing, came and sat down in the chair facing her desk.

"I'm impressed you got in here. Do you mind telling me how?"

"I had help."

I didn't say anything else. She didn't push it.

"How long have you been back? Mr Twelvetrees only made it here last week."

So he lived. No surprises there. I kept my face straight.

"I hope he had a difficult journey."

I certainly had. I don't know if I'd have made it if I hadn't had help.

Therese Delacroix folded her hands before herself on the desk.

"Anna, you look positively emaciated. Shall I send for some tea? Something to eat?"

"No. I just want you to read this."

She smiled.

"Ah! The famous truth script. It will be my pleasure. It's the least I could do for you."

For me? You think you owe me, you murdering bitch?

I kept my temper in check. I held out the script, I watched as the colours danced across her face. I wanted to know what had happened. I owed this to Francis. To Michelle and their child. I owed it to the children I'd seen die on Montmartre, I owed it to Luc and Jean-Michel and to all those people she had killed in Dream Paris.

"Why?" I asked. "Why did you do it?"

"It was us or them," she said, simply.

"Us or them? They were never a threat! They never had any interest in us."

She smiled.

"Not so far, perhaps. But that wouldn't have lasted. We had to do it, Anna. Mr Twelvetrees thought he could capture Dream Paris. I must admit, I had my doubts, but I took a chance on him. I was wrong, but there you go."

"He never stood a chance."

"Yes, and more's the pity. I never expected otherwise, but one can't help but dream... If the attack had succeeded, we wouldn't have had to drop the Integer Bomb."

"You *didn't* have to drop it!"

"Oh, Anna! Like it or not, the Dream World has opened up to our world. We have to show that we mean business. If we hadn't shown what we were capable of, we'd have every country in the Dream World attacking us by now!"

"You can't know that!"

She didn't say anything.

"There's got to be a better way!"

"You name it and I'll take it."

I opened my mouth. I closed it again. Therese spoke in a gentle voice.

"See? You think you have all the answers, but when it comes down to it, it's people like me who have to take the tough decisions.

"No! You've had years to think of this. You can't expect me to come up with the answers in minutes."

"You won't come up with an answer, Anna, because there isn't one. The only answer you'll ever come up with is mine. Attack first, feel sorrow afterwards."

"No!"

"Yes! Because you're living in a dream world, Anna, and you're dreaming; big complicated dreams of freedom and equality and brotherhood. What you don't realise yet is that your grand dreams will always be undercut by smaller, simpler and nastier dreams. It takes less imagination to think up a bigger bomb than to work out how to feed the hungry. It's always easier to build something that destroys than to sit down and figure out how to make things work properly. In the real world, Anna, dreamers like you will always be pushed to the side by people with quick answers."

"There's got to be a better way."

"Like I said, name it and I'll take it."

I glared at her. I wanted to hit her. To slap her. I wanted to do something to rip her from her smug complacency.

"No! Who are you to order all those people dead, anyway?"

"I'm the elected minister responsible."

"Elected? And do the people know what you've done?

Did they vote on your decision? I doubt the electorate would be happy to know they were complicit in your decision to kill a city."

"The bomb was what the people wanted."

She spoke the words with such sincerity. She must be telling the truth, I reminded myself, she'd read the truth script. But it *couldn't* be right.

"I doubt that," I said. "Did you ask them? Have the people *ever* been asked before an atrocity was perpetrated?"

"You know they weren't asked. How could we ask them? Even if we did, they don't know everything that I know. They'd make the wrong choice. The people don't know what they want."

Ah! So that's how she was doing it. Fooling the truth script by telling the truth, but not the whole truth. She read my mind.

"No, Anna, I'm not being disingenuous. Nothing can overrule a properly written truth script. No, what I have is something far more insidious. I have the politician's talent. Whatever I say, I *believe* to be the truth."

"You're evil."

"Say that to me in twenty years' time, Anna. We're not so different, you and I."

Why did everyone keep saying that to me? Why did everyone want me to think we were the same?

"We are different, Therese. Very different."

"Really? You're saying you wouldn't kill if you had to?"

Francis had asked me about that, on the roundabout outside the Public Records Office. I'd answered him, but it wasn't a fair answer. I'd had no reason to kill, then. There was nobody I hated enough then.

Then. I hated someone enough now.

I took the book out of my coat and placed it on her desk. Did she notice the caster sugar pattern on my hands?

"What's that?" she said.

"A book. Something from Dream Paris."

"Why have you brought it here?"

"To show you. There's a... There was a book shop in Dream Paris that sold books of fortunes. Your fortune is in here. This book is the proof that you're a liar."

No doubt flickered across her face. She remained perfectly composed as she picked up the book and tried to open it.

"Why won't it open?"

"Because I lied. That's not a book. I just needed you to pick it up."

She shook her hand, tried to let go of the thing. She couldn't. It was stuck to her. It was part of her.

"Why can't I let go?"

"It's an Integer Bomb," I said. "Just a little one."

"It won't work in here, you know. This isn't the Dream World."

But it was working. Clearly it was working. It was stuck to her.

"That's an interesting point. You see, this bomb came from the Dream World. It's owned by the Dream World. It's a little part of over there, over here. There's just enough Dream World in here for it to work. That's why it's stuck to you."

Finally, her composure cracked. Her eyes widened, just a fraction. Not much, but just enough for me to know that I'd frightened her.

"Get it off me!"

"No. I'm not sure that I could, even if I wanted to. I think there's just enough power for it to detonate. Shall we try?"

"No!"

"Oh, hush. You unleashed something like this on children. You're a grown up. You should be able to handle it."

The iBomb was bubbling now, shapes popping into existence like a cubist's pan of soup boiling over. Her hands turned to cubes… And then the effect stopped.

"Hah!" she said. "I knew there wouldn't be enough power here!" She couldn't keep the relief from her voice.

"No," I said. "I guess there isn't." And then I leaned closer. I wanted to spit in her face, but I stopped myself.

"But understand this, Delacroix. That thing is part of you now. You visit the Dream World, it will complete the detonation."

I leaned closer.

"*You bring any part of the Dream World here, it will detonate. You understand that?*"

She nodded.

I turned to go. And then I paused. I was falling into her way of thinking. Of outward politeness whilst perpetrating heinous crimes behind the scenes. But that wasn't appropriate here. This wasn't about political differences, this wasn't about different points of view. I was face-to-face with a woman responsible for the deaths of who knew how many people. Perhaps we need a little less tolerance in the world. Perhaps we accord the likes of Therese Delacroix way too much respect and perhaps, sometimes, we need to let them know what we really think of them.

So I turned and spat in her face.

THERE WAS A little green coffee van parked outside her offices. I climbed inside, next to the driver.

"All done, Miss Anna?"

"I am."

"Very good. Where to now?"

ACKNOWLEDGEMENTS

THANKS TO ISABELLE Morin-Lightfoot for correcting my French
    To Lisa Cuppello for the use of her name
    To the staff of the Portico library, Manchester, for a great place to work
    To Chris Beckett, Eric Brown and especially Jon Oliver, for their advice and feedback
    To Robin and Michael for the wealth of ideas

    And lastly thank you (as always) to Barbara, without whom…

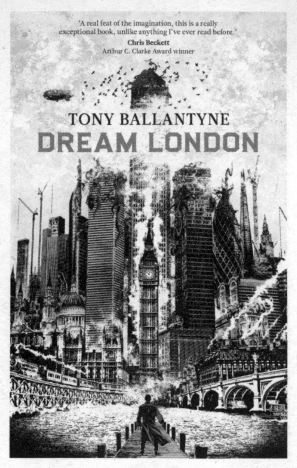

'A real feat of the imagination, this is a really exceptional book, unlike anything I've ever read before.'

Chris Beckett
Arthur C. Clarke Award winner

TONY BALLANTYNE
DREAM LONDON

ISBN: 978-1-78108-173-0 • £7.99

Captain Jim Wedderburn has looks, style and courage. He's adored by women, respected by men and feared by his enemies. He's the man to find out who has twisted London into this strange new world. But in Dream London the city changes a little every night and the people change a little every day. The towers are growing taller, the parks have hidden themselves away and the streets form themselves into strange new patterns. There are people sailing in from new lands down the river, new criminals emerging in the East End and a path spiraling down to another world. Everyone is changing, no one is who they seem to be.

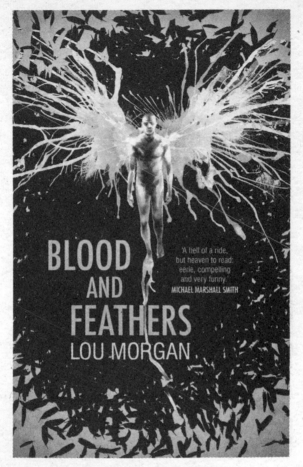

ISBN: 978-1-78108-018-4 • £7.99

Alice isn't having the best of days – late for work, missed her bus, and now she's getting rained on – but it's about to get worse. The war between the angels and the Fallen is escalating and innocent civilians are getting caught in the cross-fire. If the balance is to be restored, the angels must act – or risk the Fallen taking control. Forever. That's where Alice comes in. Hunted by the Fallen and guided by Mallory – a disgraced angel with a drinking problem he doesn't want to fix – Alice will learn the truth about her own history... and why the angels want to send her to hell. What do the Fallen want from her? How does Mallory know so much about her past? What is it the angels are hiding – and can she trust either side?

'Dark, enticing and so sharp
the pages could cut you'
SARAH PINBOROUGH
ON BLOOD AND FEATHERS

BLOOD AND FEATHERS

REBELLION

LOU MORGAN

ISBN: 978-1-78108-122-8 • £7.99

Driven out of hell and with nothing to lose, the Fallen wage open warfare against the angels
on the streets. And they're winning. As the balance tips towards the darkness, Alice — barely
recovered from her own ordeal in hell and struggling to start over — once again finds herself in
the eye of the storm. But with the chaos spreading and the Archangel Michael determined to
destroy Lucifer whatever the cost, is the price simply too high? And what sacrifices will Alice
and the angels have to make in order to pay it? The Fallen will rise. Trust will be betrayed. And
all hell breaks loose...

 WWW.SOLARISBOOKS.COM

Follow us on Twitter! www.twitter.com/solarisbooks

ISBN: 978-1-78108-048-1 • £7.99

The east coast of the USA is experiencing the worst winter weather in living memory, and John Redlaw is in the cold white thick of it. He's come to America to investigate a series of vicious attacks on vampire immigrants – targeted kills that can't simply be the work of amateur vigilantes. Dogging his footsteps is Tina "Tick" Checkley, a wannabe TV journalist with an eye on the big time.

The conspiracy Redlaw uncovers could give Tina the career break she's been looking for. It could also spell death for Redlaw.

 WWW.SOLARISBOOKS.COM

Follow us on Twitter! www.twitter.com/solarisbooks

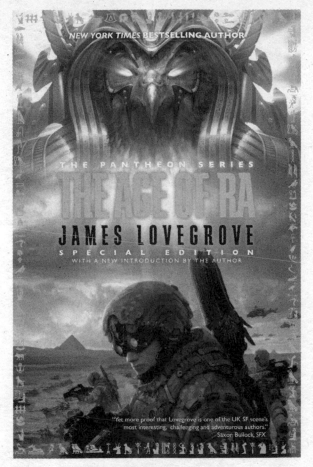

ISBN: 978-1-78108-410-6 • £8.99

The Ancient Egyptian gods have defeated all the other pantheons and claimed dominion over the earth, dividing it into warring factions, each under the aegis of a different deity. Lt. DavidWestwynter, a British soldier, stumbles into Freegypt, the only place to have remained independent of the gods' influence. There, he encounters the followers of a humanist leader known as the Lightbringer, who has vowed to rid mankind of the shackles of divine oppression. As the world heads towards an apocalyptic battle, there is far more to this freedom fighter than it seems...

 WWW.SOLARISBOOKS.COM

Follow us on Twitter! www.twitter.com/solarisbooks

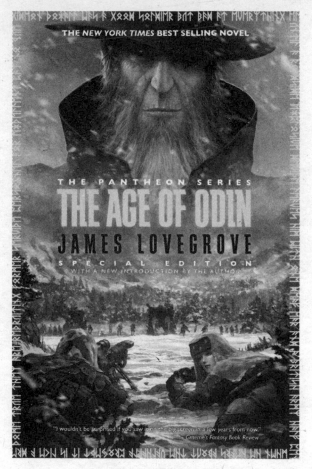

ISBN: 978-1-78108-422-9 • £8.99

Gideon Coxall was a good soldier but bad at everything else, until a roadside explosive device leaves him with one deaf ear and a British Army half-pension. So when he hears about the Valhalla Project, it's like a dream come true. They're recruiting former service personnel for excellent pay, no questions asked, to take part in unspecified combat operations.

The last thing Gid expects is to find himself fighting alongside ancient Viking gods. The world is in the grip of one of the worst winters it has ever known, and Ragnarök – the fabled final conflict of the Sagas – is looming.

 WWW.SOLARISBOOKS.COM